DARK MOON

A Legal Thriller

Deborah Hawkins

Dark Moon © 2016 by Deborah Hawkins

Formatting by Polgarus Studio

Published by Deborah Hawkins
ISBN 978-0-9889347-5-7 (ebook)
ISBN 978-0-9889347-6-4 (print)

"Everyone is a moon, and has a dark side
which he never shows to anybody."

Mark Twain

NOVELS BY DEBORAH HAWKINS

THE WARRICK-THOMPSON FILES
(Legal Thrillers)

DARK MOON
MIRROR, MIRROR
KEEPING SECRETS
THE DEATH OF DISTANT STARS

AWARD-WINNING WOMEN'S FICTION

DANCE FOR A DEAD PRINCESS

Foreword Reviews, Book of the Year, Finalist, 2013
Beverly Hills Book Award Finalist, 2014
Paris Book Festival, Honorable mention, 2014

RIDE YOUR HEART 'TIL IT BREAKS

Winner, Women's Fiction, Beverly Hills Book Award, 2015
Honorable Mention, Paris Book Festival, 2015

Contents

SARAH

CHAPTER ONE

First Weekend of August 2013, Friday Night, La Jolla

She was sitting at the bar, staring at the full moon over the glass-smooth, night-black Pacific. Her back was toward him, but Jim Mitchell could see her reflection in the mirror behind the bar. Her dark hair was very short like a child's pixie cut, and she was all eyes. They were the saddest brown eyes he had ever seen as they gazed through the window at the blank ocean.

Judging by her long, elegant legs and graceful posture, he guessed she was a model or a dancer. But no, he told himself. Models and dancers don't hang out at La Jolla's exclusive Trend Bar in conservative black couture suits and impossibly expensive white silk blouses. She was obviously a business woman. A retired model, he decided, who now ran her own modeling agency. He was glad he'd worn his business casual tan chinos and thrown his navy sport coat over his white oxford shirt. She didn't look as if sloppy appealed to her.

She was lost in thought, and she didn't turn when he slid onto the seat beside her.

He wondered what such a beautiful woman was doing alone on a bar stool at nine p.m. on a Friday night, and he wondered how many of the losers several stools away had tried to gain the place he now occupied. And he wondered how long she would let him hold it.

"Mind if I sit down?"

"Help yourself." Her eyes riveted on his, still sad but now guarded. He noticed a long scar snaking across her left cheek. He guessed it must have ended her career in front of the camera. She watched him glance down at her left hand.

"If I were married, I wouldn't be here."

"Me, either." The bartender shifted from one foot to the other, waiting for his order. "Martini, two olives. And may I get something for you? Your glass is just about empty."

"Another one of my usual."

Satisfied, the bartender scurried away to earn his tip.

"If he knows your usual, you must come here often."

"Not an original pickup line. Besides, you had me at 'mind if I sit down.' My office is just down the street. I like to come by on Friday night to wind down."

"But happy hour is long over."

"I don't do happy hour. Too crowded."

"Me neither."

"Is your office just down the street, too?"

"No. I work out of my home in Pacific Beach."

"Then why aren't you in a bar in Pacific Beach?"

"Too loud. Too noisy. And I'm too old."

He saw the first glint of amusement in her dark eyes. "You don't look too old."

4

"I'm forty-two. That's too old for twenty-something coeds."

She laughed, a deep honest laugh that he liked. "I know plenty of men your age who wouldn't agree with that."

"They have their preferences. I have mine. If I feel like a drink on Friday night, I drive up here. What about you? You could be down in PB with the party crowd."

Her eyes became serious, but her tone remained light. "Too old, too."

The bartender appeared with their drinks, and he noticed her "usual" was red wine.

"To Friday night! I'm Jim Mitchell, by the way." He held up his glass.

"Sarah Knight." And she lightly touched his glass with hers.

Afterward he said, "I'm not believing the 'too old' stuff about you."

"Thanks, but it's true. I'm four years ahead of you."

"You look ten years behind me."

She smiled. "I've finally reached the point where that's an advantage. When I first started out as an attorney, no one took me seriously."

"You're an attorney?"

"Don't sound so surprised. Lots of women are these days."

"No, no. I didn't mean that. I took you for a former model, now head of her own agency."

Sarah threw back her head and laughed. "Now that's a first. Thank you, I think. Ever heard of Craig, Lewis, and Weller?"

"Sure. They're big time rivals of my old man's stomping grounds, Cravath, Swain, and Moore."

"Well, I went with Craig, Lewis out of law school–"

"Which was Harvard, I bet."

"Wrong, Yale. And I became a partner in their white-collar crime section eleven years ago."

"A woman who looks like a model and who does white-collar crime. This has got to be a movie. I would never have guessed."

She smiled. "I think looking like a kid gave me an advantage in front of juries, particularly with the female jurors."

"So what brought you to San Diego?"

"I got tired of New York winters."

"I can relate to that."

"If your dad was a Cravath partner, you obviously grew up in New York."

"Well, not in the city. We had the regulation big house in the Connecticut 'burbs."

"And you are Jim, Junior, and your father wanted you to follow in his footsteps."

"Now, I think you're psychic. James Chapman Mitchell, III. He sent me to Andover because it was his prep school, and he sent me to Brown because it was his college, but I rebelled and went Georgetown because it wasn't Harvard, his law school."

"And did you go to work for Cravath?"

"For one miserable year. And then I joined the FBI."

"It's difficult to see that as an act of rebellion."

"As far as my father was concerned, it was."

"Why'd you pick the FBI?"

"I wanted to put the bad guys away. I thought it would give some meaning to my life."

"And did it?"

"Too much meaning as it turns out. I got very caught up in my work. Finding a lead in a cold case was like an addiction. But my partner, who was single, had no trouble leaving work at six o'clock to hang out with my wife, who was tired of sleeping alone. Five years ago, Gail handed me the divorce papers and put Josh's ring on her finger instead of mine."

"Sounds tough." Her eyes were unreadable again.

"The toughest part is being away from my son, Cody. He's thirteen, and I only get a few weeks with him every summer. He's just gone back to Baltimore where his mother lives. What about you? Ex-husbands? Children?"

"No time. Remember I made partner at a Wall Street firm at thirty-five. I couldn't date my clients, and I don't like office romances. That left the dry cleaning delivery boy and the kid who brought Chinese takeout when I got home before midnight. And I don't do younger men."

"Darn. And I was just getting ready to proposition you."

"An ex-FBI agent propositioning a criminal defense attorney? In what universe?"

"This one. I'm a private investigator now. I had to leave the Bureau after Gail married Josh. I saw and heard too much, and I couldn't take it. I'm still in love with Gail, in case you haven't noticed."

"I noticed."

"I moved out here to get a fresh start. I literally closed my eyes and stuck a pin in the map. And San Diego it was. Here's my card. I'm really good. You never know when you might need an outstanding gumshoe."

She took the card in her long, graceful elegantly manicured fingers and studied it for a moment. She seemed to be thinking something over. Finally she said, "Actually, I do need someone."

"I can't believe my luck."

"You might not think that when I tell you about the case."

"Try me."

"Do you know who Alexa Reed is?"

"Sure. The daughter-in-law of United States Supreme Court Justice Coleman Reed. She was arrested on June 3 for the murder of her husband, Michael, who was a partner at Warrick, Thompson, and Hayes, and of a psychologist, Ronald Brigman. She and Michael were locked in a bitter custody battle for their two children. Brigman seems to have been on Michael's side. The papers say Alexa was losing custody even though she had given up her career at Warrick, Thompson to be a stay-at-home mom. She snapped and killed Brigman and her ex."

"I was appointed to represent Alexa today."

"Wow! That's going to be a tough one."

"You have no idea. There's a lot more, but I can't talk about it here in public."

"Of course not."

"Are you in?"

"Definitely. Hey, I know a great little restaurant where we can talk. Tomorrow night at seven."

"Ok. And where would that be?"

"My place. Here's the address."

* * *

First Weekend of August 2013 - Saturday Night, Pacific Beach

Her second thoughts about Jim Mitchell began the moment she walked out of Trend, and they continued as she rang the bell at his Pacific Beach bungalow the following night. The house stood out from its beige stucco neighbors in a fresh coat of olive green paint with bright red begonias smiling from the flowerbeds. Not only did he seem strong and wise, seasoned in the ways of the world and his own man, he also appeared to have an artistic streak. She liked him; but, at the same time, she questioned her decision to hire him. This was a new experience for her. She had advanced in the competitive world of Craig, Lewis because she was smart and because she had excellent judgment. She rarely had any reason to think twice once she'd made a decision.

But Jim presented a number of challenges beginning with his dark hair, decisively dimpled chin, and firm, square-jawed good looks. He was six feet, two hundred pounds of well-honed muscle that any woman would have found attractive, and she never dated or slept with anyone she worked with. It was a rule set in stone. And even though Jim's background meant he knew his way around the tough world of criminal defense, he had the kindest brown eyes she had ever seen. Their empathy tempted her to open up about herself in a way she would never have considered with anyone else. But never looking back was another implacable rule. Finally, his honesty about his responsibility for the loss of his marriage and his love for his former wife surprisingly tugged at her heart, an organ that was nearly impossible to touch after years spent turning herself into one of the toughest lawyers on Wall Street. So Sarah considered telling Jim Mitchell the deal was off as soon as they had settled down to dinner on his charming patio in the remnants of the soft summer evening scented with ocean breeze and night-blooming jasmine.

But she hesitated. He was not the average private detective. Even his dress that night was not average California casual. No slouchy knit shirts and faded jeans. Instead, he wore an I-mean-business blue oxford cloth shirt, sleeves rolled back to the elbows, and impeccable tan linen slacks. Everything about him broadcast confidence and professionalism. If she searched the entire West Coast for an investigator to work on behalf of Alexa Reed, she couldn't do better than Jim. And loyalty to her client was, according to the cannons of legal ethics, her top priority.

"Where did you learn to cook like this?" She had just tasted the lamb chops in a delicate mustard cream sauce with tiny peas and braised leeks.

"You were expecting steaks from the butane grill." His eyes teased her.

"Most definitely. You do not look like a sous chef."

He grinned. "Thank you, I think. My mother came from old money. Her father was an investment banker and a Cravath client. She insisted on having a professional chef. I liked hanging out in the kitchens and learning about cooking. Drove my old man nuts because he was afraid I'd go to culinary school."

"You'd have been very successful."

"Doubtless. But in the end, I wanted to catch the bad guys more." He smiled. "My cooking skills came in handy when I was living on a government salary and couldn't afford five-star restaurants."

"And now you can?"

"In theory. My father died three years ago and left me, his only child, his fortune along with my mother's money. In trust, of course. But the monthly payments have made me financially independent. It's unlikely I'll ever need to touch the capital."

"So why keep working? And on the side of the bad guys?"

"I keep working because I love doing investigations. Every one is a new story, with a new plot, and new characters. And the clients aren't 'bad guys.' They're innocent people I'm keeping out of prison. I'm still on the side of justice. Tell me about Alexa Reed."

Sarah sighed and traced patterns on the base of her wine glass with one finger. "In the interest of full disclosure, I should let you know I didn't want this case."

"How'd you get it, then?"

"When I left Craig, Lewis and set up shop out here alone, I brought a few clients with me who are based in Los Angeles. One was accused of masterminding a Ponzi scheme, two others were indicted for insider trading, and the fourth was on the hook for racketeering."

"Isn't defending clients under the Racketeer Influenced and Corrupt Organizations Act a specialty of yours?"

She felt herself stiffen and hoped he didn't notice. "I've done a few RICO cases, that's true."

"But you won one of the most influential and toughest cases of all time, the Joey Menendez case."

Sarah's mouth went dry at the name, and she gulped a sip of wine to make her tongue work. "How'd you know about Menendez?"

"It's famous throughout law enforcement. You persuaded a jury to acquit the head of the Menendez drug cartel of six counts of murder for hire and twenty counts of extortion. No one ever thought that would happen, including the U.S. Attorney who opposed you. What's wrong? You look upset."

"No. Of course not." But she gripped the base of the wine glass to keep her hands from shaking. He was violating one of her iconoclastic rules: don't look back. She needed to change the subject quickly. "Anyway, I didn't want to defend Alexa Reed."

"So then how'd you become counsel of record?"

"In a word: blackmail. Last month I settled all but one of the four cases I started with. I've picked up one or two new ones as I've gone along, but they are all out of L.A. I haven't developed any business in San Diego. So I put my name on the list of attorneys willing to accept trial court appointments for indigent defendants. Yesterday morning, Hal Remington, who heads the appointments panel, called and insisted I come to his office at ten a.m."

"He couldn't offer you the case on the phone?"

"Apparently not." Her hands had stopped shaking, and she paused to fortify herself with a sip of wine.

"So what happened?"

"I found his office in the basement of the old Justice Building on the third try. They've hidden it pretty well. Remington turned out to be a scruffy version of Ichabod Crane, slouched behind a desk so covered in paper, I doubt he's ever filed anything in his entire career. He told me he was appointing me on Alexa Reed's case, and I said no."

Jim leaned over and poured more Australian Shiraz into her glass as he asked, "And then?"

"And then he said if I didn't take the case, I'd never work in this town. He'd personally guarantee it. I didn't know whether to believe him or laugh in his face."

"I hope you believed him."

"What do you mean?"

"People have their own way here. Money and influence talk."

"But surely they follow the state bar's ethical rules just like everyone else?"

"Some do. Some don't. Have you ever heard of Patrick Frega?"

She shook her head.

"He was a San Diego attorney. Back in 1992, he was caught by us Feds bribing two very willing superior court judges. They all three got disbarred and sentenced to federal prison. What did you tell Remington after he threatened to blackball you?"

"I told him I couldn't take the Reed case because I'm not death-qualified in California. Alexa is facing the death penalty because it was a double murder."

"And then what?"

"Remington said my death qualification in New York was enough, and I'd better take the case. Then he leaned over his desk and said, 'For a woman who graduated number three in her class at Yale, you're kind of dense. You're getting this case because you aren't qualified, and you'll lose it because that's exactly what Coleman Reed wants. He wants the woman who killed his son to die by lethal injection as quickly as possible. You and twelve citizens of this city are going to oblige him. You were hand picked because you look qualified, but you aren't."

"He actually said that?"

"I wish I'd been wearing a wire. I asked him what made him think I'd lose; after all, I did graduate number three, and I'm a quick study."

"And?"

"And he said, 'Yeah, you were editor of the law review at Yale. Big f'ing deal. That means nothing in this town. I'm *it* when it comes to handing out defense work. You want to survive professionally? Better not win Alexa Reed's case.'

"When I reminded him that was unethical, he laughed and said, 'Then go tell the state bar. You'll never prove a word out of my mouth. There's only me and you in this room, and I've been appointing lawyers for twenty years. Everyone knows me, but you're some New York hot shot who doesn't belong here. It's my word against yours, and mine will win. Why don't you go back where you belong?"

"Wow. So you took the case?"

"He made me angry. I could see if I didn't take it, she'd never get an attorney who'd give her a fair defense."

"Who represented her at the preliminary hearing?"

"Trevor Martin. I picked up her file from his office yesterday, but I didn't get a chance to talk to him. I read his withdrawal motion. He claims his mother has inoperable brain cancer, but I think he just doesn't want anything to do with Alexa Reed."

Jim reached over to refill her glass one more time, but she put her hand over it.

"No, thanks. I'm driving."

"You can stay here. I have a guest room."

She looked through the open French doors into his living room, full of an eclectic mix of old and new furniture, antiques, and Ikea pieces. Maple and mahogany and a few painted chairs and chests here and there. Cozy and comfortable. The kind of room you'd be tempted to put your feet up in and snuggle into a soft throw on the sofa. Jim was probably like that, too. Safe and comforting. She reminded herself she didn't get close to men like Jim. She had one-night stands with married men, and men she'd never see again. But men who were capable of relationships were dangerous to the self-contained, tightly controlled world she had created.

Her dark eyes locked onto his mellow, softer ones. "No, thanks. And let's get one rule very clear: I never sleep with anyone I work with."

"I wasn't inviting you into my room. There really are two." He grinned, and the tension broke. "Now, tell me what we're up against."

"June 2 was a Sunday night. Meggie, who's six and Sam, who's five, were with their father at his house on Mount Soledad in La Jolla. Alexa was alone in her rented place in Pacific Beach. Ronald Brigman, who lived about ten minutes away from Michael, had a surveillance camera recording traffic at his front door. The video footage shows Alexa arriving alone at nine p.m. but doesn't show her leaving. Brigman was killed around eleven, and Michael was shot about twenty minutes later. Around eleven-fifteen, Meggie's cell phone called Alexa's. Alexa's phone pinged off a cell tower that shows she was close to Ronald Brigman's when Meggie called. Within ten minutes of the call from Meggie's phone, Alexa's cell was dialing 911 from Michael's house. She told 911 she'd arrived to check on the children and had found him dead. The Glock .9 millimeter used in both murders was registered to her and was found next to Michael's body. There were two DNA profiles on the gun: hers and Michael's. Ballistics show five bullets in Brigman, and four in Michael, all from that Glock. That's all I know so far. I'm meeting with Martin at ten on Monday morning."

"Do you want me there?"

"No. I don't expect him to be a witness in her case, and he'll open up to me better if we're alone. But I'm going to the jail to see Alexa on Tuesday afternoon. I'll need you then. Two o'clock."

CHAPTER TWO

First Monday of August 2013 - Downtown San Diego

Trevor Martin had done well for himself, Sarah reflected, as she sat opposite his massive mahogany desk on Monday, sipping the coffee his assistant had brought in. He could afford a three-office suite on the thirtieth floor of 600 West Broadway to house himself and his two associate attorneys. The associates were tucked into the interior spaces, but Trevor's office overlooked San Diego Bay, now sparkling in the August morning as if the sun had thrown handfuls of diamond dust over the gray-blue waves.

"You aren't going to like what I have to say about this case," Trevor began.

"Try me."

"Well, to get straight to the point, your client is as looney as they come. The court declared a doubt about her mental competency to stand trial a week after the preliminary hearing. Basically, she went straight back to her cell after the prelim, curled up on her bunk, and hasn't spoken a word since."

"Wouldn't it be a bit of a shock to be held for trial on two murders, knowing she's facing the death penalty?"

Trevor shrugged. "She's a lawyer. She had to know what was going to go down from the minute she pulled the trigger on Brigman. And, as you probably know, her gun was the murder weapon; and two weeks earlier, Brigman had given Michael primary custody of the children starting in September when they went back to school."

"What did Alexa tell the police about the gun?"

"She claimed it was stolen and that she reported the theft. But there's no record of a police report."

"How can you be sure there's no report?"

"Preston Barton is the deputy district attorney who's prosecuting the case. He's the number three man in that office, and we go back a long way. He's turned over all the discovery, and no police report."

Sarah studied Trevor until he began to squirm in the silence. If you put an ill-fitting, thousand-dollar suit on a donkey and turned it into a person and then added a beer belly, you'd get Trevor Martin, she reflected. He was thin, except for the paunch, in his late fifties, with a bulbous nose, and squinty dark eyes of an undefined color. He combed his sparse gray locks over, Donald Trump-style, and wore a suit that matched his hair. Everything about him said mediocrity. Sarah reckoned he'd earned his high-class address based on cunning and deceit and not on legal talent.

"You mean you're conducting your investigation into your client's defense by relying solely upon the word of the man who's prosecuting her?"

"Look, you're making way too much out of this. I told you, Preston and I go way back. We've tried probably a hundred cases against each other. We socialize. In fact, I was at a barbecue at his house the night after the prelim. If that report had been in his file, he'd have turned it over."

Sarah tried to keep her face impassive, but she could tell Trevor was becoming more and more agitated by her disapproval. He leaned over his desk and hissed, "Don't waste your time on sympathy for this woman. She's a consummate lying, manipulating bitch."

"I'm sorry, did you just call your client a 'bitch'? What about your duty of loyalty? Did you tell her you were out partying with opposing counsel the night after she was bound over to face the death penalty?"

Trevor shrugged. "I can see you've got a lot to learn about how we do things here. This isn't New York, Ms. Knight."

"This is beginning to sound like my meeting with Hal Remington."

"Better not cross Hal if you want to work in San Diego."

"Funny, that's exactly what he said."

Trevor leaned back in his padded leather executive chair and adopted a paternal tone. "If you want to go on some sort of crusade, claiming we're all unethical, you're welcome to do it. But remember, we've all been here more than twenty years, doing our jobs, and not getting into any trouble with the state bar. If you start accusing us of shafting our clients—even if that's true—you won't get to first base. Who do you think the state bar is going to believe? You and a string of convicted felons, complaining about their trial attorneys? Or us?

"Look, Ms. Knight, Alexa Reed was a washed up associate at Warrick, Thompson, and Hayes. She got herself pregnant twice without much time between babies to hide her incompetence and to give herself an excuse to leave the firm. Michael, on the other hand, was a brilliant young lawyer who made partner in three years."

"Was he brilliant or just the son of a sitting United States Supreme Court justice who was a former Warrick, Thompson partner himself?"

"If I have to answer that question, you haven't heard anything I've said so far. Anyway, Alexa gets herself knocked up twice. The firm lets her go; and then she files for divorce, claiming Michael beat her and persuaded the partners to fire her. Ronald Brigman did her psychological evaluation in the custody case and found she was lying through her teeth. Michael did his best to work with her co-parenting the children, but she was a hostile mess. In May of this year, her instability forced Brigman to give primary custody of her kids to Michael. Two weeks later, Brigman and Michael were dead, killed by Alexa's gun. Come on, Ms. Knight. How much time do you think anyone should waste investigating this case? Don't be ridiculous. There's no way anyone can prove Alexa Reed is innocent."

"You sound exactly like Hal Remington."

"And you'd better not forget what he said: don't try too hard. Just file a few pre-trial motions to make it look good, do some cross-examination, and accept the inevitable outcome. This client is a guilty nut job and then some. You're here to make it look good and get paid. That's all.

"And by the way, this case is going nowhere fast. Alexa Reed wouldn't talk to me, and I doubt she will talk to you."

"So I gather there's a hearing coming up to determine whether she is competent to stand trial?"

"Right. On September 3, the day after Labor Day."

"And who is the psychologist who is evaluating her?"

"Percy Andrews."

"Why didn't you request someone out of L.A.?"

"Because I didn't need to. Percy Andrews has been doing court-appointed evaluations in this town for twenty years."

"And that's my point. Isn't it a conflict of interest to have him evaluating the woman accused of killing his colleague?"

Trevor Martin's mouth became a tight line, and he stood up abruptly. "I've got another appointment coming in ten minutes. I've given you all the help I can. And I've warned you. If you have any questions after you go over the file, you can call me."

But not bloody likely you'll answer, Sarah thought as she shook hands and left his office.

CHAPTER THREE

First Tuesday of August 2013 - San Diego Main Jail Downtown

A jail is nothing but gray, Sarah thought on Tuesday afternoon. She and Jim had been sitting in gray metal chairs at the gray metal table in the attorney-client interview room for a half hour without any sign of Alexa Reed. Sarah looked around to keep from being mesmerized by Jim's gentle eyes as they studied her from his end of the table. He looked good in a suit. She'd never seen him in one before. Feelings would complicate things; she couldn't have feelings. But his eyes tempted her to have them. She needed a night with David and soon to make her forget about Jim. Hadn't he said his wife was in Cabo this week? She'd call him after work and see if he was free that evening.

She took in the dust-gray walls, the gray chairs and the table where they were seated, the gray door they had come through, and the metal bars over the peek-hole window. A guard in a gun-metal gray uniform peering at them through the large glass security window completed the set. Sarah hadn't been in a jail in a long time. Her clients were all wealthy business executives who bypassed lockup with millions of dollars worth of bail.

"I think she's standing us up," Jim said.

"Maybe. Trevor said she's been curled up in a fetal position and hasn't spoken since the preliminary hearing."

"So she's incompetent to stand trial."

"I'd say yes for sure, but there's a hearing September 3 to make that determination. I'm going to interview the psychologist who's evaluating her as soon as I can get an appointment."

"You'll want me there in case he lies on the stand at the hearing."

Despite her best judgment, Sarah's eyes darted to his and remained fixed on their brown depths longer than she'd intended. "Yes, I will. Definitely."

The gray metal entrance door began to slide to the right, extremely slowly, creaking as it moved. She and Jim turned toward it, thinking Alexa was about to appear. Instead, they saw only a portly fortyish woman guard with a sour look on her face.

"Are you Sarah Knight?" she demanded. "Where's you bar card?"

Sarah tried to stifle her annoyance, knowing a rise from her was what this nameless jail official wanted; but she'd shown her state bar identification card more times in the last half-hour than she had ever displayed it in her entire career. She was tired of dragging it out of her wallet.

But she did, and the guard scanned it for several minutes as if she thought it was counterfeit.

"And you?" she demanded of Jim. "Where's yours?"

Without a word, he patiently handed over his District of Columbia bar card which showed he was on inactive status as a lawyer, and his private investigator's license. Sarah noticed he fumbled with his ex-FBI agent's association ID card for the grumpy guard's benefit.

"You used to be an agent?"

"Yeah."

"Then why are you working for defense lawyer scum?"

"Have to make a living." Jim gave her a half-smile and put his credentials away.

"Well, bad news. Your client won't get up to talk to you. She's lying on her bunk, eyes open, saying nothing. Somehow she eats enough to stay alive. But that's it."

"I'd like to go down to her cell and introduce myself," Sarah said. "She's never met me."

"It's against jail policy."

"I can get a court order if you'd rather."

The guard frowned at them both, delaying the moment when she'd have to admit defeat.

"You don't have to. I'll escort you."

The interior corridors were even grayer, Sarah reflected a few minutes later as she and Jim followed the woman to Alexa's cell. They twisted and turned through narrow hallways with the astringent smell of lemony disinfectant until they reached the tiny space Alexa Reed occupied.

Their sour guide dialed a combination lock on the door of the cell, and then used a key to complete opening it. Sarah and Jim stepped inside when it swung open, but there was barely room for them both in the small, dark space lit only by a three-by-three window high up on the outside wall.

She was a tiny bag of bones, Sarah reflected as she looked down at the woman in the navy blue prison scrubs curled up on the single cot. Her blonde hair was matted and uncombed, and apparently unwashed for weeks. Her large light blue eyes stared straight ahead, unfocused and distant. She was about five feet tall, Sarah guessed, and must have weighed all of ninety pounds.

She knelt by the cot. "Alexa, I'm Sarah Knight, your new attorney. And this is my investigator, Jim Mitchell. We've come to hear your side of things. Will you go down to the interview room with us where we can talk?"

No response. Alexa's blue eyes remained blank and fixed on the opposite wall.

Jim leaned over and took one of Alexa's small hands in his much larger one. Sarah thought she saw a flicker in Alexa's otherwise vacant eyes, but it might have been her imagination.

"She isn't going to talk to you," the hostile guard announced. "You're going to have to leave."

Jim let go of Alexa's tiny fingers and stood up. Sarah stood also and turned toward the door. Suddenly, on impulse, she paused and fished one of her business cards out of her brief case. She pressed it into Alexa's unresponsive hand.

"Here's my card, Alexa. We're here to help you."

* * *

First Tuesday Night of August 2013 - Pacific Beach

That night, Sarah found herself standing in front of Jim's olive green bungalow at seven-thirty. He'd insisted on making dinner again to give them a chance to talk over the day's events. She had called David as soon as she'd gotten back to her office, ready to cancel the evening with Jim if he was free. But his wife had unexpectedly backed down from her Cabo trip, so seeing him was out of the question. Had Tessa guessed about their relationship? That possibility nagged at Sarah as she thought of calling Jim to set up a meeting at a restaurant where she would feel more in control. But the need for confidentiality trumped her scruples about being alone with him.

He put a glass of cabernet in her hand and motioned for her to take a seat on one of the tall stools around the island in his kitchen.

"I was in the mood for burgers, although not the ones you burn over a gas grill. Feeling the French bistro vibe tonight, so I've made grilled onion confit and Bearnaise sauce and shoestring sweet potato fries."

"I'll have to work out tomorrow for sure."

He turned from stirring the onions and gave her a once over. "I doubt that. You look very Audrey Hepburn tonight in those black skinny pants and black shirt. Do people ever tell you that you look like her?"

"Once in a while. When they don't otherwise know my day job."

"I have to admit you had me fooled that night at Trend."

Was it really less than a week since they'd met, Sarah reflected. Why did she feel as if she'd always known him?

"That was tough today at the jail," Jim observed, turning back to his onions.

"Yes, it was." Sarah paused to take a long drink of her wine, wondering if she should have asked for scotch instead.

"She's barely alive."

"Trevor Martin warned me, but it was much worse than I'd pictured."

"She'll be declared incompetent to stand trial. She's completely incapable of assisting with her defense."

"Yeah, that's blatantly obvious. Still, I want to interview Percy Andrews to find out what he's going to say at that competency hearing. I've got an appointment with him on Friday at nine in the morning."

"I'll be there."

* * *

They ate in Jim's small dining room at a small antique maple table. He dialed the lights down and lit candles in clear glass holders. Sarah wondered if he considered the evening a business or personal occasion.

"How long have you been in San Diego?" he asked, as he put the plates on the table and motioned for her to take the seat opposite his.

"Since January. What about you?"

"Two years, now. It's easier being on the opposite coast." His eyes became sad as he spoke; but he gave her that gentle, honest smile that she found hard to resist. "Do you miss New York?"

"Sometimes."

"Why didn't you go with a big firm here like Warrick, Thompson?"

"I thought about it. I talked to Alan Warrick. In the end, I was tired of working for someone else."

Jim smiled. "I can understand that. Any broken hearts left behind in New York?"

"Only the ones I mentioned the other night, the dry cleaning delivery boy and the Chinese food messenger. But I doubt they miss anything but the tips. I was always generous. What about you?"

"I've tried. No luck. Still head-over-heels for Gail."

Jealousy was an inappropriate emotion, Sarah reminded herself as he refilled her wine glass. "What is she like?"

"Funny, smart, beautiful. Taffy hair, big blue eyes. Knockout figure. Grew up in Boston. She teaches third grade and loves it. Cody has a two-year-old half-sister, Brittany, whom he adores."

Sarah studied him across the table. White oxford cloth shirt tonight with navy linen pants. Such a kind, gentle face. Hard to believe he hadn't found someone else by now.

"Penny for your thoughts."

"My hourly rate is a lot higher than that."

"Guess I can't afford them, then."

"I thought you were a trust-fund baby."

He laughed. "I tend to forget about the old man's money. I did without it all those years. Ok, I'll pay your hourly rate if you tell me why you're looking at me like that."

"Like what?"

"As if you were reading my mind."

"Now that would be a useful skill for a defense attorney. But I don't do mind reading. I was just thinking a guy like you should have hooked up with someone by now."

"I could say the same about you." The tone of his voice made her tummy flutter, and she decided this conversation had to end—and quickly.

"I do see someone. From time to time."

Did he look disappointed? She wasn't sure.

"Lucky him. What's he like?"

"A busy, important CEO of a commercial real estate firm. His brother, who works for him, had a minor problem with the Securities and Exchange Commission last winter, just after I got here."

"And you took care of it for him?"

"Made it all go away."

Jim studied her in the candlelight. "There's something you're not telling me."

Sara traced the circle of the bottom of her wine glass. "Now you're reading minds."

"I've interviewed hundreds of witnesses. I know when someone's holding back."

Her dark eyes met his, and she smiled. "You're really good. I'll give you credit. David Spineli is very married."

"Ah, I see." He crossed his knife and fork across his plate in a gesture of finality before bringing his eyes back to study hers. "Then why waste your time?"

"He takes my mind off things." *But most importantly, I can't fall in love with him.* But Sarah would never say that out loud.

"Does the wife know?"

She frowned as she thought of the defunct Cabo trip. "I don't think so."

"But you're not sure?"

"She was supposed to be in Cabo tonight."

"And he was supposed to be with you?"

"But she cancelled. I don't think it had anything to do with me and David."

"Well, my luck that she stayed in town." He leaned over and started to refill her glass, but she put her hand over the top.

"I'm driving, remember?"

"And I've got that guest room, remember? This was a tough day. You need it. Let me put the plates in the sink and then join you in the living room. I've learned a lot about Alexa Reed since this afternoon. I think you're going to be interested in what I've found out."

* * *

Sarah studied Jim's display of Cody's pictures on the bookshelves on either side of the fireplace as she listened to him clinking dishes into the dishwasher. The photos took Cody from plump babyhood in an old fashioned pram to the most recent ones in a little league baseball uniform. He had Jim's dark hair and dimpled chin, but blue eyes like his mother. He looked tall for thirteen, so she guessed he took after his father in the height department. He smiled unselfconsciously at the camera as if he hadn't a care in the world.

"That's my boy," Jim said as he entered the room, carrying a folder full of papers.

"Good looking. Takes after his old man."

He smiled. "Thanks for the unexpected compliment. But I think he looks more like Gail." She heard the note of wistfulness that came over him whenever he mentioned his ex-wife's name. It was like a theme song he played forever in her memory. For a moment, she wished someone would play a theme like that for her. But only for moment.

"I gather all that is information on Alexa Reed?"

"You are correct. Since our client wouldn't tell us anything about herself, I did some research. Here, sit down and let me show you."

She would have preferred the seat across the room where she couldn't smell the clean, spring scent of his soap and the light starch in his shirt, but he had laid the folder on the coffee table between them. She caught her breath when he opened it, and she saw Alexa Reed as she'd once been.

"That's Alexa with her grandmother, when she graduated number one in her class from Georgetown. She was editor of the law review."

Sarah couldn't believe the exquisite little blonde with the enormous blue eyes, flawless complexion, and perfect cupid's bow lips was the woman they'd seen on the jail cot that afternoon. She felt Jim's eyes on her as she stared at the picture.

"Hard to believe, isn't it?" he said.

"She's gorgeous."

"She's amazingly talented, too."

"How so?"

"She was born in Fairfax, Virginia, in 1978, making her thirty-five today. Her parents died in a car accident when she was six. She was raised by her grandmother, and had a habit of winning academic honors. She was the valedictorian of her class at Jefferson High and then went to Yale, your law alma mater, on a full academic scholarship. She graduated with honors in history and then went to Georgetown for law school. She graduated in 2003 and went to work as a clerk for the D.C. Circuit Court of Appeal. Then in July 2004 she went on to clerk for Justice Paula Moreno on the Supreme Court. That's apparently when she met Michael Reed, whose father, as you know, is on the Court. Michael, who also went to Georgetown, was a second-year associate at Steptoe and Johnson.

"She and Michael got married in August 2005 and moved to San Diego to become associates at Warrick, Thompson. Michael went to work in litigation. Alexa was assigned to Chuck Reilly, their one and only appellate lawyer."

Sarah continued to turn through the photographs of Alexa that Jim had found. She was a lawyer-like, petite blonde, hair slicked into a tight bun and wearing an expensive dark suit next to Justice Moreno in one photograph. In another, she stood between Justice Moreno and her father-in-law, Coleman Reed, still wearing a professional face. In another series of shots, she was the tiny, perfect bride in satin and white lace on a handsome Michael Reed's arm.

"They were a good looking couple," Sarah observed. Michael's dark hair and green eyes were a perfect counterpoint to Alexa's blue-eyed blondeness.

"I think he was lucky to get her. She's much better looking than he is."

Sarah studied the wedding pictures again. Although Michael had a Gerard Butler boyish charm, he had also inherited Coleman Reed's too square face and stubborn jaw.

"He looks as if he could be a tough character."

Jim nodded. "Heartless might be more to the point. Alexa had Meggie in August 2007. Six months later, she was pregnant with Sam. He was born in November 2008. She tried to go back to work, but for some reason she left the firm in December. A month later, in January 2009, Michael filed for divorce, seeking custody of the children. Meggie was barely one and Sam was just a few months old."

"Trevor Martin told me Alexa started the divorce proceedings."

"Wrong. It was Michael." Jim held up a copy of the divorce petition.

"Where'd you get that so fast?"

"I have my tricks. Don't ask too many questions but don't worry. I know how to get copies through regular channels if we need them as defense exhibits at trial. But in the meantime, I knew we had to have immediate information."

"I can't believe Martin got something as important as who initiated the divorce so wrong. I wonder what else he lied about. He called her a crazy, manipulative bitch."

"I'm pretty sure that's going to turn out to be a lie, too." Jim said, looking down at Alexa's smiling engagement picture.

Suddenly Sarah's phone began to ring, and she jumped up to fish it out of her purse. David's picture appeared on the screen. She felt Jim watching her.

"I have to take this." She pressed the accept button. "Hello? I wasn't expecting to hear from you tonight. Oh, I see. Well, I'm just finishing up my meeting with my investigator. I can be at your house in, say, thirty minutes."

She looked up to find Jim's eyes still fixed on her, dark and unreadable.

"I take it that was your guy?"

"David. Yes."

"How did he break free of the wife?"

"She decided to go to Cabo after all."

"There are no flights this late."

"David's company has a private jet. She took that."

"Ah, perfect for you, then."

"Perfect." Sarah was relieved to be leaving behind the conflicting feelings he aroused in her. Things were much simpler with David. Straight up sex, no strings attached. "Thank you for all the work you've done today."

"My pleasure." But he didn't look at all happy she thought.

"So I'll see you Friday at nine at Percy Andrews' office. I'll text you the address. Thanks for a lovely dinner."

* * *

Jim stood in the cool, late summer night watching Sarah's white BMW back out of his drive, then went into his kitchen, poured himself a stiff Scotch, and threw himself onto the sofa. *You can't do this to yourself*, he thought. *You can't get emotional because she's sleeping with another man.* He hadn't liked the way she'd dismissed him as "my investigator."

But I can get emotional, he told himself. In fact, I'm powerless to stop the feelings. It's exactly the way I felt when I realized Gail was sleeping with Josh after we separated. I hated knowing the woman I wanted was with another man.

He drank some more scotch and frowned at his glass. *Wow, I've just admitted I want to sleep with Sarah*, he thought. I knew she was trouble the first time I saw her. Well, I know I can't sleep with her for a trillion reasons; not the least of which is her own rule against sleeping with co-workers. But I want to. *That's the awful part. I want to so much.* He could smell the faint trace of her perfume that lingered where she'd sat on the sofa. A flower, he thought, possibly a gardenia. He wanted to know the name of the scent.

He closed his eyes and pictured Sarah's slender body in the other man's arms just as he used to picture Gail with Josh on some of the worst nights early in their separation.

What did this David person look like? Was he handsome? Was he younger, older? Sarah had said no younger men, but he thought she'd been joking. Had she told this David character how that scar had come to be on her left cheek? Maybe it wasn't a car accident. Maybe she'd been mugged at knifepoint coming home from her office in New York too late to be out alone. She was too fiercely independent; that was for sure.

He was going through his scotch too fast. He'd better slow down. He began to reorganize Alexa Reed's photographs and put them back into the folder to take his mind off Sarah.

He paused to study a picture of Alexa with her children when they must have been about two and three. The uptight lawyer clothes were gone. She was wearing a simple white t-shirt, outrageously flattering tight jeans, and her hair was wild and free around her shoulders. It was about the color of Gail's. And she, too, had those blue, blue eyes. How had she slipped from a life devoted to over-achievement into the dark, murky world of homicide? She was obviously an exceptionally bright and clever woman. As much as Jim hated to admit it, there were ways to keep from being found out. Some people did get away with murder. And if anyone would have been good at creating the perfect crime, it would have been someone like Alexa Reed. Bright, capable, meticulous attention to detail. Then why had she been so clumsy? She clearly hadn't wanted to get caught because that meant the loss of her children. So what had gotten into her on the night of June 2?

The Joey Menendez case had looked as lost as this one did. They'd been celebrating in the U.S. Attorney's office even before the jury went out. Sarah had come up with a last minute witness who had lied through his teeth and testified Joey didn't give orders to the cartel. He'd come out of nowhere, and the U.S. Attorney, who had thought he knew everything there was to know about Joey Menendez, had been blindsided. Against all the odds, Sarah had persuaded that jury to believe her lying witness. Funny how she wouldn't talk about a truly legendary victory. Well, she had worked miracles before; Jim was betting she could work one here.

CHAPTER FOUR

First Tuesday Night of August 2013 - San Diego Main Jail Downtown

The jail was never quiet at night, but it was quieter than in daylight. Alexa Reed shifted on her cot so she could see the single star shining through the tiny window of her cell. She guessed it must be midnight. Everyone seemed to be asleep except for someone crying softly down the hall. Probably a new prisoner. Everyone cried at first until the sheer futility of grief became apparent.

Someone had come to see her today. Or was it yesterday? All the days ran together, and she couldn't remember which was which. A woman with deep dark eyes and a scar down one cheek. A ragged, unexpected scar on a beautiful face. And she'd had a man with her. He was tall, with warm hands, and the kindest eyes she'd ever seen. They said they'd come to help her. If anyone could help, they looked as if it might be them. But no one could end her waking nightmare.

If she thought too long about Meggie and Sam, she'd start to cry like the lost soul down the hall. She hadn't seen them since the third of June. It must be July by now. No, probably more like August. Wrapped in her semi-conscious state, she had lost the ability to speak, so she could not ask what day it was. There were words in her head, but none of them would come into her mouth to be made into sounds. Grief had left her mute, but it didn't matter. No one had believed anything she'd said since the day she'd married Michael Reed. Mute was better than being called a liar.

She wished she could wake up and find herself back in the rented cottage in Pacific Beach with Meggie and Sam. She would have given anything to be following the old routine of supper, bath, bedtime story, prayers, and goodnight kiss.

She could see Sam's chubby little hands playing with the cut-up bits of fish sticks on his Winnie The Pooh plate when he was just two. He had loved to wipe the bits of fish through the ketchup at least twice and then stuff them into his mouth, giggling at Meggie because he knew he was supposed to use his fork. Meggie, at three, had taken her status as older sister very seriously. She always frowned and reminded him about that fork. Then Sam would look at Alexa and giggle some more because he'd gotten the hoped-for rise out of his sister.

Alexa missed bath time, too. They loved to play with Sam's shiny black plastic submarine. Sam scooted it across the water, making what he imagined were boat noises even after Alexa reminded him subs ran silently. Meggie, who was endlessly patient and precocious, liked to take the red, green, and yellow baby subs out of the mother ship and line them up on the edge of the tub, coming up with new patterns every night. Alexa didn't mind if they splashed a little.

After the games in the tub and after trying to sing *Row, Row, Row, Your Boat* as a round, there was always that wonderful moment of lifting each precious little body out of the water, wrapping their chubby pinkness in big fluffy terry towels, and breathing in their wonderful clean soap and baby shampoo smell. Alexa marveled at each perfect finger and toe as she helped them into pajamas. Meggie could do everything except button her nightgown in the back, but Sam preferred to dance naked down the hall to escape clothes if possible.

They shared a room because their tiny rented cottage only had two bedrooms. But it didn't matter because Sam was afraid of the dark and preferred to sleep in his sister's room. Alexa sat on Meggie's bed with the two of them between her to read their bedtime story. Sam's favorite was *Goodnight Moon,* but Meggie adored *Runaway Bunny.* She loved the part where the Baby Bunny asks the Mother Bunny what would happen if he ran away, and the Mother Bunny says she'd come after him. Meggie always asked, "You'd come after us, too, wouldn't you?" Alexa thought she asked because the three of them lived every day in fear of separation. Michael used family court as his ultimate weapon of abuse.

The star twinkled down at Alexa, reminding her to stop thinking about Michael and his scorched earth litigation tactics, in order to preserve whatever remnants of sanity she had left. She could stay in her semi-conscious state, floating free from everything that surrounded her, only if she didn't think about Michael and Ronald Brigman. If those memories crept in, or worse yet if she talked about what they had done to her, she would come crashing back to the horror of being locked in this cell. That's why she was glad she could no longer speak, and that's why she was glad she couldn't talk to the man and the woman who'd come today. Or yesterday. She wasn't sure. The man's eyes haunted her. They were so kind. She hadn't seen eyes like that since her father died. She'd been just Meggie's age when her parents went off to church one wet Sunday morning and never came back.

The star twinkled down at her, taunting her with its freedom. If she'd had Meggie and Sam with someone like the man with the kind eyes, they'd still be together. Her precious star was nearly out of sight. She closed her eyes and tried to sleep.

* * *

Alexa woke with a start. For a minute, she could not remember where she was or why. Then it all came rushing back. Michael, dead. Brigman, dead. Her missing gun, the murder weapon. Sam and Meggie in D.C. with Coleman and Myrna. And the woman with the beautiful face and the ugly scar, and the man with the kind eyes, who wanted her to talk to them.

She looked up at the sliver of night sky visible between the bars. Her star was long gone. She had no idea how long she'd slept.

If she hadn't married Michael, she wouldn't be here now. Danger clung to him like a heady perfume, but that was the very quality that had attracted her the first time they met.

June 2003, Washington D.C. - The United States Supreme Court Building

She'd been sitting in Justice Moreno's outer office, waiting to be summoned for an interview for the clerkship opening in her chambers when Michael Reed walked in.

"Wait! I know you. You were in my class at Georgetown! Are you trying for Paula's job? I'll tell my old man to put in a good word for you. The Court could use some better-looking women! How about coffee when you're through?"

She didn't know whether to be insulted or amused, but his striking green eyes twinkled at her. "Not today, thanks. I'm just taking a few hours off for the interview."

"Shot down. Too bad. Where do you work?"

"I'm a clerk for Justice Steiner at the D.C. Circuit."

"Oh, Marilyn. Tell her I said hi."

"You want me to tell Justice Steiner Michael Reed said 'hi'?"

"Yeah, sure. She and my dad go way back. How come I never asked you out in law school?"

"I'm not your type."

"And what is my type?"

"Curvy and not very smart."

Michael threw back his head and roared. "Damn! The rumor mill was more accurate than I thought. So skinny blondes with brains and melting blue eyes weren't considered 'my type'?"

The door to Justice Moreno's inner sanctum opened, and the Justice herself appeared. She was about forty-five, with mousy brown hair, going gray, and fifteen extra pounds around her middle. "Miss Harrison? Are you ready to come in now?"

"I am, Your Honor."

Alexa got up to follow the Justice into her inner office. Justice Moreno looked over at Michael and gave him an indulgent smile. "Don't be developing designs on my clerks, Michael Reed, if you're looking for a date."

"I wasn't, Paula. I swear. I just came in to find a stapler; I didn't mean to stay."

And that was how it began. He found her number at the court of appeal and asked her for coffee two days later.

"So how was your interview with Paula?" They had walked a few blocks to Starbucks on her lunch hour.

Alexa laughed. "I can't get used to hearing Justice Moreno called 'Paula' or Justice Steiner called 'Marilyn.'"

"Sorry. But they socialize with my mother and father. I don't call them 'Justice' at my parents' cocktail parties."

"What's it like having your father on the Supreme Court?"

His green eyes grew thoughtful. "It has its advantages and its disadvantages."

"Such as?"

"Well, I'm pretty sure Steptoe and Johnson would not have hired me as an associate in their litigation section if my old man hadn't been on the Court. My grades at Georgetown, as you probably know, were not in your league."

Alexa sipped her coffee. "Actually, I had no idea what your grades were."

"Really? I thought everyone knew I was in the bottom third of the class."

"Not me."

"I suppose you realize everyone knew *your* GPA?"

"I'm not sure if 'everyone' knew, but I got my share of attention."

"For being number one?"

"Right."

"How does it feel?" He studied her face.

"Actually, a bit lonely. My grandmother died a few months ago. All the work I did in school was for her. Now there's no one to work for anymore."

"What about your parents?"

"They died when I was six. They were on their way to church one Sunday morning when a drunk driver ran a red light and plowed into their car. I had stayed home that day with my grandmother, my dad's mother, who lived with us, because I had a sore throat."

"Wow! So you're kind of an orphan?"

"Not 'kind of.' I am."

"That's tough." He gave her a warm, deep, sympathetic smile and squeezed her hand. Alexa's heart fluttered.

"So besides the job perks, what's it like being the son of a Supreme Court justice? Do you get a lot of dates?"

"With first-year female associates and paralegals, yes. But you wouldn't go out with me just because my father is on the Supreme Court."

"You're right. I wouldn't."

He looked disappointed. "Why not?"

"Two reasons. First, I'm seeing someone. And second, you had quite a reputation at Georgetown."

"As a ladies' man?"

"I'm not telling you anything you don't already know."

"Who are you dating?"

"His name is Josh Turner. He's a clerk for Justice Dombrosky."

"You mean 'Clarence.'"

"Justice Dombroksy goes to your parents' parties, too?"

"Everyone in D.C. goes to their parties. My dad's only been on the court four years, but he knows everyone in this town. Was Josh in our class?"

"No, he went to Harvard."

Michael's beautiful green eyes studied her thoughtfully. "You're not going to marry him."

"Don't be so sure about that."

"Has he proposed?"

"I think he's planning to. His clerkship is almost over, and he's looking for jobs here in D.C. because he knows I want to clerk at the Supreme Court."

"I'm not going to let you marry him," Michael Reed insisted.

"There isn't anything you can do about it."

"Yes, there is. Dinner, tomorrow night at Bistro La Mer."

"No, I can't."

"Yes, you can. Come on, Bistro is one of the most expensive places in the District. Don't tell me you aren't curious."

"Okay, I admit I am."

"Look, we're just law school classmates, nothing else. I'm coaching you for your follow-up interview with Paula—if your boyfriend asks. And I heard, by the way, she's going to call you back for another interview. Congratulations."

* * *

The night sky had lightened outside her slice of window. Red dawn would be coming soon, and it would bring with it the clang of breakfast carts, and metal trays being shoved through metal doors, and guards shouting insults to the inmates. But for now, she could remain undisturbed, floating on her cloud of memories.

Michael Reed would not give up on something he wanted, and Alexa found his pursuit flattering. It was much easier for Michael to make excuses to see her after she started working for Justice Moreno. He popped in whenever he stopped by to see his father. And that was often.

Josh complained, of course; but she insisted repeatedly that she and Michael were merely friends. She'd clung very hard to that fiction, possibly because she'd sensed the danger that lay just below Michael's heartbreakingly attractive surface. She knew she'd be safe if she never slept with him. The two of them hung on the phone for hours on week nights, and ate lunch as often as possible at their favorite Georgetown restaurants, and returned to Bistro La Mer so often the waiter offered to name a table in their honor. But what Alexa would not do, and what Michael dearly wanted her to do, was sleep with him. And she steadfastly refused. Josh was still her official boyfriend, and he had hinted he was going to ask her to marry him at Christmas, and he made it clear he did not like Michael Reed at all.

Justice Moreno noticed how often Michael now turned up in her chambers and tried to warn Alexa one late November afternoon. They had been working on revisions to a draft opinion that Alexa had researched. When they finished the last edit, Justice Moreno pulled off her reading glasses and looked across her desk at Alexa.

"Mind some advice?"

"Not at all." She had thought it was going to be about something professional.

"Michael Reed is trouble. So is Coleman. I know the Reeds make it look good from the outside, but you don't want to be mixed up in their mess."

Alexa felt her cheeks burning as she tried to deny what she realized must have become obvious in the last few weeks. "I understand, but Michael and I aren't dating. We're just friends from law school."

"So you're still seeing the young man I met at the Thursday night cocktail parties?"

"Josh Turner. He's finished his clerkship at the D.C. Circuit, and he's taken a job with Arnold and Porter."

"Well, I'm glad to hear that. I'm not trying to be nosey, Alexa. But I like you, and I'm certain you don't know the sordid history of the Reeds. And judging by how often Michael has dropped by these chambers since you started here, he isn't taking your relationship with Josh seriously."

"Well, he should." Alexa smiled, hoping Justice Moreno was finished handing out advice.

"Then I won't worry about you."

* * *

"I think you'd better stop coming by the office to see me," Alexa told Michael that night over dinner at Bistro La Mer. Her guilt at being out with him, knowing she'd lied to Josh about her plans for the evening, was easily assuaged by the tranquility of crisp cream linen, pale pink roses in crystal vases, good wine and the seductive smell of garlic simmering in cream and butter, while a trio of violins wafted Mozart delicately into the atmosphere.

"But I like seeing you at work!" His green eyes danced mischievously in the candlelight.

"Did you know Justice Moreno doesn't like you? Or your father?"

His face fell. "Actually, I knew she has had some problems with Coleman. She's an outspoken liberal, and of course my dad is as conservative as they come. They've had words, I understand, about professional issues. I didn't know she held her animosity toward my old man against me."

"She doesn't think you are someone I should get involved with."

His eyes went a shade darker. "I guess she's heard those womanizer rumors, too.

This is a big small town. Things get around. That's why you won't sleep with me, isn't it?"

"I'm officially dating Josh, remember?"

"I wish I could forget."

"It has to stay a friendship, Michael. There are too many other women in your life."

"There wouldn't be, if you'd be the only one."

It was a beautiful speech, and his eyes were soft and gentle as they looked into hers. She'd drunk more wine than she'd intended; and Michael's compact, five-nine frame of pure muscle was so much more attractive than Josh's six-foot beanpole. And the soft music and candlelight along with the hovering waiters ready in an instant to do their bidding made her feel safe. But instinctively she realized Michael carried that edge of risk and danger that Josh did not, and that was precisely what Paula Moreno was trying to tell her. She was in the midst of a lovely, dangerous dream. She mustn't let it seduce her into letting go of what she knew to be true.

"We agreed on friends, Michael."

"Okay, okay. And to prove I'm keeping my word, I'm inviting you and Josh to my parents' big Christmas bash. December 10. I'll make sure you get a formal invitation addressed to both of you."

* * *

Michael hadn't been in her or Josh's intellectual league. That's why the two of them had been clerking for appellate justices that winter while Michael was slogging his way through interminable depositions as the right arm of a Steptoe and Johnson civil litigation partner. But, Alexa reflected, as she listened to the clank of breakfast trays move closer, he outranked them in the cunning department. And the invitation to his parents' Christmas party had proved it.

It had been a bitter cold night. She and Josh had taken a cab from her apartment in Cathedral Heights to the Reed's impressive Georgetown townhouse. They'd arrived late because cabs had been scarce. The party was in full swing, with hearty fires roaring in all the fireplaces, massive silver trays loaded with food placed on white linen tablecloths in the dining room, and a trio of jazz musicians noodling Christmas carols by candlelight in the den. Waiters in white coats with sprigs of mistletoe circulated with trays of canapes and champagne flutes.

Alexa stayed with Josh throughout the evening, although she was deeply aware of Michael's eyes on her as they circulated through the crowd. She'd expected him to have a date, but he'd been solo. He made certain she and Josh were introduced to his mother and father. Coleman seemed to cling to their handshake a moment too long, and Alexa had felt uneasy.

Josh had not wanted to come, and only when Alexa fibbed and told him Justice Moreno expected to see her there did he relent. Fortunately, Justice Moreno spent a lot of time with them, introducing them to her colleagues. She seemed to be sizing up Josh, too. When she came across Alexa alone for a few seconds in the dining room, she whispered her approval in her ear. "You've got a good man, there. So glad you know that."

But the evening didn't end that way at all. Around midnight, when Alexa came out of the downstairs powder room, Michael stepped out of the shadows. Alexa jumped, and he caught her in his arms and gave her a long kiss that left her breathless.

"Stop that!" she pulled away.

"You don't really want me to stop." And he began to kiss her again. Alexa was torn between the magnitude of the attraction and her fear of Josh discovering her. And the footsteps behind her told her even before she turned that her worst fear had come true.

Alexa pulled away from Michael and started to walk toward Josh. "It's not what you think. I can explain."

But he shook his head and turned away. A few seconds later, she heard the front door close behind him.

In shock, she stared at the floor, wondering what to do. Michael put his hand on her arm.

"You'll need someone to take you home."

She nodded.

"Hey, look!" He put his hand under her chin and turned her face up to his. "He'll get over it. And if he doesn't, well maybe I'll have my chance now."

"That's why you did it, isn't it? You wanted him to see."

"No, I didn't think he would come looking for you."

She wanted to believe him, but she was skeptical.

"Hey, let's at least go for a walk, so you can calm down. And we'll see if we can find you a cab."

So she let him fetch her things, and they walked through the silence of Georgetown on a freezing December night at one a.m. They meandered in the cold until they reached Michael's townhouse, a few streets away.

"I haven't seen a single cab, and you're freezing. Come in for a few minutes and get warm. I'll get my car and drive you home."

But she didn't make it home. As soon as they were inside, the months of wanting tore away the last of Alexa's resolutions. She was angry with Josh for leaving her alone with Michael. And she knew she wasn't safe with him, but all the danger and risk of this beautiful man overwhelmed her. They made love over and over until they fell into an exhausted sleep.

Alexa woke several hours later. The bedside clock said four a.m. She studied Michael's peaceful face in the glow of the streetlight. He had the longest, most beautiful lashes she'd ever seen on a man. They softened his otherwise squarely masculine face. She looked out and saw flakes drift past the window in the pinkish glow of the streetlight.

She wrapped herself in a blanket and went to get a better look. The world had become a white wonderland of snowy silence.

"What are you doing over there?" Michael raised himself on one elbow.

"Looking at the snow. It's beautiful."

He smiled. "Come back to bed. I have an early Christmas present for you."

He opened a drawer in the table next to the bed as he spoke.

The bedroom was cold, and she was glad to slide next to his warmth. "Don't you want to wait until morning?"

"This can't wait." He opened the ring box, and let the diamond glitter in the frosty light from the street lamp. "Will you marry me?"

"I–"

"You can't say it's too soon. I've known you for five years. And I've known I wanted to marry you since the day I found you in Paula's office."

Alexa looked from his anxious eyes to the ring to the snow falling outside. It was true he had too many women in his life. But even a womanizer could settle down with a woman he adored. And Michael Reed had patiently protested his adoration in the face of her skepticism for months. She thought of the beautiful warm house tonight, dressed for the Christmas party, and of his polished, successful parents surrounded by

Washington's elite. Paula Moreno didn't like Coleman Reed. She'd had her reasons for suggesting the Reeds were not as they appeared. But Michael loved her, and Michael had so much to offer her, and he was offering it to her now on this magical December night.

Alexa smiled. "Yes. Yes, I will marry you."

CHAPTER FIVE

Friday Morning, Second Week of August 2013 - La Jolla

Percy Andrews kept them waiting on Friday morning. Sarah was not amused.

Jim had met her promptly at nine at Andrews' sterile glass and chrome office on the eleventh floor of the Ximed Building next to Scripps Hospital. He was way too attractive in a dark suit with a maroon tie, smelling of fresh shaving cream and laundry starch, and Sarah wished that two nights with David had done more to put him out of her mind.

"Looks like the court-appointed expert business must be pretty good," Jim observed as they sat in Andrews' glass and chrome waiting room gazing out at North San Diego, stretching flat and brown in the August heat toward the blue Pacific on the horizon.

"Agreed. Nice digs. These guys all practice the black arts for a considerable sum."

He grinned and his eyes twinkled, and her heart flip- flopped like a teen's. This, she told herself, was not good. The implacable Sarah Knight, toughest defense attorney on Wall Street, had to return at once and banish the dangerous idiot with the school girl crush on the ex-FBI agent.

"I thought defense attorneys swore by hired guns."

"So do prosecutors. I've met a few psychs with integrity, but not many."

Percy appeared at the door and summoned them to his inner sanctum. As they crossed the waiting room, Sarah heard Jim mutter under his breath, "Why do I think we are about to meet one of the latter?"

Percy Andrews, a thin balding man in his fifties wearing the cliche gray cardigan and baggy brown trousers associated with psychs, led them to his inner office which was cozier than the wasteland of his waiting room. He motioned for Sarah and Jim to sit on the large down sofa in the middle of the room, while he stretched out like a snake on a modern reclining chair opposite.

Did digging your heels into a thick, shaggy brown carpet make you want to confess your most private secrets, Sarah wondered, as her Jimmy Choos sank into the deep pile. She noticed a sand box in the corner of the room, filled with dozens of tiny plastic people and animals, where children who were caught in custody wars were, no doubt, forced to play while Percy Andrews decided their fate. She shivered at the thought.

"I'm Sarah Knight, and this is Jim Mitchell, my investigator."

"I know. Let's not waste anyone's time here. I'm going to testify she's competent to stand trial."

"*What?*" Jim nearly leapt out of his chair, and Sarah thought he was going to throttle Andrews. She pictured him standing next to Alexa's cot on Tuesday, deeply concerned.

"I said, I'm going to find her competent."

Unlike Jim, Sarah had retained her lawyer cool. "On what basis? She's practically comatose, and she hasn't spoken a word to either of us. In fact, we don't know if she can speak."

"Oh, of course she can."

"And she spoke to you when you evaluated her?"

"No, she was curled up on the cot with her back toward me."

"Then how can that be competency to stand trial?" Jim demanded.

"Meds. Give her some Lexapro, and she'll be right as rain."

"But there's a very strict United States Supreme Court test for ordering medication. And Alexa doesn't meet it," Sarah insisted.

"I don't give a rat's ass. She killed my colleague of more than twenty years, and she's going to die for it."

"But only after a fair trial in which she understands the nature of the proceedings and can assist in her defense."

"What defense? Her cell phone puts her in the neighborhood at the time of the murders which were committed with her gun. She hasn't got a defense, Ms. Knight. Ronald took her children away because she was a crazy lunatic, and she proved him right by killing him and Michael."

"Obviously you aren't familiar with the correct legal test."

"I'm familiar with *Sell v. United States*. I've been a forensic psychologist for twenty-five years."

"Then you know she doesn't meet the *Sell* standard. You can't show that less intrusive procedures such as counseling wouldn't produce the same results as forcing her to take Lexapro or some other drug."

"That's a pile of crap, if you'll excuse me for being blunt. Look, Alexa Reed is faking incompetency big time. She graduated first in her class from Georgetown. She knows if she becomes a comatose blob, she'll get sent to the state hospital, which is a lot cushier lifestyle than death row where she belongs. And she knows the state can't execute her while she's incompetent. She's counting on me to say she has to go to Patten Hospital for treatment until competency is restored, but I'm not going to play her game and let her live out her life in a medical facility when she belongs on death row."

"It's not a game," Jim spoke up.

"Excuse me?" Andrews raised his eyebrows as if Jim were an intruder without a right to speak.

"I said, she's not playing a game. She's mentally ill and unable to communicate to help us provide a defense."

"Too bad for her you aren't the court-appointed expert. She killed a close friend, and I'm not going to do her any favors."

"You mean you're biased, and you aren't going to be fair," Sarah said.

"Save your name calling for the hearing. It won't do you any good."

* * *

They were silent as the chrome elevators slipped effortlessly from the eleventh floor to the cavernous marble lobby that felt like a cathedral. When the doors opened, Sarah led the way to a quiet corner where they could talk.

"That was not what I expected," Jim began.

"I wasn't surprised after my interviews with Hal Remington and Trevor Martin."

"In other words, the legal community in this town is massed against her."

"The criminal bar is, at least."

"So what's next, boss?"

"I'm going to go to court this afternoon and request appointment of a defense expert to evaluate her."

"Got anyone in mind?"

"Jordan Stewart in L.A. I've used her before in cases that I tried in New York. She's an international expert on domestic violence, and she's one of the few who won't give an opinion just for the money. If she can't testify favorably for the defense, she won't get on the stand and perjure herself. According to Trevor Martin, Alexa told Brigman that Michael had abused her; but he refused to believe her."

"Looks like I'd better see what I can find on Michael, then. We'll need police reports for domestic violence and/or hospital visits."

"Would it be terrible to say I hope you find some?"

"Not at all. What about dinner tonight to talk over what I find?"

"Plans, tonight. Sorry."

"Wife still in Cabo?"

"Until Monday. We can talk about whatever you find on Michael in my office at nine on Monday morning."

He tried to conceal his disappointment. "Okay. See you then."

* * *

Second Friday of August 2013 - San Diego Superior Court

Judge Jay Steven Tyler III's court clerk, a harried, middle-aged woman in an ill-fitting black suit whose phone would not stop ringing, insisted between phone calls that Sarah would have to come back on Monday when she filed her motion for the appointment of an expert at one o'clock that afternoon.

"His Honor is presiding over a trial until four. He can't hear your matter today."

"It's an emergency. It will only take five minutes of his time."

"I can't promise anything. If you want to sit in on his trial and see if he has a break when he is willing to hear you, you can do that. But, again, no guarantees."

Sarah hated the idea of waiting three hours with no promise of any results, but she needed to get Jordan Stewart started on this case right away. So she tucked herself into a spot in the back of the courtroom watching a deputy district attorney and a public defender go at it over a gang shooting as she studied Judge Tyler. He was in his late fifties, with thinning gray hair, and a sharp face. His nose came to a point like a bird's beak. He frowned a great deal at his computer screen as he observed it through the half-glasses perched on his nose. He barked at both lawyers from time to time, and Sarah decided she had her work cut out for her. Either this judge lived in a state of permanent irascibility, or he was having a bad day. Still, no one ever denied a motion to appoint a defense psychological expert when the issue was competency.

After an hour and a half, the court recessed for a break; and Sarah hurried up to the bench to make her request.

Judge Tyler gave his clerk a puzzled look. "Who's this?"

"Sarah Knight, Your Honor. She's here on an emergency motion in the Alexa Reed case."

The judge stared down at Sarah who was standing behind the lectern recently vacated by the other attorneys. He was sizing her up.

"You're new in this courtroom."

"I am, Your Honor."

"Well, then, here's some information. I only hear motions on the morning docket call. This is not the morning, and this is not a docket call."

Sarah struggled to keep her anger out of sight. "I understand. But I've only been on this case a week, there are barely three weeks before the competency hearing, and I need an expert right away."

Judge Tyler frowned. She could tell he was weighing his options. He would have to hear her motion; maybe he would just decide to get it over with.

"Well, not now. We are on a short break as you can see. If there is time at four o'clock, we can go into chambers, and I'll listen. But no promises."

Sarah suppressed a sigh and resumed her spot in the back of the courtroom. Waiting gave her time to wish she hadn't turned Jim down for dinner and time to regret the coming weekend with David.

The gang expert finished droning on about "snitches" and "respect" at four fifteen. The judge apologized to the yawning jurors and sent everyone home. Sarah held her breath, hoping for the summons to his chambers to hear her motion. As His Honor stood up from the bench, he looked over the top of his glasses and saw her in the back of the courtroom.

"You're still here."

"I am, Your Honor."

"Well, come into chambers. We might as well get it over with."

The deputy district attorney and the public defender gave her sympathetic looks as she followed the judge out of the courtroom. They think he's going to tear me apart, Sarah thought as she entered the judge's chambers.

The room overlooked a parking lot at the back of the courthouse. It wasn't well lit, and it was littered with books and paper from one end to the other. She thought of Hal Remington's messy office and wondered if clutter was endemic to San Diego attorneys and judges.

Judge Tyler motioned for her to sit down, and she took the only empty chair.

He hung up his robes and sat down at his desk. She said nothing while he read her motion through his half glasses.

After he had scanned through it, he said, "Put this together in a hurry, didn't you?"

"Yes, Your Honor."

"Talked to Percy Andrews this morning, you say in here?"

"Yes, Your Honor."

"And obviously you didn't like what he said."

"He isn't basing his opinion on the facts."

"And you say the facts are you have a catatonic client who hasn't spoken since June 17."

"Actually the jail records and her medical records say that."

Judge Tyler heaved a world-weary sigh. "Motion denied."

Sarah's blood ran cold. "I'm sorry, Your Honor, did you say 'denied'?"

"In plain English. I've heard your motion, now I have to beat the Friday afternoon traffic home to La Mesa."

"But Your Honor—"

"You aren't from around here, are you Ms. Knight? You were in one of those fancy Wall Street firms, weren't you?"

"Craig, Lewis, and Weller, Your Honor."

"Like I said, fancy Wall Street firm. Our legal community is different, Ms. Knight. Percy Andrews has been doing evaluations for thirty years. Any judge in this courthouse will trust his opinion."

"But he's biased. Ronald Brigman was his friend and colleague."

"So what? It doesn't matter because your client is very guilty. Motion denied, Ms. Knight. Have a good weekend."

* * *

Second Friday of August 2013 - Rancho Santa Fe

David had invited her for dinner at his mansion in Rancho Santa Fe at eight. She parked in the gravel circle in front of the mock-French chateau, done in ubiquitous West Coast beige stucco instead of sandstone, and surveyed the acre of manicured lawns and imported palms that surrounded the house. Jim's cheerful red begonias were on her mind. Did he garden in his spare time? How had he chosen that particular shade of green for his house? Why didn't he turn all his father's money into a grand estate like this one? But she knew the answer: because he didn't need ostentation to be happy.

David met her at the front door. He was tanned, fifty, and in top shape because his personal trainer worked him out six days a week. His close-cropped blonde hair refused to go gray. He was handsome in the older Robert Redford way. When he met her in the marble entrance hall and gave her his signature Hollywood-style greeting, a hug and kiss on both cheeks, she noticed he didn't reach Jim's six feet.

"Hey, babe. Missed you. Come have a drink on the terrace while Michelle finishes up dinner."

Sarah followed him outside where a bottle of champagne waited, wondering how David's personal chef would stack up to Jim's cooking.

"Not champagne tonight. It hasn't been a celebration sort of day."

David arched an eyebrow, another annoying trait. She assumed he used it to intimidate his business staff, but she was beyond those kinds of tactics. "Scotch, then?"

"A good cab would be fantastic."

David summoned his butler to fulfill her request and poured bubbly for himself.

"Well, I'm going to celebrate Tessa in Cabo!"

"Do you think she hesitated to go because she knows about us?" Sarah gratefully took her glass of wine from the long-suffering Sam and took a big sip.

David shrugged. "Who knows? Who cares?"

"I thought you cared. Divorce would be extraordinarily expensive."

He waved his hands. "Tessa hasn't the guts to file for divorce. She loves this lifestyle far too much. We need to find her a boy toy to keep her occupied. Then we could spend a lot more time together."

How did I get involved with this man, Sarah asked herself. But she knew the answer far too well. He was superficial enough to be someone she could have sex with.

Which was the subject on his mind at that moment. "Come on, baby. Let's have a quickie before dinner."

* * *

Sarah woke at midnight in the guest room's four-poster with David beside her. She refused to sleep in the bed he shared with his wife.

She got up, wrapped herself in a white silk robe, and crossed the room to the French doors, open onto the cool, deep blue August night. She sat down in one of the chairs on the terrace that ran the length of the back of the house, and stared up at the stars and the newly waning moon in the soft night air. Her ghosts surrounded her, and she couldn't push them away.

"I don't want to be here," she told the Universe.

"'Here' as in 'here with David' or 'here' as 'at this point in your life'?" the stars asked.

"Both."

"Well, the David part you can fix in a heartbeat. The other part is going to take some time."

"I don't want to go through that."

"You don't have a choice."

She heard the sheets rustle, and then David called out, "Where are you, babe?"

"Out here."

He got up and pulled on his own robe and came outside. He looked puzzled. "What are you doing outside? Come back to bed."

Sarah shook her head. "Not yet. I need time to think."

"About what?" He pulled her to her feet and tried to kiss her, but she turned her head away. "Hey! What's this? Don't waste the little time we have being moody."

"I'm not moody. I've just gotten this big new case, and there was a hearing today that didn't go well. I'm upset."

"Hey! Remember the rules. No wife-talk. No work-talk."

I remember, Sarah thought. I made those up. And now I regret them because I need someone to talk to. And you are not that someone.

"Come on, back to bed."

She let him lead her out of the cool night, away from the friendly stars and the moon, into the bedroom where she didn't resist when he went through the motions of sex one more time. She wanted to go home, but it would upset more apple carts if she did than if she just stayed until morning. It was what he expected, and it was easier just to go along. When he was quiet at last and ready to sleep again, Sarah lay awake and watched the stars through the open doors and thought about Jim.

CHAPTER SIX

He arrived at her office in La Jolla at eight forty-five on Monday. He was carrying two grande Starbuck's lattes and a paper bag containing scrambled egg and bacon sandwiches. He wished his heart didn't beat so fast at the sight of her in jeans and a simple black blouse.

"You're early."

"I thought you'd be hungry."

Sarah smiled and took a fortifying sip of coffee from the covered paper cup. "I can't argue with that."

He sat down in one of the two chairs in front of her desk and opened the sandwich wrapper. Sarah noted his uniform of casual khakis and starched shirt, sleeves rolled up to the elbows. He saw her take in his attire.

"Real men do wear pink."

"I wasn't disputing that. It looks good on you."

"Thanks. And I'm admiring those jeans."

"I'm not headed to court today. Thank, God. I can get away with these out here."

"But not back on Wall Street, I take it. So what happened on Friday?"

She recounted the debacle in Judge Tyler's chambers.

"That bad?"

"Yeah. And the funny part is, I thought he'd play fair and say yes."

"This isn't 'Play Fair' world."

"I'm beginning to understand that. I feel like Alice in Legal Wonderland. I'm expecting to see the Red Queen sitting on the bench at any minute."

"So what are you going to do? Take a writ to the court of appeal and demand an order to get an expert appointed?"

"No. As I was leaving, Tyler reminded me he plays golf with Justice Wilmont, the presiding justice of the court of appeal, every Tuesday afternoon. I have a feeling I'm going to be up there seeking a writ before this case is over, so I'd better pick my spots."

"Go up too often, and you look like a whiner."

"Exactly."

"Well, I've got some more bad news for you." He licked the last drop of ketchup off his fingers as he spoke and noticed she had eaten a third of her sandwich and put it down. "Don't you like the chow, by the way?"

"No, it's great. Thanks. Talking about Judge Tyler took my appetite away. What's your bad news?"

"I didn't find any incidents of domestic violence on Michael Reed. Nothing. Nada. Zip."

"Wow, and I assume you've illegally checked the Bureau's data bases. So we are big time out of luck on that one."

"For now. You don't know what Alexa is going to say when she wakes up."

"Oh, you mean when they med her to make her talk to us."

"Look, I agree they'll be acting illegally. But at least she'll talk to us."

"Meds are not a cure-all. Sometimes the clients hallucinate; and when they talk to you, you can't tell what's real and what's fiction. And meds make them zombie-like in front of the jury."

"Sounds like more issues for the appellate attorney."

"Do you read lawyer fiction?"

Jim smiled. "Some of it."

"Know what Scott Turow calls an appellate attorney? 'The designated loser.' I hate to think my sole function as trial counsel is creating a case for another attorney to lose on appeal."

"So what are we going to do about an expert for Alexa?"

"I'm going to hire Jordan Stewart out of my own pocket. We don't have any other choice. And we should go see Alexa every few days. Frequent visits might turn her around enough to talk to us. I'm also thinking how often I've tried to get her to cooperate might become a subject at the competency hearing."

"You mean they'll say you didn't try hard enough?"

"As you know, the defense attorney gets blamed for everything."

"I'd like to say you're being paranoid, but you're not. So when do we go to see her again?"

"Let's meet at the jail at two o'clock on Tuesday afternoon."

* * *

Second Week of August, 2013 - San Diego Main Jail Downtown

The man and the beautiful woman with the unexpected scar on her cheek kept coming to see her. It must be every couple of days. Alexa wished she could talk to them and explain there was nothing they could do. They spoke in soft, concerned voices, urging her not to give up hope, begging her to talk to them. But her words stayed in her head and refused to go into her mouth. Besides, if she spoke, she'd wake up in hell instead of drifting in the out-of-body world she had managed to retreat to.

Sometimes she could hear Meggie and Sam's voices calling to her. "Mommy, Mommy. You said you'd come after us, Mommy."

* * *

Fourth Monday in August 2005, Michael Reed's Townhouse, Georgetown

At four o'clock Alexa sat alone in the living room of her new husband's townhouse, surrounded by boxes that the movers had packed that day. All their belongings were going to be loaded onto a moving van headed to San Diego in the morning. The house had been sold; the new owners were taking possession as soon as their things were on the truck.

It was far too late to heed Justice Moreno's warning even though the memory of buying the one-way ticket to San Diego made her nauseous. When she'd said 'yes' to Michael in December, she'd had no idea she was going to be torn away from everything familiar by August and forced to move to a place she'd never seen.

They announced their engagement in January, with the wedding set for early August after Alexa's clerkship ended in July. Alexa had expected to have a job waiting for her at one of Washington's prestigious boutique appellate law firms when she left the Court. In February she had talked to the hiring partners at Harper, Spalding and at Williams, Pogue; and both firms had been very interested in offering her a job. She'd been excited about her starting salary at either firm, and about the prospect of being on the fast-track for partnership. She was also glad to be joining some of her fellow clerks from the D.C. circuit and some of her current colleagues, also leaving the Court with her in July, who would be scattered throughout both firms. It would be good to be working with people she liked and respected.

But all of Alexa's expectations for her future changed radically one evening in May. Michael had pressured her to give up her apartment in Cathedral Heights and move in with him in March. Alexa hadn't liked giving up her independence; but, at the same time, now that the news was out, she realized the world expected her to marry Michael Reed. Backing out would be embarrassing and would open the door to some unpleasant speculation and gossip.

Michael had come home around midnight, angry and upset. Alexa had never seen him in such a dark mood before.

He slammed the front door and hurried into the living room to pour himself a scotch from the drinks tray. Alexa, dressed in pajamas, hurried downstairs to welcome him home. But the welcome died on her lips when she saw his face.

"What's wrong?"

"I've been fired."

The news hit her like a punch to the gut. "You've been what?"

"Fired. Let go. Oh, not immediately, but I was told tonight I'm not ever going to make partner at Steptoe, and I'd better start looking for a new job."

"But I thought—"

"You thought they'd want me forever because Coleman is on the Court?"

"I—well, you always said your father's job was important to Steptoe's hiring decision."

Michael gulped his scotch and poured another. Alexa suddenly realized he'd had way too much before he came home.

"Go easy on that. You've already had quite a bit."

"Don't tell me what to do!" He threw the tumbler across the room, sending glass shards flying everywhere, and grabbed her by both wrists and shook her hard. "Don't you fucking tell me what to do, you little whore!"

Alexa had never experienced this kind of violence before. It sucked all the air out of her lungs and made her feel as if she were floating above her own body, looking down.

"Michael, calm down."

"Don't you tell me what to do!" He screamed, twisting her left wrist painfully as he jammed his face into hers.

Alexa held her breath as a sharp pain stabbed her arm. Michael, still inches from her face, began to laugh hysterically.

"Didn't like that, did you, bitch? I can fix the other one for you, too!" He started to twist her right hand, but something occurred to his drunken brain at that moment. "Oh, wait. You'll tell your big, bad boss Moreno that I hurt you. Can't have rumors about me floating around the Supreme Court."

Abruptly he let her go, throwing her across the room backwards so that she lost her balance and fell against the coffee table, bruising her ribs.

"Didn't expect that one, either, did you? I can take you, Alexa Harrison! Don't think you can get away with doing anything other than what I tell you to do!"

Alexa lay still where she had fallen, waiting for him to leave the room. After he had poured himself another scotch and had gone upstairs, she found blankets and pillows and made herself a bed on the couch where she cried herself to sleep.

By morning he was sober and sorry. He brought her breakfast he had cooked himself. He was in tears as he begged her forgiveness. But she hadn't given him an answer. She was still in shock. She stopped at a drug store on the way to work and bought an elastic brace for her sprained wrist. She left her suit jacket on in an attempt to hide it, but Justice Moreno's sharp eye caught it right away.

"What happened?"

"I tripped and fell."

Paula Moreno gave her an odd look, and Alexa had the distinct feeling she didn't believe her. "You're sure that's what happened?"

"I'm sure."

Alexa was glad the Justice was in conference during lunch and didn't see Michael hurrying into her office with a blue box from Tiffany's. She probably would have guessed the truth if she had seen him.

"I know I don't deserve to be forgiven, but I at least wanted to give you something to say I'm sorry. I don't deserve anyone as wonderful as you. If you want to call off the wedding, I understand."

The normally powerful, confident Michael Reed was now an embarrassed schoolboy, shifting uncomfortably from one foot to the other as he stood in front of her desk. In the end, it wasn't the diamond bracelet that melted her heart. It was what appeared to be his genuine anguish over what he had done.

They went to dinner that night at Bistro La Mer. She wore the bracelet over her elastic support bandage, and Michael offered her a thousand mea culpas until she was desperate to talk about something else.

"Well, then, I'll give you the good news. I've been offered a job at my father's old firm in San Diego, Warrick, Thompson, and Hayes."

"You've been offered another job that quickly?"

Michael grinned. "Maybe I'm not as bad a lawyer as Steptoe thinks. But to tell the unvarnished truth, Coleman set it up for me. He brought a lot of clients to Warrick, Thompson when he left Eliot, Fitzgerald in New York. In fact, his clients represent forty percent of the firm's annual billings. Coleman was the firm's biggest rainmaker before he went on the bench."

"So he used his influence to get you a job in San Diego?" Alexa's stomach tightened at the thought of moving so far from everything she knew.

"I wouldn't put it like that. His clients haven't gotten the attention they received when my father was with the firm. He called Alan Warrick today and told him I need to be there to look after them the way he did. It's a great opportunity. I'll be a partner in no time."

"But where does that leave me? Does Warrick, Thompson have an appellate department?"

A cloud passed over Michael's face. "Um, no. They only have one partner who does appeals, Chuck Reilly. They're going to offer you a job working for him. I told my father we are a package deal."

Alexa frowned. "That's not the job I'm looking for when I leave the Supreme Court. I want to work for Harper, Spaulding or Williams, Pogue."

Michael frowned. "But I'll never be offered anything like this opportunity in D.C. My father doesn't have a stable of clients here to pass on to me."

Alexa wanted to say *then find your own clients the way everyone else does*, but the memory of the prior evening stopped her. "I don't want to live in San Diego. I grew up in Fairfax. Northern Virginia is my home."

"I don't want to leave D.C., either. But, I can't pass this up."

Alexa frowned. "But the best job for me is here."

"And the best job for me is in San Diego."

And, in the end, Alexa reflected ruefully as she lay on her cot in the jail, Michael got his way. That was his specialty: getting what he wanted. She had tried to hide her elastic bandage under long-sleeved blouses in the inferno of an unseasonably hot spring while the sprain healed. She'd felt deeply and horribly ashamed, as if she were the one who had reacted violently and not Michael. She often wished she had the courage to tell Paula Moreno the truth, but Alexa was sure Paula would think less of her for not heeding her warning about Michael Reed. She was certain her boss thought her engagement was a mistake because she had never offered congratulations.

* * *

Last Week of August, 2013 - San Diego Main Jail Downtown

The man with the kind eyes and the woman with the scar on her cheek kept coming to see her, now accompanied by a tall, thin blonde woman with patient hazel eyes. She, too, begged Alexa to talk to her; and when she didn't, the blonde woman looked at the man and the woman with the sad eyes and said, "I think they might have to give her meds." And the man and the woman always said, "No! No!"

But Alexa knew the answer was *yes, yes*. But not for the reason the kind blonde woman thought.

* * *

Last Week of August, 2013 - Sarah's Office La Jolla

On the last Thursday of August, Jim, Sarah, and Jordan met in Sarah's conference room to put the final touches on their preparation for the competency hearing on Tuesday. Sarah sat at the head of the table with Jordan on her left and Jim on her right. They had just come back from their last meeting with Alexa.

"Nothing changes," Jordan began.

Jim liked her for being honest. Jordan was tall and lean, in her mid-forties with blonde hair and gentle hazel eyes that invited confidences. Her husband taught psychology at UCLA, and they had three teenage daughters.

"Agreed." Sarah sighed. Her dark circles were that much darker, and she wasn't eating. Jim wondered how many nights she'd spent with David Spineli but knew he couldn't ask.

"I think Alexa is suffering from Post-Traumatic Stress Disorder," Jordan began. "When the mind encounters more than it can process, it shuts down."

"Are you willing to give an opinion that she should be committed to the state hospital for treatment until she regains her competency to stand trial?"

"Yes," Jordan said. "I know you said Percy Andrews will insist she can go to trial on psychotropic drugs; and honestly, she is so depressed they might have to use those in the beginning just to get her to speak to a psychiatrist. But I think she needs counseling sessions before she can stand trial. She's been through a lot that we don't even know about, and right now she can't tell us any of it. Drugging her is only putting a tiny band-aid on her condition."

* * *

Jim drove Jordan to Solana Beach to meet her five o'clock train to Los Angeles. Sarah remained behind to work on her cross-examination of Percy Andrews.

As Jim swung his black Range Rover onto the I-5 North, Jordan asked, "Have you known Sarah long?"

"Only a month. We ran into each other in a bar in La Jolla one night, and she happened to be looking for an investigator."

"Sarah never gets involved with anyone."

Jim glanced quickly over at her, and then turned his eyes firmly back to the road. "Am I that obvious?"

"I don't think you are to Sarah. I've known her a long time. She's the most work-oriented person I know. But, yes, I can see you've got a thing for her."

"Has she ever told you how she got that scar on her cheek?"

"No."

"And you've always had the good manners not to ask, right?"

"In my profession, we wait to be told. If the client doesn't want to talk, we wait for them to be ready."

"Except Percy Andrews isn't willing to wait for Alexa Reed."

Jim pulled into the parking lot at the train station and got out to help Jordan with her brief case and overnight bag. "What time are you arriving on Tuesday? I'll meet your train."

"I'm coming down Monday night, arriving at eight. I'm paranoid about being late for the hearing next morning."

"I'll be here to pick you up. I have a guest room. Want to use it? I make a better breakfast than a five-star hotel."

CHAPTER SEVEN

Labor Day Weekend, August-September 2013, San Diego Main Jail

The memories were worse at night. They flew at her, thick and fast, like bats in the dark.

The guards had been talking about who was off on Monday, so Alexa guessed the calendar had reached September and Labor Day. That was the weekend in 2005 when Michael had insisted they put the offer down on the house on Mount Soledad in La Jolla. They'd been in town a week, and they were scheduled to start work at Warrick, Thompson on Tuesday.

Alexa had wanted to buy a smaller, older home in the historic Kensington neighborhood that felt more like the Virginia community where she'd grown up. But Michael was adamant that his new position as overseer of Coleman's clients required him to have the five-thousand-square-foot mansion with the breathtaking ocean view. Coleman and Myrna had lived in La Jolla, and Michael insisted they must live there, too.

Alexa tried to embrace her new job with enthusiasm, but from day one she could see that working for Chuck Reilly was not going to be the equivalent of working for Paula Moreno, who had been a professor at Yale before she went on the Court; nor was it going to be comparable to working for any of the partners at Harper, Spaulding or at Williams, Pogue. Chuck was in his late fifties, with thinning hair, and a slight stoop because his six-feet seemed to be collapsing from being at his desk too much. He had gone to law school at UCLA, made law review, and clerked for a justice on the California Supreme Court. But despite his academic credentials, he wasn't in the intellectual league Alexa had just left behind. And he was a loner through and through. He had never had an associate working for him before, and that was because he didn't want one. He'd started in Warrick, Thompson's litigation department, had done middling work in their law and motions practice, and then had decided to call himself an appellate specialist to avoid ever having to try a case.

Alexa wilted with boredom at her desk each day. Sometimes she went home at four o'clock to the big empty house and sat out on the back patio, staring at the ocean and drinking cold white wine in the sharp September sunshine. One day in early October, she realized she was not only living in Michael's mother's former neighborhood, she was developing Myrna's fondness for excessive alcohol to dull the pain of loneliness. Like Myrna, she never saw her husband. Night after night, Michael was on "business development" dinners with his father's clients while she was home alone.

She wanted to talk to him about it, but the violence of that May night remained etched in her memory. Michael was obviously happy in this new life. She obviously was not. And more obviously, he did not care. Alexa wracked her brain to figure out how to make her situation more bearable. Starting with finding a new job.

She made discreet inquiries but found there were no boutique appellate firms in San Diego. When a trial lawyer lost a case, he or she simply filed his or her own brief in the court of appeal. She quickly deduced that Chuck Reilly fed like a vampire off his litigation partners' losses. And since Warrick, Thompson did not lose many cases, she realized to her horror that Chuck Reilly was significantly underemployed.

Deeper research into the problem demonstrated Alexa would have to go to Los Angeles or San Francisco to find the job she wanted. One night in October when they had been at the firm a little over a year, she broached the subject to Michael when he came in very drunk and reeking of perfume. He laughed in her face. Instinctively she'd realized if she pushed the subject, she'd see the frightening, violent Michael she'd seen in D.C. She was too afraid of him to say more.

There were rumors in the firm that he was dating other women. She tried to ignore them, but the scent on his clothes and the hours he kept confirmed their truth without her having to ask. Alexa held her head high but stayed mostly in her office. When she asked Chuck Reilly for work, he apologized and said he'd try to find something. Only he never did.

November 2006, Law Offices of Warrick, Thompson, San Diego

Then one Friday afternoon, a week before Thanksgiving, the horrible truth came into her office around three o'clock.

"Mrs. Reed, I have to talk to you."

Alexa looked up from one of the small research projects she had finally wrestled from her boss to find a curvaceous red-head in a form-hugging black suit standing in her office doorway.

"Have we met?"

"I've seen you a few times at firm cocktail parties. But, no, we haven't met. I'm Stacy O'Connor, I'm a litigation paralegal."

Alexa's stomach tightened. "You work for my husband." She immediately recognized the perfume, the scent of too many roses in a small space.

"Yes, I do. I need to talk to you."

"If you want to talk about Michael, I'm not going to listen to anything you have to say."

"Please. I'm frightened."

Alexa studied her face. She was in her late twenties, she guessed; and her dark eyes were full of terror.

"I can't help you." Alexa wanted her to go away.

"Maybe you can; maybe you can't."

"I'm not making any promises. But I'll listen."

Stacy came in, closed the door, and took one of the chairs in front of Alexa's desk. She twisted her hands together as if summoning the courage to speak. "I've been having an affair with your husband."

Alexa willed herself not to display any emotion.

"I see. For how long?"

"Since late September. Not long after I started working for him."

"And didn't you know he was married?"

"Yes, of course. But he said it wasn't happy. He said you'd be leaving him soon and going back to D.C."

"And then?"

"He promised we'd be married." Stacy pressed her hands together tightly. "Look, I know how this sounds. And I had a boyfriend, too. But Michael—I mean Mr. Reed—well, he just—"

"Swept you off your feet?" Alexa asked dryly, thinking of that December night when she'd let Michael drive Josh away and had been vulnerable to his ridiculous proposal like something out of a really bad romance novel.

Stacy nodded, looking down at her hands, now motionless in her lap.

Alexa leaned back in her chair and willed this interview to end. "Okay, Stacy. I understand. I hope this confession has helped you in some way. I don't want to listen to any more."

"But there is more!" Stacy looked desperate. "I'm pregnant!"

Alexa closed her eyes and let the blow sink in. Then she opened them. "And how can you be sure my husband is the father?"

"Because I haven't slept with anyone else."

"What about your boyfriend?"

"We broke up because I was seeing Michael. I mean, Mr. Reed."

Alexa waived her hands impatiently. "I don't care what you call him. I can't help you."

"Look, I just came to ask for one thing."

"And what is that?"

"Michael says I have to have an abortion. He says the firm is going to pay for it. And then I'm getting a big severance check to leave and find a new job."

Alexa was incredulous. "He told you the firm would pay for your abortion?"

"I have the check right here. See? A cashier's check made out to the Women's Health Center."

Alexa took the paper from her as if it were a snake. It was, indeed, exactly what she said.

"And this is the severance check. Fifty thousand dollars." Stacy handed her another piece of paper, and Alexa stared at it.

"Fifty thousand dollars? But you don't make that in a year. Why is the firm paying you that much to terminate you?"

"I don't know. Michael just said I had to leave, but he'd see that I was well looked after."

"If you have all this money, why are you here in my office claiming to be terrified?"

"Because I'm scheduled for the procedure tomorrow. And I'm afraid I'm not going to make it."

"*What?*" Alexa stared at her. "That's ridiculous!"

"I wish it were. But I heard Michael arranging things. The clinic is one of his clients. I heard him say he was expecting 'the outcome he wanted.'"

Alexa tried to focus on Stacy's words even though her world was spinning.

"You're reading too much into a simple statement."

"Maybe. But I'm still terrified."

"I can't help you."

"But you can. I'm not going through with the abortion. I'm from Seattle. I'm going to head out tonight for home and have the baby there. No one will ever know. But just in case something happens to me, I wanted you to know the story and to see these checks."

Alexa stared at the paper in her hand. "They're drawn on the firm account, not on Michael's personal account."

"Right. He said he was so important to the firm that it had to pay for everything."

"What?" Alexa stared at her.

"He said his father's clients bring in forty percent of the firm's revenue. His father sent him here to look after those clients; so the firm will do what he wants, including paying for my abortion and severance."

"I can't do anything about this, Stacy."

"Yes, you can. I'm giving you these checks to keep."

"But then you can't cash them."

"I don't want to cash them. Michael will find me if I do."

"But why give them to me?"

"Because if anything happens to me, you'll be able to prove Michael was involved."

"Are you saying your life is in danger from my husband?"

"Yes. That is exactly what I am saying."

* * *

November 2006, San Diego

She would return to D.C. She'd been a fool to go through with the wedding, but she didn't have to go on being a fool. She could salvage her career, even if there'd be questions because she was going to be Coleman Reed's ex-daughter-in-law. She hid Stacy's original checks in the bottom of her jewelry box with the diamond bracelet that she'd worn only once: the night of the make-up dinner at Bistro La Mer. Looking at it made her remember the terror of Michael's attack and how humiliated she'd felt afterward. All weekend, she planned her escape while Michael spent hours on his cell phone.

He seemed distracted and upset; and on Sunday night, around ten o'clock, she passed the bedroom that served as his home office on her way to bed and heard his voice loud and angry through the door.

"What do you mean you haven't found her? She didn't show up at the clinic on Saturday morning. The checks I gave her were never cashed. She's got red hair and a body to die for. She stands out in any crowd. You can't be much of a private investigator if you can't find Stacy O'Connor!"

Suddenly the door opened, and an angry Michael Reed found her standing in the hall in her pajamas. Alexa's heart began to race. His eyes went from angry to cold and hard, the way she'd seen them that night in Georgetown. She braced herself for a blow.

But it never came. His face softened, and he asked, "How much did you hear?"

"Enough to know what's going on. Stacy came to see me on Friday, and she told me everything."

"That's why you've been so quiet this weekend."

"I'm going back to D.C., Michael."

He nodded in defeat. "Of course. This hasn't been much of a job for you, has it?"

"No."

"If it makes any difference, I didn't know. Chuck claimed he had a busy practice, and you'd have lots to do."

"If he said that, he lied."

"Then he lied. What did Stacy tell you?"

"Everything. The affair. The baby. The money you gave her drawn on the firm's account."

"That's just a loan. I'll have to pay it back when I make partner."

"I don't believe you."

"Well, you will someday when I have to pay it all back."

"How did you know Stacy's checks were drawn on the firm account?"

"She showed them to me."

"They haven't been cashed. Any idea where she is? I'm worried. Alone, pregnant with a married man's child. Who knows what she'd do?"

"I have no idea," Alexa lied. "I'm going to bed."

"Would you let me talk to you for a few minutes first?"

"You're not going to change my mind about leaving."

"I know. But I'd like to apologize. I can't do it properly standing here in the hall."

She hesitated for a split second but agreed. He followed her to their bedroom.

A pair of matching love seats faced each other with the fireplace in the middle. Alexa sat down on one, Michael on the other. She was amazed to see tears in his eyes.

"You're crying. I've never seen you cry."

"What else can I do?" His green eyes met hers, dark with pain. "I've lost the person I love most in the world, and it's all my own stupid fault."

"But surely you knew what would happen if I found out about Stacy? And how could you have believed you'd get away with it when we work at the same place?"

Michael wiped away a tear that had fallen on his cheek. "Arrogance. Plain and simple. And stress. I've been worrying about whether I could live up to Coleman's expectations. Look, I admit being fired from Steptoe shook my confidence. I've had nightmares about Coleman's clients leaving because I wasn't giving them the attention they expected."

"But you don't actually handle all that work. It's distributed throughout the firm to other attorneys."

"Right. But Coleman expects me to make sure they are all happy with the service Warrick provides. I'm supposed to watch over all of their accounts."

"So where does Stacy O'Connor come in?"

"She came on to me."

"That's not the impression I got from her."

Michael nodded in defeat. "So you believe her and not me? I'm not surprised after what I've done. But for the record, she pursued me."

"Why?"

"To put it bluntly, she wanted to be a partner's wife."

"And you didn't tell her you were married?"

"I didn't have to. Everyone knew. But she kept after me. Working late. Tight dresses. Backrubs at my desk when my shoulders were tense from worrying."

"She said you knew she had a boyfriend and got between them. The way you got between me and Josh."

"Okay. I admit I planned everything that night at my parent's party. I wanted to get you alone and ask you to marry me."

"So you staged that kiss for Josh to see?"

"I admit I did. But I didn't do anything to come between Stacy and her boyfriend. If he broke up with her, it was because she was pursuing me." Michael got up and came to stand in front of her. He went down on one knee dramatically.

Alexa frowned. "I already told you that you are not going to change my mind about leaving."

"I know. But I just want a chance to explain. I'm sorry if you think my proposal was a dirty trick. But I fell in love with you the first time I saw you in Paula Moreno's office. And I loved being with you. I tried to find any and every excuse to see you. Come on, you have to admit, you enjoyed being with me, too."

"I did, but I felt guilty because I knew Josh wouldn't want me seeing you."

"And Paula didn't approve of me, either."

"Please get up and sit down."

"Can I sit beside you?"

He looked so contrite that she agreed. He gave her a little smile as he settled next to her. "Thanks. When are you leaving?"

"Tuesday morning. I want to miss the Thanksgiving rush at the airport."

"Would you consider staying until after the holiday?"

Alexa eyed him suspiciously. "What for?"

"Well, you don't have any family back in D.C. to celebrate with. And I'll be alone here and missing you terribly if you go on Tuesday. We could at least part friends and have one last nice time together. And I also want you to stay because I have a proposition for you to think over."

"Such as?"

"One of Coleman's clients just lost a very, very big appeal in the Ninth Circuit, and wants the firm to take it to the Supremes. Chuck Reilly thinks that's going to be his case, but I can get it for you."

"Why would you do that?"

"Can I be honest?"

"I don't want to be lied to anymore."

Michael winced. "I deserved that one."

"Then why are you trying to do something nice for me after ignoring me for more than a year and getting another woman pregnant?"

"To do more than just say I'm sorry and that I love you. To show you, too."

"I'll have to think about it."

"Of course."

"Will you put off leaving for a week?"

"That depends. Tell me why Stacy said she was afraid for her life."

"You mean she thought I might do something to hurt her?"

Alexa nodded.

"That's ridiculous. My whole career would be over. Why was she paranoid enough to think I'd harm her?"

"Because she overheard a call you made to the abortion clinic telling them you expected the outcome you wanted."

"That's ridiculous. I wanted everything to go well for her. Do you believe me?"

Alexa studied his face, tear-streaked and sad. Her heart ached for him and for her. She remembered all the good times they'd had at their own personal table at Bistro La Mer. She remembered how funny and charming he could be, and how much she had enjoyed having him pursue her. "Yes, I do. I didn't think I did, but I believe you."

"Good. And will you stay? For another week? And think about taking that case. You could still have it, even if you go back to D.C. I can make that happen."

"Okay, I'll stay another week."

"May I hug you?"

He opened his arms, and she went into them. She smelled his deep, musky aftershave, and her body remembered all the times they'd made love. He clung to her like a drowning man, and she settled closer, grateful for his warmth. He was now all the family she had. Deep in her heart, she didn't want him to be Bad, Cruel Michael Reed. She would far rather believe he was the husband who loved her and was genuinely sorry.

Later they made love, and afterwards Michael held her close. "Does that feel like I love you?"

"Yes."

"So you believe that I do?"

"Yes."

"And do you trust me?"

"Yes."

"Then will you tell me where Stacy has gone?"

"Why do you need to know?"

"If there's going to be a child, I want to do the responsible thing and pay my share. I won't interfere in her life. But I owe her child support."

"Seattle. She grew up in Seattle."

They made love again and again until they were exhausted and drifted into sleep.

CHAPTER EIGHT

First Tuesday in September, 2013, San Diego Superior Court

Sitting at the defense table with Jim next to her on the Tuesday after Labor Day, Sarah stared up at The Honorable John Charles Tomlinson and tried to quiet the butterflies in her stomach. Judge Tomlinson was the opposite of Judge Tyler, who had been thin and sharp. He appeared to be around Sarah's age, and he had no angles. He was slightly portly, with an open, round face, kind gray eyes, and a thatch of light brown hair sparsely streaked with gray. He treated everyone in the courtroom with the upmost politeness. He had been more than willing to listen to Jordan Stewart, although Sarah had entered the hearing very worried about whether her witness would be allowed to testify.

As expected, Percy Andrews had opined only drugs would render Alexa able to stand trial. And he lied, claiming to be unbiased when Sarah tried to demonstrate his loyalty to Ronald Brigman. Then Jordan's turn came, and she explained why, even if Alexa were given drugs, she still wouldn't be competent to assist in her defense.

"She's been through too much trauma. She lost custody of her very young children, and that was a shock. And then she was the one who found Michael dead that night, and that was a shock."

"But it was a shock only if she didn't kill him." Judge Tomlinson broke in.

"At this point, Your Honor, we have to presume she's innocent," Sarah reminded the judge. "She reported finding Michael to the police, didn't leave town, and went in voluntarily for questioning."

"Okay. For the moment, I'm going to make that assumption. But haven't you also testified, Dr. Stewart, that she's so depressed it will require medication to get her even to talk to a counselor? Why put her in the hospital if meds will make her able to talk to her attorneys and assist with her defense?"

"Because there's no guarantee medicating her will restore her to competency. She can only be competent after she heals from the underlying trauma. Drugs might make her able to talk again, but healing requires being able to talk about the traumas and working through her emotions. Right now she's so overwhelmed by her feelings, she's completely nonfunctional, and she will still be overwhelmed even if she's no longer too depressed to talk."

"I see." Sarah watched the judge make notes on his yellow legal pad.

He continued to scribble furiously after Jordan stepped down. After a few more minutes of writing, he looked directly at Sarah.

"Ms. Knight, I have a few more questions for Dr. Andrews. Would you object to allowing Mr. Barton to recall him briefly?"

I object with every fiber of my being, Sarah thought. But she could tell Judge Tomlinson had taken Jordan's testimony seriously, and she didn't want to risk making him angry by saying no. "That's fine, Your Honor."

Percy Andrews slithered from the back of the courtroom and wrapped himself around the chair on the witness stand after being resworn.

"Dr. Andrews," the judge began, "you've heard Dr. Stewart's opinion. She believes medication alone will not restore the defendant. In Dr. Stewart's opinion, Alexa Reed needs counseling. Do you agree?"

"Not at all. A good drug like Lexapro will have Alexa Reed ready to assist her attorneys in her defense within two weeks. I've already said she's faking mental illness to avoid being tried. She's a very bright, clever young woman."

Judge Tomlinson frowned. "I'm not seeing evidence of faking on this record."

"That is my professional opinion," Andrews insisted.

"Very well. I need a few minutes in chambers to look over the expert's reports before I decide."

Sarah watched Tomlinson's round figure waddle off the bench. She and Jim stood up, and Jordan came from the spectator section of the courtroom to join them.

"I'm pleased he didn't buy the 'faking' it line from Andrews," Jordan said.

"I'm holding my breath." Sarah was as taut as a wire.

"Whatever happens, I thought both of you did a great job," Jim observed.

"Thanks," Jordan smiled, but Sarah didn't look at him. She was staring at the bench with a dazed look in her eyes as if she were reliving some horrible memory.

"Are you all right?" Jim asked.

"Of course." She turned to him and smiled, although he thought it was forced. "I've got to make a phone call. I'll be out in the hall. If the judge comes back, let me know."

"She's letting this get to her," Jordan remarked as Sarah vanished through the courtroom doors. "I've never seen her this worried about an outcome."

* * *

Thirty minutes went by before Judge Tomlinson resumed the bench. Sarah had paced in the hallway the entire time, hoping against hope the delay meant a favorable ruling. Jim, who had remained in the courtroom, came to tell her the judge was ready to rule.

"Everyone can sit down," Judge Tomlinson said.

Sarah was grateful to feel the chair under her. She was so nervous her legs were shaking.

"Your expert makes a good case for hospitalizing Mrs. Reed." The judge's mild gray eyes met hers. "Whatever the truth is about the night of June 2, she suffered a significant trauma. And being separated from her children certainly has to be a factor in her breakdown.

"I think from a medical/psychological standpoint, Dr. Stewart has the better recommendation. But the trouble is, the law isn't asking what is best for Alexa Reed. The law is asking how to make her able to assist in her defense and to understand the proceedings at trial. And from that point of view, Dr. Andrews' opinion better answers the question. So I'm going to adopt Dr. Andrews' recommendation and find there is no less intrusive procedure."

"Your Honor, I have a request," Sarah spoke up.

"And that would be, Ms. Knight?" His mild demeanor never changed although it was clear she was going to challenge him.

"I want to take this up to the court of appeal on a writ."

Again, Judge Tomlinson was unfazed. "I'm not surprised. You're very set against using these drugs on her, aren't you?"

"She's on trial for her life. It's not fair to put her in front of a jury looking like a drugged-up zombie."

The judge looked over his half glasses at Percy Andrews, who was sitting next to Preston Barton's bald fifty-something paunch in an ill-fitting suit. "Do you agree the drugs will alter her demeanor?"

Sarah expected him to lie and deny they would have any effect. To her surprise he didn't. "I can't say for sure, but patients on these meds do have a rather flat affect. They don't seem to feel anything, and they can appear distant and detached. On the other hand, not every one of these medications has that effect on every patient."

"Okay." The judge looked back at Sarah. "Here is my ruling, Ms. Knight; and I'm taking into consideration your concerns. I'm going to order the jail psychiatrist to prescribe the appropriate medications for Mrs. Reed. We'll have another hearing in thirty days to hear from Dr. Andrews to see if, in his opinion, she is competent to stand trial and if the drugs alter her demeanor significantly. And I will be happy to hear from Dr. Stewart, too, if you want to bring her back. That is my order."

* * *

First Tuesday of September 2013, San Diego Main Jail

The woman with the beautiful face and the terrible scar and the man with the kind eyes had come to see her today.

"We lost, Alexa," the woman had said. The man with the kind eyes squeezed her hand, while the beautiful woman continued, "The jail psychiatrist is going to prescribe antidepressant medication for you. Then there will be another hearing to see if you are able to stand trial. I'm so sorry. I wanted to win this one as much as I've ever wanted to win anything."

* * *

Alexa waited for her star to appear that night through the tiny window. She wished she had been able to speak earlier when the beautiful woman and the man with kind eyes had come to tell her what they thought was sad news about the drugs. They couldn't know what Alexa knew all too well: her situation was hopeless. Michael had stacked the deck so completely against her she had no means of escape.

It was the end of January 2007, after Stacy O'Connor's departure in November, when she'd realized her period hadn't come in December. She had prayed it wasn't a pregnancy. She wasn't ready for a child, and she was still uncertain about where her marriage was headed. During December, Michael had seemed to rebound into the old Michael who had courted her in D.C. He'd come home early from work. He'd taken her to San Diego's most expensive restaurants. He'd wrenched the promised case away from Chuck Reilly and seen it assigned to her. He'd taken her to a beautiful San Francisco bed and breakfast for the week between Christmas and New Year's. And he'd made love to her night after night, telling her how much he cared about her and wanted her to be happy. But as January had dwindled toward February, he had gradually slipped into his old pattern of staying out late and coming home to sleep on the foldout couch in his home office.

Alexa, bored at work and tired of Michael's indifference, had been ready to pack for D.C. when the awful truth dawned on her: she might be pregnant. A pregnancy test next morning confirmed the news she didn't want to hear. She stared at the blue line in horror, and hated herself for letting her guard down in the face of Michael's considerable charm. She'd given him yet another opportunity to make a fool of her, but this time she wouldn't let him get away with it.

She waited up that night. She reserved a hotel room and packed an overnight bag, planning to leave as soon as she'd confronted him. He came in around one o'clock, tie undone, bathed in jasmine perfume. And he was more than a little drunk.

"What are you doing up?" He slurred.

"Waiting for you."

"Well, whatever it is, you can tell me in the morning. I'm going to bed."

"I won't be here in the morning."

"Don't be dramatic."

"I'm not being dramatic. I'm leaving now. For good."

Michael laughed. "You've got no place to go."

"I've got a hotel room, and I'm giving my two weeks' notice at the firm tomorrow."

"Hey, slow down. You don't mean that."

"Look at you, Michael. Of course, I mean it."

"Come on, Alexa. Client development is my job."

"Her name is Amanda George, not 'client development.' And she's your replacement for Stacy. The whole firm is talking about my husband and his new paralegal."

"So what? She's a hell of a better fuck than you."

Alexa stiffened. "That's fine. I'm getting out of your way. Goodbye, Michael."

She turned and walked toward the front hall where she'd left her bag. She reached into her purse for her car keys when she felt the first blow from behind. She reeled backward into the wall. She looked up into a pair of savage green eyes.

The second blow hit her on the left cheek and felt like a knife cutting through her jaw. She realized he was aiming a third blow at her belly. She lashed out with her fist to protect her unborn child and connected with his left eye.

"You little bitch!" he screamed, grabbing his face. "You hit me! You hit me! I can't believe you hit me!"

"It's not as if you weren't about to hit me–again!"

"You liar!" he screamed. "I didn't hit you. You stumbled and fell against the wall."

Alexa couldn't believe what she was hearing even as she felt the knot growing at the base of her skull. "No, you hit me from behind. And then you tried to hit me in the stomach. I'm pregnant, Michael."

But he didn't seem to be listening. He pulled out his cell phone and dialed 911. Alexa heard the operator answer. "911, what's your emergency?"

"My wife has attacked me. We're at 6518 Soledad Terrace."

He gazed at her triumphantly. "I'll teach you to hit me, you little bitch!"

Suddenly Alexa's head exploded with the force of another blow. She found herself sprawled in the hall, stunned. A siren sounded in the distance. In a few minutes, she heard footsteps, and the doorbell rang.

Michael opened it, and Alexa could see two uniformed policemen standing on the front step.

"What happened here?"

"My wife, officers," Michael gestured toward Alexa sprawled on the floor. "She hit me, here."

"Wow, buddy, you're going to have quite a shiner tomorrow!" The older officer peered at Michael's eye as he spoke. Alexa felt a hot wave of shame wash over her as the two policemen stared at her as if she were some sort of zoo animal.

"Why'd she hit you?" the younger officer asked.

"I came home late from work, and she was drunk and accused me of having an affair."

Alexa concentrated on catching her breath, waiting for the moment when they'd come inside, and she could tell her side of the story. Then they'd see she was hurt. But they never came in. They exchanged a little more conversation with Michael outside on the porch and then turned away after he handed them his business card and said, "I'd really appreciate it if you didn't write a report. She's an attorney at Warrick, Thompson–where I also work–and my father is a justice on the U.S. Supreme Court. It would be embarrassing to everyone if this got around. It could end her career."

Michael closed the front door carefully and looked down at her with utmost contempt. "When are you going to admit what a loser you are?"

A moment later, she heard the door to his office close. She hurt everywhere. She knew she couldn't walk down the hall to her bedroom, but when enough breath returned so she could crawl, she made it to the living room sofa and tried to sleep.

* * *

If she could have talked, Alexa would have told the beautiful woman and the man with the kind eyes that was the moment when everything changed. Never again would Michael woo her with apologies and presents. Instead, he would call her "violent," "irrational," and "crazy."

By the end of February, Alexa was desperate to get away from her husband and his hostility and contempt. She still had almost nothing to do at work, and her own efforts to drum up clients by speaking at seminars had proved fruitless. She made discrete inquiries at Harper, Spaulding and Williams, Pogue; and both firms were still very interested in hiring her.

So on a blustery late March day, still queasy with morning sickness, she walked to the offices of Harris, Harris, and Gomez at 600 West Broadway. Diane Gomez, an attractive dark-suited attorney in her early forties, listened to the history of her marriage.

"And so you're pregnant?"

"Yes."

"How far along?"

"Four months."

"And what do you want me to do for you?"

"I want you to file for divorce. I've been offered a job at two appellate law firms in Washington, D.C. I have no work here at Warrick, Thompson. And my husband has been violent toward me since even before we were married."

"Why did you marry him, then?" Diane spoke sharply as if she didn't believe her.

"I-it's hard to explain. I felt pressured because his father is a Supreme Court justice. The engagement had already been announced when Michael hit me the first time. I think I was afraid to back out. And I thought he wouldn't do it again."

"But you say he did?" Her tone was still skeptical and unsympathetic.

"Yes."

"How many times?"

"The time I told you about in D.C. and now again in January."

"So twice?"

"Yes, and I also think he's responsible for another woman's death."

Diane frowned skeptically. "You're accusing him of murder, too?"

Alexa realized the story of Stacy O'Connor and the checks hidden in her jewelry box sounded more soap opera than legal rationalism. A wave of shame washed over her as she told the story.

"So this Stacy person went back to Seattle to have a child you believe was your husband's, and she gave you two checks you claim were drawn on your law firm's account?"

"Yes."

"So what makes you think she was murdered?"

"When I found out I was pregnant, I tried to get in touch with her."

"And did you?"

"No. She had been killed a week after she got to Seattle. That was a week after I told Michael where she was."

"So?"

"So she was stabbed while she was withdrawing money at an ATM."

"A robbery?"

"Yes."

"I don't see the connection to your husband. Was he in Seattle when she died?"

"No. He never left San Diego. But when I found out she was dead, I looked for those checks. And they were gone. No one knew about them other than me, Stacy, and Michael. So he had to be the one who found where I'd hidden them."

Diane Gomez frowned. "Mrs. Reed, I'm sorry, but I'm finding all of this hard to believe. If you graduated first in your class from Georgetown and clerked at the Supreme Court as you say, you would have to know your story is just that–a story. You have no independent evidence that your husband had anything to do with that woman's death."

Alexa swallowed hard and fought back her morning sickness. "But it's all true."

"Well, even if it is, you can't prove it. And even if you could, it would not matter in the least to a judge in family court. The law expects you to co-parent that baby."

"But how? With a man who's attacked and beaten me?"

"He hasn't attacked and beaten the child, Mrs. Reed. The court expects you to put aside your feelings and share the child with its father."

"But I have high-paying jobs waiting for me in Washington. My career is never going to go anywhere here."

"I'm sorry to hear that. Maybe you should consider an area other than appeals." Diane Gomez looked pointedly at the clock on her desk. "I've given you more than the hour that I normally provide free to prospective clients. Here are your options, Mrs. Reed. You can go back east, but your husband can get an order for full custody as soon as the baby is born and can bring the child back to California. Courts here will not look favorably on your decision to leave the state and deprive your husband of access to his child. Your contact with the baby will be minimal, if at all. Or you can make the best of your situation here and share the baby with its father. I'm sorry, but I can't give you any more time."

CHAPTER NINE

First Tuesday in September 2013, Train Station, Solana Beach

Jim drove Jordan to the train in Solana Beach that afternoon after the competency hearing. Despite her protests she didn't need any help, he carried her overnight bag across the parking lot to the gunmetal gray, half-cylinder station, surrounded by red, white, and blue Amtrak kiosks and a single Coffee vender under a green umbrella with gold fringe.

"Thanks for putting me up," Jordan said. "You were right about the breakfast. Michelin would give you six stars if they knew about you."

Jim grinned. "For that I have to buy you coffee. You've got time before the train, and Amtrak isn't stellar in the coffee department."

They stood by the chain link balcony overlooking the tracks below, basking in the mild afternoon sun and the cool salt breeze as they sipped lattes from paper cups with lids shaped like toddlers' tippee cups.

"Sarah is taking this loss pretty hard," Jordan observed.

"I haven't worked with her long enough to know how she usually reacts."

"She's normally unfazed. Actually, sometimes I think she's too unfazed. She doesn't seem to show much emotion except when she's in front of a jury."

"Some people aren't upset easily."

Jordan shook her head. "This is more than that with Sarah. It's as if feelings bounce off of her. Or as if they are embedded so deeply inside her, she can't experience them."

"Any idea why?"

"No. She never talks about her past. As far as I know, she went to Yale, and then spent all her days and nights at Craig, Lewis, and Weller until she came to San Diego in January. I will say, she seems more tightly wound here than when she was in New York. Something seems to have been bothering her in this town even before she took Alexa Reed's case."

"Most likely the stress of starting her own practice."

"Maybe business stress is the answer."

"And then, too, I suppose you know about David Spineli?"

"The married-millionaire, realty tycoon, owner of Spineli Development? Well, I will admit that has gone on longer than her usual very-short lived relationships."

Jim tried not to show any emotion, but Jordan was too quick for him. "Look, we've already established you have an interest in her. You don't have to pretend the David Spineli business doesn't make you unhappy."

"Ok, busted. It makes me unhappy. Have you met him?"

"I have. Picture stereotypical West Coast, over-forty male trying to look late twenties. The wife is a plastic surgeon's version of blonde Barbie, boob job, nose job, and Angelina Jolie lips. No kids. I'm sure she wouldn't want to spoil her figure for nine months."

Jordan downed the last of her coffee and tossed it into the trash can. "The train will be here soon. I'd better get down on the platform, so I can get a good seat in business class. Why don't you stop by Sarah's place tonight and check on her? I'll text you the address."

* * *

He waited until seven-thirty to drive to the cottage in La Jolla Shores. She was three streets from the beach in one of the small stucco houses that had been built in the forties and probably had all of eleven hundred square feet. Hers was the same shade of beige stucco as its neighbors, but the windows had deep terra cotta shutters that gave it a personality of its own. Land values had made these tiny homes worth millions; and every one, including hers, was an expensively landscaped gem with strategically placed potted palms in clay pots, pink bougainvillea vines trailing up the walls, and a jungle of feathery maiden hair ferns in the flower beds.

He was as nervous as a kid on his first prom date as he stood on her front stoop in his jeans, loafers, and yellow knit shirt after ringing the bell. No one answered. The butterflies in his gut began to swoop and soar. This had been a stupid idea. What if she was tucked up with that Spineli character? He didn't embarrass easily, but he'd not get over that one in a hurry, especially because they worked together.

But he wanted to see her, so he threw caution to the wind and rang again. This time, he heard someone shuffling toward the door and felt himself being scrutinized through the peep hole before he heard the click of the deadbolt's release.

She was barefoot, wearing black yoga pants, a black camisole, and no makeup. Her pixie hair was tousled as if someone had run fingers through it. Jim thought of David Spineli once more with foreboding.

He licked his dry lips and tried to sound nonchalant. "I thought I'd come by and offer to take you out for a drink. I was thinking you might want to unwind after the hearing today." He wished he could add, "Are you alone?" but, of course, he couldn't.

"Thanks, but I'm pretty exhausted." His hopes fell. But she went on, "Why don't you come in, though, and have a drink here?"

The butterflies had left his stomach and were flying around his heart. He was weak with gratitude and relief. She was alone.

He followed her down the hall, his loafers clattering slightly on the polished, golden hardwood floor. She led him through the living room, where no lights were on and where he had a quick glimpse of casual but sophisticated white slip-covered Pottery Barn furniture. She led him through mahogany French doors that were opened onto a miniature stone patio surrounded by palms and bougainvillea mixed with more ferns and bright blue morning glory vines and red hibiscus.

She had been sitting on one of the redwood lounge chairs covered in crisp white linen cushions, apparently killing a bottle of expensive California red zin by herself in the deep pink twilight. She motioned to the other lounge chair and said, "Sit down. I'll go get another glass. And another bottle of wine."

"Have you eaten?"

"I'm not hungry."

She'd been thin when they met, but she'd lost weight in the last month. Another reason to worry about what this case was doing to her.

"If I cook, you'll be hungry."

"But there's nothing here to cook. I–I haven't had time to go to the market."

He bet she kept little in the house to eat as a general rule. "I'm a food wizard. Let me take a look."

She led him back through the living room to the miniature but very modern white tile and stainless steel kitchen. He opened her refrigerator to find butter, eggs, brie, an onion and some mushrooms.

"One of my amazing omelettes will fix you right up."

She opened the second bottle of wine and poured him a glass. She watched in silence as he transformed her scant variety of ingredients into two omelettes that they ate on the patio in the deepening, brine-scented twilight.

"I like it here," Jim said, as he put his empty plate on the table between the two chaise lounges where the bottle of wine now also stood.

"I wanted to be close to the water. The previous owner remodeled just before I bought it. Everything's new. I was lucky."

"You never asked how I found your address."

"You're an ex-FBI agent turned private investigator. I didn't have to ask."

"I hope you don't mind that I came by. I thought you might want company because today was a tough loss."

She shrugged and sipped her wine. "But not unexpected. Although, I will admit Judge Tomlinson got my hopes up when he wanted time to think it over. Jordan did her usual brilliant job."

"Unlike the opposition."

"True. But we have one more crack at this at the next hearing in thirty days. Meds may not bring her back enough to stand trial."

"Good point." He could smell her gardenia perfume across the small space that separated them. Like a high school kid, he wished they were side-by-side on a sofa where he could casually drop his arm across the back, hoping for skin-to-skin contact.

"Great food, again, by the way."

"I have the feeling you need a personal chef."

"Maybe. I can't cook. I burn everything up. No patience."

"Patience to do complex legal work but not to follow a recipe?"

"Yeah, go figure." For the first time, she let her eyes meet his, and she smiled. His heart was like a runaway freight train on the downhill.

"I think that's the first personal thing you've ever told me about yourself."

"What? That I can't cook?" She laughed, but he sensed she was uncomfortable.

"I've told you about the two people who mean the most to me, Gail and Cody. You never mention anyone."

"That's not true. I told you about the Chinese take-out boy and the dry cleaner's messenger that I left pining for me in New York."

Jim reached out and took her hand and looked directly into her eyes. "Be serious."

Sarah pulled her hand away and frowned. "I am serious. I could tell you about my partners at Craig, Lewis. I'm sure they miss my billable hours."

"Why did you leave New York?"

"I told you that night at Trend. I got tired of the winters."

"I have a feeling that's not the only reason."

Her eyes became expressionless, and Jim remembered Jordan's remark that her profession waited for confidences, rather than probed for them.

"I'm afraid your intuition let you down on that one."

He looked up at the stars, and wished she weren't so determined to keep him locked out of her world. He wondered how much she shared with David Spineli.

"Why date a married man?"

"For the same reason you're still in love with your ex-wife."

"But I've tried to move on."

"And maybe for me trying to move on is too dangerous."

Jim frowned. "I don't understand."

"And I can't explain."

He studied her face in the low light. Her mouth was set in a determined line, and some sort of inner conflict was playing out in her eyes.

"If you ever change your mind, I'm here to listen."

"Thanks, but I won't. Anyway, the most important item on my agenda is finding some sort of defense for Alexa Reed. Her family law attorney, Bob Metcalf, has agreed to meet with me on Friday. I'd like for you to be there. He might turn out to be a witness."

* * *

That night, Sarah lay awake in the wee hours reminding herself that telling was not an option and wishing for the unattainable was a waste of time.

CHAPTER TEN

After midnight, First Tuesday in September, 2013, San Diego Main Jail

Her star was gone. It had passed over to be replaced by the backdrop of infinite darkness, and now Alexa would have to wait another twenty-four hours for its tiny beam of hope to shine through the bars of her window.

She wanted to sleep but the memories had brought anger licking like fire through her veins once more. After she left Diane Gomez's office that day, she'd begun to research California custody law, and what she found appalled her. She was virtually a prisoner of the state until her child turned eighteen.

It was at least some comfort that she rarely saw Michael. He came home to change clothes and to sleep in his home office, but he left her alone. She found herself indifferent to his affairs. She welcomed the news that the coming child was a daughter and busied herself furnishing a nursery and struggling to find appellate work. But she was ever mindful of the need to avoid conflict with her husband.

Margaret Louise Reed arrived on a hot August day at ten in the morning. The long hours of labor seemed to transform Michael into the loving, supportive man she had thought she'd married. As they sat together that afternoon, taking turns cuddling Meggie's exquisite perfection, Alexa began to hope their daughter's coming was the magic that would make them a family at last.

But her hope faded within days of returning home from the hospital. Michael had resumed leaving early for the office and coming home in the wee hours. Overwhelmed by the work of caring for a newborn, Alexa had little time or emotion to waste on wondering what he was up to.

It was hard to leave Meggie at six weeks and return to the boredom of life as Chuck Reilly's associate. But she'd been fortunate to find an excellent Mexican nanny through another attorney in the firm who had used Guadalupe for her own children. Alexa wanted motherhood, but she also wanted her career. Besides, she knew how dangerous dependency on Michael would be.

Still, as she sat at her desk day after day with little to do, she wondered if the separation from her child was worth it. And then, one morning when Meggie was three months old, Harold Pogue of Williams, Pogue called from D.C. to tell her the firm would still like to have her as an associate. It was an out-of-the-blue surprise that she hadn't dared to wish for. It lifted her sagging spirits.

That night she sat in Meggie's pink and white Pottery Barn nursery, lit only by the pink bear night light, watching her baby sleep under the mobile of pink clown bears that rotated slowly over her crib. Meggie liked to stare at the bears until she fell asleep. Alexa smelled her daughter's warm, clean, baby-bath scent and watched her tiny rosebud mouth quiver and smile as she dreamed. Her birth fuzz had grown into a crop of unruly blonde curls that swirled around her head like a halo. She had one tiny hand around the paw of her favorite white rabbit. Alexa loved her so much that her heart hurt.

She looked around the expensively furnished room with its shelves overflowing with dolls and books and stuffed toys. Michael had complained about her extravagance, but outfitting Meggie's nursery had kept the knowledge that she had become a prisoner because of her child from crushing her. That night she realized she could bear it no longer. She had known for some time Michael didn't care about her, but she had come to realize he wasn't attached to Meggie, either. He'd been an only son, and he'd wanted an only son. Meggie was not worth coming home to. Surely she could negotiate a divorce that would let them both start over.

She heard the front door open and close. She glanced at the pink and blue ballerina clock on the wall. Midnight. Michael had come back early. But he'd be drunk and not in any shape for a rational discussion about their future. Better to avoid a confrontation. She decided to stay where she was until he'd gone to sleep in his study. Then she'd creep down the hall undetected to the master suite that she now occupied alone.

But her luck didn't hold. Suddenly the door burst open, and Michael stumbled in.

"What are you doing in here?"

"Sitting with Meggie. I heard her cry out, and I came to check on her." A lie was better than the truth at that moment.

He ambled unsteadily toward the crib, and Alexa realized to her horror he meant to pick Meggie up.

"Michael, don't! She's sleeping!"

He turned and gave her a cold stare. "I'll pick her up if I want to pick her up."

He leaned down and pushed his hands under the baby who began to squirm and frown.

Alexa smelled the alcohol on his breath, and she began to panic. "Michael, please! Leave her alone!"

But he was now roughly lifting Meggie off the mattress, her head lolling backward, her eyes now wide with surprise. She began to scream.

Alexa ran to the crib and tried to support Meggie's head as Michael continued to hoist her at arm's length out of the crib. She felt his elbow connect with her ribs, and she went flying across the room and fell against the rocking chair she had just vacated. The sharp end of the rocker cut into her back, but she was far too worried about Meggie to care.

"You tried to hit me!" Michael shrilled. "You tried to hit me while I was holding my daughter! You violent bitch!"

Suddenly Guadalupe appeared at the door, wrapped in her bathrobe. She stared in disbelief at Alexa on the floor, and Meggie dangling in Michael's grasp. Without a word, she crossed the room to Michael and held out her arms for the screaming baby.

Alexa was relieved when he handed her to the nanny without resistance, but then she realized in one sickening moment why he'd given Meggie up so easily. He crossed the room in a single stride and smacked her so hard on her left cheek her ears began to ring.

"Don't you ever try to hit me again! And don't you ever try to keep me from holding my daughter! If you do, I'll make sure you never see her again!"

He strode out of the room and slammed the door to his office. Alexa got up slowly, and sat down in the rocking chair, and held out her arms for Meggie, who was still wailing. Guadalupe laid her in Alexa's lap.

"Don't you want me to get her back to sleep, Mrs. Reed?"

"No, I'll do it."

"I'm going to the kitchen then and make a bag of ice for you to hold on your jaw."

"Thanks, Guadalupe."

Alexa rocked Meggie slowly as she hummed a nameless tune that she hoped would calm both of them. Her entire body was shaking. It felt as if something evil had invaded all of this pink baby tranquility and as if her child's nursery would never feel safe and secure again.

Against her shoulder, Meggie snuffled and yawned and began to drop back into the first stages of sleep. When her breathing became regular and deep, Alexa laid her back in her crib.

Guadalupe appeared with the ice bag. "Here, Mrs. Reed. You go get some sleep."

"I can't leave her. I'll sleep on the pullout bed." Alexa pointed to the small pink and white print sofa that converted into a twin bed.

"Let me stay with her tonight," Guadalupe insisted. "I don't think he'll be back. He's probably passed out by now. But if he does come again, better for him to find me than you."

* * *

The next morning she didn't go into the office because she could not cover the bruise with makeup. And she called Harold Pogue to thank him for the offer that she couldn't accept.

CHAPTER ELEVEN

Next day, Wednesday, First Week of September 2013, San Diego Main Jail

"Hi, Alexa, I'm Dr. Yager. I'm the jail psychiatrist. I'm here to get your medical history and to help you get well."

He looked like a monkey, Alexa thought. He was bean-pole thin in a rumpled brown suit, and his ears stuck out like Curious George's.

"Why don't you sit up and eat some of your breakfast, and let's talk a little?"

Alexa didn't stir on her cot, but her eyes darted toward the box of dry cereal and the cup of warm milk on the metal tray. Even if she'd been hungry, it didn't look edible.

She could see Yager was on the verge of irritation. He reminded her of Ronald Brigman. All oily unctuousness until he realized she could see through his treacherous pretense of friendship. Then his claws came out.

"Now, Alexa, you must cooperate with me. I need a complete medical history including any known allergies to medications."

Alexa rolled over and faced the wall.

Sam. Her adorable little Sam, who loved Curious George only a shade less than his favorite bear, Mr. Wiggles, had been born on the first of November, 2008. He was a long, thin, dark-haired baby with a thoughtful expression in his green eyes. Michael had grabbed him out of her arms in the delivery room, and she had had the uneasy feeling he considered Samuel Harrison Reed his personal property. Only Michael's intense desire to have a son had brought him back to the marital bed. Briefly. It had been unpleasant, and Alexa had been relieved when he'd lost interest. Meggie was only a few months old, and Alexa was struggling to get to work each day. And to keep the bruises hidden.

But then she found herself pregnant with Sam. And even though the timing was bad, she was glad Meggie wouldn't have to grow up alone in a house always on edge, waiting for Michael's next explosion.

Her maternity leave ended on the eighteenth of December. She'd kissed her babies goodbye and headed back to the office. Friday was an odd day to end her leave, but Alan Warrick himself had set it as the date for her return. Alexa's skirts still wouldn't zip, and she felt fat and uncomfortable as she sat at her desk at nine that morning waiting with baited breath for Chuck Reilly to give her something to do. As she waited for Chuck, who never came into the office before ten, she dreaded the thought of the firm Christmas party that night at the Hotel Del Coronado. The last thing she wanted to do was stuff herself into an evening dress and leave Meggie and Sam again after being at the office all day.

But it was not Chuck Reilly who appeared in her doorway at nine-thirty. It was Alan Warrick himself.

Although Alexa liked Alan, she gazed at him uneasily. A name partner in your doorway on your first day back was likely not a good sign.

But she stood up and smiled anyway. "Good morning, Alan."

"No, no sit down. You look wonderful, by the way. How's the baby?"

He slid his six feet of solid muscle, even at sixty-two, into one of the two chairs opposite her desk and smiled.

"He's fine. Just beautiful."

"Good. Glad to hear that. I'm sorry I'm going to have to give you some bad news, and I hope you don't mind that I had you come in to the office. I didn't feel right discussing this over the phone."

"No, it's fine, Alan. What bad news do you have for me?"

He sighed. "I've been over this a hundred times while you've been out on leave, but there is no other conclusion that I can come to. Chuck's practice just isn't big enough to support having an associate."

Alexa's stomach tightened. She wondered if her face betrayed the panic she felt.

"I've never been able to work the hours here that I've wanted to."

"I know. But you've also been out sick quite a bit. I'm not blaming you, but obviously your billable hours can't be what they should be if you're not well."

Alexa sat very still and concentrated on Alan's face, willing herself not to cry. She wanted to say, I wasn't sick. I was too ashamed of the bruises to let anyone see them. But she said nothing.

"Anyway, I've been thinking it over, and this seems like a good time to give you a leave of absence from the firm."

"Leave of absence?"

"Say a year or two. You've got two very young children, and you don't know how tough it is to go from one child to two. My wife said it was the most difficult thing she's ever done."

"But I have a live-in nanny. Actually, she's the one Maribeth Washington in the tax section used. Maribeth has three children, all close together, and with Guadalupe's help she made partner right on time."

Alan shifted uncomfortably in his chair. "I'm sorry, I wasn't suggesting a leave because your children are young. I was just trying to get you to see the advantages of it for you. You are a fine attorney, Alexa; and I would never suggest something like this if we had enough work for you."

"Can't you give me six months to build a client base of my own?"

He shook his head. "You've had two years already. I'm sorry. Things will probably pick up for appellate work in the next couple of years. By then your children will be older, and you'll be feeling better."

Alexa looked around her office, still trying as hard as she could not to cry. "So I should have my things out of here by this afternoon?"

"Oh, no. Take your time. The party's tonight. You don't want to be moving out today. Come in next week and box it all up, and I'll have the firm's movers bring it over to your place."

He smiled and uncoiled his large frame from the small chair. Alexa felt the first tears begin to flow as he closed the door behind him.

* * *

She fought desperately for control. She couldn't cry now. She had to think. Being completely dependent upon Michael and at the whim of his moods terrified her. Her heart hammered hard as she tried to decide what she should do.

Finally a coherent thought emerged. She would have to find a job in a firm that had enough work for her, like Williams, Pogue or Harper, Spaulding back in D.C. Diane Gomez had said she could not prove Michael had hit her because there were no witnesses, but now there was Guadalupe. Her heart began to slow as she realized she had a way out at last.

* * *

By midnight, Alexa was so tired she could barely stand. The cocktail party in the Del's lobby followed by dinner in the Crown Room and then dancing on the terrace had taken the last bit of strength she had. She was relieved when the musicians began packing up their instruments, forcing the Warrick, Thompson tide of attorneys and spouses to surge toward the parking lots.

She assumed Michael would go straight to his office and fall asleep on his couch, the way he always did. He'd virtually ignored her at the party as usual, but she hadn't cared. She'd needed all her wits and poise to field questions about her departure from the firm. Apparently she had been the last to hear the news.

But he followed her into their bedroom, and she had the uneasy feeling he wanted what she hadn't the slighted interest in giving him at that moment.

"Not tonight, Michael. It's still too soon after the baby. And I'm exhausted after today."

She saw the fire spring up in his eyes, and she tried to fight back the tide of rising panic.

He grabbed her left arm and yanked her toward him. "You are not going to say no to me! Understand?" Suddenly his foot shot out and knocked her feet out from under her. He slammed her hard against the parquet floor and threw his weight on top of her. She heard the bone snap as she hit, and she screamed with pain. She felt Michael freeze and then get up slowly.

"Come on, don't be a baby. I didn't hurt you."

Alexa sat up and cradled her useless left arm with her right hand. The throbbing pain was nearly unbearable.

"Get up!"

"I can't."

She watched his rage turn to fear as he realized he'd done something that would now expose him for what he was.

"Is it your arm?"

"It's broken. I heard the bone snap."

"No. It's just twisted." He leaned down and steadied her as she got up. "Here, let me move it a little."

"No!" The fiery pain stabbed harder when he put pressure on her arm. "Stop! You'll make it worse."

Guadalupe had awakened and was standing in the hall as they left for the hospital. Alexa knew she understood what had happened, but she said nothing except the children were sleeping soundly, and she would look after them until they got back.

A million thoughts whirled through Alexa's head as they drove through the night. Beside her, Michael was grimly silent. Her arm hurt; but now, at last, she had an undeniable ticket to freedom with her children. There was light at the end of this long road even if for the present it meant the pain of a broken bone.

Michael parked in the hospital lot; but instead of getting out, he hit the automatic lock button so the doors wouldn't open.

"What are you doing?"

He leaned across the BMW's soft leather seat and pushed his face into hers.

"When they ask you what happened, you say you tripped and fell. If you tell the truth, you'll never see Meggie and Sam again."

* * *

A week later, now sporting a cast, she paid another visit to Diane Gomez. The family law attorney listened intently, her dark little gimlet eyes darting from Alexa's face to the cast.

"Again, Mrs. Reed, what exactly are you wanting a family law attorney to do for you?"

"To file for divorce and full custody of my children. I have no work here. I still have excellent opportunities in D.C. And now there's a witness to what Michael has done to me."

"You mean your nanny?"

"Yes, Guadalupe."

"But what did you tell the emergency room doctor about your injury?"

"I told you. Michael threatened me with loss of the children if I didn't say I tripped and fell."

"And did your nanny witness that threat?"

"Well, no. But–"

"I'm sorry, Mrs. Reed. But the court will not be impressed by your story. If the medical records say you tripped and fell, then the court will believe you tripped and fell. And, quite frankly, in the eyes of the court, your nanny is useless as a witness."

"You mean because she's a Mexican national? That's ridiculous."

"No, no. Although, if she's undocumented, you might have a problem there. But the court will think you put her up to lying for you. You really can't prove what you say your husband has done. Courts regard a wife's claim she is being abused as a fabrication to get full custody of the children and more child support. I'm very sorry for you, Mrs. Reed. But you'd still be better off to go home and try to get along with your husband."

* * *

The next morning at ten o'clock, INS agents in full uniform came for a terrified Guadalupe. Alexa phoned Maribeth, whose children thought of their old nanny as a grandmother, and begged her to get one of the immigration attorneys at the firm to help.

Maribeth called that afternoon to say no one in the immigration section had had time to go see Guadalupe, and she had been sent back to Mexico without even the usual cursory proceedings. In short, Maribeth said, it was clear someone wanted her out of the country immediately.

Two weeks later, after Alexa had secretly hired a relief babysitter three mornings a week, she found a gun shop in National City, bought a Glock nine millimeter, and signed up for lessons on how to use it. She thanked her lucky stars she was right-handed.

CHAPTER TWELVE

First Friday in September, 2013, Downtown, San Diego

Bob Metcalf had a seedy little office in a ratty brick building, two blocks down from the family law courthouse. Sarah led the way with Jim following up three flights of narrow dingy stairs to Suite 312, etched on the frosted glass door. Inside they found an empty receptionist's desk, a cheap plastic couch with two matching gold plastic chairs, and some tattered magazines on a rickety coffee table.

Before they could sit down, the door to the inner office opened, and Bob himself appeared. He was in his late fifties with a thin, wiry build, a high forehead and a receding hairline. He was wearing a cheap gray suit and a light blue tie that bore the stains of a lunch, either past or present.

Sarah and Jim took the seen-better-days, chipped, pressed-wood chairs in front of Bob's desk and declined his offer of bottled water from the dorm-room fridge wedged into a corner.

"Thanks for meeting with me," Sarah began. "This is Jim Mitchell, my private investigator."

Bob shook all hands offered and sat down behind his desk. Sarah noticed a stack of thick folders in front of him.

"Are all those files Alexa's case?"

He nodded. "If she got the children to Michael's for visitation fifteen minutes late, he'd drag her to court over it. He litigated *everything*. How is she by the way?"

"Not good." Sarah briefly recapped the hearing in front of Judge Tomlinson.

"Sorry to hear it. She's a sweet woman, but she ruined her life by marrying a class-A dick like Michael Reed."

"Her former criminal defense lawyer called her a 'lying, manipulative bitch.'"

Bob Metcalf waved his hands impatiently. "Well, he didn't talk to me, then. He must have been talking to Michael's lawyer. Michael hired Tara Jeffers, the nastiest family law attorney in San Diego County, to make all out war on her. Alexa came in here just trembling the first time we met. She'd been served with one of the most vicious sets of divorce pleadings I've ever seen. Obviously you can tell I don't have high end clients," he waived his arms around the small office, full of sagging book cases, with the view of a pay-per-hour parking lot below. "The truth is, none of the attorneys who are able to stand up against Tara would take Alexa's case because she couldn't afford them, and they didn't want to be crosswise of Coleman Reed's son."

"Why did you take it?" Jim asked.

"Truth be told, at first I thought I'd get some attorney's fees out of it. Not from her, of course. Michael had tied up all their money, so she couldn't touch a cent. But judges usually award attorney's fees out of the deepest pocket. Since Michael had all the money, I figured he'd have to pay for Tara and me, too."

"But I gather that didn't happen?" Sarah said.

"No. This was the damnedest case I've ever seen. Right from the get go."

"What do you mean?"

"The judge threw her and the kids out of the family home in La Jolla and gave it to Michael. That's unheard of. At the time, she had a one-year-old and a two-month-old, and she was a full-time stay-at-home mom because she'd just been let go from Warrick, Thompson. No judge makes the primary parent move out of the family home. But that was just the beginning."

"Was that when you realized you weren't going to get any money out of the case?"

He nodded. "I made the usual request everyone makes at the end of the hearing, and I thought Judge Watkins was going to hold me in contempt. He said, 'Mrs. Reed graduated first in her class from Georgetown. She's perfectly capable of getting a job that will pay your fees. I see no reason why she should sponge off the plaintiff.'"

"Wow!" Sarah breathed. She noticed Jim wince as he sat beside her taking notes on a yellow pad.

"Yeah, nasty stuff. And, again, remember she was unemployed with two babies, and Michael was on track to become a full equity partner at Warrick, Thompson. In most cases like that, the judge awards the wife a huge chunk of child support and temporary alimony. Alexa got a little, but nothing like what she was entitled to."

"So why did you stay on the case?"

Bob shrugged. "I thought, why not? Most of my other clients pay me pennies on the dollar. She was so sweet and grateful, and I knew she was in a desperate situation. We worked out a deal. She'd prepare papers for me, memoranda, briefs, things like that. I'm a rotten writer, and I barely passed the bar after going to an unaccredited law school. She made me look really good on paper for the first time in my career."

"So what happened next?"

"I tried to negotiate a settlement with Tara Jeffers. It would have been in everyone's best interest to settle. Alexa needed to focus on her babies and finding a job. Michael had no use for kids; his career and his women were his life. Do you know about the paralegal he knocked up in his first year at Warrick, Thompson?"

"No."

"Her name was Stacy O'Connor, and she worked for Michael. He insisted she have an abortion, but she gave him the slip and went home to Seattle to have the baby."

"Did Alexa know about Stacy?" Sarah asked

He nodded. "Stacy came to see her as she was about to leave town. She gave Alexa the two checks drawn on the firm's account that Michael had given her. One was for the abortion; one was for severance pay."

"You mean Warrick, Thompson paid for her abortion?" Sarah frowned. "That doesn't sound like something Alan Warrick would do."

"You'll have to talk to him about that. I only know Stacy gave Alexa those two checks. She didn't want to cash them because she didn't want Michael to find her. Stacy thought if anything happened to her, Alexa could prove Michael was involved because she had those checks."

"Where is Stacy now?" Jim asked.

"Dead. She was stabbed while taking money out of an ATM in Seattle a week after she got back. Alexa blamed herself for her death."

"Why?" Sarah frowned.

"Because Stacy swore her to secrecy about where she was going, but Michael wormed it out of Alexa, anyway."

"Was there any evidence linking Michael to Stacy's murder?"

"Nothing you could use in court. But Alexa found the checks missing from their hiding place, and she assumed Michael had found them and destroyed them because other than Alan Warrick, Michael was the only person who knew those checks existed. And, of course, they tied him to a dead woman."

"How did Ronald Brigman come to be involved in Alexa's case?" Sarah asked.

"Ah, that's where the plot thickens. When she first came to me, I thought Michael just wanted to dump his inconvenient family and be free to do his fooling around on the books instead of off. He was a good looking guy, as you know, and attractive to women. He was on track to become a partner *and* he was the son of a sitting United States Supreme Court justice, and all that made him hotter than George Clooney. So I thought he'd just pay Alexa off, do a couple of pro forma visitations a year with the kids, and let everyone go about their business. I had no idea he'd go after custody of the children."

"But he did."

"That's right. As soon as I tried settlement negotiations with Tara Jeffers, I knew something really sinister was up. She laughed in my face, and two days later filed a motion to give Michael full custody of the children."

"But he couldn't raise them. His career wouldn't let him do that. Alexa was at home with them."

"Right. And she was their primary caregiver, and that should have been the beginning and end of the matter. But it wasn't. Michael didn't want the children, he wanted to use them to control Alexa. For men like Michael Reed, it's only about power and control."

"So what happened?"

"I tried to knock it out of the water at that first hearing on custody, but I never had a chance. The court ordered both parties into psychological evaluations. As a practical matter, that meant Ronald Brigman would decide who got the children."

"Isn't that something only a judge could decide?"

"That's what the law says, but the family law judges here thought Brigman was the voice of God. They just rubber-stamped anything he said. When Alexa told him about Michael and the abuse, he labeled her a chronic liar and said she had borderline personality disorder. What Brigman called borderline personality disorder was post traumatic stress from all the beatings."

"But a judge can't rubber-stamp an expert," Sarah insisted. "Wholesale adoption of expert opinion is an unauthorized delegation of judicial power."

"You graduated in the top of your class like Alexa. That's exactly what she said. I doubt anyone practicing family law in this bar is even aware of that rule. But Alexa and I took it to the court of appeal. And lost. Some of the judges up there had been on the family law bench before they were kicked upstairs. They knew how much they liked to have a so-called expert decide the tough issues, so they didn't have to split the baby themselves. They didn't want to take that way to escape making the decision away from their brother judges still on the hot seat."

"So Brigman gave full custody of the children to Michael?"

"Not at first. Michael didn't want that in the beginning because if he had gotten the kids from the get go, he would have lost his power to torment Alexa. No, what Michael wanted was to humiliate her over and over again in the place where a lawyer like Alexa should have been most respected–in the judicial system. And he wanted to torture her by taking the children away little by little. So he dragged her to court every chance he got to build a record of what a lousy mother she supposedly was. He got to abuse her in public instead of knocking her around at home."

Bob paused to open the top file on his desk. "Here's a couple of examples. A hearing on February 15, 2009, because she was ten minutes late bringing the kids for visitation. Her excuse: Sam pooped in his diaper as they were leaving the house and she had to change him. Court reamed her out. The next month, March 18, 2009, she was a half hour late because Meggie was crying and too upset to get in the car. Alexa's explanation: Meggie was beginning to have nightmares because she had to sleep in a strange bed at Michael's. The court told her it would hold her in contempt if she ever again referred to the bed at Meggie's father's house as a 'strange bed.'" Bob let the file drop shut and looked at Sarah and Jim with his mild, watery eyes. "That went on from 2009 until the day Michael died."

"How did Alexa manage?"

"She tried to hold up—at first. She obviously knew even better than I did that almost every word out of the judge's mouth was a violation of her and the kids' federal constitutional rights. All three of them were being forced by a psychologist to deal with a man who was using the courts to terrorize and control them. They lived in constant fear of being separated forever. Con Law is one subject I never understood when I was in law school. But Alexa had it down. Like you, Ms. Knight."

"Sarah, please."

"She'd sit up late, drafting motions and supporting memoranda in her case. Beautiful things. And I'd file every one of them. And then Tara Jeffers would come to court and snarl about how Alexa was just a lush who was demonstrating she had the smarts to go back to work as a lawyer, but who was trying to live off her ex to punish Michael for divorcing her and showing the world what a crazy psycho she was."

"And the court bought that?"

"Every time. I could never get the judge to listen to the legal merits of Alexa's motions because Tara would turn every hearing into a character assassination. Little by little, defeat by defeat, it started to wear her down."

"How was she supporting herself?"

"Alan Warrick and a couple of sympathetic partners sent her some contract jobs to do. Research and writing. But they did it on the down low."

"Why in secret?"

"I don't know. Alan will have to explain. I only know Alexa would have lost the work if anyone found out. And no one else would give her anything to do. The legal community here is really just one small town. Full of backstabbing and politics. Michael poisoned every well where she could have possibly gotten a job."

"And how do you know that?"

"Again, that's something Alan told Alexa, so you'll have to talk to him about that."

"So Tara Jeffers would stand up in court and claim Alexa was a lazy freeloader who wouldn't go back to work, while Michael was making sure she couldn't get a job in this town?"

"Exactly." Bob nodded.

"And she couldn't get a job out of town because Michael wouldn't let her take the kids?"

"Right. And Michael kept subpoenaing her bank records to see what her sources of income were so he could go after them. That's why Alan paid her in cash."

"Did you subpoena Michael's?"

"I tried, but he wouldn't turn them over. He claimed they were covered by attorney-client privilege."

"His *personal* bank records? How in the world did he get away with that?"

"He claimed he deposited client funds into his personal accounts before they went into the firm's trust account."

"But it's unethical to put client money into anything other than a trust account."

"I know that, and you know that, and the state bar knows that. But Judge Watkins bought Michael's claim every time we tried to see his bank records."

"So Alexa eeked by on the secret work from Alan and the little bit she got from Michael?"

"Right. And then her world went up in flames."

"How?"

"Well, Meggie and Sam didn't want to go visit Michael. I mean, kids that little don't want to leave their mothers in regular families. But the stress on those babies was horrible. They cried, they wet the bed, and Meggie stopped eating for a while."

"And Brigman blamed Alexa?"

"Who else? He claimed she was working to alienate them from Michael."

"When they'd never been bonded to Michael in the first place."

"Common sense was never part of Ronald Brigman's approach to life. He was also a colossal control freak. I think he enjoyed tormenting Alexa as much as Michael did. She was smart enough to know everything Brigman did was illegal, so he loved rubbing her nose in the fact she couldn't do anything about it."

"So what happened?"

"Well, Michael kept her in court pretty continually from January 2009 to July. Then fate got a little kinder to Alexa for a bit. The actual divorce went through in July, and Michael made partner in August. He was so hot on the dating market that, for a while, he forgot how much fun he was having in family court."

"But he'd only been at the firm for three years in July 2009. No one makes partner at Warrick, Thompson in three years," Sarah said.

"I know," Bob agreed. "I can't explain it. That's something else you'll have to talk to Alan Warrick about. But the odd thing about this case is Michael started cancelling a lot of his visits with the kids. And that should have been enough to keep him from getting full custody."

"But it wasn't?"

"No."

"They managed to get through the rest of 2009 and a lot of 2010 without much happening except for those times when Michael would drag her to court, exaggerating some trivial complaint.

"Michael was dating and enjoying himself. Alexa was living in a little rented cottage in Pacific Beach with the children, looking after them full time and doing her piece work for Alan. But then, in November, Michael lost it with Sam, who was going through the terrible twos. Michael knew he was always at risk of beating somebody up, so he usually had a girlfriend over when the kids were with him. But one Saturday night, his date fell through, and Sam ran all over the house after his bath and wouldn't come put on his pajamas. Michael took the kids home on Sunday and told Alexa the bruises on his arms were from a fall in the backyard; but Meggie, who was three, had seen the whole thing and told the truth."

"So wouldn't proving Michael was the abuser help Alexa's case?"

"In a normal family law situation, yes. But not in this one."

"So what happened?"

"Alexa and I went to court to reduce Michael's time with the children, and I pointed out this was evidence Alexa hadn't lied about Michael's abusing her. But Judge Watkins denied my motion and referred the whole thing to Brigman again for another psychological evaluation. And, predictably, he turned it all against Alexa. His report said she bruised Sam, and she coached Meggie to lie for her. He ordered her to go to anger management counseling with some court-appointed hack like himself. It was one of Michael's finest acts of humiliation."

"Did you appeal?"

"No. Alexa thought that if she'd quietly dance to Michael and Brigman's tune, she'd get to keep the children. And she loved them above all else. I mean, she was literally going through hell for them. And there was no chance of her starting a new life. No man in his right mind would have wanted to get mixed up in that mess and have his own character assassinated in court."

"So she did as she was told?"

"Yes."

"Wasn't she angry about being treated this way?"

"Of course. That's where Brigman really got her goat every time. Any normal person would have been furious at being repeatedly humiliated and harassed and called a liar. And she was. But every time she showed even the slighted hint of anger, Brigman would put another 'crazy' label on her and talk about Michael's 'well-regulated' personality."

"But he wasn't 'well-regulated.'"

"No, not at all. In January 2012, Michael lost it again, this time with Meggie. She was five and Sam was four. Brigman did exactly the same thing: he turned the incident around on Alexa and blamed her for coaching Meggie to lie. But this time he went even farther. He ordered the kids to go to counseling to 'improve' their relationship with their father. When he got it 'improved' enough, he was going to 'enlarge' their time with Michael. In lay terms, he was brainwashing the kids against their mother a little at a time to prepare them to go live with him full time. And she was helpless to stop it."

"Who was the therapist who was working on the kids?"

"Brigman himself."

"But that's a blatant conflict of interest. Not to mention it's a violation of the federal constitutional right to privacy to order involuntary psychotherapy to change a child's bond with its parent."

"Again, that's what Alexa said. And we went back to the court of appeal."

"And lost?"

"And lost. She did a magnificent job at oral argument. Alan Warrick came, too. He had tears in eyes when it was over. But he got out of there before Michael and Tara Jeffers saw him."

"And after that?"

"I told her to pack her bags and get out of this town."

"You mean, leave her children?"

Bob nodded grimly. "She was never going to have a life here. Michael and Brigman would see to that. I told her better a clean break with the kids than losing them a day at a time for years and years and never knowing when the final blow would fall. She had the credentials to make partner in one of those big Wall

Street firms. I told her to go back East and rebuild her career, get married, and have some more kids with someone else."

"What did she say?"

"That she'd never leave Meggie and Sam."

"I can only admire your endurance, Mr. Metcalf. And hers."

"Bob, please."

"But there's one more thing I need to know," Sarah said. "How did she come to own a Glock nine?"

"I don't know. She had it when she first came to me. Michael had made death threats–of course nothing on the record that you could prove–and I told her to get a gun and learn how to use it. She told me she already had one."

"In your opinion, was she capable of killing Michael and Ronald Brigman?" Jim asked.

"Without any doubt. She had every reason to. But there's one thing you have to remember, Mr. Mitchell. She didn't have that gun in June when Michael and Brigman were killed. It had been stolen."

"How do you know?"

"She called me in late May on a Sunday afternoon, crying because the gun was missing. She kept it in the trunk of her car where the children couldn't get to it. She had no idea how anyone could have gotten into the car, but it was gone. I told her to file a police report."

"Trevor Martin told me there was no police report," Sarah said.

Bob shrugged. "I can't say I ever saw one. But she told me she reported it, and she said the officer told her he'd write a report."

"Was late May about the time Brigman ordered full custody of the children to Michael?"

"Yes. He ordered the change to take place in September when they went back to pre-school and after Michael had had time to hire a nanny. That summer was the last one Alexa was going to spend as the primary caregiver of her children. Instead they were going to be raised by Michael's hired help."

"So wouldn't that be enough to make her snap and kill Michael and Brigman?" Jim asked.

Bob nodded grimly, "More than enough. I wanted to kill them, too."

CHAPTER THIRTEEN

First Friday Night in September, 2013, Pacific Beach

"You're very quiet, tonight," Jim observed.

Sarah was sitting on the stool in his kitchen with a glass of wine, watching him pound chicken for piccata. She was miles away, lost in thought. She'd looked so tired and drained after the session with Bob Metcalf that he'd insisted she let him cook dinner for her. At first she'd protested she had to go home and work, but he was relieved when she'd responded to persuasion.

"What? I'm sorry, I wasn't listening."

Her lovely eyes were clouded as she gazed at nothing in particular. The dark circles under them stood out more than they usually did. Her translucent skin looked like very fine, white paper stretched over her cheekbones, making her scar stand out more than usual. She had taken off her suit jacket and was wearing a navy silk blouse and a black skirt. He wanted to hold her and tell her everything was going to be all right. But, of course, he couldn't.

"I said you're very quiet tonight."

"Am I? I guess I'm thinking about what Bob Metcalf told us."

"That was hard to listen to," Jim said. "I can't imagine what it must have been like for Alexa to live it."

She said nothing, but gazed into her wine glass, still a million miles away.

Jim quickly browned the meat, completed the sauce and served their plates with the chicken and pasta along with steamed broccoli with brown butter. He motioned for her to follow him to the dining room where he put the plates on the table, refreshed her wine glass, dimmed the lights, and lit candles.

When the lights went down, she looked across the table at him and frowned slightly.

"I thought this meal needed some atmosphere to take your mind off whatever you're worrying about."

"I'm not worrying."

"Your eyes are giving you away."

Sarah sighed and sipped her wine. "I keep trying to figure out a defense."

Jim paused between bites. "I'd say Battered Women's Syndrome. It looks like losing her children to her abuser was the last straw. It sent her over the edge, and she decided to kill Michael and Brigman."

"But her gun was stolen."

"There's no police report to back that up. When Brigman ordered that custody change in late May, she decided to kill them. She pretended it had been stolen and lied about making a police report."

"But why not get another gun that wasn't registered to her?"

"Because she didn't know how. She wasn't exactly in a position to know where black market guns are sold."

Sarah frowned. "But we only have the prosecutor's word to a defense attorney who was in his hip pocket that there was no report."

"I have some contacts at the San Diego Police Department. I'll see what I can find out."

"I hope you find one." She was still upset and drinking too much, he thought; and there was a desperate edge in her voice.

"What's wrong with using Battered Woman's Syndrome? She clearly had it. And post traumatic stress disorder, as Bob said."

"Because you know BWS will get her convicted of manslaughter. She'll still spend twenty-two years in prison, and her children will grow up without her. I have to get her back to her children." Still that urgency.

"Only an acquittal will do that. And that's impossible on these facts."

"There's jury nullification. Sometimes the jurors say, we don't care what the law is; we don't think this defendant deserves to be convicted." Still that desperate edge.

"That's the equivalent of a Hail Mary pass."

Sarah sighed and drank more wine.

"You're not eating, and I know it's wonderful because I'm eating mine."

She gave him a small smile. "No, it's fantastic. Really."

"You are also going to have a problem driving home if you don't dilute some of that wine with my amazing piccata."

Obediently, she picked up her fork and began to eat again.

Jim watched her for a few minutes in the dim light and thought about how beautiful she was even with that horrible scar. Then he said, "We should talk to Alan Warrick."

"I know. I'll set up an appointment next week."

"Do I come, too?"

"Yes. It sounds as if he and Bob are going to be witnesses."

Jim finished eating and stacked his knife and fork together in a gesture of finality. He noticed Sarah had put her fork down again and was staring into space, apparently lost in some painful thought, by her expression. He wanted to bring her back to the present.

"What about the children? Has anyone talked to the children?"

"No!" Did she say that a little too fast and a little too loud, he wondered. What emotion was driving her tonight?

"Not even the police?"

"No," she had found her professional voice again. "Coleman and Myrna Reed took them back to D.C. the day Alexa was arrested. Coleman Reed got a protective order so no one could talk to them."

"But didn't I read in the police report that Alexa said the children told her they heard Michael arguing with a woman just minutes before the shots were fired?"

"That's true."

"Then we need to know who that woman is."

"Right now we need to talk to Alan Warrick. Why did the firm pay for that abortion? And why couldn't Alexa get a job in San Diego? And why did Alan have to send her work in secret after the divorce? Why couldn't he bring her back to the firm? And did he know Michael washed client money through his personal accounts before depositing it where the state bar said it belonged from the beginning?"

"Let's have dessert on the patio."

"I don't eat dessert."

"You'll eat this one. Coconut flan with raspberry sauce. No one can resist it."

* * *

It was a warm night for September, and the air was heavy with the scent of night-blooming jasmine. Sarah allowed herself to put aside her worries about Alexa as she sipped espresso and listened to the ocean rolling onshore in the distance while Jim spoke passionately about Cody's love of model trains and Lego blocks. She knew she'd drunk a little too much wine, but the alcohol had finally taken the edge off the misery of hearing Bob's story. And now the warm coffee and the joy of being too close to Jim on the little love seat under the stars lulled her fears and made her wish she could sit with him forever. He'd brought one plate of flan with two forks, and he'd been right. The soft pudding was irresistible, the ultimate comfort food.

"He has a huge train layout in Josh and Gail's basement," Jim explained. "And he uses the Legos to build cities for the trains to run through and to create the people who live in them. Every time he comes to see me, he wants to go to Legoland to get more ideas for his projects."

"What's Legoland?"

"Oh, I forgot. You don't have kids. You know what Legos are, right?"

She felt that sharp stab of pain whenever anyone reminded her she was childless. But she kept her mask in place and nodded, so he wouldn't know he'd said anything amiss.

"The company is based in Denmark. They've built an amusement park here at Carlsbad with rides and slides, and tiny cities and people made out of the blocks."

"And you like to go?"

"With Cody, yes." His eyes clouded over as he spoke.

"When do you see him again?"

"Thanksgiving and Christmas. If I'm lucky. More and more he doesn't want to come because he has things to do with his friends. He's beginning to be interested in girls. When he gets a girlfriend, he won't come at all unless she can come, too. And you know her parents will say no."

"It hasn't happened, yet. Don't borrow trouble. Besides, I'm going to have to send you back to D.C. to interview character witnesses for Alexa. If the worst happens and she's convicted of both murders, we'll have to find people who can tell the jury enough about who she really is, so they won't give her the death penalty."

"Won't you come, too?"

I'll want to, she thought. But too much time with you isn't good for me. "It depends on what's happening here."

He smiled as he put the empty plate on the little table next to the love seat. "Too bad you didn't like it."

"You won me over. Normally, I don't like sweets."

He grinned, happy at his triumph. But then his face clouded. "You know, the toughest thing for me is knowing Cody's happy in a world I can't belong to. I mean, I'm glad Josh filled the void in Gail's life my stupidity created, but the pain never ends for me. Every day I think about Cody getting up, going to school, doing his homework, playing with those trains without me. And all I can do is send him more trains and more Legos, but I can't build them with him or watch them run. Another man gets to do that."

His pain was so raw and so real that without thinking, Sarah put her hand over his. His dark eyes held hers, and he leaned toward her, his lips inches from hers. She wanted him to kiss her, but she knew it would change everything. And everything couldn't change. Ever. Her cell phone in her bag in the dining room suddenly shrilled, and she jumped up and ran inside to answer it.

* * *

What had he been thinking? Jim asked himself as he followed her inside and watched her frown into her phone. He knew she was involved with someone, and he'd been stupid beyond stupid to turn tonight into a show of his personal feelings. Still, how to control himself on a gentle summer night with the ocean purring on shore and the jasmine in full bloom and her own gardenia scent overwhelming his senses?

But now she was frowning into the phone with her lawyer face on, and the moment had passed forever.

He heard her say, "Very well. I understand. I'll be right there."

She ended the call with a decisive click.

"What's wrong?"

"That was the jail. Alexa Reed is in the hospital and not expected to make it."

Jim's mouth went dry, and the bottom dropped out of his stomach. "I thought they had her on suicide watch?"

"They did. It wasn't suicide. It was a reaction to the medication the jail psychiatrist prescribed for her. They took her to UCSD in Hillcrest. I have to go down there. She doesn't have any family that I know about."

"You'd better let me drive."

* * *

"Here, Alexa."

Curious George was standing by her cot, holding a small paper cup full of pills and a cup of water.

"I've prescribed Lexapro for you. Here's the first dose. You'll be feeling better in no time."

CHAPTER FOURTEEN

First Friday Night in September, 2013, UCSD Hospital, Hillcrest

Hospitals are white and barren at night, Jim thought, as they headed down the white linoleum corridor on the third floor where they'd been told they would find Alexa's room. Sarah raced along, her face set in a mask of grim determination. The gigantic circle of a clock pinned to the white tile wall said eleven-thirty.

A deputy sheriff in a khaki uniform was on guard outside Alexa's room. He stopped them as they tried to enter.

"You can't go in there."

"Yes, I can. I'm her court-appointed attorney, and this is my private investigator." Sarah flashed her bar card as if it were a light saber and went in.

Jim took several seconds to find his own identification and to display it to the frowning deputy. Then he followed Sarah. She had frozen by the bed, her arms wrapped around herself, staring down in disbelief, crying and whispering, "No, no, no, no."

Surrounded by a forest of life support machines, Alexa looked even tinier. Jim saw tubes down her throat, the wound from the tracheotomy, and an IV line running into one arm. The machine was breathing for her.

Still crying, Sarah reached out for the hand not attached to the IV, leaned over, and lovingly stroked Alexa's tangled hair off her face. She felt Jim standing close behind her and turned, her eyes full of pain. "This can't be happening."

He put his arm around her and gave her a reassuring hug. "I know, but it is."

"Here," he handed her a tissue from the box by the bed, and she wiped her eyes.

The door opened and a fortyish woman in dark gray scrubs with tired eyes and wisps of hair escaping what had started her shift as a bun came in.

"Who are you? You can't be in here."

"Yes, we can," Jim said quietly. Sarah was still fighting back tears and couldn't speak. "This is Alexa's attorney, and I am her investigator. She doesn't have any family that anyone knows of. We came to see how she's doing."

"When the jail called, they said she'd had a reaction to the drug they gave her," Sarah had found her voice but was still holding Alexa's hand. "Didn't they check for allergies before they prescribed it?"

"I have no idea. I work *here*, not at the jail. You'll have to ask the people downtown what they knew about her medical history. Look, don't give me a hard time, ok? I'm just supposed to check her vitals and fill in her chart and note that she's still alive. Barely. Now if you'll step aside, I have to put the blood pressure cuff on."

Sarah frowned and moved away, bowing to the frazzled woman's exhaustion.

After the nurse left, Sarah tried to sit down on the side of the bed, but because of all the machines close by there was no space. Jim pulled up one of the two chairs for her.

"Here."

"Thanks." Sarah sank into it as she reached for Alexa's lifeless hand once again. Jim watched the occasional tear continue to trickle down her cheek. "We need to do something for her."

"I don't think there is anything we can do," Jim said softly.

"There has to be something." Sarah was crying openly again, her body shaking. "If I hadn't lost that hearing—"

Jim laid a hand on her shoulder. "It wasn't your fault."

But Sarah shook her head and sobbed.

Jim knelt down in front of her and put both hands on her shoulders. He put his face close to hers. "Listen to me. You didn't cause this. Stop blaming yourself."

She looked up at him and then at Alexa. "We should at least find a priest for her. That's more than the hospital staff is willing to do."

"Okay. Do you know if she's Catholic?"

"Pretty close. Episcopalian. I read it in her file. Brigman made a big stink about her wanting to raise the children in her church supposedly to alienate them from Michael, who wasn't religious."

"I'll go see if there's any kind of priest on duty. Will you be okay if I leave you?"

She nodded. He watched her touch the lifeless form on the bed. "Hurry. It doesn't look like we have much time."

* * *

When the door closed behind Jim, Sarah sat in the dim room and watched the respirator mechanically and rhythmically push Alexa's lungs up and down as if she herself were resisting continuing to live. Why save her for the purpose of killing her, Sarah wondered. What would happen to me if I pulled the plug on the machine? I could say I tripped. I could end all of this in a split second. She stared at the tangle of wires, wondering which one would free Alexa Reed forever.

This is when you pray, Sarah reminded herself. But she had prayed once. No, not once. She had prayed every day for hundreds and hundreds of days. She had worn out her knees proving there was no God because if there had been, her prayers would have been answered. But God was merely a figment of suffering people's imaginations. He was no more than an effort to explain the unexplainable horror of unbearable suffering. Besides, if there were a God, he would have not created Alexa Reed's personal hell. Or hers.

Suddenly, the door swung open, and Jim appeared with a thirtyish man in a priest's collar and black suit.

"Sarah, this is Father Richard Morely. He's a Catholic priest, but he's on duty right now as the night chaplain."

"She needs the last rites, Father," Sarah said. "She's Episcopalian. Can you still do that for her?"

"Of course. Do you know if she was ever baptized? That's the more important sacrament."

"No, we don't know. I'm her attorney. We don't think she has any family. Her file says she grew up Episcopalian, so I'd bet she was baptized. I know her children were."

"I'll do both, just to be very sure. I'll need to fetch some holy water from the chapel and anointing oil. I'll be back in ten minutes."

The door swooshed shut behind the priest, and Jim's gentle eyes met hers. "Here's another tissue."

"Thanks. And thanks for finding him."

"Of course. I didn't know you were religious."

"I'm not. But Alexa is. Or was."

He walked over and gently stroked Alexa's tangled blonde hair as if she were a child. He said, "I was religious once. Gail wanted Cody to be raised Catholic because she is. I went to mass with them every week. I thought of converting. But then Gail hit me with those divorce papers, and I lost what I loved best in the world. I wondered why God didn't at least send me a warning. After that, I wasn't so sure about Him anymore."

"A benevolent God would have Alexa Reed home safe and sound with her children right now." Sarah could see the bitterness in her voice startled him. "I'm sure it's a pretty safe bet that heaven is the empty hole we think it is."

The door swung open, and Father Morely came back with his priest's stole, holy water, and anointing oil. As he began his preparations, Jim said, "I'll be back in a few minutes. I want to see if I can get anything out of the night nurse."

* * *

When the priest was finished, he took a few minutes to pack up the vials of holy water and oil in his little black leather sacrament case. Then he removed the stole from his neck and folded it over his arm the way a maitre d' carries a napkin.

"Thank you, Father."

"Of course. That's why I'm here. I'm on duty all night, so if things change, please call me. I think prayer over a departing soul eases its passage."

I wish I believed in souls, Sarah thought. But aloud she said, "I'm sure you're right."

After the door swung shut behind Father Morley, Sarah sank into the chair by the bed once more and took Alexa's dry, papery hand. The puke green curtains turned the blank walls their sickly shade of death and disease in the low light. Sarah listened to the whir and thump of the ventilator, and watched it labor to keep Alexa Reed on this side of eternity. She considered once more what would happen if she eased its plug out of the outlet.

The door swooshed open again, and Jim reappeared looking upset and angry.

"Is the priest finished?"

"Yes, he just left. I'm thinking there's not anything else we can do tonight. We should probably go get some sleep and be here early tomorrow."

He shook his head and pulled the remaining chair up close to Sarah's and sat down. He leaned very close and spoke softly. "No, we shouldn't leave her alone. I have to keep my voice down. I don't want the deputy outside to hear what I'm going to say."

A new wave of apprehension washed over her as she fought down the emotions that being close to him always aroused. "What did you find out?"

"That the jail shrink gave her a drug he knew she was allergic to."

Sarah frowned. "But surely he wouldn't knowingly do something like that. It has to be negligence."

"No, listen. The night nurse told me Alexa's private doctors were all affiliated with UCSD and this hospital, so all of her medical records are in their system. They show that back in '09, a few months after Michael started the divorce war, the stress got to her. Her own doctor referred her to one of the psychiatrists here, and he gave her a low dose of Lexapro. She had a mild allergic reaction and couldn't take it anymore."

"But that doesn't prove the jail psychiatrist tried to kill her."

"Yes, it does. I haven't finished. My little red-headed friend out there said the jail shrink requested all of Alexa's records a few days ago; and privacy laws notwithstanding, they handed them over. She showed me the computer entry the hospital made when it sent her records to Yager."

"They should have contacted me before doing that."

"True, but you know what the jail people think of defense attorneys. Anyway, at the time Dr. Yager handed her the Lexapro, he knew she was allergic; and he gave her a much larger dose than he should have, so her reaction was bound to be far more acute than before."

"I'm still seeing negligence here, not intent to murder."

"Wait, there's more."

"More?"

"It only took a few minutes for her airway to start to close. Yager hadn't left the building. In fact, he was out in the hall, probably hanging around to see her crash. When the guard summoned him because she was in trouble, he instructed her to wait to call the paramedics. Apparently he wanted to make sure they couldn't do anything for her when they arrived. When the ambulance did get there, she was almost gone. The only thing that saved her was the emergency tracheotomy one of the EMTs was able to do at nearly the last second. It wasn't negligence. It was deliberate."

"You're saying Dr. Yager tried to kill her."

"In a word, yes. You looked stunned."

"I am. Although, Yager, like Percy Andrews, is part of that mental health community that included Ronald Brigman. His attitude toward her was probably the same as Andrews'. But they can't make another attempt on her here. The hospital staff doesn't care a thing about Brigman."

"I know, but we don't know who else might have been involved with Yager in setting her up for this." He gestured toward the door. "There's a deputy, out there, for example, whom I wouldn't trust any farther than I can see him."

Sarah looked down again at the wires and plugs for the laboring machines. Jim followed her eyes and said, "See what I mean? All the opportunity in the world to finish what Yager started."

"I see your point. What should we do?"

"We shouldn't leave her alone. You're exhausted, and you've had two big shocks tonight. I'll stay here, so you can get some sleep. I'm going to call you a cab to take you back to my place to get your car. Be back tomorrow at nine, and we'll take turns watching her. We can't leave her alone until she wakes up."

"If she wakes up."

CHAPTER FIFTEEN

First Saturday in September 2013, UCSD Hospital, Hillcrest

Sarah slept fitfully and was up by eight to slip into comfortable gray yoga pants and a white t-shirt. She put some work into her briefcase and headed for the hospital to relieve Jim at nine as promised. She found him dozing in the chair next to Alexa's bed, a never-before-seen growth of stubble on his chin. She laid her hand lightly on his shoulder to let him know she had arrived. A stray, wicked thought asked what would it be like to wake him up every morning.

Her touch startled him, and for a moment he looked around blankly, apparently having forgotten why he was there. His eyes went from the ventilator to Sarah's face, and then he gave her a small smile.

"Didn't mean to go to sleep."

"I'd say that was unavoidable. Looks as if nothing's changed."

"The doctor came by this morning before I dozed. He hadn't expected her to make it through the night. But even though she's still hanging on, he wasn't optimistic about the future."

"What do you mean?"

"He thinks she'll have some sort of brain damage if she does wake up. At the very least, memory loss."

"So she may never be able to tell us why she went to Brigman's that night?"

"Exactly. The brain throws out the most traumatic memories first."

"You need some sleep. Go home and rest."

"I'll be back at six."

* * *

Sarah grew used to the rhythm of the ventilator as it pumped air into Alexa's lungs. Her chest rose and fell rhythmically, driven by the machine. The bright September sun streaming in through the windows had banished the sickly green glow from the walls, and now the room was pristine white again. Nurses came and went and gave her polite, but puzzled, looks as they checked Alexa's vital signs and made notes in her chart.

Around noon, a man in a priest's collar came in. He was in his early fifties with thinning gray hair and a round, open face.

"I'm Father Bennett," he said. "I'm the Episcopal chaplain. Father Morley told me he'd been here last night. Were you the one who summoned him?"

Sarah nodded. "She seemed near death."

"Any improvement?" Father Bennett looked at the lifeless form on the bed as he spoke.

"Nothing I can see."

"You look tired. Have you had time to eat?"

Sarah hadn't stopped for breakfast and hadn't thought about food during her bedside vigil. But suddenly she realized she was hungry. "No, but I can't leave her."

"I'll stay for a bit. Go down to the cafeteria and have lunch."

* * *

When she came back thirty minutes later, she found Father Bennet quietly reciting the Episcopalian version of the rosary as he sat next to Alexa. He turned at the swish of the door opening, and his excited eyes met hers.

"She opened her eyes," he said. "Only for a second or two. But she opened them. I told the nurse."

"What did she say?"

"Not much. But it's a good sign. We have to keep praying."

"I don't pray."

His kind brown eyes looked puzzled. "But you summoned Father Morley last night."

"Only because I respected Alexa's beliefs. I have no use for God."

He remained unperturbed. She had the feeling he'd had this conversation dozens of times. "Well, He has plenty of use for you."

"*No—He—does—not.*" She spoke each word slowly and distinctly as if passing judgement for all eternity. "Didn't they tell you why they're trying to keep this woman alive? So they can murder her by lethal injection in twenty years when her appeals are exhausted."

Again the priest was unmoved by her bitterness. "All the more reason to keep praying for God to spare her life entirely. Were you raised in any particular faith?"

Sarah wanted to bite back a scathing "no," but for some reason his kindness in the face of her anger made her tell the truth. "Yours."

"Well, then, here." He handed her the rosary. "You can put it to good use. And call me if anything changes." He pressed his card with his cell number into her hand along with the beads, gave her a smile, and left.

Sarah slipped the business card into her brief case and sat down again by the bed. She stared at the onyx beads with the silver cross at the center in her left hand and wondered what to do with them. She was suddenly sorry her connection to Alexa had brought the sore subject of religion back into her life.

Her mother had given her a blue crystal rosary after her confirmation when she was twelve. And she'd prayed it over and over and over through all those dark years until the day she'd thrown it into the Pacific, officially telling God she didn't buy the myth of Him any more. So why now was she tempted to try to remember the prayers?

She held the large bead above the cross and tried to recall the words she was supposed to say. No clue. *The Lord be with you.* No, that was the priest's invitation to the congregation at the beginning of the Eucharist, not the beginning of the rosary. And there was some sort of answer the congregation chanted back, but she couldn't remember it. She couldn't remember the rosary prayers, either. What had Jim said? The most traumatic memories are the first to go.

She studied the beads again and wondered what to do with them. As she was about to slip them into her brief case to be carted to the Pacific for disposal, she looked over at Alexa's lifeless hand. She looped the beads over the thin wrist like a bracelet and laid the silver cross against her palm.

"Wake up," she heard herself say. "For Meggie and Sam. Wake up."

* * *

Jim was back at six, rested and clean-shaven in fresh jeans and a white knit shirt. He pulled the second chair next to Sarah's and sat down. She was immediately aware of the masculine energy he brought into the room. She wanted to put her head on his shoulder and feel his arms around her. This wasn't good. She couldn't have these thoughts. She had to stay focused on Alexa.

"Any change?"

She told him about Father Bennett's observation.

"But nothing since?"

"No."

"And I gather the nurse wasn't especially impressed when Father Bennett told her Alexa had opened her eyes?"

"No, she wasn't."

"You need to eat."

"I'm not hungry."

"I said, 'you need to eat.' This case is taking its toll on you."

"Ok. I'll run down to the cafeteria for a little bit."

"Or you could go home and get some rest."

"No. I want to be here if there's any change."

* * *

For the entire evening, they sat side-by-side next to Alexa's bed while the machines hummed and pumped and kept her alive. The stray, wicked thought came back, slightly altered from the morning: what if she and Jim could sit side-by-side in companionable silence every evening, like an old married couple. No, no. Never that. Never. Be quiet, she told her brain. You know the rules. She forced herself to concentrate on the work she had brought. But by eleven, she was too tired to do any more.

Jim, too, had put down his files. "You've been here all day. You should go home."

"I keep thinking she'll open her eyes again."

The door swooshed and a new nurse appeared with her stethoscope draped around her neck and a blood pressure cuff in her hand. She appeared to be in her late twenties, very attractive with large dark eyes and long blonde hair that was confined to a surprisingly flattering on-duty pony tail. Sarah noticed she caught Jim's attention as she crossed the room to check Alexa's vital signs.

"Any change?" Jim asked.

"Her pulse is weaker. I'm going to call the doctor on duty."

Suddenly Sarah's heart began to race as if she could make up Alexa's deficit with her own. She tried to rein in any show of emotion in front of Jim, but she had believed all afternoon Alexa was going to turn the corner because she'd opened her eyes for Father Bennett. She didn't want to give up her shred of hope.

The door swooshed more abruptly than before. The attractive nurse had returned with a harried doctor who waved Sarah and Jim out of the room.

"Sorry. You'll have to leave."

They stood in the hall under the deputy's suspicious gaze, waiting for news. Ten minutes felt like ten hours.

Sarah leaned against the wall and closed her eyes to keep from showing tears.

She felt Jim watching her.

"It's ok to feel something," he said.

She shook her head. "No, it's not. I never get involved emotionally with a case."

"You'd have to have a heart of stone not to be involved in this one."

"The thing is, I can't decide if it would be better if she lived or died. Her children need her, but we've got almost nothing to work with for a defense."

"That's what they said about the Menendez case."

"This isn't the same thing!" She knew she was speaking too sharply, but she didn't want to talk or even think about Joey Menendez ever again.

Before Jim could say anything else, the doctor came out of Alexa's room, rattling off instructions to the pretty nurse who eyed Jim sideways as she listened. Sarah read his name badge for the first time. Dr. S. McCord. He was in his early forties, she guessed. Dark hair, a few streaks of gray. She bet Dr. S. McCord had two preteens at home and a Mrs. S. McCord who grocery shopped in tennis skirts and ran his house to perfection.

He finally noticed them standing in the corridor. "Are you her family?"

"Her legal team. We don't think she has any family," Jim said. "How is she?"

"We're going to lighten up on the sedatives to see if her blood pressure will come up. But honestly, I'm not optimistic. The nurses say you've been here around the clock since last night. You should go home and get some sleep. You both look exhausted."

But Sarah shook her head. "No. I'm responsible for her. I can't leave. She opened her eyes around lunchtime. She might do that again, tonight."

"It's not likely. Coma patients often open their eyes for a few seconds at odd times. It's not a sign she's going to come out of it or that she hasn't suffered brain damage."

"But you don't know that."

"True. At this moment, I'm just trying to keep her from crashing. If you both insist on staying, why not take turns sleeping? There's a chair that converts into a make-shift cot in the Family Waiting Room."

* * *

In the wee hours, Sarah sat with Alexa, watching an IV drip into her arm. The pretty nurse returned often with the blood pressure cuff. She always gave Sarah a reassuring smile as she went about her business, but never said a word. Her name tag said, "D. Murphy." D for Diana or for Dorothy or for Deirdre because Murphy was Irish? Odd how irrelevant details could calm your mind in moments of crisis.

Sarah sat beside the bed and held one dry, lifeless hand. "Stay for Meggie and Sam," she whispered over and over again through the dark hours. "Stay for Meggie and Sam."

She eyed the rosary often and was tempted to take it back and try to remember some prayers. At least until she had realized there was no such thing as *Our Father* and no such place as *Heaven*, praying made her feel as if she could influence the outcome of a situation. But that had just been an illusion, as she now knew far too well.

Fatigue had settled into her bones like drying cement. She sat in her chair and held Alexa's hand and chanted her mantra, until Jim came to relieve her at four a.m. He tapped her lightly on the shoulder and smiled as he slid into the chair beside hers.

"I'm here. Go get some sleep."

And she was so delirious with grief and so relieved to see him that she kissed him lightly on the cheek. Later, as she lay on the fold-out chair that smelled like him, too exhausted to think, she tried to decide if he had really kissed the scar on her own cheek in return. Or was she so tired she was hallucinating?

CHAPTER SIXTEEN

Second Sunday in September, 2013, UCSD Hospital Hillcrest

Alexa Reed was swimming upward from the bottom of the darkest ocean. Her eyelids felt like lead as she tried to force them open to see if she had surfaced yet. She worked to move her lips to speak, but she was still deep under water.

Her mouth was dry, and her throat hurt. As she struggled through the darkness hoping to reach the light, she imagined ice water tingling on her tongue. She concentrated on the weights on each eyelid, willing them to vanish so she could see how much farther she had to go before she'd break free of the dark. But then there'd be the problem of swimming to shore. Her limbs were heavy, and she couldn't imagine having the strength to keep going much longer. Something was pushing on her chest. Was she wearing scuba gear? But a scuba tank didn't push the air into your lungs. Was she still alive or was this death?

* * *

Around eight on Sunday morning, Jim saw Alexa's eyelids flicker. He held his breath as he waited to see if she'd open them. His back was stiff and sore from the makeshift cot and from being in the chair by her bed for so many hours. The stubble on his chin itched, and he longed for a hot shower and a razor. He had been about to go for a brief walk in the hallway to limber up, but now he stayed put.

Suddenly Jim was looking into Alexa's deep blue eyes; and they weren't blank the way they'd been while she'd been lying on the jail cot. They were a mixture of confusion and anxiety. The doctor apparently had been right: her memory was gone, and she had no idea how she'd wound up here.

Jim got up and hurried over to the bed.

"Alexa?"

Her eyes met his, and tears began to flow. They streamed down her face, a torrent of unchecked emotion.

He sat on the side of the bed and did what he could to gather her into his arms. She was attached to so many machines, he couldn't hold her very close, and he doubted the professional propriety of what he was doing, anyway.

But professionalism wasn't the point, he reminded himself. Alexa Reed needed human contact at that moment, and fate had put him there to provide it.

"It's ok, it's ok," he whispered over and over, patting what was left of her thin little body. "You're going to be ok, now."

But, of course, that wasn't true.

The door opened and Sarah appeared, her eyes puffy from lack of sleep, her short hair sticking up wildly, and her clothes wrinkled from being slept in. Jim wasn't sure if her eyes went wide with shock because Alexa was awake or because he was holding her in his arms. He felt even more uncomfortable.

"She just woke up."

Sarah nodded but said nothing.

"We'd better ring for the nurse."

She remained silent but reached for the call button.

Jim eased Alexa back onto her pillows and awkwardly dabbed at her eyes with the end of the sheet.

"Here." Sarah handed him a wad of tissue from the box by the bed.

"Thanks."

Alexa's eyes were now fixed on Sarah's face as if she were seeing her for the first time. Jim's heart sank. Significant memory loss for sure.

A crisp, newly on-duty morning nurse answered their call and quickly shooed them out of the room while she took Alexa's vital signs and summoned a doctor. Once again, they stood in the corridor and waited for news.

"Why didn't you call me?"

"She had just opened her eyes. When she started to cry, I didn't have time to think."

Jim's empty stomach knotted because Sarah looked skeptical.

They stood in awkward silence, waiting for the doctor. Finally, he appeared. His name badge said Dr. P. McMillan. Sarah noticed Dr. McMillan was ten years younger than Dr. McCord of the previous evening but no less jaded and not particularly optimistic.

"Dropping her sedation has allowed her to wake up."

"So is she going to be ok?" Sarah demanded.

"Too soon to tell. We need to wean her off the ventilator."

"How long will that take?" Sarah asked.

"I can't say. Some patients can breathe on their own in six to eight hours. Others, it's a long process."

"When can she talk to us?"

"Not for several days, and that's assuming the weaning process goes quickly. She's going to have a sore throat, and the tracheotomy has to heal."

Jim saw Sarah's shoulders sag.

Dr. McMillan noticed, too. "Look, these things take time."

"I know. I know." She frowned. "But we don't have a lot of that."

* * *

"I'm not letting them send her back to the jail," Sarah said that night as she sat once again on the stool in Jim's kitchen as he made omelettes. They had spent the day watching over Alexa, who had mostly slept.

"Red or white?" Jim asked, pulling a wine glass out of the cupboard.

"Red."

He felt her eyes on him as he opened a bottle, poured the wine, and handed her a glass.

"You look fierce when you say that."

"I feel fierce. They are not going to do anything else to her. And I want to force Judge Tomlinson to face the consequences of his order. God, how I hate these shrinks!"

Jim stopped beating the eggs and studied her face.

"What's wrong?"

"Nothing. It just sounded personal to me."

"What?"

"Your feeling about the mental health types. It sounded personal."

Her eyes grew darker and more guarded. "I'm just reacting to so many years of seeing them spout off dishonest opinions."

He poured the eggs into the pan and concentrated on when to add the mushrooms, ham, cheese, and onions. His masterpiece was finished in seven minutes. He slid it onto a plate and sliced it in half. One half went on her plate, the other on his. He picked up both and said, "Come on. Let's eat in the dining room while it's hot. I hate cold eggs."

He thought of the last meal they shared there, as they sat down. But candlelight didn't feel appropriate tonight. He could sense she was still as shaken as he was over the events of the weekend.

"The bigger question is, how are you going to keep her out of jail," he observed as he watched her eat. He was happy to see she was devouring her half. "She's charged with special circumstances, so she has no right to bail."

"She has a right to a bail hearing," Sarah said.

"Yes, but you have to show the evidence of her guilt is not 'substantial' to get her out on bail. And that's impossible in this case."

Jim watched her eyes darken. "We don't know that for sure. We need to talk to her to find out why she was at Brigman's that night."

"But we have no idea when she can talk to us or even what she remembers. You could put Jordan on for Battered Women's Syndrome. There's some pretty substantial evidence she's guilty of manslaughter, not murder."

"I don't want her convicted of manslaughter!" Sarah dropped her fork on her plate in frustration. Suddenly there were tears in her eyes.

Jim got up and came around the table to put his arms around her, but she shook her head. "No, don't. I'm sorry. I'm too emotional about this."

He went back and sat down, wishing she hadn't refused his comfort. Disappointment sat on his shoulder like an old friend. "As I said, earlier, you'd have to have a heart of stone not to be touched by this case."

She wiped her eyes, and drank a long, deep gulp of wine. "I can't make tactical legal decisions based on my feelings. We shouldn't leave her alone at the hospital. Can you look in on her this week? I've got a full calendar of hearings and motions. I can stop by in the evenings."

"Of course," Jim said. "I'll check on her in the mornings and afternoons. It's really my job, anyway, as your investigator."

"I'm going to calendar a bail hearing tomorrow in front of Tomlinson. Will you take statements from that night nurse who told you about the medical records, the ER nurse who was on duty when they brought her in, and the EMT who saved her life?"

"Of course."

"And we're going to need the name of the guard at the jail who followed Yager's orders to wait to summon help."

"That's going to be harder to come up with. But I'll get it."

"Judge Tomlinson is not going to like this story, but he's going to listen to it, anyway."

* * *

Second Monday in September 2013, La Jolla, California

Sarah drove back to her office in La Jolla the next morning at eleven o'clock, having persuaded Judge Tomlinson to hold a bail hearing on October 1. Preston Barton, in his neat gray suit and round bald dome, had been apoplectic.

"Your Honor, don't let her waste everyone's time! She can't possibly make a showing that the evidence of Alexa Reed's guilt is not 'substantial.'"

Judge Tomlinson looked over his glasses at Sarah.

"He's got a good point, Ms. Knight."

"The jail psychiatrist tried to kill her. You *cannot* send her back there."

The prosecutor began to sputter. "Really, Your Honor! She has no proof!"

"Try me!" Sarah whirled on her opponent, her eyes fierce. She took a deep breath and reminded herself not to lose her professional composure entirely. She looked back at the judge. "Give me that hearing date, and I'll show you what I can prove."

* * *

She smiled as she swung her BMW into the underground parking garage at her office. She wished Jim had been there to see the prosecutor's face when Judge Tomlinson granted her request. She needed to call him as soon as she got upstairs.

She parked and hurried to the elevator. Even though there should have been no one in the waiting room, she decided to slip in through the back to give herself a few more minutes of privacy before facing her long-suffering law clerk, who also doubled as a receptionist.

She reached her office undetected, took off her suit jacket, and hung it on the peg behind her door. She sat down at her desk and reached for the phone; but before she could dial Jim, her clerk, Martin Browning, appeared in the doorway.

"What's up, Martin?" He was tall and thin, with unruly red hair and freckles spattered across his nose and cheeks. He was in his third year of law school at the University of San Diego, and Sarah would miss him when he graduated because he was patient with her whims and did excellent legal research.

"I heard you come in. Hope the hearing went ok."

"It was fine. I got everything I wanted. I need a few minutes to make a phone call. Would you mind running downstairs and fetching me a latte from Starbuck's?"

"No problem. But you might want me to bring back two coffees."

"Why?"

"There's a woman in the waiting room who's been sitting out there for at least two hours to see you. Her name is Tessa Spineli."

Damn, Sarah thought, and quickly ran through her options. Only she didn't really have any options other than to accept the inevitable confrontation with David's wife.

"Two coffees sound about right. Go ahead and show her in."

Tessa sashayed into her office a few minutes later like an angry Barbie in a red Versace suit with Angelina Jolie's lips.

"You're sleeping with my husband!"

Remain cool, Sarah reminded herself. "Would you like to sit down? My assistant has gone to fetch coffee."

"I don't want any coffee."

"Well, what about a seat, then?"

Tessa shook her blonde layers like a Farah Fawcett throwback, and eyed the chair in front of Sarah's desk as if it were a booby trap. After a few seconds, she folded her thin body into the chair and crossed her long legs.

"Do you know who I am?"

"Of course. Tessa, David's wife."

"Emphasis on 'wife.'" She flashed the four carat diamond on her left hand at Sarah.

"Mrs. Spineli, I'm sorry someone has given you false information, but I'm not sleeping with your husband."

"Lying won't help," she snarled. "The household staff tells me what goes on when I'm not there."

Shit, Sarah thought. I warned David about conducting an affair in his own house. Remain calm, she reminded herself. "I'm very sorry if someone close to you is trying to hurt you, Mrs. Spineli. But I'm not sleeping with your husband. I've had dinner with him a few times because he hired me to straighten things out for your brother-in-law with the Securities and Exchange Commission."

"You did more than have dinner with him."

Martin knocked and entered with the two coffees.

"Thank you," Sarah smiled as if everything were going her way. He looked over at Tessa curiously and left the room.

"Now, Mrs. Spineli, as I said, I am not having an affair with your husband."

"It's been going on for months."

Sarah decided seizing the offense would get rid of her. "I refuse to keep repeating myself. I'm not sleeping with your husband, and that is all there is to it. Your story about being tipped off by the household staff is completely false. Your husband pays them, Mrs. Spineli. They are not going to give you any information that would put their jobs in jeopardy. Blackmail is a crime. Now please get out of my office. We have nothing more to discuss."

"Oh, don't we?" Tessa reached into her cavernous Gucci bag, pulled out a folder, and held up the photo on top.

Sarah's mouth went dry. It was a picture of her with David on the terrace outside the guest room on the night Tessa had wavered about going to Cabo.

"Okay, so the staff didn't tell me. That's true. I hired a private investigator to catch the two of you."

"I repeat, blackmail is a crime, Mrs. Spineli."

"I'm not here for money. I get plenty of that from my husband."

"Then what are you here for?"

"I want you to stop sleeping with my husband."

"You won't publish those pictures and risk upsetting David. You need your allowance from him too much."

But Tessa was unfazed by the insult. "Oh, I'm not going to do anything to upset my husband. You're right. I depend on my allowance. But if you don't leave him alone, there are a number of accidents that could happen to you."

With that, she got up and left the room, making sure to slam the door hard.

Sarah sat back and closed her eyes. She had been ready to end the affair with David, anyway. She didn't enjoy his company, and the sex wasn't great. And it wasn't the first time she'd been confronted by an angry wife. Until today no one had threatened her life, but she didn't take Tessa seriously.

The photos, though, were a different story. She doubted Tessa would publish them because that would very likely end her marriage. But just knowing they existed made Sarah uneasy. If they did get out, it would damage her professional credibility. And she needed every ounce of that right now to defend Alexa Reed.

She opened her eyes and stared blankly at the autumn-blue ocean stretching vast and infinite toward the lighter sky. The guilt pangs that had wracked her since Alexa came out of the coma had subsided for the first time during the hearing that morning, but they were back now and stronger than before. She'd drawn a peacefully departing spirit back into a hellish world of lies, bribes, and probably certain death in twenty years under the vengeful eyes of a roomful of strangers. And she'd done it in the name of reuniting her with her children, even though that was a promise Sarah could never keep. What had possessed her to tell Alexa to stay for Meggie and Sam?

CHAPTER SEVENTEEN

Second Monday Night in September, 2013, La Jolla, California

Jim headed out of the parking lot at the hospital that night at eight o'clock and navigated the winding side streets of Hillcrest until he reached Washington Street and merged onto I-5 North to head home. He'd spent a large part of the morning with Alexa and then had come back tonight. She was making rapid progress, and the doctor was optimistic she'd be off the ventilator soon.

He had waited all day to see Sarah. He had hoped she'd come by as promised. But, in the end, his only contact with her had been by phone. She'd called twice to give him the hearing date and to get a progress report on Alexa. Driving along in the lonely dark toward his empty house, Jim knew how much he wanted to see her. Suddenly, as he drove down Garnet Avenue, just minutes from home, he abandoned the road toward home and headed up the back of Mount Soledad toward La Jolla and Sarah.

* * *

There was a black Porsche 911 S Turbo Cabriolet in her drive. Stay calm, he thought. You don't know who it belongs to, and you have no right to be upset. But he turned back toward home, tired and preoccupied.

He was surprised when his phone went off just as he parked in the garage. It was Sarah.

"Are you still at the hospital? Can you come by?"

"Actually, I just got home. But give me a few minutes, and I'll be there."

"Thanks."

* * *

She was wearing black leggings and a gray hooded sweatshirt that seemed to have swallowed her when she opened her front door for him twenty minutes later. The night air was chilly, and she invited him inside quickly to keep out the sharp breeze.

She looked uncharacteristically shaken by something, and he wondered what had ruffled her normally unflappable exterior.

She looked down at the plastic container in his hand. "What's that?"

"My world famous beef stew. I figured you hadn't had any supper. I'll warm it up in the microwave while you tell me what's up."

He followed her into the kitchen where he heated the stew, and she poured him a glass of wine.

"How is Alexa?"

"She had a good day. The doctor thinks she'll be off the ventilator pretty quickly."

The oven beeped, and Jim opened the door and pulled out the container with the potholders Sarah handed him.

"It smells heavenly."

"It is." He poured it into the bowl she had provided, and smiled. "Eat."

"Ok. Thanks. Come sit in the living room."

She perched on one end of the sofa and described Preston Barton in court that morning while he sat on the other end and listened.

"Should I say congratulations?"

"No, not yet. It's going to be an uphill fight to keep her out of that jail. Barton did tell the judge Yager has been put on administrative leave."

"With pay, I bet."

She nodded. "Absolutely. That community covers each other's asses." She frowned and studied the black and white dhurrie rug on the floor as if thinking hard about something.

"You seem upset."

Her eyes met his again, and she ran her fingers through her close-cropped hair.

"To be honest, I am."

"Want to tell me about it?"

"I really shouldn't talk about it."

"You can if it helps. I'm guessing you called because you wanted to tell me what's upsetting you."

"It's the David Spineli thing." She told him about Tessa's visit that morning.

"She threatened your life; you should call the police."

"No, I can't. Those photographs were not fakes, but her threats were."

"You can never be too sure."

"I'm sure. And David was too."

"David?"

"I asked him to come by tonight before I called you."

So David Spineli drove a 911 S Turbo Cabriolet. Useless piece of trivia. "And?"

"He laughed about the whole thing and said he'd buy the photographs from her."

"What if she won't sell?"

"As David said, Tessa always has her price."

"Well, then, you are both off the hook."

"Except David wants the affair to continue after he's acquired Tessa's pictures, and I don't."

Jim was careful not to show how happy that news made him. "Well then, let Mrs. keep the photographs because she'll have no reason to use them."

* * *

Sarah was restless after Jim went home around ten thirty. Her demons didn't haunt her in his presence, but they came roaring after her the minute she closed the door behind him. She poured herself another glass of wine, hoping it would help her silence the inner voices and go to sleep.

But she was still grappling with her guilt over Alexa when the phone rang at midnight.

"Hey, babe."

"David, it's late, and there's nothing more to talk about."

"Wrong. There's plenty to talk about. I came back by around nine-thirty to tell you the news, but I saw you were otherwise occupied."

"You have no right to spy on me."

"Yes, I do. I bought Tessa's pics and her silence for half a mil."

"I didn't ask you to do that."

"Doesn't matter. You owe me. Don't get the idea you can dump me for someone else. My relationships end when I say they do. Period."

"I've had enough threats for one day. Good night."

"You'd better take mine seriously. Dinner, my place on Friday. Eight sharp."

"I have plans."

"Then unmake them."

* * *

Second Tuesday in September, 2013, La Jolla, California

The phone woke her at six the next morning instead of her alarm. She had drunk enough the night before to give herself a headache, and she thought about not answering. But it might be Jim. And it might be another emergency with Alexa. So she rolled over and picked up the receiver and said, with great effort, "Hello."

"Good morning, Ms. Knight. I believe it's morning where you are. It's lunchtime in D.C. This is Coleman Reed."

Sarah sat up and forced her hungover self to concentrate. "What do you want, Justice Reed?"

"Well, first to congratulate you. You've actually persuaded the judge to set a date for a bail hearing in a capital case."

"I don't for one minute believe that is the purpose of this call."

"You're very acute, Ms. Knight. I remember you in oral argument in the Berger versus New York case, three years back. Fourth Amendment. Illegal search. You won for your client."

"No thanks to you, Justice Reed. You wrote the minority dissent."

"Like I said, you're very acute. Talented, even. Your work in the Joey Menendez case is legendary. As you know. And you turned six of my colleagues against me in the Berger case. Because of you, Myron Berger, an international drug dealer, walked away a free man. It's too bad they appointed you to defend my daughter-in-law. You're going to lose, and that will tarnish your considerable reputation."

"I don't think you called to discuss my standing in the legal community."

"Maybe I did, maybe I didn't."

"Let's get to the point."

"You might not like that."

"I'll take my chances."

"You can't win against me, Ms. Knight. Haven't you figured it out, yet?"

"I have to do my job, Justice Reed. You know that."

"And how do you define 'do your job'?"

"This isn't oral argument. I don't have to explain. Go read the Sixth Amendment."

"'A criminal defendant is entitled to the effective assistance of counsel.' I know what it says. But 'effective assistance' doesn't mean you have to commit professional suicide."

"What does that mean?"

"I don't want Alexa out on bail. And you're the kind of attorney who can make the impossible happen. So I've called with an offer."

"An offer?"

"Withdraw your request for bail. And stop defending Alexa like an angry pit bull."

"I don't think the Sixth Amendment allows me to do that."

"Of course, it does. Trevor Martin told you what to do in this case. File a few pre-trial motions that you will lose. Do some cross-examination. Make it look good, but don't try to win. No one expects you to."

"Throwing a case is not my job, Justice Reed."

"What if your life depended on it?"

"I'm sorry. Is that a threat?"

"You can call it what you want. No one will ever believe it came from me. Back off, Ms. Knight. I understand your business hasn't grown much in San Diego. I can get you a partnership at Warrick, Thompson."

"I've already turned down Alan Warrick's offer of partnership. I like having my own shop."

"Well, then, I still have a number of clients using Warrick who are loyal to me. I can send them your way. Alan and I aren't seeing eye-to-eye right now over Alexa. I would love to damage his bottom line on your behalf."

"Isn't that a conflict of interest, sending me your clients if I violate my duty of loyalty to Alexa?"

"You are not going to be her attorney forever, Ms. Knight. And the sooner she's tried and convicted, the better for all of us. No one will ever know about our arrangement."

"If anyone found out I'd made a deal with you for my own benefit, her conviction would be overturned in a heartbeat. And I'd be disbarred."

"You know, Ms. Knight, I'm going to have to give you some advice. You and Alan take the Rules of Professional Responsibility way too seriously. The Law Office of Sarah Knight will go down in flames if you play by the ethics rules. You aren't in a Wall Street firm any more where you can afford to dither about what the state bar thinks. Things are different in the local bar, as Hal Remington has probably told you. Business is based on who you know. If you don't play the game right, no one is going to send you any work; and an attorney's bottom line is based on referrals from other attorneys. If you aren't a team player in that community, you're going to starve. What the state bar wants you to do for Alexa Reed, and what the legal community wants you to do, are two very different things. I can make you rich beyond your wildest dreams, Ms. Knight. Your solo practice could grow into a firm as big as Craig, Lewis, or Warrick, Thompson. Or bigger."

"In exchange for Alexa's life?"

"She's already a dead woman. Save yourself."

"I'm sorry, Justice Reed, is that a threat?"

"It certainly is."

CHAPTER EIGHTEEN

Tuesday, October 1, 2013, San Diego County Court House

Jim watched Sarah put on their witnesses, the two nurses, the EMT who had saved Alexa's life, and the jail guard who was a decidedly hostile witness. Judge Tomlinson rocked back and forth in his creaking chair and listened thoughtfully. He asked each witness a few questions and then turned his attention to Preston Barton's examination of Sheriff Denis Hughes, who evaded taking responsibility, but promised Yager had been fired and would never be back, and Alexa would be safe in custody now.

Jim saw Sarah's face turn white with anger, making her scar stand out against her otherwise perfect cheek. She was wearing a deep purple suit that highlighted her dark hair and large dark eyes. She looked sleek and elegant. On cross-examination, she made Hughes admit he didn't know why Yager had deliberately overdosed Alexa Reed, and he couldn't say for sure it wouldn't happen again.

In closing argument, Preston Barton had harped on Alexa's intelligence which Barton had insisted gave her the ability to fake mental illness, only to be sharply interrupted by Judge Tomlinson.

"Are you claiming, Mr. Barton, this woman faked the need for an emergency operation in the back of an ambulance after the administration of Dr. Yager's prescription?"

"Uh, no, Your Honor."

"Well, I'm glad to hear that because for a moment I thought you had taken leave of your senses. Get to the point, Mr. Barton."

Although Jim had spent most of his FBI career working on the prosecutor's side, he enjoyed watching this particular one squirm. He sensed Preston Barton realized the need to hurry up and sit down.

"My point, Your Honor, is that Mrs. Reed should not be allowed out of custody. She is an extremely clever woman, and there is a high likelihood she won't show up for trial if she's released. And above all, Ms. Knight has not shown any possibility that her client may be innocent, and without that showing Mrs. Reed is not eligible for bail."

Judge Tomlinson turned quickly to Sarah, who had replaced Preston Barton at the podium. "I'd like to hear you address that last point, Ms. Knight. What evidence can you point to that might acquit your client?"

"At the moment, the best evidence I have is protected by attorney work product, Your Honor. I'm not prepared to give away my theory of my client's defense this morning, but I can assure you I will have a case to present at trial."

"So I'm just supposed to take your word for it that your client might not be guilty?"

"I'd suggest you look at the facts as we know them," Sarah said. Jim marveled at the way her voice never wavered. "She called the police when she found Michael Reed, she notified them of her whereabouts, she went in voluntarily for questioning. She is a woman of considerable achievement as an attorney and is an officer of the court in several jurisdictions. She is not the profile of a multiple murderer."

The judge leaned back in his chair and studied Sarah thoughtfully for a few minutes. "Do you have anything else to add?"

"Only that the interests of justice are best served if my client survives to go to trial, and the jail has created significant doubt about its ability to make that happen."

"What if I lift the medication order?"

"If you don't, I'm going to take an immediate writ to the court of appeal and demand that the order be terminated, regardless of the outcome of this hearing. Alexa Reed should never have been given medication, and ordering more drugs will just give the state a second chance to accomplish what it failed to do this time."

Jim could see her tough tone surprised His Honor. Judge Tomlinson opened his mouth to say something and then closed it again. After a little pause, he said, "I'm going to retire to chambers to consider what I am going to do."

Ten minutes passed while Sarah scrolled restlessly through the messages on her cell phone, and Jim tried to resist the spell of her gardenia perfume. To take his mind off Sarah, he concentrated on Alexa's face as he'd said goodbye to her in the hospital last night.

"Do you think we'll win?" She looked wistful and sad. "I don't know how I'd be able to handle another day in that cell."

Jim patted her hand and tried to give her a reassuring smile, although he guessed she knew how uncertain he felt. "If anyone can get you out, Sarah can."

Suddenly the door to the inner sanctum opened, and the clerk announced Judge Tomlinson had ordered the attorneys into his chambers. Jim saw Sarah's hands shaking as she stood up.

"Do you want me to come?" he whispered, noting that the sheriff, who had been sitting with Preston Barton at the prosecution's table, was following him toward Judge Tomlinson's chambers.

"Yes."

The attorneys took the chairs closest to the judge's desk. Jim and the sheriff sat behind them. Judge Tomlinson frowned as he scribbled away on his legal pad, allowing the silence in the room to lengthen into palpable tension for everyone present. Finally he whipped off his half-glasses, put down his pen, and rubbed his eyes with his chubby fists as if he was unbearably tired. Then he looked at them.

"I'm not happy with this situation." The judge looked directly at Sheriff Hughes, who opened his mouth only to be admonished, "Don't say anything! You had your time on the witness stand. I just want to make it clear that my job is not made easier by the obvious bias a segment of the mental health and legal community holds against Mrs. Reed. My job is to see she gets a fair trial. I didn't enter that order for medication to have it used the way it has been. I don't want anyone ever to think I knew this was going to happen or that I entertained any possible bias against a defendant in my courtroom. And if you think so, Ms. Knight, you know your job: recuse me."

"Yes, Your Honor." Jim noticed Sarah was gripping her pen to keep her hands steady.

"Judge, I hope you are not suggesting that I knew–" Preston Barton began, but Judge Tomlinson raised his hand.

"I didn't invite you to speak, Mr. Barton. Argument, like testimony, is closed." Judge Tomlinson leaned over his legal pad, folded his hands and said, "This is what I am going to do, and I don't like doing it. But I've been left with little choice. I'm going to release Alexa Reed to the custody of her attorney on house arrest with GPS monitoring."

"And the amount of her bail, Your Honor?" Preston Barton frowned.

"I'm not setting bail. She can't afford any. I already know that because she has appointed counsel. This is house arrest!"

"But you can't do that."

"Well, then go get yourself a writ from the court of appeal and tell the justices up there the jail nearly killed her before she ever got to trial because your expert insisted she be medicated, and I listened to him. Go right ahead, Mr. Barton!"

Jim saw the prosecutor swallow hard as he realized he was out of options.

"Now, Ms. Knight. I don't have to tell you about your responsibilities here."

"No, Your Honor."

"And I'm not going to be generous with continuances. I've had to let a defendant out of custody who probably should be in jail, so I'm going to keep that time to a minimum. That means if you ask for a continuance, you'd better have impeccable grounds to support your request. Do you understand, Ms. Knight?"

"I understand."

"Your Honor?"

"Yes, Sheriff."

"I'd like to have some of my deputies stationed outside Mrs. Reed's residence."

"And what will that get you? Another chance to put her in the hospital?"

"Your Honor—"

"If it weren't for your negligence—and I'm being polite when I use that term—we wouldn't be here right now. And I wouldn't be making an order that very well may be illegal. But it's an order that I know none of the guilty parties are going to challenge because they know who did what, and they don't want to go explain themselves to the court of appeal. Now let me be very clear about this: for the rest of these proceedings, everyone—and I mean *everyone*—will operate by the book. Am I understood?"

"Yes, Your Honor," the lawyers intoned.

"I'm setting Friday, October 18 as the date to reassess Mrs. Reed's competency to stand trial. And, assuming she is competent, I'm going to arraign her on the charges and set a trial date."

"But, Your Honor," Sarah spoke up. "Isn't that rather soon to be calendaring a case like this for trial? It's a capital case. For the defense, that's like having to prepare for two trials instead of one."

"I'm setting a date, Ms. Knight. I told you I wasn't going to be generous with continuances."

ALEXA

CHAPTER NINETEEN

Evening of October 1, 2013, UCSD Hospital Hillcrest

Sarah waited until seven-thirty to go see Alexa. She knew Jim was already there. Over the last three weeks, he'd developed the habit of visiting her twice daily, making sure to share supper with her. She was too thin, and she didn't like the hospital food; so he took her some of his own cooking night after night.

He also brought her books and a laptop and movies to watch and a Lexis password because she wanted to do legal research on her case. He arranged for a hairdresser to style her hair; and bought her new pajamas and a robe when she was able to shed the hospital gown.

Sarah stood outside Alexa's door and took a deep breath before pushing it open. Jim was by far the most empathetic and caring man she'd ever met. Gail had done herself and her son a vast disservice by not giving him the second chance he'd craved. She tried not to be jealous of the bond that had grown up between Jim and Alexa over the last three weeks. At first, Sarah had tried to make all the nightly visits, too. But over time, watching the two of them grow close as they shared their common memories of living in D.C. and of studying at Georgetown and of being parents, wore her down. It was especially hard to listen to them talk about Meggie and Sam and Cody. So she'd made more and more excuses not to stop by and had left them alone to enjoy each other's company. But tonight she had a duty to report on the hearing to Alexa, although she knew Jim had already given her the good news.

Sarah took a deep breath and pushed open the door. Alexa was sitting up in bed, wearing the robin's egg blue silk robe Jim had bought her. He had the chair by the bed. Their used supper dishes were stacked neatly on a table. They were laughing together about something. They both looked up as the door opened, slightly startled by her interruption. Sarah felt like an intruder, but Jim recovered impeccably and quickly stood to offer her the chair closest to the bed as he pulled up another for himself some distance away.

Alexa smiled warmly at Sarah. "I can't say thank you enough!"

Sarah sat down on the chair Jim had vacated and patted her hand. "I'm relieved that you're going home tomorrow." Sarah and Jim had been amazed to discover Alexa's landlady had left everything in her cottage exactly as she'd had left it when she'd gone to the police station on the morning of June 3. Mary Whitehurst believed passionately in her tenant's innocence.

"The somewhat bad news is that Judge Tomlinson has said he's going to set a date for trial when we go back on October 18. I tried to tell him that's too soon for us to prepare adequately, but he wouldn't listen. We need more time to find more facts we can work with for a defense."

Alexa's smile faded. "I keep trying to remember that night. Jim has shown me the surveillance video a dozen times. I see myself going into Dr. Brigman's, but I have no memory of it."

"That's what the overdose did to her," Jim said a touch bitterly. "The neurologist said he would testify to that."

Sarah nodded. "What can you remember?"

"I remember driving in the car. It was dark. I don't know why I was driving in the car. And then my phone rang, and it was Meggie. She was crying because Michael was arguing with someone, and she and Sam were afraid."

"Did you tell the police Meggie said Michael was arguing with a woman?" Jim asked.

Alexa fixed her wide blue eyes on him and shook her head. "I may have said that, but I don't remember now what they told me. It wasn't much because I wanted to get them calm enough to go to sleep. I figured I'd talk to them the next day to find out what they'd seen, if anything. But then I was called to the police station that morning and wasn't allowed to go back to them." Her voice broke slightly, and Sarah saw a tear slip out of the corner of her eye.

"What else can you remember?" Sarah asked.

"Seeing Michael lying there in all that blood. And finding the children huddled in the closet in Meggie's room and thinking I had to get them out of there without letting them see Michael."

"Anything else?"

"No. I have no idea why I went to Dr. Brigman's that night. The only reason I ever went there was to drop the children off for the so-called 'therapy' Brigman tried to do on them."

"You didn't tell the police that you went to Brigman's."

"Didn't I?" She frowned. "I don't remember much of what I told them."

"Do you remember telling them your gun was stolen and that you had reported it?"

"Yes. I kept it in the trunk of my car where the children couldn't find it. I checked on it every few days. One day I opened the trunk, and it wasn't there. It was close to the time the children's pre-school ended in May. Ronald Brigman had just announced he was giving Michael ninety percent custody when school started again in the fall."

"And you're sure you made a report?"

"Yes, I called that afternoon, and an officer came out and took my statement. He wrote down everything I told him, and he said he was going to file a report."

Sarah studied Alexa's puzzled face in the soft light. "So you don't remember being at Ronald Brigman's at all that night?"

"No." She frowned. "It feels as if there is something I should remember. But I can't. I must have been very upset to have been driving around alone late at night."

"And in Michael and Brigman's neighborhood, too."

Her lovely blue eyes seemed to have a mist over them. "Yes, right. I don't know why I was there before Meggie called. I think I used to know. But I don't remember now."

"Why did you have a gun in the first place?"

"I got it after my nanny was deported. I was afraid of being alone in the house with Michael. As long as Guadalupe was there, I had a witness to what he did to me. And to the children. But after they took her away, we were alone with him."

"When was she taken?"

"Late December 2008, the year Sam was born. My maternity leave ended on the day of the big Warrick, Thompson Christmas party. That morning when I got to the office, Alan told me he was letting me go because there wasn't enough work for me. He called it a 'leave of absence.'

"Michael got mad when we came home from the party that night because I didn't want to have sex with him. It was too soon after the baby, and I was exhausted by everything that had happened that day. I was pretty upset about being fired. He tried to force me and wound up breaking my arm. When we got to the hospital, he said if I told the ER doctor the truth about how I'd been hurt, I'd never see the children again. So I lied.

"A week later, I went to see Diane Gomez, a family law attorney whom I'd seen before right after I found out I was pregnant with Meggie. That first time, she told me there was no way I could prove Michael had abused me; and if I left California and took a job in D.C., Michael could get an order for full custody of the baby as soon as it was born. In other words, I was a prisoner of the state because I was pregnant.

"A week after Michael broke my arm, I went to see her with the cast on. I told her that now I had a witness, Guadalupe; and I wanted to take the children back to D.C. where I knew I could get a job in one of the top appellate firms. But she said no one would ever believe Guadalupe because she was my nanny. A judge would think I had put her up to lying about Michael, so I could have full custody of the children.

"And then the day after I talked to Diane Gomez, the INS came for Guadalupe. I suspect Michael or Coleman found out I'd seen Diane, and they arranged to have Guadalupe deported, so I couldn't file for divorce and tell the truth about Michael. After Guadalupe was gone, I decided to buy the gun and learn how to use it."

"Were you a decent shot?"

"I got really good at it."

"Did Bob Metcalf ever try to find Guadalupe?"

"No. He didn't know how; and honestly, I don't think she would have cooperated anyway. She was terrified when the INS came to get her."

"Where did they take her?"

"To a holding cell, briefly. I called the attorney at the firm who'd used Guadalupe for her own children and asked her to get some of Warrick's immigration attorneys involved. But no one had time, and the next day—without even a hearing—they sent her back to Mexico."

"So someone wanted her to disappear quickly," Jim said.

Alexa nodded. "I assume Coleman arranged the whole thing because Michael asked him to. But I've never said that to anyone because I couldn't prove it."

She was fading. "You look tired," Sarah said as she stood up. I'd better go so you can get some rest. They are coming at ten in the morning to fit the ankle monitor, so we should have you home by lunchtime."

Alexa looked over at Jim, who smiled. "I'll be here to bring you breakfast," he said. "And I'll help you get comfortable for the night now."

Alexa smiled up at him, and Sarah saw what a dangerously charming woman she was on the way to becoming once again. Her razor sharp intellect was hidden under a veneer of naive, sweet femininity. No wonder Michael Reed had pegged her for the role of long-suffering wife who would never object to any of his affairs.

As Sarah gathered her bag, she watched Jim arrange the pillows at just the right angle so Alexa could sleep comfortably with her head elevated. He also made sure the pitcher of ice chips was within her reach. He was still helping Alexa when Sarah got to the door. He turned quickly and said, "Wait. I'll walk you to your car."

But she shook her head. "No, I'm fine. You stay and make sure Alexa is comfortable. I'll meet you here in the morning at nine-thirty."

* * *

It was eleven thirty when Sarah got home. She had stopped at Trend for a drink in an effort to forget Jim and Alexa. But sitting at the polished bar, staring out at the dark ocean and fending off pick-up artists, had not made her forget a thing. She'd kept wishing that by some miracle Jim would walk through the door.

You could call him, she told herself, as she sipped her wine and watched the waves dance under the stars. And if he'd made it home by now, he'd probably drive up from Pacific Beach and join her. But she knew she wouldn't feel any better because she would spend their time together thinking about the way he'd settled the pillows behind Alexa's head, and Alexa's smile of anticipation when he'd said he'd be back in the morning.

She sat in her dark car in her dark garage for a few minutes, summoning her courage to go inside and face the too quiet house where her own thoughts could swarm unchecked. Suddenly she felt tears like pin pricks behind her eyes, so she got out of the car quickly and hurried into the kitchen to self-medicate with more wine before she could actually begin to cry. That was another one of her hard and fast rules. Never look back; and above all, never cry. She poured a large glass of cabernet and took a few quick gulps before going into the bedroom and slipping into her black silk pajamas.

She crawled into bed and settled comfortably against the down pillows. She tried to concentrate on the mystery thriller she was reading. But the picture of Alexa and Jim in the hospital continued to haunt her.

Bob Metcalf was right about Alexa. She was a sweet woman. Sarah thought they would probably have been friends if they'd had jobs at the same law firm. Craig, Lewis always liked to recruit former Supreme Court clerks as associates, and the ones who went the distance with the firm always became partners. Sarah would have liked having a young associate in her practice who knew constitutional law as well as Alexa did. She would have enjoyed mentoring her to partnership in the firm. If only she hadn't thrown away her career and her life by marrying Michael Reed.

"It's your job to get them back for her," the Universe reminded her in the too-quiet house.

"I know. But I've already told you, I don't want that job."

"Too bad because it's yours."

"But I want off this hook."

"Want away, but you have to come through for her. It's your only hope of redemption."

Suddenly her phone began to ring. The clock said midnight, and her heart began to flip-flop like a teenaged girl's, hoping Jim was calling.

"Hey, babe!" David Spineli. Her heart stopped dancing and became as still as stone. "You've been ignoring me these last three weeks."

"No, I haven't. I meant it when I said it's over."

"And I meant it when I said it's not over until I say it's over. And I haven't said it's over. Tessa used her half mil to buy herself a boy toy. We'll have lots more time together now that she's happy."

"I'm not interested. I'm trying to save a woman's life."

"And does that just happen to include sleeping with your investigator?"

"I'm not sleeping with anyone. But if I were, it would not be your business."

"Wrong again. It is my business, and I've got my man watching you right now. You're lying to me about that investigator."

Sarah shivered. "I'm going to get a restraining order for you and anyone connected to you first thing Monday morning."

David laughed. "Please do. You know those orders aren't worth the paper they're printed on."

And that was only too true.

"Don't cross me any more, Sarah. You don't want to get hurt. And no one would ever know I'm responsible. I've done it before, and I can do it again. Why do you think Tessa stays in line so nicely?"

She shivered once more but said firmly, "Good night."

A wave of raw terror washed over her as soon as she put down the phone. She crept through the silent house and peeked through the blinds in the front hall without opening them. Some sort of generic white car was parked in front of her neighbor's house. It hadn't been there when she'd come home.

She stood in the hall trembling and considering what to do. One part of her wanted to call Jim, but yet another part of her knew she should not become dependent upon him. She had always fought her battles alone; nothing had changed in that department. She moved silently down the hall and into her bedroom. She decided not to turn out the light because she didn't want whoever was in the white car to think she was going to sleep. She picked up her phone and dialed the San Diego police.

"911, what's your emergency?"

"I live in La Jolla Shores and there's a suspicious car that's been parked in front of my neighbor's house for over an hour. My neighbor isn't home, and I think the driver is casing the place for a burglary."

"Ok, ma'am. We'll get right on it."

And ten minutes later, Sarah smiled as she watched the police shine a bright light into the private investigator's car. Five minutes after that, he was gone.

CHAPTER TWENTY

Third Wednesday in October, 2013, San Diego Office of Warrick, Thompson, and Hayes

Exactly two weeks to the day after they had settled Alexa in her tiny Pacific Beach cottage, Sarah sat on the couch in Alan Warrick's glass-walled corner office high atop the Emerald Plaza building in the storied Emerald Shapery Center in the heart of downtown San Diego's power district. Jim occupied the opposite end of the sofa. He wasn't looking at her. Instead, he was lost in thought, studying the city thousands of feet below as it shimmered in the brilliant blue October sun. She'd seen little of him since Alexa got out of the hospital. When he hadn't been with Alexa, he'd been back in D.C., interviewing Justices Steiner and Moreno, both potential character witnesses in the penalty phase of Alexa's trial if the jury found her guilty. And he'd had a visit with Cody that seemed to disappoint him.

Sarah listened to the quiet shuffle of feet in the corridor and the low, intense tones lawyers use to greet each other and realized she had forgotten what it felt like to be inside the halls of a major law firm. She had forgotten the sense of power it had given her to have hundreds of support staff ready to do her bidding at the snap of a finger. Suddenly she regretted her decision to work alone with only poor long-suffering Martin to collect the mail and answer the phones. She wished she were defending Alexa with a team of Warrick, Thompson's finest, instead of sailing her boat solo into the raging waters of Coleman Reed's desire for revenge.

Alan Warrick appeared at that moment, hurrying across his enormous office to shake her hand and then Jim's. He had remained a handsome man, Sarah reflected, even at sixty-eight. His square-jawed good looks and expressive dark eyes would always endear him to juries. Sarah wondered if he still tried cases. He had been a legendary securities litigator in his time. He and David Thompson had built the firm against all odds after doing a few years as associates at Latham & Watkins. Gerald Hayes, the third name on the letterhead, had been ten years older than Alan and David. He'd been a Latham partner before the two young bucks persuaded him to join their venture in creating an international law firm with a reputation for excellence.

"Sit down, please," Alan said, after the handshakes and introductions. "My secretary is right behind me with coffee."

Sarah sipped the intoxicating brew of Blue Mountain beans in the solid black ceramic mug and regretted serving her clients Starbucks in paper cups with plastic lids.

"So how is Alexa doing?" Alan asked as he took off his suit jacket and settled opposite them in his shirt sleeves with his own mug.

"Things have been rough," Sarah said, and gave him a quick rundown of events since her appointment. "We're going back on Friday for a redetermination of her competency to stand trial. And Judge Tomlinson has threatened to set an early trial date."

"You certainly have the odds against you," Alan agreed. "How can I help?"

"We have a lot of questions, starting with why did you fire her?"

Alan shook his head. "That was not one of my finest moments. I've made personnel mistakes over the years, but letting Alexa go was the biggest."

"Why did you do it?"

"I'm going to give you a completely honest answer, but some of the things I'm going to say will have to remain private. I can't testify to anything covered by attorney-client privilege."

"I understand," Sarah nodded.

Alan took a sip of coffee and leaned back in his chair. "There are two explanations for why I let Alexa go. And I didn't fire her, by the way. It was a genuine 'leave of absence.'" The public explanation is there wasn't enough work for her. And that was true. Chuck Reilly, our appellate partner, has always had trouble keeping himself busy. Sometimes he's had to take depositions for the litigation partners to make his billable hours quota. So, in truth, he never really had any work to give her. And that is exactly what I told Coleman Reed when he insisted I hire both Alexa and Michael. I told him Alexa wouldn't have anything to do."

Sarah frowned. "What did Coleman Reed have to do with your hiring decisions?"

Alan grimaced and put the cup down. "Okay, here's the part that has to stay private, and it's something neither I nor my partners are proud of. We allowed ourselves to be owned by Coleman Reed."

Sarah noticed that Jim, who had been taking notes, stopped writing, and studied Alan's face for a minute. Then he asked, "How could one man 'own' a firm as big as this?"

"Coleman was a young partner at Eliot, Fitzgerald in New York with the reputation of being a genius rainmaker. Gerald Hayes got to know him because they represented some plaintiffs in a big class action suit against some drug companies. Gerald liked him, and learned that Coleman had a huge portfolio of clients. Gerald persuaded me and the other founding partner, Dave Thompson, to bring him into the firm as a full partner. Big mistake." Alan stopped and refreshed his lukewarm coffee from the pot.

"Why?" Sarah asked.

"Because before long Coleman's clients grew to be forty percent of the firm's business. Whatever Coleman asked for, we had to give him. And Gerald, Dave, and I didn't like what he was asking for."

"Which was?" Jim looked up from his notes again.

"Coleman played fast and loose with the ethics rules. He liked to put big sums of client money into his personal bank accounts before putting them into the firm's Client Trust account where they belonged. The three of us talked to him about it many times, but he always laughed and said he'd never get caught. And then he'd remind us we weren't in a position to lose forty percent of the firm's business. Of course, we suspected he was money laundering, but we couldn't prove it. And even if we could, the scandal would have destroyed the firm."

"So what did you do?" Sarah asked, pouring more coffee into her own cup.

"My partners and I decided to open up our checkbooks and get him kicked upstairs to a federal judicial appointment. We started handing out campaign contributions to every senator we could think of who could get him nominated to the Ninth Circuit Court of Appeals. But, then, as luck would have it, in 2003, a vacancy opened up on the Supreme Court. So we started writing checks to presidential candidates or potential candidates. Having him in D.C. would be even better than booting him up the road to Pasadena because it was all the way across the country."

"You mean you bought Coleman Reed a seat on the United States Supreme Court?" Jim looked up again from his notepad as he spoke.

"If you want to put it that way, yes. Campaign money talks. Don't pretend you don't know."

"What about Michael? If you'd wanted to get rid of Coleman, why'd you hire him and then make him a partner in only three years?" Sarah asked.

"To be honest, no one wanted to. Coleman relies on his cunning, but he's also a very intelligent lawyer. Michael, on the other hand, washed out of his job as an associate at Steptoe for a reason: he's just not that bright. And, although he's clever, he's definitely not in his father's league when it comes to the ability to manipulate people and situations.

"But Coleman wanted us to hire him, and we did. And Coleman forced us to make him a partner, too. What I didn't realize until it was too late was that Coleman's reason for sending Michael here was to have someone to watch over Coleman's stable of clients. Pretty soon, Michael was making demands on all of us just like his father used to."

"And he was also depositing client money in his own bank accounts before putting it in the Client Trust account," Sarah said.

"How did you know?"

"Bob Metcalf, who represented Alexa in the divorce, said they tried to subpoena Michael's bank records but could never get them because he claimed they were covered by attorney-client privilege."

Alan nodded. "That sounds about right."

"So is that why you cut those checks for Michael on the firm account for the Stacy O'Connor business? In essence, Michael or Coleman or both could blackmail you, if you didn't go along?"

"Yes. I realized the firm was right back where it had been when Coleman himself was here. I was too ashamed to tell Gerald and Dave. It should have been obvious what Coleman was after when he made us hire Michael."

"Who in the firm knew about the O'Connor checks?"

"Just me. I ordered them from accounting and gave them to Michael. Later, Alexa told me how she wound up with them."

"Do you think Michael destroyed them?"

"Without any doubt. When Ronald Brigman labeled Alexa a liar over them, I wanted to come forward on her behalf."

"Why didn't you?"

"Coleman made it clear Michael would walk with all his clients if I did anything for Alexa. Including give her a job."

"So that's why you had to pay her cash under the table for the work you sent her?"

"Right. Michael was constantly subpoenaing her bank records, trying to figure out where she was getting the little money she had."

"Did Michael pressure you to let Alexa go after Sam was born?"

"He and Coleman. Michael gave me this long song and dance about how the second baby had made her emotionally unstable and how she couldn't cope at home with two children. And I blew him off. But, then, Coleman called from D.C. with his usual series of threats. And, in truth, there wasn't enough work for her. But it wasn't her fault. She's a very fine lawyer, and I contributed to destroying her career. I regret that more than I can say."

"So that's why you sent her work?"

"Yes, and I tried to help her find another job here in town behind Michael's back."

"So that's how you knew he'd poisoned the well against her?"

"Right. Every hiring partner I talked to said they'd heard she was unstable and didn't want her. When I pressed them for their source, it was always Michael. That's the way Coleman loves to work, too. By bribes and threats. I'm surprised you haven't heard from him, Sarah."

"Oh, I have."

Jim looked up sharply from his notepad. "You didn't tell me!" It was an accusation, not a question.

"There was no reason to. Threats are routine when you practice criminal defense. Some unhappy client or prosecutor always wants you dead."

"An unhappy United States Supreme Court justice is different," Jim insisted.

"I'd agree with that," Alan said. "Coleman is a force you cannot reckon with."

"Well, I can; and I have to. For Alexa's sake. He was very disappointed when he offered me a partnership here and found out I'd already turned that offer down. He seems to think he still owns Warrick, Thompson."

"He doesn't," Alan said. "I had to work hard to make it happen, but we merged with Drake and Lockyear in Dallas in January, and their client base cancels out Coleman and Michael's portfolio. If every Coleman Reed client left tonight, our bottom line would still be healthy tomorrow."

"Did you have any indication Michael was abusing Alexa?" Sarah asked.

Alan sighed and leaned forward to put his empty cup on the table. "This is the part where I blame myself the most. Sarah, you know the firm does some pro bono work with domestic violence clients. I know the profile by heart, and I should have seen what was happening to Alexa and asked more questions. She obviously didn't get to be a law clerk for Marilyn Steinberg and Paula Moreno by taking sick leave. I should have realized something was going on after Meggie was born when she started to miss so many days of work. She had a full-time nanny, so the baby wasn't keeping her home.

"But the biggest red flag came right after I let her go. Brenda and I ran into her in the grocery store in La Jolla with a cast on her arm. Her story about tripping and falling the night of the firm party didn't sound genuine. I should have put together the picture: repeated abuse and an over-controlling partner who gradually isolated her from everyone on the outside."

"How much of this could you testify to?" Sarah asked.

"I could certainly explain how Michael pressured me to let her go, but my conversations with other hiring partners, as you know, can't come in because they are hearsay."

"Maybe we could get them in as evidence of Alexa's state of mind since you told her about them," Jim suggested.

Sarah looked annoyed. "That only fuels Preston Barton's claim she killed them."

"Yes, but it helps the Battered Woman's Syndrome defense," Jim insisted. "It shows why she finally snapped."

"And I told you I don't want to use BWS!" Sarah shook her head sharply.

Alan studied them both thoughtfully. Then he said, "I've read the papers. It doesn't look good. Her gun, Brigman and Michael killed within minutes of each other, just after the custody change order, and her cell phone and surveillance data put her at the scene of both murders. I mean, Michael had plenty of enemies who would have loved to kill him, including me because I wanted ownership of my firm back. But Michael and Ronald Brigman had only one person in common with a motive to kill them; and that, unfortunately, was Alexa. As much as I don't want to say this, Sarah, your investigator has got a point about BWS."

"But she'll never see her children again if she's convicted of two counts of voluntary manslaughter. BWS is not good enough. We've got to find something better."

"What does she say about that night?"

"The near-death episode wiped most of her memory about recent traumas."

Alan looked disappointed. "Not much help, then."

Suddenly Jim spoke up. "I'm assuming you can't give us the records of the transfers from Michael's personal bank account to the Client Trust account?"

"Right. As wrong as the practice was, it is covered by attorney-client privilege."

"Did Michael have a firm credit card?" Sarah asked.

"He did. And he used it for personal as well as business charges."

"Could you give us those records?"

"Yes. And tell Alexa, I've got plenty of work to send her when she's feeling up to it."

Sarah brightened. "That will be good for her. It will help take her mind off things."

"And tell her she has a job here when it's over. And my offer to you is still open."

"Thanks, Alan, but you know what we're up against. As much as I don't want to admit it, the odds are not in our favor."

"You can beat the odds, Sarah. You've done it before. If I were sitting where Alexa is right now, you're the one I'd want next to me at counsel table."

CHAPTER TWENTY-ONE

Third Friday Night in October, 2013, Alexa's Cottage, Pacific Beach

The last few rays of daylight were turning into long fingers of twilight as Sarah sat with Alexa in the living room of the cottage that Sarah thought looked like something straight out of a fairy tale. The little white house sat at the end of a cul de sac named Crescent Court, well away from the Pacific Beach traffic. It was nestled under gigantic pine trees, with a white picket fence meandering around the yard and a curving stone path leading to its bright blue door. Matching blue shutters on the windows seemed to give the little house solemn eyes that watched the street.

Alexa was curled up on the threadbare sofa, a blanket over her legs. Sarah occupied the shabby, overstuffed chair opposite. It was five-thirty, and Sarah was telling Alexa about the details from the competency hearing that morning while they were waiting for Jim to arrive with groceries for Alexa's pantry. Since she could not go out and Sarah was too busy, Jim stocked the larder each week.

They had fallen into a routine, Sarah reflected. Jim checked on Alexa night and morning and stayed in the evening to make supper and eat with her. Sarah came by for a few minutes in the evenings but did her best to find reasons to turn down the invitation to stay for the meal. Alexa and Jim had grown even closer, and Sarah didn't like being in the middle of their evenings together. Jealousy wasn't appropriate, but she was only human.

"So Judge Tomlinson has reversed his earlier order finding you incompetent to stand trial. And I entered a not guilty plea on your behalf."

Alexa had waived her right to be present for arraignment on the charges.

"The bad news is the judge set December 9 as the trial date. That doesn't give us much time. Fortunately we have interviewed Justices Steiner and Moreno. And Alan Warrick. He's very much on your side. And he wants to send you some work to do."

Alexa smiled. "How like Alan. He thinks work will fix everything. But I'd like to have a project."

"He offered you a job—"

"Don't." Alexa held up her hand. "Don't talk about what comes after the trial. I can't think about it. I don't want to think about it."

"We're going to find a defense."

"I don't see how you can unless I remember that night. I keep trying. The only reason I ever went to Brigman's was to drop the children for those horrible therapy sessions. And they weren't with me that night, so that can't be it. Maybe he made me go over there so he could gloat because he'd given my children away to Michael. Brigman liked to remind me he was all powerful over my life. There was the humiliation of losing in the courtroom, and then there was the humiliation of being interviewed for those so-called psychological evaluations."

"Which were nothing more than character assassinations," Sarah observed.

"I didn't think I should say that."

"Well, that's what they were. I've read them. And that reminds me, there is something I should bring up about Meggie and Sam."

"I think you're going to say I have the right to speak with them over the phone."

"Yes."

"I know. I thought a lot about it when I realized I might not have to go back to jail."

"I can get a court order for telephone visits. You know that."

"I do, but I don't think it's a good idea." Her lovely eyes held Sarah's, and she realized once more what a compelling presence Alexa Reed could be. "What could I say to them? They'd ask me when they can come home. You know, I can see by their room, Coleman didn't let them take anything but the clothes on their backs. Meggie's favorite Miss Janey doll and Sam's beloved Mr. Wiggles the Bear are still there. They would never have left willingly without them. Coleman wants to finish what Michael started: to obliterate me from their lives."

"But that's just it. If the jury acquits you, it will take a custody battle to get them back. The court would want to know why you didn't at least ask for phone visits."

Alexa looked away toward the fireplace that she'd filled with dried flowers in happier times. After a minute or two, she said slowly and carefully, "I know you are right. But the odds of being acquitted are slim to none. The best I can hope for is prison time. And it would be a lot of prison time. I can't do something now that would hurt them by getting their hopes up that I'm coming back when I know what the real story is."

"I understand," Sarah said quietly.

Alexa gave her a small, twisted smile. "You're lucky you never had children."

Suddenly Sarah wanted to scream. She wanted to run out of the front door and stand under the emerging stars, and howl at the unfairness of it all. And then that tiny voice inside said once again, "Saving this woman is your only hope of redemption."

At that moment, Jim appeared, carrying two large bags of groceries. He set them on the counter in the kitchen and continued on into the living room where he turned on a lamp.

"What are the two of you doing here in the dark?"

"We were busy talking and didn't realize the sun had set completely. I was telling Alexa about the interview with Alan."

"He's going to turn over the records for Michael's firm credit card. We might find something there that will help," Jim said.

"And I've subpoenaed Michael and Brigman's bank records," Sarah added.

"You won't get them," Alexa shook her head.

"I'll get Brigman's. His ex-wife is the executor of his estate. She lives in Tel Aviv. I notified her New York attorneys of the subpoena and not a peep out of them. So I don't think she cares. I agree we won't get Michael's. Coleman is his executor, and he's lined up a team from King and White who've filed a motion to quash my subpoena. There's a hearing next Thursday. I've asked Bob Metcalf to come. You'll need to be there. And Jim."

Alexa nodded.

"You look tired," Sarah said. "I'd better go. I'll be by tomorrow." She stood up and gathered her brief case and her purse and turned toward the front door just as Jim stepped into her path.

"I think you should stay. You need to eat. I'm making my famous sauce bolognaise."

"Not tonight."

His wonderfully kind eyes look down at her and every resolve she had to leave began to melt. "You should stay."

"I–I can't. I have some plans," she lied and fled while her legs were still willing to take her through the enchanted blue door.

* * *

Later that night, Sarah's house, La Jolla Shores

Jim finished cleaning up the kitchen at Alexa's at eight-thirty. She liked to dry the dishes after he washed them, but she'd been too tired tonight. She still had a long way to go in her recovery. He'd sent her off to get a good night's sleep.

He turned out all the lights in the living room except for the small one he always left on in case of an emergency. He was glad he lived only five minutes away.

He backed his Range Rover out of the drive and headed for home. But Sarah was on his mind. He hadn't really had a chance to talk to her alone since Alexa had left the hospital and since his trip back to D.C.

He was relieved when she answered on the first knock because it was more likely she was alone. He hadn't bought her earlier excuse that she had plans that night. She was wearing soft gray sweat pants and a black t-shirt, and she was barefoot. She was cradling a thick file in her arm like a baby.

"Is everything ok?" She was obviously surprised to see him.

He wanted to say *no, why are you shutting me out this way.* But he knew better.

"Fine, just fine. I wanted to talk about the hearing this morning."

"Better come in, then, and have a drink. How is Alexa?"

"Asleep. She was ready for bed as soon as she finished eating."

"Poor thing. I'm not surprised."

He followed her into the living room where he could see she'd been curled up on one end of the sofa, doing legal research on her laptop and scribbling on a yellow pad. She motioned for him to take off his suit jacket and lay it across one of the chairs.

"Here, have a seat, and I'll get another glass."

He noticed the open bottle of wine on the coffee table and a half eaten sandwich wrapped in deli paper.

Instead of the chair facing her, he deliberately chose the other end of the sofa, but she was unfazed when she came back from the kitchen.

"I thought the hearing went pretty much the way I thought it would." She handed him the glass of wine. "She's now competent to stand trial. No surprises except that December 9 trial date. That's too soon."

"We've got to work fast," Jim agreed. "And we need to talk to the Reed children."

"No." Sarah shook her head emphatically. "That's too big a risk. They're only five and six. We don't know if they actually saw anything at all. Alexa found them hiding in a closet."

"What we really need is a female other than Alexa who had a motive to murder both Michael and Brigman," Jim observed.

"Alan called today and said he'd have those credit cards records to us by Monday. And then we'll have Brigman's bank records on Friday. So you'll have a lot to look at next weekend. Of course, it would help if we had the numbers of Michael's bank accounts. Without those, we can't see what kind of financial relationship Michael and Brigman had."

"Alexa might have Michael's account numbers. I'll check with her in the morning."

"Sounds good."

Her tone told him she wanted him to leave. But he wanted to stay. "Why don't you come over to Alexa's for breakfast in the morning?"

"No, sorry. I've got to work tomorrow."

"You could work after breakfast."

But Sarah shook her head.

"Let me make you something then before I leave."

"No. I had a sandwich." She motioned toward the sad little concoction next to the wine bottle.

"I'm not sure that merits the name."

"Well, you won't even find eggs in the fridge tonight. Anyway, I have to read four more cases before I can call it a day."

She was a champion at keeping her distance, Jim reflected sadly as he got up to leave.

She walked him to the front door. "I'll try to stop by Alexa's sometime tomorrow."

"Come for dinner."

But Sarah shook her head. "Can't. I'll probably drop by around midday. I have to go into the office in the morning."

He turned away, disappointed, got into his car, and started to back out of her drive. But then he noticed something that made his blood run cold. There was a black Nissan SUV parked in the shadows directly across from Sarah's, and the man in the driver's seat had binoculars trained on her house. Jim patted his revolver in his shoulder holster. Then he pulled up behind the car and turned his headlights on high beams. A few seconds, later, the Nissan's engine came to life, and it went roaring down the street.

Jim gunned his Range Rover and chased it in and out of traffic until he lost it just before the entrance to I-5. He hadn't gotten close enough to get the license plate number.

He drove past Sarah's house to make sure the Nissan hadn't returned. Then he checked Alexa's cottage where all the lights were out except the one he always left on in the living room. Satisfied for now, he went home and slept an uneasy sleep.

CHAPTER TWENTY-TWO

Fourth Thursday in October 2013, San Diego County Court House

It did not take the two King and White attorneys in their identical black power suits long to get Judge Tomlinson to agree that Michael Reed's bank records could not be given to the defense because they contained confidential attorney-client privilege. Moreover the dark-haired one, who seemed to be the leader of the two, insisted that Michael's records contained so much confidential information that nothing would be left to turn over if the privileged entries were redacted. His blonde counterpart nodded constantly while his colleague spoke, apparently for emphasis. Sarah thought he looked like a bobble-head doll.

What intrigued her far more was the presence of Tara Jeffers, next to Preston Barton at the plaintiff's table. Alexa had had a physical reaction when she saw her, and Sarah had leaned over and whispered, "I had no idea she'd be here. Don't worry." She saw Jim squeeze Alexa's hand under the table.

Tara remained tautly grim-faced throughout the brief King and White presentation. Sarah thought it was probably because her plastic surgeon had eliminated any possibility of smiling a couple of facelifts ago. Everything about Tara was so sleek she looked plastic. Her dark hair was pulled into the tightest bun on record. Her cobalt blue suit appeared to have been steamed within an inch of its life to remove every wrinkle. She looked as if she never touched food, and her French manicured nails were so long she could barely pick up a pencil. Every bit of her screamed that she was trying too hard.

When the King and White twins had left the courtroom, Judge Tomlinson looked over at the prosecutor.

"Mr. Barton, the motion to quash has been concluded. I'm not sure why you are here since this was not your motion, and I am not sure who is sitting with you at counsel table."

"This is Tara Jeffers, Your Honor. She's my witness on my motion to quash the subpoena for Ronald Brigman's records."

"What motion to quash? Did you receive a copy, Ms. Knight?"

"No, Your Honor."

"I have it here," and Preston Barton's round little frame waddled over to the bailiff who distributed the papers.

Sarah barely glanced at it. "Your Honor, the defense objects. This is untimely filed, and Mr. Barton has no standing to oppose our subpoena."

"It is untimely," Judge Tomlinson observed, looking over his half glasses at the prosecutor.

"It's very straightforward. I would ask the court to waive the time requirements."

"Well, even if I could do that you still don't have any standing to file it. You remember standing don't you, Mr. Barton? Civil procedure, first year of law school, the person or entity who has the right to bring an action before the court."

"But, Your Honor," the prosecutor bleated, "the state is opposed to disclosure to the defendant of the sensitive personal documents of the victims. I represent the victims, and Ronald Brigman is a victim of Alexa Reed!"

Sarah felt Alexa flinch as she sat beside her. She saw Jim give her hand another reassuring squeeze under the table.

Sarah stood up. "If I might be heard, Your Honor?"

"Yes, Ms. Knight."

"Ronald Brigman's financial records aren't going to be disclosed to Mrs. Reed. They are coming to me, as counsel of record. And Mr. Barton represents the People of the State of California, not Ronald Brigman."

"I'm afraid Ms. Knight is correct, Mr. Barton. To the extent you've even filed a motion, it is denied."

"Your Honor, wait!" Tara Jeffers leapt to her feet while the prosecutor folded his lawyer tail and sat down.

"Ms. Jeffers, I thought you were here as a witness?"

"Well, I represent Michael Reed and Ronald Brigman. I'm here on their behalf to oppose disclosure of their personal bank records."

"Hm." Judge Tomlinson's kind gray eyes studied Tara's taut eagerness intently. "I'm sorry, Ms. Jeffers, I'm afraid you've got a bit of a problem. Your purported clients are both dead. That means they no longer have standing to oppose anything. The representatives of their estates can offer an opposition on their behalf, but Dr. Brigman and Mr. Reed are no longer able to be litigants in a court of law."

"Yes, but I represented Michael in his family law matter."

"Yes, but you aren't in family court this morning. You are in my court, and you don't represent his estate. Those two gentlemen who just left are the attorneys for his father, who is the executor of his estate. Besides, you are wasting the court's time. We've already settled the matter of Michael's records. The defense doesn't get them."

"But they can't have Ronald Brigman's either!" Sarah noticed an unprofessional note of hysteria in her voice.

"Your Honor," Sarah stood up. She was glad she'd worn black. It made quite a nice professional contrast to Tara's electric blue. "Ms. Jeffers has no standing, either, to oppose our subpoenas. She doesn't represent Ronald Brigman's estate. I sent notice to the estate's lawyers, Silverstein and Greenberg in New York. And you see they are not here, today."

"She's quite right, Ms. Jeffers."

"I–I well, he was a friend. He would not want his personal records turned over to Alexa Reed."

"I think we covered that point, Your Honor. The records are coming to me." Sarah remained standing at counsel table, enjoying Tara's increasing discomfort as she realized she'd waded into legal waters where she didn't belong.

"Ms. Jeffers, you are wasting the court's time. This hearing is over!"

"But, Your Honor!" Tara was on the edge of hysteria. There's something she really doesn't want us to see, Sarah thought. Good, maybe we'll get a break at last.

"Wait, please. There were privileged communications in those records."

"In Michael Reed's, yes." Judge Tomlinson agreed. "But not Ronald Brigman's. He wasn't an attorney."

"But I talked to him. Things that Michael told me, I told him!"

"And these communications are in Dr. Brigman's bank records? That makes no sense on many levels, Ms. Jeffers. If you disclosed the confidences Michael Reed made to you to Ronald Brigman, you have waived the attorney-client privilege, and anything Michael Reed said is no longer confidential. Why do I feel as if I'm instructing a bunch of first-year law students? Has everyone on the prosecution side taken leave of his or her senses this morning?" Judge Tomlinson glowered at that side of the courtroom.

Tara made one last-ditch effort. Sarah could smell her fear under her overly controlled grooming. She was willing to make herself look foolish to try to keep the records out of the defense's hands.

"Sorry, Your Honor. The point is Alexa Reed should not profit by her decision to kill her husband and Dr. Brigman. Mrs. Reed is a lying, devious, manipulative individual with a psychopathic borderline personality disorder, whose only goal in life was to live off her husband's money. She—"

"Wait, Ms. Jeffers! Just wait, please!" Judge Tomlinson held up his hand. "I am not persuaded by character assassination. Is that clear?"

"Yes, Your Honor. If I might finish?"

"You are finished, Ms. Jeffers. I did my tour as a judge in family law court a few years back. The kind of language you are using disgusted me then, and it still does. I feel like levying a hefty sanction on you for wasting my time this morning. If you'd done your legal research, you've have known you had no standing to move to quash these subpoenas. If you will kindly fold up your papers and exit now, I won't impose the two thousand dollar fine I'm considering."

Sarah thought she heard a slight whimper from Tara as she swept her legal pad into her Louis Vuitton brief case and headed for the back door. She could see Bob Metcalf, who was sitting behind them, trying to suppress a smile.

After Judge Tomlinson had left the bench, Sarah turned to Jim and Alexa.

"There are going to be way too many reporters outside in the corridor. Let's go out together, but I'll linger and offer a few sound bites while the two of you get past them as fast as you can."

Jim nodded. He put his arm around Alexa's waist protectively as he shepherded her toward the door.

Her plan worked. As soon as the reporters saw Sarah make herself available, they lost interest in watching Jim hurry Alexa out to the car.

Sarah was well-practiced in the art of answering a question without actually giving an answer. Within twenty minutes, the throng of reporters had dispersed to take up positions on the courthouse steps where they taped their solemn recitations for the evening news.

Relieved to be alone in the vast lobby of the courthouse, Sarah headed toward the front doors. Suddenly, Tara Jeffers stepped into her path. She looked even meaner up close than she had while making her ridiculous arguments in the courtroom.

"I want to talk to you," she snarled.

"We have nothing to discuss." Sarah kept on walking.

"Yes, we do!" Tara carefully placed one of her Manolo Blahniks in her path.

Sarah stopped and turned to face the bright blue demon glaring at her. "I'm going to summon a bailiff." Sarah nodded toward the gaggle of khaki-uniformed officers standing by the metal detectors.

"Listen to me!" Tara hissed. "Stay away from Ronald Brigman's bank records."

"Is that all you have to say?"

"No, it's not. If you want to stay alive, leave those records alone!"

* * *

Midnight, Jim's Bungalow, Pacific Beach

She was afraid he'd gone to bed. She had taken a desperate chance, driving over to his house at midnight just because she wanted to see him. She'd been drinking alone at Trend for hours and driving herself crazy thinking about the way he'd squeezed Alexa's hand so reassuringly that morning during Tara's diatribe and the way he'd held her close to push past the throng of reporters. Finally, she could stand it no more.

He was wearing gray sweat pants and a white t-shirt and holding an empty glass that she guessed must have held scotch. It was the most casually dressed she had ever seen him. She reminded herself that nothing would have been possible with him even if Alexa hadn't been in the way. But the mounting threats were starting to wear her down, and Jim had become her anchor in the swirling intrigue that surrounded this case.

"You haven't been home to change since the hearing this morning!"

"I had meetings with prospective clients this afternoon and then I went to Trend for a drink."

"Alexa and I were hoping you'd show up for dinner."

Alexa and I. The words hurt. He seemed to read the sadness in her face. He pulled her inside and said, "Never mind. I'm sure you haven't had a thing to eat."

"I'm not hungry."

"Yes, you are." He led the way into his dark kitchen, snapped on the light, and pulled out a stool for her at the island in the center. Without asking, he took her briefcase and purse and began to unbutton her suit coat. He didn't care if he was inappropriate. He was sailing on too much scotch, and he'd missed her, and right now nothing mattered more than having her here with him.

"What are you doing?"

"Making sure you don't dribble brie and mushroom quiche on your very expensive jacket. Chanel?"

"No."

"Then designer Who?"

"Does it matter?"

"You were the best looking one in the courtroom this morning."

Sarah gave him the first smile he'd seen that day.

"Aren't you going to make a crack about real men and quiche?"

"No. I'm going to be happy you let me into your house at midnight and are willing to feed me. The suit is Marc Jacobs, by the way." *I've had too much to drink,* Sarah thought. *I shouldn't have come here. But I'm so happy to see him that it hurts. I only hope I don't do something stupid.*

"Should I pour wine or make coffee?"

"Wine." Ok, Sarah thought. That was stupid. I'm already over my limit.

He opened a bottle of cabernet and poured two glasses. "Go slowly on this. The quiche will be ready in a few minutes. I brought it back from Alexa's. We had some for dinner." He told himself not to be distracted because she was wearing a lacy black camisole under the discarded jacket.

"How was she tonight?"

"Worried that she isn't going to remember why she was at Brigman's. I'm wondering if I took her to the scene, if it would help."

"We'd have to get Tomlinson's permission. She's on house arrest. But I'm pretty sure he'd give it."

"It might be worth a try. You're going to have those bank records to give me tomorrow?"

"Yes. There's bound to be something in them. Tara Jeffers stayed behind to threaten me after the reporters left."

Jim's face was grave. "Threaten you how? The same way Tessa and David Spineli threatened you? And Coleman Reed?"

"Pretty much."

He set the plate of quiche in front of her. "Here, eat up."

"Thanks."

He watched her wolf it down. Unlike the inedible stuff she brought home in saran wrap, she always ate his food, and that made him happy.

"That was fast. I bet you haven't eaten all day."

She looked up guiltily from the empty plate. "Do the pretzels at Trend count?"

"Definitely not. Here, one more piece." He fought down the wave of feelings that washed over him as he sliced another serving and heated it in the microwave. She needed someone to look after her. She needed him.

"Thanks." Sarah attacked her second helping more slowly, savoring every bite.

"It's wonderful as usual."

"I still say you need a personal chef."

She laughed. "Wouldn't work. My hours are too irregular."

"There would at least be something in the fridge for you to heat up when you finally got home." His light tone changed. "Listen, Sarah. About those threats—"

She waived her hand impatiently. "You know people in my business are always being threatened."

"But these aren't empty threats."

His tone made her look up from her plate. "What are you talking about?"

"When I left your house last Friday night, a black Nissan SUV was parked across the street, watching. I chased it as far as I-5 but couldn't get a license plate number."

She put down her fork, but said nothing.

He studied her face. "So you see why I'm concerned?"

She sighed. "I don't want to tell you this, but that's not the only time there's been someone watching my house. Except I know who was responsible the first time."

"Who?"

"David. It was the night of the bail hearing. He called right after I got home from the hospital and demanded to see me. When I said no, he told me he had an investigator outside watching my house. I called the police and pretended the car was there to case my neighbor's place for a burglary. When the cops started shining lights inside, he got out of there."

"Have you heard from Spineli since?"

"No, but I've seen him following me sometimes in traffic. I mean, he doesn't exactly drive a low-profile vehicle. He wants me to see him. He thinks it will intimidate me. I'd say whoever you saw last Friday night was linked to David."

"How dangerous do you think he is?" Jim frowned as he asked.

"Hard to tell. He bragged, of course, that he could get away with hurting me. I do know his legitimate business has some unsavory ties. That's what got his brother in trouble with the Securities and Exchange Commission."

"I'd tell you to go get a restraining order, but they're pretty worthless."

Sarah nodded. "Maybe it's just a nosey reporter who thinks he might get a shot of me coming and going from work."

But Jim shook his head. "I highly doubt that. No one can take a decent photo at midnight. Do you have a gun?"

"No."

He frowned. "Someone in your position should have a gun."

Sarah shrugged. "Well, I don't."

"I'm going to get you one."

"No, thanks." She had finished the last of the quiche. She was suddenly overcome by the desire to sleep.

"Hey!" Jim caught her as she was slipping off the stool.

"Sorry. Food. Wine. I'm tired, now. I'd better go home."

"Well, you can't drive. And to be honest, neither can I. I've killed quite a bit of scotch tonight."

"No, I can drive. I'll be fine," she insisted.

"You will not be fine. Guest room, now."

"No. I have to go home." *Because something will happen if I stay. And tomorrow at the cottage, when I see you with Alexa, my heart will break all over again.*

Jim sighed. "Then I'll call a cab for you."

Within ten minutes, he bundled her into the bright yellow taxi and then stood in the drive watching it vanish into the dark.

CHAPTER TWENTY-THREE

First Friday in November, 2013, Law Office of Bob Metcalf, San Diego

"Did you know?" Jim asked Bob Metcalf at three-thirty on the first Friday afternoon of November. He and Sarah once again occupied the pressed-wood chairs in front of Bob's messy desk and once again had turned down bottled water from the dorm-room fridge.

Bob leaned back in his chair and studied them both thoughtfully. "Alexa and I suspected, but we had no way of knowing. You're sure?"

"Positive," Sarah said without hesitation. "Michael was bribing Ronald Brigman."

"And it looks to me as if Michael's attorney was in on the scheme, too," Jim added.

"What makes you think that?"

"Because Michael paid Tara a retainer on January 12, 2009, of twenty thousand dollars. And on the same day, he paid Ronald Brigman the same sum, even though Brigman wasn't appointed by the court to be the evaluator in the case until early March."

"And you discovered all this from Brigman's bank records?" Bob asked.

"Yes. Alexa fortunately had Michael's account numbers. I could track the money he paid Brigman. Once Brigman got appointed on the case, Michael paid him four thousand a month."

"But the court made Michael responsible for the psychological evaluation fees and for the cost of the therapy Brigman ordered for the children," Bob said.

"Right. But those sums are all distinct from those four-thousand-a-month payments. You can tell by reading the court's orders which payments the court ordered and which ones Michael was making on his own. Brigman, by the way, was raking in a fortune from Michael."

Bob looked stunned, although he said, "I shouldn't be so surprised. There have been rumors for years that Tara had a deal going under the table with certain evaluators and judges. Her well-heeled clients always wound up with full custody even in the face of a string of DUI's or a history of drug abuse. And she used Ronald Brigman in a lot of those cases."

"By any chance did she use Percy Andrews in the others?" Sarah asked.

"In fact, she did. The bar joked about her pet evaluators."

"Did she sleep with either of them?" Jim asked.

"I doubt she slept with Percy. He's married, and there have never been any rumors that he strayed from the wife. Brigman, of course, had been divorced for years; so I'd say there's a good chance they were an item from time to time. Tara was also notorious for sleeping with her clients."

"So there is a distinct possibility she slept with Michael Reed?" Jim asked.

"Absolutely, and I know the person who can tell you if she did. She's Tara's ex-secretary, Marilyn Mosell. Tara underpaid and abused her for years, and finally Marilyn got sick of it and quit. She works for a friend of mine, Brett Williams. His office is at 600 Broadway. You've got time to stop by this afternoon, if you want. I'll call and let her know you're coming."

* * *

First Friday in November, 2013, Alexa's cottage, Pacific Beach

Sarah arrived at Alexa's cottage at five p.m., but there was no sign of Jim. She had hoped he would be right behind her, but apparently his interview with Marilyn Mosell was taking longer than anticipated. Sarah had gone ahead to make sure someone checked on Alexa at the usual time.

She sat in the drive for a few minutes studying the solemn eyes of the little house and hoping against hope Jim's Range Rover would pull in. But it didn't, so she got out and headed up to the minuscule front porch where she knocked.

Alexa's lovely blue eyes clouded with disappointment the moment she realized Jim wasn't there. Sarah stepped inside and smelled a rich stew simmering on the stove.

"That smells delicious."

"Coq au vin. I told Jim it was my turn to cook for him," Alexa smiled. "You should stay for supper."

"No, I can't. I have plans later," she lied smoothly. "We have some news to share, and then I have to meet a friend for a drink."

Alexa didn't look disappointed by her excuse.

"Can I pour you a glass of wine while we wait?"

"Sure. How are you feeling?"

"Better all the time. I seem to tire out pretty easily though. I took a nap today because I knew I wanted to make dinner tonight."

"Well, keep resting. Those days in trial are going to be long and grueling. You'll need all your strength."

Alexa nodded. "I know."

Suddenly a key scratched in the lock, and the front door opened. Jim came in grinning, and Alexa brightened.

"I've got some really interesting news."

They gathered in the living room with glasses of wine and a fruit and cheese plate Alexa had arranged. She sat next to Jim on the sofa while Sarah took the shabby chair opposite. They look like they belong together, Sarah thought as Jim began to run down the details of Michael's bribes to Ronald Brigman. As he talked, an odd look came over Alexa's face.

"Is something wrong?" Sarah asked.

"No, nothing's wrong. But it's starting to come back to me. That night. June 2."

"What do you remember?" Sarah asked.

"I remember Michael picked up the children at five, and they were upset because they didn't want to go. He made a scene. I cried after that for a long time because it all seemed so hopeless. Then around eight-thirty my phone rang, and it was Dr. Brigman. He said I had to be at his house by nine if I ever wanted to see my children again.

"I just knew it was some kind of set-up to take away the little bit of time I had left with them. I was terrified. I called Bob to ask what to do, but he had his cell turned off. Finally I decided I'd better go."

"What happened when you got there?" Sarah had pulled a pad out of her purse and began to jot down notes as she concentrated on Alexa's answer.

"At first I thought he was going to make a sexual come-on. He mentioned he knew the children were with Michael and offered me a drink. I said no, and he started to get upset."

"What did you do?"

"I said, ok, a glass of wine and then just held it without drinking anything. I was just so sure he was setting me up. I knew I needed to be very careful."

"What happened next?"

"He insisted we sit down on his couch. I got as far away from him as I could. He noticed and laughed at me. He said, 'Don't worry. You aren't my type. I don't like smart women.'"

"And then?"

"He told me Michael was paying him four thousand a month for the children. He said Tara set it all up when Michael first retained her before Brigman was even appointed. He said he offered his services for a price for Tara's clients who had money to burn and who wanted to make sure they got full custody of their children."

"How did you feel?"

"Scared. Upset." Alexa shrugged. "Hopeless, too. I realized I'd never had a chance of keeping them. Then I asked Dr. Brigman why he had decided to tell me."

"What was his reason?"

"He said Michael was months behind on his payments. So he had decided if I could come up with two thousand a month, he would give them to me. He said he knew they'd be miserable with Michael, and he felt guilty about making them go live with him."

"What did you think?"

"I was horrified, and he laughed at me. He warned me not to think about trying to get relief from Judge Watkins because Michael was paying him off, too. Although apparently, according to Dr. Brigman, the judge wasn't making as much as Brigman himself."

"What did you say to his offer?"

"I told him I didn't have that kind of money. He just laughed at me again and said I'm giving you 'the single-mother discount.' He said all I had to do was get my job back at Warrick, Thompson, and I could easily afford his arrangement."

"What did you do then?"

"I decided to leave. I still thought he was trying to set me up for the complete loss of Meggie and Sam."

"What time did you leave?"

"I'm guessing nine-thirty."

"Where did you go?"

"I drove around La Jolla and Pacific Beach. I wasn't really going anywhere. I just didn't want to go home and be alone. At one point, I parked and tried to call Bob again, but he still didn't answer."

"What did you do next?"

"I kept driving; and as I drove, I thought about what he'd said. I decided to go back and accept his offer and beg Alan to take me back at the firm. Even though I wouldn't see a lot of the children with a full time job at Warrick, Thompson, I'd still see more of them than I would if Michael got ninety per cent custody."

"What time did you get back to Dr. Brigman's?"

"About ten-thirty. I thought it was odd he wasn't there. I decided to drive some more and come back again to accept his offer."

"Did you go back?"

"No. I kept driving around more or less in circles until Meggie called and said she and Sam were afraid."

"But you were driving in the vicinity of Michael and Brigman's houses?"

"Yes. I couldn't go home until I'd told Dr. Brigman I'd find the money to pay him for custody of Meggie and Sam."

Sarah looked over at Jim, who looked grim. Alexa followed her gaze. Her deep blue eyes looked like an animal's when it realizes it is caught in a trap. "Remembering this doesn't help us, does it? It just adds to my motive to kill them."

"I'm afraid you're right," Sarah said.

"Wait, maybe it does help," Jim frowned as he concentrated. "Alexa can testify that Brigman called her to come over, and he was alive when she left at nine-thirty. And he wasn't there at ten-thirty when she went back, so she couldn't have killed him then. If she'd been angry over the bribes, she would have rushed back a lot earlier than ten-thirty. And we know Brigman didn't die until eleven. And I learned something today from Tara Jeffers' ex-secretary. Tara was sleeping with both Brigman and Michael."

"Did they know?" Sarah asked.

"Brigman did. And he wasn't happy. Marilyn said Michael wasn't really interested in Tara, but she pursued him relentlessly. She knew he had a lot of girlfriends and she didn't like that."

Sarah glanced down at her watch. Seven-thirty. "I've got to get going." She said it so convincingly that even she believed she had someone to meet somewhere.

"You should stay and eat," Jim said as she gathered her belongings.

"Not tonight."

CHAPTER TWENTY-FOUR

First Friday in November, 2013, Alexa's Cottage, Pacific Beach

Sarah hurried to her car and got in. She sat behind the wheel for a moment and wondered where to go. She decided not to drive through the heart of Pacific Beach because on a Friday night at seven o'clock, the partiers would be taking over the streets. Her nerves were like frayed electrical wires, snapping and arcing, and she was not in the mood to worry about hitting jaywalking drunks.

She navigated her way back to Felspar Street which led on to Mount Soledad Road. She decided it would be easier to drive over the mountain and through downtown La Jolla to go home. As she swung up the mountain's long steep grade, she considered stopping at Trend for a drink. The bar offered half-priced appetizers on Friday night, and it was a big draw for businessmen in the office buildings near by. Maybe she'd pick up someone to spend the night with, and maybe he'd be interesting enough to take her mind off Alexa cooking supper for Jim.

But that was the trouble with Trend. She couldn't go in now without wishing Jim were there, too. The bar had always been one of her favorite spots for picking up the men who rotated quickly through her life, but her feelings for Jim had ruined that for her.

She reached the top of the mountain and began her descent toward La Jolla. The BMW purred happily along the sharp bends and twists on the downward slope. She steered into the curves and let herself admit the truth: she wanted off this case. The emotions it conjured up slammed her to the ground, day after day. It brought back the dark days of Joey Menendez, a place of horror she never wanted to revisit.

She was now on the steepest part of the descent. Her feet reached for the clutch and the brake to slow the big car into the hairpin turn. The brake depressed, but her speed didn't change. Automatically she pumped the brake. Craig, Lewis had required its high-profile criminal lawyers to learn advanced driving techniques. She felt confident even in the emergency.

But the brakes remained unresponsive. She still had the clutch engaged, so she pulled the stick back to third gear. But nothing happened. Suddenly she was covered in cold sweat without time to think. The brakes and her clutch were gone, and she was hurtling toward a hairpin turn at sixty miles an hour. She frantically pumped the brakes and tried to steer away from the stone wall directly in her path. At the last minute, the car somehow made it around the turn without flipping over. Another lay just ahead.

She continued to hold the wheel as she reached for her last hope, the emergency brake. But, it too, was gone. The car continued to pick up speed, and she braced herself for the coming turn. And then nothing.

* * *

After Sarah left, Alexa went to the kitchen to finish preparations for dinner. Jim followed and poured more cabernet for both of them. He noticed she was wearing very flattering dark jeans and a medium blue cashmere sweater that set off her lovely eyes. She was recovering, he thought with satisfaction.

They ate in the tiny dining table in the alcove off the living room that pretended to be a separate dining room. The food was good, the wine relaxing, and Alexa's spirits had been lifted by her ability to remember the night of June 2.

Jim insisted on helping her with the kitchen cleanup, and then they took the last glass of wine of the night into her living room and sat side-by-side on the couch.

"Like an old married couple," Jim smiled, and then realized he'd had a hair too much to drink, and the alcohol was talking.

But she was not offended. "Too bad we didn't cross paths at Georgetown."

"Except that I was about ten years before your time."

"True. Still, we could have been very good friends."

"Well, I'd say that we are good friends now." Why was he throwing caution to the wind? He knew better.

Alexa smiled. "Yes, we are. And not many people have stayed my friends."

"It only takes a few really good ones, you know."

Alexa looked up at him with her clear blue eyes and then gently laid a hand on his shoulder. "Thank you."

"For what?"

"For everything. For believing in me."

She was so small and beautiful and alone in the world. And he hurt for her. His feelings were about to get the best of him. He should leave before he said or did something he shouldn't.

"It's after eleven, and I've kept you up too long. You need your sleep." He stood up and smiled down at her. "Thank you for dinner."

She got up, too, and he realized once more how tiny she was. How could any man lay a hand on her in anger?

"I'm glad you liked it. You should let me cook for you more often."

She followed him to the front door. He paused just before he opened it.

"Lock up as soon as I'm gone. And keep your phone with you. Leave the little light on in the living room."

She smiled. "I will, of course."

"Goodnight. I'll see you in the morning." And he leaned down and gave her a kiss on the cheek.

* * *

Jim hurried home, downed a fast tumbler of scotch, and fell into bed. When his phone went off at one a.m., he opened his eyes long enough to see the call wasn't from Alexa. He didn't recognize the numbers, so he pushed the dismiss button and went back to sleep. But the phone shrilled again, determined not to let him rest.

"Hello."

"This is Scripps Memorial Hospital in La Jolla. Someone whom we believe is a friend or relative was in a car crash tonight. The police found your name among her things. She's here in the hospital. Her name is Sarah Knight."

Panic seized him. How badly was she hurt?

* * *

She was sitting on the side of her bed, trying to sign something with her left hand. She had a white gauze bandage wrapped around her forehead, and her right arm was in a sling. She looked angry and annoyed.

"What are you doing here?"

"Making sure you're ok."

"How'd you find out I was here?"

"The hospital called. My name was the only one they could find in the car. Apparently you don't carry the names of your next-of-kin on you."

"That's because I don't have any."

"Well, I'm filling in tonight. Get back in bed. What are you trying to do?"

"I'm signing myself out and going home."

At that moment the door whooshed open, and Jim remembered all the recent nights with Alexa in the hospital. He'd had enough of them, but he knew Sarah should stay put.

"I'm Tom Barrett," the forty-something, square-jawed, salt-and-pepper haired doctor in the white coat strode in with a smile and an out-stretched hand. No wedding ring, Jim noticed, and the kind of face women found irresistible.

"You must be Mr. Knight?"

"No, a professional colleague."

Was that a spark of relief in the meltingly handsome doctor's eyes? Jim didn't want to think about it.

"Well, Sarah here has had quite a blow to the head. She's lucky to be alive at all. Very lucky. She's sprained her right arm; but more importantly, she's got a mild concussion and shouldn't go home tonight. Maybe you can get her to see reason."

Tom Barrett turned to Sarah who was frowning at his handsome face. "Put that down and let me take a look at you."

"I'm fine."

"You are not fine. Any nausea or dizziness? Double vision? How's that headache?" He proceeded to shine a light in her eyes, in the face of her silence. He smiled, "You aren't going to tell me, are you?"

"I'm going home."

"You are not going home. You can't drive."

"I'll call a cab. I'm going home."

Tom Barrett sighed and turned to Jim. "See if you can talk some sense into her."

Jim sat down on the chair beside her bed as the door closed behind the doctor.

"Hand me the paperwork."

"Not, yet. Tell me what happened."

"The car hit a wall going over Mount Soledad on my way home."

"Were you drinking?"

"No, I only had one glass of wine at Alexa's."

"So why did the car go out of control?

"Don't know. The BMW people took it to the shop. Ask them."

"I will. But you know what happened. Tell me."

"Hand me the papers."

"Not until you tell me."

"Ok, ok. The brakes failed."

"And you have a manual transmission. Why didn't you down shift?"

"I did."

"So no clutch, either."

"Right."

"Someone just tried to kill you."

"I'm aware of that."

"And now you want to sign yourself out of the hospital and go home in the middle of the night?"

"Don't argue with me. Hand me those papers."

Jim studied her wiry, determined form, swallowed by the white tent of the hospital gown. He watched her try to scribble with her left hand.

"Come to my place instead. I'd rather know you were in my guest room."

"Nope. Going home."

"So there's nothing I can say to change your mind?"

"Nothing."

"Okay. Then I'll drive you."

* * *

She was fading, Jim noticed, as they turned into her drive. Her fierceness was no match for the medications Dr. Barrett had given her. He wondered if she'd fall deeply enough asleep to let him take her home with him. She had not been able to get her clothes on alone, so the hospital had let him wrap a blanket over the cavernous hospital gown she still wore.

She seemed to read his mind about taking her back to his place. Her eyes popped open. "Don't even think about not letting me go inside."

"You just seemed to have passed out here in the car."

With a mighty effort, she heaved open the passenger side door with her left hand.

"Wait. Let me. Where's your key?"

"In my purse."

"Come on, then. Lean on me. If you don't, you're going to fall and send yourself right back to Dr. Barrett."

She gave him a small, mischievous smile. "I think he'd like to have me back."

"He definitely would like to have you back. He knows you need to be in the hospital."

"No, he *liked* me. I could tell. He liked me."

"You're on a lot of medication right now."

"Doesn't mean I don't know when an attractive man likes me."

"Okay, okay. He liked you. Why don't you let me take you straight back to the hospital then?"

"Because I'm tired, and I want to sleep in my own bed. He'll call me tomorrow. He has to find out how I am."

Jim suppressed his annoyance and helped her make her way up the walk in the chilly November morning dark. He realized the drugs were talking and exposing the lonely, vulnerable side of her life, something she kept expertly hidden from the world.

She leaned on him while he turned the key in the lock. He stepped into the hall, drew her inside, and closed the door behind them. She smelled of antiseptic and her usual gardenia perfume. He put his arms around her and thought of a bird's small bones as she sagged against him.

"Come on, then, let's get you into bed." He reached out and flipped the switch for the hall light.

"Oh, my God!" Sarah lurched toward the living room, which had been turned upside down. Lamps lay smashed on the floor. The end tables had been overturned. Someone had used a knife to rip open all the sofa cushions and scatter down everywhere.

Jim tried to grab her before she got beyond arm's reach but was not successful. She stopped in the doorway, and Jim saw her legs sag as she grabbed the doorframe.

He hurried to put his arms around her before she could fall.

"Turn on the light," she commanded.

"No, don't look."

"I want to see."

Reluctantly Jim reached out and switched on the overhead recessed lighting.

She shook her head in disbelief. He saw tears in her eyes. But his training immediately made him pull her close.

"We have to get out of here," he whispered in her ear.

"No."

"Sh-h-h. We don't know who did this. And we don't know who might still be here."

She opened her mouth to say something, but he picked her up and hurried out to the car. He didn't have time to go back and clear the scene, and it would be dangerous to do that alone, anyway.

He bundled her into the car, and backed out of the drive quickly, still afraid someone might yet be in the house. Shock on top of the medications had silenced Sarah. She slumped against the passenger's door and closed her eyes.

Jim's mind raced through the possibilities of who could be responsible. Had the same person who'd cut her brakes been the one who'd gone through her house? And what about Alexa? He'd left her ready to sleep. Had they gone after her, too?

He drove through the dark, deserted streets wondering if he should swing by Alexa's. But it was three-thirty in the morning, and she'd been instructed to call if anything seemed amiss. Right now getting Sarah to rest had to be his top priority.

He pulled into his garage, closed the roll-up door behind him, and got out of the car. Fatigue and fear had finally gotten the best of her. He carried her into his guest room, pulled back the sheets, and tucked her in. She smiled in her sleep but never woke up.

CHAPTER TWENTY-FIVE

First Saturday in November, 2013, Jim's Bungalow, Pacific Beach

Sarah opened her eyes and wondered where she was and why her head felt as if someone had taken a sledge hammer to it. The bright light streaming into the bedroom hurt her eyes, and she closed them. It felt like the worst hangover on record, except she couldn't remember being at a party last night.

The door opened, and Jim appeared with a small tray.

"How are you feeling?"

"Awful. Where am I?"

"My guest room."

"How did that happen? I left Alexa's, and then I don't remember–"

"You don't remember crashing your car? Or the very handsome Dr. Barrett at Scripps?"

Sarah frowned at the tray. "What's that?"

"Breakfast. Scrambled eggs and toast. Just a little until we see how you're doing."

She frowned. "I don't think I'm hungry."

"Well, try. Sit up." She moved slowly. "Ow. Every bone in my body aches. And the light hurts my eyes."

He settled the tray on her lap and closed the blinds. "There." Then he sat down on the chair by the bed.

"You're watching me eat."

"True. I want to see how you're feeling."

"Really awful."

"Do you remember being at Alexa's last night? She remembered why she went to Brigman's that night."

She considered for a moment between bites of egg. "Yes. In fact, it's coming back to me now. The car crashed on the other side of Mount Soledad as I was driving home. And someone went through my house. And Dr. Barrett is the one who bandaged up my head."

"Yeah, you hit so hard the air bag gave you a mild concussion. But it also saved your life."

She closed her eyes and lay back against the pillows. "Sorry, can't eat any more. I'm dizzy. Has Dr. Barrett called to find out how I am?"

"As a matter of fact he has."

She smiled. "Good."

But suddenly she opened her eyes and tried to sit up.

"Hey, what are you doing?" He gently pushed her shoulders back against the pillow.

"I've got to go home and see what's missing. Some of my confidential files on Alexa's case were there."

"I think you should make a police report."

"Thanks for the advice, but no. I need to go home and see if they took my file."

"And the only way you'll get there is if I drive you."

"If you don't, I'll call a cab."

"Well, then rest until early afternoon. We'll go at three o'clock. I need to run out now and make sure Alexa is still okay."

"All right." Sarah settled back against the pillows and closed her eyes.

Not long after she heard the front door close behind Jim, her phone began to ring.

She smiled. Wrecking the car and banging her head were not preferred ways of meeting attractive men, but Tom Barrett was exceptional and single. Maybe he would take her mind off Jim.

"Hello."

"I'm not happy with you."

Sarah stiffened at the sound of Coleman Reed's voice.

"You're not telling me anything I don't already know."

"I'm not responsible for the car. My man who was tailing you saw it, though. He called the paramedics. He thought you were dead. Would have been a nice benefit for me if you had been."

"So I guess you'll try on your own next time."

"Maybe. When Raoul saw them haul you off in the ambulance, he went over to your place. Found your file."

"Couldn't he have done that without destroying everything?"

"Well, he could have. But I told him to create maximum impact. Just in case you had survived the crash."

"I'm not feeling well, Justice Reed. I'm going to hang up now."

"Not yet. I've got another proposition for you."

"Not interested."

"Are you interested in staying alive?"

"Depends on the day. Right now I'm in a lot of pain."

"I've read your file. You don't have a defense, and you'll never find that nanny."

"We've learned Michael was bribing Ronald Brigman for custody of the children."

Coleman laughed. "Big, f**ing deal. Michael was fully justified. He knew how unstable Alexa was. She'd be bad for the kids."

"Number one at Georgetown. Clerkship for your colleague, Justice Moreno. Nothing in Alexa's history is unstable."

Coleman was silent for a long time. Then he said, "I've got an out that will save your career."

"Such as?"

"How would you feel about ten million dollars in your name in an offshore account by midnight tonight and guaranteed partnership at Warrick, Thompson? In exchange, you go in on Monday and tell that clown Tomlinson you're too ill to continue."

"I told you before. I've already turned down a partnership at Warrick, Thompson."

"But it didn't come with a ten million dollar tax-free signing bonus."

"Not interested."

"Look, I happen to know you've sunk everything into starting that law practice out there, and you're very short of cash."

"Big deal."

"And you're only going to make peanuts on this case."

"So what?"

"You need ten mil and a spot at Alan Warrick's place a lot more than you need to be the lawyer who sent Alexa Reed to death row."

"She's not going to death row."

"In your dreams. The offer is open until midnight. You know where to find me."

PRETRIAL

CHAPTER TWENTY-SIX

Second Friday in November, 2013, Sarah's Office, La Jolla

"Here's what I can testify to." Jordan Stewart sat at the far end of the conference table in Sarah's office the following Friday. Sarah sat at the other end with Jim in the middle. Jordan had come down on the train from L.A. that morning to meet with Alexa at the cottage. Now she was ready to give Sarah and Jim her conclusions.

"Let's hear it," Sarah said. She still had a bruise above her right eye, and she was wearing a brace on her right hand, but she refused to acknowledge the car accident in any other way. She was happily aware that she had a date with Tom Barrett for drinks at eight-thirty at Trend.

"I can testify she has the symptoms of Post Traumatic Stress Disorder, which will support my opinion that she was battered."

"But you only have her word that Michael abused her," Sarah said.

"That's true. Without third-party corroboration, a jury might decide she's lying."

"Or the judge might rule you can't testify if she doesn't. And I don't want her on the stand."

"I had a lead on that nanny in Guadalajara, but it hasn't panned out," Jim said. "Still looking."

"We're running short of time," Sarah gave him a pointed look.

Jim frowned, and Jordan looked from one angry face to the other, but said nothing.

"I can testify Michael's repeated batteries made her hyper vigilant where he was concerned and that's why she killed him. It wouldn't have taken much from him to trigger her fear reaction and make her believe she needed to defend herself."

"That's not a great defense," Sarah said.

"I know. And it is much harder to apply PTSD and Battered Woman's Syndrome to Ronald Brigman's death. But I think I can say legitimately, based upon the research, that Brigman's emotional battery became one in Alexa's mind with Michael's physical battery, and she reacted to him the same way. But Battered Women's Syndrome requires facts that show Alexa reacted to what she perceived as a threat of immediate danger. Neither Michael nor Brigman was armed. Instead, it looks a lot more like she got fed up with the custody proceedings and drove across town on a night when she didn't have the kids and shot both of them."

"But she says she didn't have her gun," Sarah observed. "If she didn't have that gun, she didn't kill them. What did you find out about the police report she said she made?"

Jim frowned. "Nothing. Yet. My contacts at the San Diego Police Department couldn't verify or rule out a written report."

"So in short, all we've learned is that Michael was bribing Ronald Brigman. And that fact doesn't help our case!"

I've never seen Sarah this angry, Jordan thought.

"I can't make facts out of thin air!" Jim's tone was too sharp. The tension was getting to both of them. "We need to interview the possible eyewitnesses, Meggie and Sam Reed."

They were squabbling like high school students, Jordan thought. "Fighting isn't going to help Alexa's defense," she said mildly.

Sarah and Jim eyed each other uncomfortably.

"We've got to come up with something better than Battered Women's Syndrome," Sarah said.

"It fits the facts we have," Jordan observed. "I have no doubt she was physically and emotionally abused by Michael and Ronald Brigman."

"But if she didn't have her gun, she didn't do it!" Sarah insisted. "What about Tara Jeffers? She was sleeping with both of them, and they weren't happy about it."

"I ran that down," Jim said. "Tara was at a fund raiser for the San Diego Symphony that night. She was even photographed around eleven p.m. with a large group of patrons."

"Are you sure?" Sarah demanded.

"I'll send you the time-stamped photographs if you don't believe me!"

* * *

Jim drove Jordan to Solana Beach to catch the five o'clock train.

Jordan was silent for much of the trip, but just as he exited I-5 onto Lomas Santa Fe, she said, "How long have you and Sarah been at each other's throats?"

"We aren't."

"Would you like to give a truthful answer this time?"

"Okay, okay. Someone tried to kill Sarah last Friday night by tampering with her car and then ransacked her house and stole her confidential file. She refuses to ask Judge Tomlinson for a continuance of the trial which begins in less than a month."

"Does she need a continuance?"

"She's a ball of nerves, as you can see."

"But would she be any less on edge about this case in another six weeks or two months?"

Jim parked in the lot at the train station, turned to Jordan, and frowned. "Is this the part where the therapist shows the client how unreasonable he's being?"

She smiled. "Your emotions are too mixed up in what needs to be purely professional. You've lost the ability to be objective."

"No, I haven't."

"That's not what I'm seeing."

He took a deep breath and leaned back against the driver's seat. "Look, the Reed children could be important witnesses, and Sarah refuses to interview them. And that's unacceptable given that there's a small, fragile, emotionally vulnerable woman who's lost everything and whose life is hanging by the thread of Sarah's ability to persuade a jury she didn't kill her two tormentors. Doesn't Alexa have a right to an attorney who's had time to get over the emotional toll of an attempt on her life?"

"Sarah always does a good job."

"I question her ability to do a good job right now. You have to understand. She's been the target of multiple threats for months, and last week it became more than a threat."

"And that has to be because someone who is afraid she'll win is putting pressure on her. Don't underestimate Sarah."

* * *

After dinner that night, Alexa and Jim settled side-by-side on her threadbare couch to finish the bottle of zinfandel. She was wearing her blue sweater and tight jeans, and Jim wished yet again that they had met under different circumstances.

She smiled up at him, and he had to fight the urge to kiss her. She was so sweet and intelligent and much less complicated than Sarah, who was full of secrets. But that was part of the trouble. The secrets made her so intriguing.

"Tell me about the meeting with Jordan today."

"She just went over the outlines of her trial testimony."

"And you could see I don't really have much of a defense."

Jim winced, and she smiled. "Don't be afraid to be honest. You know I know the truth."

He frowned. "Yeah, unlike the average client, there's no way to sugar coat it."

Alexa took a thoughtful sip of wine and wrapped herself protectively in the soft turtleneck collar of her sweater. She looked so sad that Jim's heart ached, and his anger flared. It was all so unfair.

"It's 11:30. You need your sleep." He stood up and smiled down at her. "I'll see you tomorrow."

She smiled and got up, too, and followed him to the front door.

"Lock up as soon as I'm gone. And keep your phone with you, and call if you even think something suspicious is going on."

"Of course."

"I'll be back in the morning." And he gave her what had become their nightly ritual, a kiss on the cheek. Then he headed out into the night to confront Sarah.

CHAPTER TWENTY-SEVEN

Midnight, Second Friday in November, 2013, La Jolla Shores

"Should you answer that?"

Someone was knocking loudly on Sarah's front door, and it was close to midnight.

She had questioned her decision to invite Tom Barrett to come home with her after drinks at Trend. But her inner fire of loneliness was burning more intensely than usual, so she took a chance.

They had been sitting side-by-side on her sofa, polishing off a bottle of merlot, while he talked about his work as a neurosurgeon. He was telling her about an operation scheduled for Monday morning on a thirty-two-year old mother of three to remove a malignant tumor. She was attracted to more than his square-jawed good looks. He was not just a highly skilled medical technician. He was a healer who cared deeply about the people who came to him in pain.

"I'm hoping it's small enough to get all of it. I'd like to help her."

Sarah smiled. "You care about us patients, don't you?"

"Of course. But you are no longer on the patient list since we are sitting here having this conversation."

He smiled, and Sarah noted with satisfaction that her heart at least flip-flopped when his dark eyes met hers. Maybe something could develop here. After David Spineli, she was deeply tired of superficial sexual encounters.

But at that moment the knocking interrupted them.

Sarah hesitated, as the replay of the accident rushed through her head. Someone wanted to kill her, and that someone could be standing on the other side of her front door. On the other hand, Tom's black Mercedes was sitting in her driveway, so it was obvious she was not alone.

"I'd better see who it is."

She opened the door to find an obviously furious Jim Mitchell glaring at her.

"I need to talk to you!" he bit off each word.

"Not now. I have company, as you can see."

"No, I need to talk to you!"

"Have you had too much to drink?"

"Maybe. Possibly. I don't care!"

"Go home and sleep it off, and I'll meet you at my office at ten in the morning."

"No. We have to talk now!"

She guessed he'd just come from Alexa's. What had happened there to transform the usually unflappable Jim Mitchell into this angry, almost unrecognizable man?

"Okay. Maybe you shouldn't be driving anyway. I'll put on some coffee. You remember Dr. Barrett. He's in the living room."

Sarah stayed in the kitchen until she had a mug of hot, rich dark coffee to put in front of him. She was hoping the even conversational tones that she could hear between Tom and Jim were evidence Jim was calming down.

Tom looked up when she entered with the coffee, a slightly hurt and puzzled look on his face.

"I guess I'd better go."

"Do you want some coffee?" Oddly she didn't want to be alone with Jim, and she was sorry he was forcing Tom to leave.

"No, thanks. I enjoyed tonight. Maybe dinner next week? I'm off on Wednesday."

"I'd like that." She smiled, relieved that Jim's appearance hadn't ended his interest in seeing her again and relieved that she actually looked forward to it.

She returned after seeing Tom to the front door, and poured the last of the merlot into her glass on the coffee table. She sat down on the sofa and looked at Jim, sitting in the chair opposite, sipping coffee. His eyes were still dark and angry.

"So what is so important that you had to interfere with my evening?"

"I've been thinking about Jordan's presentation today."

"And?"

"And you haven't got a defense for Alexa! We need to talk to Meggie and Sam."

"I told you before we don't have enough evidence to get the protective order lifted."

"Yes we do! They were the only ones in the house when Michael was killed!" Jim couldn't control his anger any longer.

Sarah sat back on the sofa and sipped her wine thoughtfully, letting silence cleanse the atmosphere of his outburst. Finally she observed quietly, "I think it might be time to let you off this case. You've lost your objectivity."

"What do you mean?" He looked as if she'd hit him with a brick.

"You know what I mean. Do you really want me to spell it out?"

"Yes, I do." His anger was rising again.

"You've developed feelings for Alexa. You're no longer functioning as a professional."

"That's not true." This time he spoke calmly. "She's become a friend, but that's all. She's a charming, interesting woman. I'm surprised you aren't closer to her."

She doubted he realized the extent of his "friend" feelings for Alexa.

"Better to keep my objectivity," she insisted. "I agree she's very charming, and I've imagined what it would have been like to have her as a junior associate at Craig, Lewis. I would have enjoyed working with her."

"I don't think we've done enough yet to develop a defense." He had reverted to the quiet tone he normally used.

"You mean *I* haven't done enough."

"If you insist on putting it that way." He was immediately testy again.

"What should I do then?"

"Just what I said. Interview Meggie and Sam."

"No."

"What do you mean 'no'?"

"We've already been over this. You didn't have to rush over to my house at midnight while I was seeing someone to go back over old ground."

"It's not old ground. What Meggie and Sam saw is the key to this case."

"I told you before, we don't know if they saw anything at all. Alexa found them hiding in a closet."

"They know who the woman was that Michael was arguing with."

"We don't know that for sure. All we know is they heard a female voice."

"You're afraid it was Alexa. It wasn't."

"Those are your feelings talking."

"I already told you—"

"Don't. I don't want to hear it again."

She watched him polish off the coffee and set the mug on the sofa table.

He stared at the black night through the French doors for a long time before he spoke. Finally he said, "If there wasn't a protective order, I'd already have interviewed Meggie and Sam myself."

"Well, there is one, and I can't ask that it be lifted based upon guesswork. They are very young children and talking to them about that night will most likely upset them. And we don't know how much of whatever story they may tell us has been influenced by Coleman."

"You are going to lose this case as it stands now. And when you lose, it will go up on appeal for the next twenty years."

"That's standard procedure in death cases."

"But there are going to be at least two more attorneys appointed for Alexa, the attorney who does the appeal and the attorney who does her habeas petition."

"And that is standard, too. Why are you running my date off and going through elementary capital criminal procedure with me at one in the morning?"

"Because your work is going to come under fire on appeal if you don't interview the Reed children. You'll be accused of providing ineffective assistance of counsel. They're the only possible witnesses to the murder."

Sarah put her empty glass on the table and sat very still. Absently she fingered the scar on her left cheek, lost in thought. Finally she said, "Okay. I'll ask Tomlinson to lift the order. He might not, but asking for it will mean I won't be accused of letting Alexa down. I want you to leave now."

"I will. But one more thing."

"And that is?"

"You need me with you when you interview them."

"What makes you think I'm going to keep you on this case?

"Because you know you need me."

CHAPTER TWENTY-EIGHT

Third Monday in November, 2013, Washington, D.C.

At ten-eighteen p.m. on the following Monday night, the United Airbus 320 roared upward from the runway at Lindbergh Field like an angry dragon. Spitting fire and flame and flexing its wings, it launched itself westward over the vast black Pacific, like a predator on the hunt. But suddenly, as if sensing that no prey was to be found over those dark cold waters, the dragon spit one long last tail of flame into the heavens and banked to the right, rolling gracefully in the night sky as it began its seven-hour journey through darkness across the United States. It would land at Dulles at six a.m.

Sarah vowed to ask the flight attendant for a red wine the minute the captain turned off the seatbelt light. She wished she'd had one in the airport before boarding. Beside her, Jim huddled under an airline blanket, his eyes closed and his earbuds in even though his iPad was turned off because they had not reached cruising altitude. He was still an angry man, presumably because she had pointed out his feelings for Alexa on Friday night and had suggested it was time for him to resign.

The cabin lights were out and most of the one-hundred passengers were also settling in for some shuteye. Sarah was too restless to sleep. The hearing in front of Judge Tomlinson that morning kept replaying itself.

He'd invited her into his chambers at eleven a.m., during a recess in the trial he was hearing that day. He'd motioned for her to take the seat in front of his desk. Sarah had the right to bring her motion without the prosecutor present to preserve the confidentiality of her thoughts and her theory of Alexa's defense.

Judge Tomlinson put on his half glasses and read her motion. He pulled them off when he finished and looked at her on the other side of his desk.

"Why ask to lift the protective order now?"

"Because—"

"Don't answer that. Because we're less than a month from trial, and you don't have a defense."

Sarah remained silent. She'd spent the entire weekend since Jim had stormed off on Friday night going over every scrap in Alexa's file, hoping against hope she would find something that would keep her from sitting in this chair on Monday morning.

"Your Honor, as far as we know, the children were the only people in the house when Michael was killed. They were never interviewed by the police. Coleman Reed took them back to D.C. and had this order entered before anyone could talk to them."

"You say in this motion Meggie Reed said her father was arguing with a woman when she called her mother that night."

"Yes, Alexa's description of Meggie's call is in Alexa's police statement."

"Didn't Meggie tell her mother who the woman was?"

"No. The children were too upset to talk when Alexa got them home that night, and the police summoned her to the station the next day before she had a chance to go over what had happened at their dad's house."

"And then Coleman Reed scooped them up and took them to D.C. so the police couldn't talk to them."

"Right."

Judge Tomlinson put his glasses on the desk and rubbed his eyes. He sighed and studied the parking lot across the street. Finally he looked back at Sarah.

"Do you honestly believe the children have anything that will help you?"

"I can't say for sure."

Judge Tomlinson sighed again and got up to pour himself a cup of coffee from the Mr. Coffee on the bookshelf across the room.

"Want some?"

"No thank you, Your Honor."

The judge made his way back to his desk and sat down again. He was quiet for a few minutes as he sipped coffee and studied Sarah's written motion. She could see he was lost in thought.

Finally he looked at her for a few seconds before he said, "I don't want to grant this because I'm sick of Coleman Reed's phone calls."

"Phone calls?"

"Don't tell me he doesn't call you, too."

"I don't think I should answer that."

"You don't have to. Everyone knows Coleman wheels and deals."

"Are you saying that a United States Supreme Court justice is calling you, the superior court judge on this case, to influence the outcome?"

Judge Tomlinson leaned back in his chair and thought about his response. "I'm not sure I would go that far. But Coleman calls frequently and makes his wishes known. That doesn't mean I give in to him."

"Has he ever threatened you?"

"More to the point, has he ever threatened you? Did he have anything to do with that accident you had?"

"I don't think I should answer that."

"You don't have to. And believe me, I've heard plenty from Coleman Reed about putting his daughter-in-law on house arrest."

"It's still hard for me to believe that Coleman Reed would be trying to influence you privately."

"You don't know about him, do you? I keep forgetting you didn't 'grow up' as an attorney in this town. Everyone here knows about Coleman Reed."

"Knows what?"

"That when he was in practice, he preferred bribes and deals brokered under the table to honest litigation in a courtroom in front of a jury. Anyone who has ever had a case with Coleman has been propositioned and threatened. The Warrick, Thompson partners didn't like the way he did business, but he had them over a barrel because he brought in so many clients. You should go talk to Alan Warrick about Coleman."

"Actually, I did. Now I need to talk to Alexa's children."

"I'm inclined to say no. I'm tired of flack from Coleman. Lifting this order will make it worse. Besides, you probably won't get anything out of them. They aren't very old."

"Six and five. But both of them are brilliant by all accounts, like their mother. They will have information, I'm sure."

"But not necessarily favorable information. I'm going to deny this."

"But Your Honor, wait!" Sarah leaned forward in her chair and reached out to keep the judge from putting pen to paper to write "denied."

Judge Tomlinson looked up at her, surprised. "You're going a bit far, Ms. Knight. Please get your hand off my desk."

"Sorry, Your Honor." Sarah put the offending hand back in her lap.

"Look, I'm sure you brought this motion to cover your ass. You're afraid the state bar will punch your ticket for ineffective assistance of counsel if you don't interview the children. If I were in your shoes, I'd be worried about keeping my license, too. But, look, there's a way to make this a win/win for you and me both."

"And that would be?"

"I'm going to deny this motion. Coleman won't call me or you in the wee hours, and you won't have to go see him in D.C. Win/win. And your bar card won't be in jeopardy because you brought the motion, and I denied it. The state bar won't find you ineffective because I said no."

Sarah shook her head slowly. "I'm sorry, Your Honor, but if you deny my motion, you'll just wind up delaying the trial."

"How so?" He looked worried at the prospect. "I don't want any delays. I want to never hear from Coleman Reed again."

"If you deny that motion, I'm going to have to go ask for a writ of mandate in the court of appeal. And if they say no, I'll have to go to the California Supreme Court. I would be ineffective if I walked out of here with a denial from you and did nothing more."

"Is that a threat?"

"Doing what I was appointed to do cannot be interpreted as a threat."

"Sorry, Coleman Reed has me on edge. And unfortunately, you're right. The only way I can make this go away forever is to grant your motion."

Sarah flagged down the flight attendant and procured her drink. She hoped it would make her able to sleep. She didn't look forward to confronting Coleman Reed next day at his house at the appointed hour of three p.m. But Jim was right. They had to talk to Meggie and Sam.

CHAPTER TWENTY-NINE

Third Tuesday in November, 2013, Washington, D.C.

A middle-aged woman in a simple navy dress and long grey sweater, who identified herself as Clara Norton, the housekeeper, answered the door at the Reed's Georgetown townhouse on Tuesday afternoon. She invited them in and led them through the formal living room furnished in eighteenth century antiques into the cherry-paneled den at the back of the house.

Myrna Reed, in gray slacks and a white cashmere sweater accented with a green Hermes scarf tied at her throat, sat at one end of the long beige sectional sofa. Coleman, in dark brown corduroy slacks, gray checked shirt and black sweater vest, stood by the fireplace, his back to the room. It was a bitter cold, rainy winter day, and the roaring fire was welcoming even if the hosts were not.

Coleman turned when he heard Sarah and Jim enter. She studied her adversary as he took her measure. He had not aged much since oral argument three years ago. He didn't look his sixty-five years. He had a full head of dark brown hair, keen brown eyes, and obviously worked out daily. At six feet, he looked as powerful as he was.

"Come in," he commanded. He walked over and shook Sarah's outstretched hand. "You haven't changed, Ms. Knight."

"This is Jim Mitchell, my investigator."

"We've never met. Former FBI, I understand."

"That's correct."

"And this is my wife, Myrna."

Mrs. Reed merely nodded regally in their direction but said nothing. She was Coleman's age, but like her husband, looked younger. Her hair was dyed a becoming honey blond, and her deep-set green eyes had been expertly lifted to banish at least ten years. Still, she looked tired as she sat silently on the sofa, watching Sarah and Jim.

"Where are the children?" Sarah asked.

"We'll get to that, all in good time. But first, sit down. We have to agree on some ground rules for these interviews."

"The ground rules are Judge Tomlinson's order." Sarah tapped her briefcase where she carried a signed original. "I'm allowed to interview Meggie and Sam Reed with my investigator present. Period."

"They are quite fragile emotionally," Coleman insisted. "Your order doesn't allow you to endanger them."

She and Jim had perched on the sofa as far away from Myrna as possible. Sarah said, "An interview with the attorney appointed to represent their mother is not going to endanger the children. Arguing about this is simply going to prolong the process. It would be better for everyone to get it over with."

"I'm going to set the rules," Coleman insisted. "They are my responsibility, and I will decide when someone is not acting in their best interests. Now here are my requirements. Myrna and I have to be present, and no probing for details. If they say they don't remember, that's the end of the interview."

Sarah had had a sinking feeling since getting on the airplane yesterday that Coleman was going to make sure this trip was a waste of time. "I'm sorry, but these have to be confidential interviews. Attorney work product is confidential. You know that, Justice Reed."

"So fly back to San Diego and complain to Judge Tomlinson. In the meantime, you do it my way or not at all."

Sarah saw Jim's jaw set. He was furious.

At that moment, a very attractive brunette in her early thirties knocked on the open door to the den. She was wearing flattering tight jeans, expensive knee-high boots, and a silky violet cashmere sweater that hugged all the right curves and accented her dark brown eyes. *She was the definition of voluptuous*, Sarah thought. Obviously Coleman had not hired her solely for her child care skills. Sarah wondered how Myrna felt about her, but her face remained impassive.

"You wanted me to bring the children down, Justice Reed?" She had a crisp British accent.

"Yes, Louise."

The beautiful woman stepped aside and ushered in Alexa's children. Meggie looked like her mother, with blonde hair and blue eyes. She was wearing a red plaid jumper, black tights, and classic Mary Jane shoes. Sam had Alexa's round open face, but Michael's dark hair and green eyes. He wore blue jeans, a buttoned up blue plaid shirt, and miniature Nike sneakers. They walked single file across the room, casting only one quick, curious look at Sarah and Jim before presenting themselves to their grandfather, still standing before the fire.

"Say hello to Ms. Knight and Mr. Mitchell," Coleman instructed the children.

They turned like little robots and faced Sarah and Jim. "Hello," they said, not quite in unison. Sarah's stomach turned over. Each child had a faint blue mark across the left cheek which, without any doubt, was a fading bruise.

"And this is Louise Baker, our nanny."

"How do you do?" From her tone, Sarah deduced she'd been told she and Jim were there to do the devil's work. "Shall I leave the children with you, Justice Reed?"

"Please. For a few minutes."

He gave her a look that didn't disguise his interest. Sarah glanced at Myrna again, but she remained stoic in her corner.

Coleman sat down in the oversized armchair that faced the sofa and motioned for the children to stand on each side of him. Sarah thought she saw them flinch when he put his arms around their shoulders. *This interview is a travesty*, she thought. Coleman was taking great care to demonstrate he owned the children.

"Now, Ms. Knight, what do you want to know?"

Sarah had hated Coleman Reed since the moment she'd been appointed on this case, but her hatred doubled and then tripled. Still, she was careful to keep her face impassive as she made eye contact with Alexa's children.

"I'm happy to meet you, Meggie and Sam."

"Have you come from San Diego?" Meggie asked. She saw Coleman squeeze her abruptly. "Ow! That hurt!" But he ignored her.

"Yes, we have. We want to know what you each remember about the last night you spent at your dad's house."

Meggie looked over at Sam, who frowned as Coleman squeezed them both a little harder.

"Ow!" Sam said. "I can't breathe."

"I just want to make sure you aren't feeling upset," Coleman soothed. Both children frowned.

Finally Meggie said, "We don't remember anything."

"That's right," Sam chimed in. "We don't remember anything."

"Not even calling your mother to come and get you?" Sarah asked.

Meggie opened her mouth to speak but was silenced by a look from Coleman.

"No," she finally said. "No, we don't remember."

Coleman kept the children next to him, but released his grip on their little bodies.

"I'm afraid that's it, Ms. Knight. They can't tell you anything."

At that moment, as if on cue, the nanny appeared.

"Ms. Knight and Mr. Mitchell are ready to leave," Coleman said. "Would you show them out, Louise, and then take Meggie and Sam upstairs?"

"Of course, Justice Reed. This way."

* * *

Although their hotel was just a few blocks away, it was too cold to walk. The air said it was going to snow. Jim hailed a taxi, and they rode in silence for the five-or-six block journey. The cab lurched to a halt in front of the hotel, and Jim paid the driver. They hurried into the warmth of the lobby where a fire burned invitingly in the bar.

"Feel like a drink?" Jim asked.

"Absolutely."

They found seats in the booth nearest the flames and peeled off their overcoats. Jim ordered scotch, and Sarah followed suit.

"That's strong for you."

"These last few days have been rough."

"I'd say these last few months."

"That, too."

He smiled his amazing, gentle smile; and her heart lit up.

"I'm sorry I jumped on you Friday night. I got emotional sitting with Alexa after dinner. I started feeling helpless, and that feeling sent me over the edge."

Sarah took her glass from the waiter and frowned into it. She took a sip and let the alcohol warm her.

"You hesitated to interview the children because you thought we'd run into something like this, didn't you?"

"That and I'm still afraid Coleman has tainted their version of events."

Jim frowned. "You have a point. Did you notice those cheeks?"

Sarah nodded.

"So you were thinking what I was thinking?"

"Michael was an abuser, so that means it's likely he learned that behavior from Coleman."

"And Sam is now going to learn it from him, too, unless we can think of a way to get them out of there."

"Unfortunately, the last time I checked, kidnaping was not an option."

He gave her another one of his heartwarming smiles. "If you're joking with me, does that mean you aren't going to kick me off the case?"

Sarah felt her stomach twist at the thought of seeing him with Alexa again.

His face became serious. "Why are you hesitating?"

"I just want you to be careful about feelings. This is a tough case not to get wrapped up in emotionally."

"I think your emotions are wrapped up in it as deeply as mine are."

Sarah looked up at him over her nearly empty glass in surprise. "What makes you say that?"

"How tightly you're wound. How much you drink. The fact you don't eat. And you worry, worry, worry. It's like watching someone being eaten by a demon from the inside out."

His voice was so soft and gentle that it made her want to cry. To her horror, she felt her eyes mist over.

He reached out and put his hand over hers. "It would be okay to let the tears out sometimes."

"No, it wouldn't."

"Why not?"

"It just wouldn't. I can't talk about it."

"You mean you won't talk about it."

"That, too."

Sarah took back her hand and drained the last of her scotch. Jim signaled the bartender for two more.

"Is that a good idea?" she asked.

"What else have we got to do at five o'clock on a freezing Monday night in D.C.? I called Cody, and he has something going on at school and no time to see me tonight. I thought we could go into the restaurant for dinner after drinks. It's not five-star dining, but it's pretty cold to be taking a cab to the Four Seasons."

"Eating here is fine." *Am I allowed to think how glad I am that you are with me and not with Alexa tonight? No, I'm not allowed to have that thought.*

* * *

They had the dining room almost to themselves. The braised short ribs and polenta were hearty comfort food on the freezing night, and Jim ordered a bottle of red wine. The snow had started to come down, dusting the sidewalks a pristine white.

For a while they didn't talk about the case, and Sarah felt as if it was the closest thing they'd had to a date. He asked questions about her family and about her life before he met her, and she wished she could give him truthful answers. But she had the comfortable old lies down pat, and he believed them. Her parents were college professors. They died in a car accident the year she joined Craig, Lewis. She had no brothers and sisters. Thankfully he listened and didn't ask questions, so she relaxed and sipped her wine as she watched the snow begin to fall outside the restaurant's bay windows and pretended she could have a life with Jim when the case was over.

But they could not stay away from the problem of Meggie and Sam for long.

"I felt sorry for them in that house today," Jim said. "It reminded me of how I grew up, surrounded by household staff and ignored by my parents."

Sarah nodded. "I felt sorry for them, too. If I were a child, I would much rather be raised by a blonde princess in a fairy tale cottage with a blue door by the sea."

Jim smiled. "You see Alexa as a princess in a fairy tale cottage?"

"Well, only metaphorically. But the whole setup made me think of the dark side of fairy tales where the evil magician casts a spell on the princess and she has to leave the castle and hide in the woods."

He looked thoughtful. "There's something to that. She was hiding there, dreading the moment she'd lose the children. Brigman and Michael's black magic was going to work its spell no matter what she did to try to stop it."

Sarah nodded. "She's a strong woman, but she was helpless against those two."

"And now we seem to be helpless against Coleman."

"Judge Tomlinson told me everyone in the San Diego bar knows he operates by dirty tricks. The judge, by the way, has been getting midnight calls from him. That's why he didn't want to grant my request to interview the children."

"And you get those calls, too, don't you?"

"I don't want to talk about it."

But Jim would not give up. "Did he admit he had your brake lines cut?"

"He says he didn't. But he also admits he had someone following me."

"To make sure you were dead."

"He said his man called the paramedics for that reason."

"So if he'd known you were alive he wouldn't have bothered."

"That's the message I got."

Sarah wanted to forget about Coleman Reed and bask in the warmth of the fire, the buzz the wine had created, and in Jim's presence. Alexa was thousands of miles away, and he was looking at her with those brown eyes that made her soul melt. At that moment, more than anything in the world, she wished he'd ask her to come upstairs to his room. What would it be like, just once, to be with a man she really loved? Even if it could never be for more than one night, didn't everyone deserve one night?

But no, not if he's in love with someone else. At that moment, Jim's cell went off, and they could both see the call was from Alexa.

"Hello." Sarah noted the warmth in his voice.

She apparently asked if he had time to talk.

"No, I'm not busy. Sarah and I are just sitting here finishing dinner. Long day."

Sarah guessed Alexa had asked how the interview with the children had gone.

"You know, Sarah should answer that. Here she is."

And suddenly she was holding Jim's phone to her ear listening to Alexa's gentle Southern vowels on the other end.

"Hi, Sarah. How were Meggie and Sam?"

"Very quiet. Coleman wouldn't let us see them privately."

"So they said they didn't remember anything?"

"Coleman had coached them."

"Is he hitting them?"

Sarah frowned. She didn't want to answer because Alexa was living in a deep enough nightmare already.

"Your hesitation says it all."

Her voice was so level even under the intense emotional pressure. *She'd have been a top attorney,* Sarah, thought, given the chance. She admired the courage and poise of this tiny woman.

"Look, we're not giving up. Jim and I are sitting here trying to think of other ways to approach them."

"I know, but I don't think there's much else that will work besides getting an order from the California Supreme Court directed personally to Coleman."

"It's an option I've been considering."

"And they might not give it to you. He is, after all, a sitting U.S. Supreme Court justice."

"Evidence that shows you are innocent outranks even Coleman Reed. The California Supreme Court knows that. Don't worry, Alexa. Jim and I haven't given up."

CHAPTER THIRTY

Third Tuesday in November 2013, Washington D.C.

At one a.m., Myrna Reed lay awake alone as usual in her mahogany four-poster. The room was too cold because her husband insisted on turning the heat off at night, but she was seething, and her rage warmed her nicely. Coleman might think she didn't know who was in his bed down the hall, but she wasn't a fool. Or maybe she was because she'd given up her early ambitions to be an investment banker and married Coleman Reed.

It had been so long ago that no one remembered that part of her story. She'd been one of the first women in the seventies to break into the white-male dominated world of investment banking in New York with a degree from Princeton. But over a long conference table on an unforgettable Tuesday afternoon, she'd met a dashing young Harvard law graduate, a dynamic third-year associate at Eliot, Fitzgerald with his eyes fixed firmly on partnership. She'd lost her heart; and later, she would realize, her freedom.

Coleman's career skyrocketed while hers plummeted. Old-line clients resisted having women handle their portfolios. Myrna drifted through various investment banking houses, but nothing stuck. Coleman, on the other hand, easily became a partner at Eliot, Fitzgerald because of his already legendary skills at attracting clients. But then, as if to crown his success, the West Coast firm of Warrick, Thompson, and Hayes came calling; and Coleman happily took their offer to become a partner in San Diego. Face it, he told Myrna, your professional life has long been over. Forget your sorry excuse of a career and come to California where it's warm. Stay home with Michael and learn to play golf.

Myrna wiped away tears of rage. Was a mother allowed to tell the truth about a child, even when she was alone and seething at one in the morning? She had regretted the horror of her marriage when she'd realized Coleman regarded infidelity as his birthright. But a child who tortured his pets until she refused to have any more, who bit and scratched the long suffering nannies, who set fires to terrorize, and who lied much too cleverly was more than she could bear. By the time Michael was Meggie's age, Myrna had found herself trapped in a world where she was only window-dressing for her husband and saddled with a child whose main joy in life was inflicting physical and psychological pain on others.

Coleman began to beat her when she suggested counseling for Michael. When her son's specialty became date rape in high school because he had learned a powerful attorney's son could not be touched by legal proceedings when the right bribes were applied in the right places, Myrna pleaded with Coleman once more to put Michael in counseling. For her trouble, Coleman knocked her senseless, giving her a concussion that kept her in the hospital for a month. He blamed the fall on her drinking and locked her up at Betty Ford, giving lip service to her need for rehab. But in reality, he didn't want her to stop drinking.

When Betty Ford finally let her go, Myrna realized it was easier to retreat into the boozy world she'd created for herself. Coleman kept her well supplied because bourbon kept her quiet about his affairs and Michael's problems. The three of them entered into an uneasy truce that allowed Coleman and Michael their freedom to do whatever they wanted so long as they left Myrna untouched with a well-stocked liquor cabinet. Coleman's money and prestige bought his and Michael's way out of any trouble they created, and the arrangement worked quite well until Michael fixated on Alexa Harrison. Myrna had wanted to tell her the truth and to warn her that their appearances were just that: appearances. But she knew the price she'd pay for snitching on Coleman and Michael. Instead, she decided to keep to herself in an alcoholic trance throughout the wedding plans and festivities.

But that night, the aged bourbon straight up didn't help her ignore the fact her husband was sleeping with her grandchildren's nanny just two doors down the hall.

At least before Meggie and Sam had arrived, Coleman had been required to conduct his affairs off-premises to maintain plausible deniability. It had been easier to nod and smile when he'd said a meeting ran late or that he'd missed a flight and booked a hotel. Myrna had welcomed any excuse that keep the wobbly wheels of their so-called marriage grinding along.

But when Michael died, Coleman had been given the perfect scenario to bring one of his mistresses into their house. Myrna realized it was heresy to be glad her only child was dead, but Michael was an exception to the rule of motherly love. It sickened Myrna to think of all the people her son had hurt, but none more than the mother of his children. If Alexa had killed Michael, she didn't deserve to die. She deserved a medal for ridding the world of a soulless predator. Myrna would be willing to get on the witness stand and testify to that. But now that she was a well-known drunk, no one would believe her. There was only one thing she could do to help Alexa. And she was willing to do it.

* * *

Third Wednesday in November 2013, Washington D.C.

Sarah's cell phone went off at four a.m. She struggled to push back the heavy curtains of alcohol-induced sleep to open her eyes. Her mouth was dry and papery. Her head hurt. The phone kept ringing.

"Hello?"

"Ms. Knight, this is Myrna Reed."

The sleep cobwebs vanished in an instant. "Yes, Mrs. Reed."

"I would apologize for what happened in my house yesterday, but this hasn't been my house for a long, long time. My son was a monster, and if Alexa killed him, she had every reason for what she did."

For a moment, Sarah doubted the voice on the other end was the real Myrna Reed.

"I'm sorry, Mrs. Reed. It's very early in the morning. Perhaps I could come over later and–"

"No!"

The terror in that one word was real enough for Sarah to believe in the authenticity of her caller.

"Coleman has surveillance cameras on every door. If he knew you'd been here to talk to me–well, I don't want to even think about that."

"Of course, Mrs. Reed. I wouldn't want to jeopardize your safety or that of the children."

"But you need to talk them, and I'm willing to let you."

"Where, then, if not at the house?"

"This is the nanny's day off. At least, that's the euphemistic term for the day of the week Louise and Coleman spend together in his suite at the Four Seasons. Are you shocked, Ms. Knight?"

"Jim and I saw the lay of the land when we were there. You have all my sympathy."

"Don't bother. I married him, and I've thrown away all my chances to escape. But I want to help Alexa."

"So how can we talk to the children undetected by your husband?"

"I always take them to the Smithsonian on Wednesdays. We arrive at ten and stay until around three. Be there at ten thirty and ask for Noel Dean. She's an assistant curator for the Americana collection and a friend of mine. She will let you use her office to interview Meggie and Sam. I'll wait elsewhere in the museum. I know it needs to be a private conversation. When you are through, Noel will know where to find me."

"Thank you, Mrs. Reed."

"You don't have to thank me. You should have been allowed to talk to them long before now."

"Do you know anything about what they might say?"

"No. They've never brought up that night, and Coleman put the fear of God into them when he found out you and your investigator were coming. They may yet be too afraid to talk about it."

"I understand. I'll make every effort to make sure your husband doesn't know you helped us."

"Thank you, but he'll probably find out, no matter what you do. I'll just have to cross that bridge when I come to it."

"But your life could be in danger."

"Honestly, Ms. Knight, I don't care if it is."

* * *

Third Wednesday in November 2013, The Smithsonian

At ten thirty, Sarah and Jim were waiting in Noel Dean's office as instructed. She was a pleasant-faced woman in her early forties. She looked like a museum curator in a dark suit and oversized tortoise shell spectacles with her auburn hair pulled into a tight bun. Her office had a small sofa flanked by two small chairs. She motioned for Sarah and Jim to take the chairs while she went to fetch the children.

Sarah had been unable to go back to sleep after Myrna's call, so she'd made a not-very-good pot of coffee on the little machine in her room and had waited until six to ring Jim with the news.

"Frankly, I didn't think she had it in her," Jim had said at eight thirty over breakfast in the hotel's restaurant. "It's no secret in this town that she drinks too much."

"I would, too, if I were married to Coleman Reed and had Michael for a son. She called him a monster."

"That sounds about right."

* * *

And now, two hours later, the door opened and Noel reappeared with Meggie and Sam. Yesterday's snow had been only flurries, but it was still unbearably cold. The children were dressed in jeans and turtlenecks and identical navy puffy coats with hoods. They eyed Sarah and Jim carefully as they crossed the room and sat down on the sofa. Meggie reached over and took her little brother's hand as if to reassure him.

"I'm in a meeting in the conference room next door," Noel said as she was leaving. "Just knock when you are done, and I'll fetch Mrs. Reed. She said there's no rush. Take all the time you need."

"Thank you." Sarah smiled at her retreating back and then smiled at the skeptical children. "Hello, again."

"Hello." Meggie didn't smile.

"You know that I'm an attorney, and this is my friend Jim who is helping me find information to help your mother."

"When can we see her?" Sam suddenly demanded.

It was the question Sarah had dreaded. "I don't know when."

"Coleman says we'll never see her again," Meggie said.

"You're supposed to call him 'Grandpa,'" Sam corrected her.

"Louise calls him 'Coleman' when she thinks no one is listening."

Sam eyed Sarah and Jim suspiciously. "Grandpa said we aren't supposed to talk to you. He said he'd hit us again if we did."

"So I take it he hit you before we came to warn you not to talk to us?"

"That's right." Meggie put her hand up to her left cheek with its fading bruise.

"Does he hit you often?" Jim asked.

"When we do something he doesn't like," Meggie said. "Our dad used to hit us. Our mother never did."

"We want to go home," Sam said. "Grandpa wouldn't even let me take Mr. Wiggles. I miss him. I wish you had brought him."

"We couldn't bring him, Sam. Your mom is keeping him safe for you."

"Okay."

"What we need to talk about is that last night you spent with your dad," Sarah said.

"Meggie, why don't you go first and tell us what you remember."

"One of my dad's girlfriends was there. He had a lot of girlfriends."

"Yeah," Sam chimed in. "A lot. Some of them he paid for. Some he didn't."

Sarah frowned. "How do you know that?"

"Because the paid-for ones used to argue with him over how much they were supposed to get," Meggie said. "He would give them an envelope, and they would count the money and then say it wasn't enough."

"Do you know if the one that night was a paid-for girlfriend?" Jim asked.

"I think so. We said hello to her when she got there, and my dad handed her the envelope."

"Did she say it wasn't enough?" Jim asked.

"No. She counted it, but she didn't say anything about it. "

"So what happened after you said hello to the girlfriend?" Sarah asked.

"We went to bed," Meggie said. "It was summer and school was out, and our bedtime was nine o'clock."

"Did you go to sleep?"

"Not at first," Sam said. "My dad tried to make me sleep in a room by myself, and I didn't like that because at home Meggie and me had the same room. So I sneaked down the hall to Meggie's room."

"Did you see your dad or the girlfriend when you went down the hall?"

"No."

"And what did you do next?" Sarah asked.

"I made him a bed on the floor with my blankets," Meggie said, "because I only had a little bed at my dad's, and there wasn't room for both of us. Then we went to sleep."

"And when you woke up what did you hear?"

"Our dad and a woman, yelling at the top of their voices."

"Could you hear what they were saying?"

"No."

"Did you go down the hall to see who your dad was fighting with?"

"No, we were too afraid."

"Could the woman have been your mother?" Jim asked.

"No," Meggie shook her head emphatically. "Our mother never went into our dad's house. She always let us out in front. She was too afraid of him to go inside."

"So what happened after the arguing woke you up?"

"The shouting went on for a little bit, and then Sam and I heard thumping like something being dragged, and then we heard bang, bang, bang."

"Yeah," Sam agreed. "Bang, bang, bang."

"What happened after that?"

"The house got very quiet," Meggie said. "So I decided to sneak down the hall to see what was going on in the living room."

"And what did you see?"

"My dad was lying on the floor, and he wasn't moving. And there was a gun next to him that looked like my mom's. I was afraid the person who shot him was still in the house and would find me and Sam and shoot us. So I ran back to my room and hid us in the closet."

"Is that when you called your mom?" Sarah asked.

"Yes. While we were hiding, I used my phone to call her. She got it for me because she was always afraid something might happen to us at my dad's."

"What happened to your dad's girlfriend?"

"I don't know," Meggie said. "I didn't see her in the living room when I was there after the gunshots."

"Did you go back into the living room after you called your mother?"

"No. We stayed in the closet. It was safer."

"So that's where your mother found you when she got there?"

"Yes."

"How long did it take her to arrive?"

"I don't know," Meggie said.

"It seemed like a long time," Sam spoke up.

"How did you know that your mother had a gun, Meggie?" Jim asked.

"We weren't supposed to know. But she kept it in the trunk of her car, and sometimes me or Sam would see her checking on it. She had it because my dad was going to kill her."

"How do you know that?" Sarah asked.

"Because when we were at his house, he would get on the phone with Coleman. And he would talk about killing my mom."

"Why did they do that?"

"I'm not sure." Meggie paused to wrinkle her nose in thought. "I heard my father say things like 'I'm paying too much right now to keep them. If she were out of the way, I wouldn't have to worry about paying anymore.' But I don't know what that means."

"It's okay. We do. Did your mother talk to you about her gun?"

"Yes.

"She told us never to touch it, and she said she needed it to keep us all safe."

"Only, it didn't work," Sam piped up. "Our dad stole her gun, so she had nothing to protect us with."

"How do you know he stole it?"

"Because we saw him," Sam said.

"When did he steal it?"

"It was the day our school was out. Our dad came to get us at our mom's, and after he put us in his car, he walked over to our mom's car and took the gun out of the trunk.

"How did he get into the trunk?"

"He had a key. He told us he was taking her gun because he was afraid she'd hurt herself with it. But Sam and I knew he was taking it so he could use it to hurt her."

"Did you tell your mother what you'd seen?"

"No," Sam shook his little head emphatically. "Our dad said he would hurt us if we told on him."

"Did your mother ever ask you if you knew where the gun was?"

"No," Meggie said.

*　*　*

Third Wednesday in November 2013, Dulles International Airport

The United Airbus lifted off from Dulles at seven-thirty that night. They would be in San Diego at midnight, West Coast time. As the big jet roared and gathered speed to hurtle itself

305

into the night sky, Jim said, "You missed your dinner date tonight."

Tom Barrett had been the last thing on Sarah's mind as the cabin shook with the effort of take-off.

"We rescheduled for Friday. He had an emergency operation tonight, anyway."

"Sounds like your kind of guy."

Sarah smiled. "It was a nice change to call him to say I can't make it and have him completely understand."

"We have to find Michael's call girl. I noticed some of his neighbors have surveillance cameras. I'll see if any of them are willing to share their footage. They might have picked up her arrival at the house."

CHAPTER THIRTY-ONE

Last Friday in November 2013, Pacific Beach

Sarah was deliberately avoiding Alexa. Jim didn't want to believe that, but the conclusion was inescapable. She had given her a summary of the interview with Meggie and Sam by telephone and had left it to Jim to go to the cottage to talk to her about it in person. It did not help Jim's mood that nothing had gone his way in the week since their meeting with the Reed children, either in his investigation into Alexa's case or in his private life.

As far as the case was concerned, all of Brigman's neighbors with surveillance cameras were out of town at exotic destinations over Thanksgiving. And he couldn't find any leads on Michael Reed's call girl. As far as his own life was concerned, Cody had decided not to come for a Thanksgiving visit; so he had spent yesterday with Alexa, trying not to depress either her or himself because they both missed their children. Sarah, as usual, had begged off dinner with the two of them; and he suspected she'd spent the day with Tom Barrett.

Now they were sitting in her office, going over the bits and pieces of Alexa's defense. Sarah looked worn and thinner than ever. The blue half-moons under her beautiful dark eyes said she didn't sleep. She was casually dressed in gray yoga pants and a deep green sweater, and she kept fiddling nervously with a pen as they talked.

"You need to see Alexa."

"I've talked to her on the phone."

"But you need to talk to her in person. We're less than two weeks from starting trial."

"Don't tell me how to do my job!"

"I'm not telling you how to do your job." He tried to keep his own anger in check, but the frustrations of this case were becoming overwhelming, Every lead turned to dust and crumbled between his fingers. "You haven't been to see her since the trip to D.C. You're avoiding her."

She reached up and traced the scar on her cheek and stared out at the ocean. He'd come to associate that gesture with extreme stress. Abruptly she brought her eyes back from the water and fixed them angrily on him. "Ok, what do you want me to do?"

"I'll make dinner for the three of us tonight at Alexa's place. Seven o'clock."

* * *

Neither woman had eaten anything, Jim reflected as he watched them on opposite ends of Alexa's shabby sofa after dinner. Alexa's golden hair glowed in the dim light like a halo around her face as she fixed her thoughtful eyes on Sarah, who was still wearing her casual outfit of the morning. Sarah was staring at the threadbare carpet, lost in thought.

He said quietly, "Have you talked to Alexa about how our meeting with Meggie and Sam changes the defense theory of the case?"

Sarah studied his face for a moment and then looked at Alexa. "We'll need to call Meggie and Sam as witnesses. We need them to testify that Michael took your gun."

Alexa frowned. "I don't want them involved. They're too young."

"We don't have a choice," Jim said gently. "They're the only ones who know how your gun went missing."

But Alexa shook her head. "There's a police report. You still need to find it. Besides, you know as well as I do, Coleman is not going to comply with any subpoena issued for Meggie and Sam."

"But he won't have a choice," Sarah insisted. "A court order is a court order."

"Not if you are Coleman." Alexa shook her head. "Haven't you learned that by now?"

"He's not above the law," Jim observed.

"But he thinks he is," Sarah said. Alexa was becoming upset, and she needed to step in to calm things down. "Alexa has a point. And, too, the children are only six and five. It is very likely Coleman would lean on Judge Tomlinson to find they aren't old enough to testify."

"You still have to try to get them here," Jim insisted.

"No, I don't. It is not ineffective assistance of counsel to refuse to do something that is impossible."

"But you don't *know* it would be impossible!"

"Wait," Alexa interrupted, looking from one angry face to the other. "I'm the client, and I have the final say in this."

Jim frowned. "We need the children, Alexa. You know the defense desperately needs them as witnesses."

"I can't let you do anything that would hurt them," Alexa said. "They're too young, and they'd be terrified in the courtroom. And they'd see me and not be able to touch me or talk to me, and that would terrify them even more. And if the jury convicted me, they'd blame themselves for the rest of their lives. No, Jim. I don't want anyone to involve Meggie or Sam as witnesses."

Jim looked over at Sarah, who sat ashen-faced on the couch, lost in thought. He wondered if she'd even heard what Alexa said.

But she had. "We're two weeks from trial. We have to go with Jordan."

"That's worse than no defense." Jim kept his eyes on Alexa, whose expression of calm determination never changed.

"Even if it is," Alexa spoke in a quiet, steady voice that twisted his heart with admiration for her courage, "it's all we've got." Sarah's phone buzzed, and she pulled it out of her purse and read the text message. Then she stood up abruptly, obviously relieved to have an excuse to escape. "Tom wants to meet at Trend for a drink. Don't worry, Alexa. Jordan can win this for us."

Seething, Jim got up, too. "I'll walk you out. I'll be back, Alexa, to help clean up the kitchen."

Once outside, Sarah hurried toward her car without looking at him. Being ignored made him angry, so he reached around and put his hand on the driver's side door to keep her from opening it

"Let go of the door." Her voice was level, but infuriated.

"In a minute. I want to know why you keep holding out false hope that Jordan can win this for us."

She spoke in an exasperated parent voice. "Because she can."

"You don't believe that!" He told himself to regain control and let her leave before he did or said something he shouldn't.

She leaned against the car, her face sharply outlined by the bright light of a full moon. She looked up at him, and studied his face in the silver light. "I'm not sure what I believe, anymore.

"We need Meggie and Sam!"

"Alexa says no."

"Then we need that police report and that call girl!"

"What we really need is a miracle." She reached for the door handle, and he withdrew his hand. He watched her get in and drive away before he went back into the house.

* * *

Alexa sat on the couch alone with the last glass of wine from the bottle Jim had opened for the three of them at dinner. He had left at eleven, after they had cleaned up the kitchen following Sarah's exit. Dinner, Jim, kitchen cleanup. It had become an almost daily ritual that she clung to like a tiny island of peace in the ocean of fear and unpredictability that her life had become. She sipped the last of the cabernet and closed her eyes, listening to the stillness. She could pretend Meggie and Sam were sleeping in their bedroom, and in the morning they'd be up at seven and ready for the usual school-day ritual. Breakfast, backpacks, sweaters, and lunch money, then fastening seat belts for the ride to kindergarten and preschool. She imagined a quiet morning with the sunlight dappling the worn carpet while she sat here in the living room working on her laptop on a project for Alan. She'd have until eleven when she'd have to be at preschool to pick up Sam. Then lunch here at home and a nap for him while she worked a few hours more before going to fetch Meggie. She had never taken that life for granted, but it seemed doubly precious now that it was lost.

She had not asked many questions about Jim and Sarah's visit with her children. The details would have been too painful to hear. And she had hated listening to them argue about whether Meggie and Sam should be called to testify. As their mother, she had to put their well being first. And being witnesses in their mother's murder trial was not putting them first.

It wasn't surprising that Michael had kept a key to her car or had taken her gun. Nothing in her life had been safe from him or truly hers from the moment she'd married him. The control he'd exercised over her during their marriage had been more bearable than the control the court had given him over her and the children through the divorce.

Jim. His kind voice and gentle smile floated in the darkness behind her eyes. She looked forward to the evenings they spent together. Going back to jail held many horrors, not the least of which was never sitting here on the sofa with him again, listening to him talk about Cody and how much he missed his boy. Alexa tried to reconcile herself to what she knew was inevitable. The best Sarah could do would be to convince the jury she killed Michael and Brigman in a blinding moment of post traumatic stress, and she would go to prison. Even with a manslaughter verdict, Meggie and Sam would be grown up by the time she was released.

But more likely the jury would believe she murdered Michael and Ronald Brigman. Her blood ran cold at the thought. Still, the state couldn't execute her for as much as twenty years; and she was, after all, an exceptional attorney. She could work from prison to try to clear her name, and there were Innocence Projects at a number of law schools that might be interested in helping a former clerk to a United States Supreme Court justice. She tried to make herself believe all was not lost and maybe she could make another life for herself some day, maybe even with someone like Jim. But nothing could change the fact that Meggie and Sam would grow up without her.

TRIAL

CHAPTER THIRTY-TWO

Second Sunday in December, 2013, La Jolla Shores

At midnight, Sarah sat in her living room, drinking a good bottle of red zinfandel and going over her notes. Tomorrow was the first day of Alexa's trial. They would begin jury selection in the morning. Because it involved the death penalty, it would take weeks to pick a jury.

"I never wanted this case," she reminded the Universe aloud as if breaking the silence would relieve her of the responsibility for Alexa's life that overwhelmed her.

"No, but it's yours." The voice was unrelenting.

"Why me?"

"You know why. I've told you before. It's your only chance at redemption."

"Then why drag me into this mess and give me nothing to work with? I could win if I had a defense."

"I gave you Jim Mitchell."

Sarah closed her eyes and tried to get the voice out of her head. As if on cue, her phone began to ring. "Hello?"

"Sarah, it's Jim. I'm outside. I didn't want to knock without warning you it was me. We need to talk."

* * *

He hurried into the living room and looked for a place to put down a folder he was carrying. Sarah had covered every open spot with the juror questionnaires she was studying.

Jim frowned and laid his papers on top of the littered coffee table. He was wearing jeans and a gray hooded sweatshirt, and Sarah wondered if he'd just come from making a late supper for himself and Alexa. She willed her jealousy demon to be still.

"I thought you might have company," he said.

"Company as in trial preparation," Sarah gestured toward the papers as she poured some wine into the glass she had brought back from the kitchen for him.

"Thanks."

"How is Alexa?"

"You should call her and ask."

"Haven't you been by tonight?"

He shook his head. "She wanted to be alone. She said it would help her get ready for tomorrow."

"Is leaving her alone a good idea?"

"She doesn't need to be on suicide watch, if that's what you mean. She just said she wanted some time by herself."

Sarah watched his eyes as he talked about Alexa; his feelings were obvious.

"She's very brave," Sarah observed. "She knows we don't have much going for us."

Suddenly Jim brightened up. "But I think that's all changed as of tonight! I found something in Michael Reed's credit card statements."

"What do you mean?"

He tossed back half his glass of wine excitedly and opened the folder he'd brought.

"Come sit here beside me, and I'll show you."

Sarah left the chair opposite and took the place next to him on the sofa, willing herself not to be dazzled by his proximity. "Okay, what have you found?"

"Look at this charge on June 2."

"Elite Call Girls, one thousand dollars."

"Don't you see? The 'girlfriend' the children described was someone from this escort service!"

"But I thought Meggie said he paid his girlfriends directly in cash."

"He did. The thousand is the fee the service charged for setting up the date. Then the girlfriends pay a percentage of their individual take to Maria Chavez, the owner, who calls herself the 'Executive Director.'"

"How do you know?"

He frowned. "Oldest investigative technique in the world. I called and posed as a potential client."

"But how are you going to get the name of the girl who was with Michael? You know agencies won't reveal names because they don't want their employees prosecuted."

"I persuaded the 'Executive Director' to meet with me at a coffee shop near my place on Saturday morning. She obviously operates out of her house and doesn't want me to know where she lives. I'm going to tell her I won't make any trouble for her if she gives me the name of Michael's 'date' on June 2."

"I'm still not sure why you came over after midnight to tell me all this. You know as well as I do, you may not get the name of this girl."

"I came because I wanted you to know we're going to have a case after all, and because you'll need to ask for a continuance tomorrow."

"But Judge Tomlinson is not going to continue this trial."

"What do you mean?" He spoke sharply.

"I mean exactly that. He warned us when he put Alexa on house arrest. He wants all of this to be over." Her finger spun faster and faster over the scar on her cheek as she spoke.

"Why do you do that?"

"Do what?"

"Show off your scar that way."

"I don't understand."

"When you're upset, you play with the scar with your finger. And you keep your hair short to make sure everyone notices it. Hasn't your boyfriend told you a plastic surgeon could erase all that in a few hours?"

"Tom Barrett isn't my boyfriend!"

"Isn't he?"

"My social life is none of your business."

"You haven't answered my question. Why?"

"Why what?"

"Show off that scar?"

"Because it's *mine*!" Sarah drained her wine glass and set it next to his on the coffee table. "And I want you to leave!"

"Fine. I want to go. But you have to promise you'll get a continuance tomorrow."

"No. I won't. Even if I asked for it—and I'm not going to—the request wouldn't be granted. Now please, leave!"

Why did I say that, Sarah asked herself. She felt tears well up, and she fought them back hard.

"Why are you about to cry?"

"I'm not. I never cry."

"Then you need to."

"You have no right to say that!"

He caught her lightly by the left wrist so that she had to turn and face him on the sofa. She felt as if the bottom were dropping out of her stomach, and her heart was racing.

"Yes, I do." He spoke each word, slowly and deliberately like an insult.

She glared at him. "Let me go."

"Okay." He pulled his hand away. "But I have a right to say that you can't hold in grief forever."

"And what would you know about that?" she demanded.

"Enough," he said. "Enough."

* * *

Jim spent the week watching Sarah and Preston Barton argue over prospective jurors while he did his best to provide support for Alexa. At ten on Saturday morning, he pulled on jeans and his gray hooded sweatshirt and walked the few blocks from his house to Café Aroma on Cass Street. The sun was lingering behind the morning-gray clouds, and the ocean-scented breeze was cool and sharp against his cheeks.

He chose a table as far from the others as possible but with a view of the door, so he could see Maria Chavez when she arrived. If she arrived. He ordered a café Americano and a scrambled egg sandwich, then settled back to wait. The soft yellow walls warmed up the cool gray sun streaming in through the deep blue curtains that framed the plate glass windows.

Fifteen minutes past ten. Then twenty minutes. As the time ticked away, Jim's heart sank second by second. He could make trouble for her if she didn't show, but the trouble he could make would involve the police and then he would never get the information he needed.

Finally at ten thirty-five, just as he'd finished his sandwich and was about to pay the bill, the door opened and a five-foot-six blonde in an expensive brown leather jacket and skin tight jeans and boots with six-inch heels walked in. She was carrying an oversized black leather purse, and Jim could see the corner of a black notebook protruding. Maria Chavez had promised to bring her records, and she appeared to have kept that promise.

Jim stood up, and she walked over to his table.

"Mr. Mitchell?"

He nodded.

The woman offered her beautifully manicured hand for him to shake. "Maria."

As she drew up a chair and ordered a latte, Jim studied her face. She had a slightly square jaw, making her look formidable, but her large brown eyes softened her otherwise unsympathetic face. He guessed she'd been in the United States for sometime because she had only a faint trace of a Mexican accent left. She was wearing a light, floral perfume that must be very expensive, but he didn't like it as well as Sarah's gardenia scent.

"Sorry to be late. It is a weekend, and I have many dates to arrange this morning. Remind me again. You are not police, but you used to be?"

"Former FBI agent. Now a private investigator."

"But you have connections that will shut me down, if I don't cooperate?"

"I would hate to do that. I'd far rather have the name of the call girl who was with Michael Reed on the night of June 2 this year."

Maria took a sip of her latte and made a face. Jim wondered if she was reacting to the coffee or his threat or both. "I have a policy not to give out my girl's names."

"But Alexa Reed's life depends on my contacting your girl— as I explained."

Maria sipped her coffee and shrugged. "Too bad for her. Maybe she killed the ex. You say he was a bad man. And even if I give you her name, she may not help you. In fact, I doubt she will. I can't force her to talk. You know that."

"I do."

"So all I have to do is give you the name, right? You won't report me to the cops if she refuses to see you?"

"As long as you don't influence her not to cooperate."

Maria waved her hand impatiently. "I have no reason to do that. Talking to you is up to her."

"Then give me her name."

"Elaina Morales. Michael Reed liked her quite a bit. He regularly asked for her."

"What did she think of him?"

"Elaina never gets involved with clients. She does her job and goes home. Like you, I bet." She gave him a flirtatious grin that he immediately decided to ignore.

"And where can I find Elaina?"

"She lives in Tijuana. She works for me on both sides of the border. I've brought you a phone number." Maria handed him her business card with a phone number written on the back.

"How about a picture?"

"I thought you'd ask, so I brought the book." Maria took the large black notebook out of her bag and turned to a pre-marked page. "This is Elaina." She was pointing to the pictures in the top row as she handed the book to him.

Without realizing it, Jim sucked in his breath audibly.

"Beautiful, isn't she?" Maria gave him a conspiratorial smile. "You can see why Michael Reed called her for many dates."

Jim studied the row of photographs as he imagined how often Maria met men in coffee shops to let them choose a "date." In the first picture, Elaina was wearing a bright red dress that highlighted her well endowed cleavage. In the second, a white bikini set off her creamy, caramel skin. Finally in the third, Elaina sat on the edge of a swimming pool, her back to the camera, looking flirtatiously over her shoulder, wearing nothing at all. The last photo highlighted her large dark eyes, provocative smile, and masses of thick dark curls cascading around her shoulders.

Jim closed the book firmly and handed it back. "I need an address, too."

Maria frowned. "That I don't have. It's too dangerous for my girls if I ever get raided. I have only phone numbers."

"But if I call, she might not answer."

"True, but I'm afraid that's a risk you are going to have to take." Maria took her last sip of coffee and grew thoughtful. "Tell me something, Mr. Mitchell."

"Okay."

"Do you like me?"

"Like you?"

"Do you find me attractive? I ask because sometimes for very especial clients, I am the escort for the evening. Would you be interested?"

"I couldn't afford you."

Maria leaned over and placed one slender, beautifully manicured hand on his arm. "For especial clients, I offer especial discount."

"Even with that, I'm sure you're out of my price range. I still need a physical address for Elaina Morales."

Maria leaned away, obviously disappointed. "Tell you what, I'll check her schedule and text you the address of her next appointment on this side of the border. And I'll let her know who you are and why you need to see her. How's that?"

"Thanks."

Maria leaned back and studied him for a few seconds. Then she said, "What about a date with me—no charge? I've fallen in love with your eyes."

Jim was caught off guard and realized he must look as uncomfortable as he felt. "I'm sorry, Miss Chavez–"

"No, it's ok. You have the air of a man who has a great love in his life with someone whose soul connects to your soul. You are very lucky, Mr. Jim Mitchell, to find someone so especial. I wish I had been that one. But I am not; so now, I must go. I feel that you are a man of your word and that I can trust you. Good luck with Elaina. I bet she, too, will fall in love with your eyes."

CHAPTER THIRTY-THREE

Third Sunday in December, 2013, La Jolla Shores

By Sunday night, Sarah was a ball of frayed nerves. Jim had been scrupulously polite to her in court all week, but it was obvious their relationship was strained. His failure to call her to report the outcome of his meeting with the director of Elite Call Girls was a clear sign they were seriously at odds. It also didn't help that she felt overwhelmingly guilty about having to rely on Jordan Stewart and Battered Women's Syndrome as Alexa's defense.

She allowed herself only two glasses of wine that night, knowing she couldn't be dealing with the effects of a hangover in the morning. At midnight, she was finishing the second and trying to concentrate on a boring late-night movie, when her phone finally rang. She switched off the television and grabbed the receiver, relieved Jim had finally called.

Only he hadn't.

"Good evening, Ms. Knight." Coleman Reed had obviously been drinking. "Thought I'd see how jury selection is going for the defense."

"I have nothing to say to you, Justice Reed. You should not be making these calls."

Coleman Reed laughed so loudly Sarah had to hold the phone away from her ear.

"Don't like to hear from me, huh? That means you are worried about tomorrow."

"I'm always well-prepared. You know that, Justice Reed. I've been in your courtroom."

"That you have. But up until now, you've always had a case to prepare."

"We have a case for Alexa." Sarah kept her voice emotionless and even. She felt like an old West gunslinger staring down her opponent at high noon.

He laughed again. "Jordan Stewart is your case. I read your file."

"I'm not going to discuss this with you."

"Fine. I didn't call for a discussion. I called to offer you one last chance to save your career. I'll up my offer to twenty million in an off-shore account and partnership at Warrick, Thompson, if you'll make sure you don't win this one. It's too late for you to withdraw as counsel, but you can do the minimum and put Alexa on death row where she belongs."

"Why throw your money away? According to you, we have no defense."

"If it were anyone but you, Ms. Knight, I wouldn't be worried. But you've been known to do miracles in a courtroom."

"I'm not accepting any bribes, Justice Reed."

"It's not a bribe," his drunken voice mocked her. "It's a fee for a legal service rendered. All lawyers charge fees, Ms. Knight. You know that."

"Not for selling out their clients, Justice Reed. You know that."

"Alexa is a dead woman no matter what you do. Make a few bucks for yourself. Get your face fixed."

Sarah stiffened. "This conversation is over."

"Not until I tell you one more thing: Mr. Barton is going to have a big surprise for you in the morning. He's not the sharpest tool in the shed. No way he's in your league as a lawyer. But he's teachable. I've explained some things to him. Good luck, tomorrow. You've just turned down the best and last offer of your career. When this case is over, you'll be lucky to get appointed to misdemeanor cases in juvie court. Your office will be a box at Postal Annex."

* * *

"Your Honor, I have an objection to one of the defense witnesses on Ms. Knight's list."

They had just returned from lunch next day. The morning had been spent with more wrangling over which jurors should be selected for trial. They were spending the afternoon arguing over the admissibility of evidence. Sarah noticed that Judge Tomlinson consistently ruled in Preston Barton's favor.

Although Jim had voted for what he called "the mommy look," Sarah and Alexa had decided Alexa should wear a suit at trial so that she would look like the former United States Supreme Court clerk that she was. Sarah was relieved her client's color had finally come back; and she looked beautiful that day in her white silk blouse and charcoal gray skirt and jacket. She was sitting between Sarah and Jim at the defense table, and out of the corner of her eye, Sarah saw her tense up when Preston Barton spoke.

"And which witness does the prosecution have a problem with?" Judge Tomlinson asked.

"Dr. Jordan Stewart."

Judge Tomlinson scanned the witness list he was holding. "Oh, here she is. She's an expert on Battered Women's Syndrome. So what is your objection, Mr. Barton? Her resume shows she's well qualified to testify on the subject."

"I'm objecting on the grounds of collateral estoppel, Your Honor. Whether Michael Reed abused his wife was fully litigated in the Reed divorce, and Dr. Brigman determined Mrs. Reed was lying about being abused by her husband. That finding is binding on Mrs. Reed. She can't turn around and claim all over again she's a battered woman when Ronald Brigman already investigated her claim and found she's lying."

Judge Tomlinson looked over his half-glasses at Sarah. "Let me hear your response, Ms. Knight."

So this was Coleman Reed's big surprise. She should be able to dispose of it quickly because Preston Barton had the rule of collateral estoppel all wrong. She stood up and moved toward the podium. Although Preston Barton had spoken from the fortress of the prosecution's table, she wanted to be closer to the judge. She had opted for her serious black Marc Jacobs suit today. Tomorrow she would break out the jewel-toned outfits. Changing colors daily with a large accessory like a lapel pin or a bold necklace always garnered positive juror attention.

"Your Honor, my short response is the rule does not apply in this case."

"And how is that?" He leaned back in his chair and studied her thoughtfully.

"Because for collateral estoppel to apply, the parties have to be identical in both court actions."

"And you're saying they're not?" The judge leaned his fist on his hand and studied her.

"Of course they aren't. In the divorce, the plaintiff was Michael Reed, and the respondent was my client. In this trial, the State of California is the plaintiff, and my client is the defendant. The parties aren't the same, and if they aren't the same, the rule doesn't apply. Mrs. Reed has every right to present evidence Michael Reed battered her as part of her defense to the murder charges."

"Your Honor!" Preston Barton practically leapt up from the prosecution's table and shoved Sarah away from the podium. "The state wants to be heard!"

"That's fine, Mr. Barton." The quiet tone of his voice showed Judge Tomlinson was unmoved by the prosecutor's urgency. "What do you have to say?"

"Your Honor, the issue of domestic violence has already been litigated between the parties. The state objects to giving Mrs. Reed another chance to claim she was abused by calling Jordan Stewart."

Judge Tomlinson looked over at Sarah, who was now standing at the defense table.

"Anything more you'd like to add, Ms. Knight?"

"Ronald Brigman's report which concludes there was no abuse is inadmissable because it is all hearsay. And I can't call Dr. Brigman as a witness and cross-examine him on his conclusions to demonstrate to the jury they are false."

"Your Honor!" The prosecutor's face was red with indignation. "Dr. Brigman is not available because the defendant killed him. She shouldn't be able to profit by her own wrongdoing and get a second chance to make false claims against her ex-husband. Dr. Brigman's conclusion that there was no abuse in the marriage is binding on Mrs. Reed."

"And what is your response?" Judge Tomlinson turned to Sarah, who was still standing.

"My client hasn't been convicted of murdering anyone. Mr. Barton's argument destroys the presumption of innocence guaranteed by the federal constitution. Collateral estoppel cannot keep Jordan Steward from testifying because it doesn't apply, and the Sixth Amendment says Mrs. Reed has a right to call witnesses in her defense."

"Okay, I hear you, Ms. Knight. But I'm going to rule in Mr. Barton's favor. I do believe all the ink that was spilled in the divorce over abuse and the finding it never happened bars evidence of Battered Women's Syndrome in this trial. And Mrs. Reed's Sixth Amendment rights are not being violated because you are quite welcome to call Dr. Stewart on other issues, if you like."

Sarah felt as if she'd been dealt a heavy blow to the chest, but she was determined not to let Preston Barton see her reaction. He'd report it to Coleman Reed, who'd be laughing over his manipulation of a legal rule that didn't apply. She said, "Thank you, Your Honor," and sat down, keeping her eyes on her yellow pad, so she wouldn't have to look at either Jim or Alexa. She hoped they didn't notice how hard her hands were shaking. And she was still furious with Jim for not filling her in on his investigation into Michael's call girl, whom they needed now more than ever.

* * *

"Now you have to ask for a continuance," Jim said as they walked to their cars that afternoon. "We don't have a defense."

"I thought you were going to bring me Michael's call girl and give us one. You never reported the outcome of your meeting with the Executive Director of Elite Call Girls."

Sarah spoke sharply, and Alexa looked at both of them anxiously. *I'm being unprofessional to let her see us fighting*, Sarah thought. *But maybe I'm too angry to care right now.* Her normally cool brain had been in a blind panic all afternoon.

"I have to take Alexa home," Jim said tersely.

"Then I'll meet the two of you at the cottage in an hour, so we can talk about what to do."

* * *

Sarah stood in the drive outside the cottage under the pines in the damp, ocean-scented darkness and prepared to face Alexa and Jim. The moon was yet to rise, so the only spear of light came from the porch light that she assumed Alexa had turned on for her. I've blown this case, Sarah thought; and I don't deserve even this small incandescent greeting from a woman whose life is on the line.

She knocked, and Jim opened the door. He was wearing jeans and the gray hooded sweatshirt. She was immediately overwhelmed by the clean scent of his soap and the faint hint of starch that clung to him even when he wasn't wearing a dress shirt. But she could see Alexa standing behind him, also now in jeans and the blue sweater that highlighted her lovely eyes

"Come in," he said. "Alexa has poured some wine, and I've ordered pizza. No one felt like cooking." He sounded tense and formal.

And I don't feel like eating, Sarah thought as she settled on Alexa's sad little sofa with a glass of cabernet and ignored the open pizza box on the coffee table.

"You didn't see this coming, did you?" Alexa asked, as she curled herself in the chair opposite with her own glass of wine. Alexa didn't feel like eating either. She'd taken a few bites of pizza and left the rest untouched.

"No, I didn't because you know as well as I do collateral estoppel doesn't apply here. That's first year civil procedure. Judge Tomlinson should have known better. And I think he does."

"Coleman is responsible for this," Alexa said.

Sarah nodded. "He called me late last night to gloat over 'a surprise' that he was putting Preston Barton up to."

"But why is he bothering to get Jordan excluded?" Jim frowned as he ate. He was the only one with an appetite. "I thought he said you didn't have a defense if you relied on her testimony."

"I don't think Coleman prompted Preston Barton to exclude Jordan because he thought she'd win this case," Alexa observed quietly. "I think it's because Coleman doesn't want the world to hear the truth about Michael."

"You're right," Sarah agreed. She turned to Jim. "You haven't given me any information about your meeting with the 'Executive Director' of Elite Call Girls." Sarah knew she sounded angry, but she didn't care.

"Maria Chavez and I met. She gave me Elaina Morales' phone number, but she either did not have Elaina's address in Tijuana, or she had it and wouldn't hand it over. She volunteered to text me the address of Elaina's next job on this side of the border, but so far no text. Having Jordan excluded as a witness isn't the only reason we have to ask for a continuance," Jim insisted. "I need time to find Elaina."

"You probably aren't going to find her," Sarah said. "After all, you've been looking for months, and you haven't found Alexa's old nanny."

"This is different. Maria said Elaina comes to San Diego several time a week for 'dates.' I'll find her."

"But so far she hasn't given you any help, and Coleman Reed doesn't want her found. And above all, you have no idea what she'll say when you do find her, or if she'll even talk to you. I can't ask for a continuance. It would be futile, and it would make Judge Tomlinson angry."

"What about doing a writ of mandate?" Alexa spoke up. "You could ask the court of appeal to order the trial court to allow Jordan's testimony."

Sarah nodded. "That's what I was thinking on my way over here."

"But we're in the middle of jury selection. Who has time to write a writ?" Jim frowned.

"I do," Alexa said. "I thought about it all afternoon. Appellate lawyers specialize in writs, and I'm really, really good at them. I can get started right now."

Sarah looked over at the beautiful, soft face of Alexa Reed and saw hope renewed in her lovely eyes. She was ready to do battle again, as she had once done for her children in family court. Only this time, she was ready to write and research and put her very competent legal work on the line to save her own life. A huge wave of emotion swept over Sarah as she studied her client's face, now set in fierce determination. She could see why Jim found it impossible not to love Alexa Reed.

* * *

Alexa banished Jim and Sarah into the cool dark, so she could go to work. Jim followed Sarah to her car.

"I'm sorry I didn't call you with a report on my meeting with Maria."

"You should have."

"You're right, and I was wrong. But please change your mind and ask for a continuance tomorrow."

"No. Alexa is right. A writ is our only option."

And she got in and drove away without looking back.

CHAPTER THIRTY-FOUR

Third Friday in December 2013, The Court of Appeal, San Diego

On Friday at noon, Sarah was summoned to the chambers of The Honorable Richard Elliott Wilmont, III, Presiding Justice of the Court of Appeal. His law clerk showed her into the justice's office on the fourth floor of Symphony Towers.

"His Honor is in a meeting in the main conference room, but he asked me to offer you coffee while you wait."

"No thank you."

The atmosphere of the court of appeal was so different from superior court, Sarah reflected as she sat down in one of the two, small, leather Queen Anne wing chairs in front of Justice Wilmont's massive mahogany desk. Instead of the constant patter of pedestrian traffic through the halls, there was only silence. The view from the window was not a parking lot, as in Judge Tomlinson's chambers, but pale blue sky and clouds, and everything was so quiet Sarah felt as if she were drifting along on a cloud, high above the hustle and bustle of the real world.

Instead of stale brew baking on a Mr. Coffee, Justice Wilmont's office smelled faintly of lavender and lemon furniture polish. And unlike Judge Tomlinson's paper-strewn cave, Justice Wilmont's desk was barren, except for Alexa's writ, sitting exactly in the center of its gleaming surface.

Judge Tomlinson had denied Sarah's request for a continuance on Tuesday morning. He'd looked over his half-glasses, as she stood behind the podium and frowned.

"I'm not delaying this trial so that you can go up to the court of appeal." His tone said he was not open to further argument on the topic.

"Thank you, Your Honor." Sarah said the mandatory words to acknowledge the court's ruling and shot Jim an I-told-you-so look as she resumed her place at counsel table. At least by making the gesture she'd always known would be futile, she had gotten Jim off her back.

Alexa had written the writ in the wee hours of Monday and Tuesday nights asking the upper court to order the lower court to withdraw its limitation on Jordan's testimony. Sarah had filed it on Wednesday morning, and at four o'clock on Thursday she'd received the summons to appear at noon the next day.

The door opened, and Sarah stood up as Justice Wilmont came in.

"No, sit down. I'm sorry I was late. I was trying to get you over here during the lunch break in your trial. I figured Charlie Tomlinson denied your request for a continuance."

"He did."

"Sounds about right." Justice Wilmont sat down at his desk and smiled at her. He was only forty-five and had been on the court for just three years. He'd left a very lucrative corporate practice at King and White to go on the bench. According to the rumor mill, he'd taken up the duties of presiding justice because, after eighty-hour work weeks in private practice, he'd been bored by the slow pace of the appellate court. He was the stereotypical aging surfer, fit and tanned with sun-bleached blonde hair. Sarah guessed the impeccable dark suit was left over from his days rubbing shoulders with CEO's of successful biotechs.

"How are things going so far? Have you finished picking a jury yet?"

"No, Your Honor."

He smiled again, and Sarah began to feel as if he might, by some miracle, be on her side. "Takes a while. I heard a rumor Preston has got a jury consultant on this one."

"He has, Your Honor." And Sarah didn't have to guess who was paying for that.

Judge Wilmont shrugged. "I'm not a litigator, but I've never believed those people were worth their fees."

"It's pretty obvious the prosecutor is trying to keep young women around Alexa's age, particularly those with children, off the panel."

"And he didn't need an expensive consultant for that." Justice Wilmont opened the cover of the writ and studied the Table of Contents. As he looked at the document he said, "How are you liking San Diego, Ms. Knight? Do you miss New York and Craig, Lewis? I always enjoyed working with your partners, there. Fine attorneys." He looked up at her as he said the last words and gave her another charming smile.

"Thank you, Your Honor. I'm still getting settled in."

"Right. You've only been here since, what? January?"

"That's correct."

"And this is your first appointment as a member of our trial panel?"

"Yes, it is."

"Hal Remington talked to you about this case when he appointed you, didn't he?"

Sarah began to feel uneasy. "He said quite a few things that day."

Justice Wilmont closed the cover of the writ and fixed his mild green eyes on Sarah as she sat opposite. "So he told you there are some special interests involved?"

"You mean Coleman Reed."

"Have you met Justice Reed, by the way?

"I argued a case before him a few years back. And recently my investigator and I interviewed Alexa's children, who are living with their grandparents in D.C."

"Ah, good. So you understand Coleman is a very–ah–persuasive–personality?"

"I've learned he had quite a reputation here in San Diego before being appointed to the Court."

Justice Wilmont looked down at the writ on his desk and then back at Sarah. "This is quite a fine piece of work, by the way. You must really be Super Woman to write like this at night after working on jury selection in a capital case all day."

"I didn't write it. Alexa did."

He smiled. "She's highly talented. Too bad things have gone the way they have for her."

"Your Honor, the defense needs Jordan Stewart's testimony."

"I don't doubt you do, but the writ panel has denied your request."

Sarah felt her stomach knot. "But, Your Honor, the Sixth Amendment says Alexa has a right to call witnesses on her behalf."

"And no one has said she can't call Dr. Stewart."

"But calling her will be useless if she can't testify about Battered Women's Syndrome."

He shrugged. "Sorry, but your trial tactics are up to you. Judge Tomlinson has not violated your client's Sixth Amendment rights."

"But collateral estoppel doesn't apply here. The parties in the criminal trial are not the same as the ones in the divorce proceeding."

"Right. I know that. And the writ panel didn't deny your request on that ground."

"Then why?"

"Because the application of the collateral estoppel rule is the kind of issue that should be brought up on appeal. It's really not suitable for a writ."

"But—"

He held up his hand. "This isn't oral argument, Ms. Knight, and I didn't make this decision. The three-judge writ panel did."

"Then why did you want to see me?"

He smiled again. "Curiosity in part. I've heard you're quite a force in the courtroom. You've done the unheard of by getting a capital defendant out on house arrest."

"The jail psychiatrist tried to kill her."

"And I've heard that, too. A very unusual case, wouldn't you say?"

"Your Honor, we need Jordan Stewart."

"And you have her. Just not exactly the way you want her. It's nearly one o'clock, and I'm guessing you are going to resume jury selection at 1:30."

"That's right."

"Well, best of luck to you. But remember what Hal Remington said. Don't make yourself unemployable in this town."

* * *

Jim's number lit up her cell at ten that night. She was in bed in her gray silk pajamas with a book she couldn't concentrate on and a glass of wine that wasn't making her sleepy.

"I'm leaving Alexa's," he said "and I want to stop by for a few minutes and talk to you."

And what if I don't want to talk to you, she thought when he knocked ten minutes later. But she let him in and led him into her dark living room, turning on lights as she went. He was still wearing his suit.

"You haven't been home to change."

"No. Alexa and I made dinner together. I wanted to take her mind off having the writ denied. She's blaming herself, saying it wasn't good enough." He sat down on the sofa as he spoke.

"It wasn't her work. It was Coleman again. Justice Wilmont as good as told me that and gave me another warning about trying to win this case. Which is currently impossible to do, of course, without Jordan. Want something to drink?"

"No, thanks. Alexa and I had wine with dinner."

"What are you here to talk about?"

"Well, first I want to say I'm sorry I woke you up."

"I wasn't asleep. In fact, I'm not sure I will sleep tonight. The writ was our only hope."

"Maybe not. Elaina Morales has a 'date' next Monday night here in San Diego. Maria Chavez sent me the details."

"I don't think Elaina's 'date' is going to let you into his hotel room for a little chat with her."

"His name is George Dunn. He's taking her to dinner first at the Neptune in La Jolla. I'm going to try to see her there."

"Well, whoever he is, he's got a lot of cash to throw around."

"Maria only serves high end clients."

"Like Michael Reed."

"Exactly. So what's your plan?"

"Their dinner reservation is at eight. I'll be waiting when they walk in. I'll pretend I know Elaina and see if I can spend a few minutes alone with her."

Sarah shook her head. "I doubt a man who has paid ten thousand dollars to see her alone for the evening is going to cooperate."

"Maybe. But I've got to try."

"All of this doesn't make our current situation any better. We are close to swearing a jury, and I've got to come up with some sort of opening statement. But I don't have anything to say because I have no idea what our defense is going to be without Jordan."

"You don't have to make an opening statement. You can reserve until after the state rests."

"I've never had to do that before. I've always had something to say for my client on the first day of trial. Not making an opening is like admitting I've lost before the trial has even begun."

Jim's soft eyes studied her quietly, and Sarah thought *I wish you'd stay and sleep with me. I'd feel safe enough to sleep if you were here.*

"You need to take better care of yourself. Eat regularly. Drink less."

"Thanks for the advice."

"I'm serious, Sarah. You look as if you're burning up from the inside out."

And maybe I am, she thought. *Maybe I'll be a pile of ashes by morning, and I'll be free of you and Alexa and the torment of this case.*

"I'm ok."

"No, you are definitely not ok." He watched her quietly for a few more moments and then asked, "Do you have any plans for the Christmas recess next Wednesday, Thursday, and Friday?"

"Not at the moment. But that could change."

"You and Tom?" Did his eyes look just a tiny bit hurt or was that her own wishful thinking?

"Possibly. It's more likely I'll be working, trying to figure out some sort of defense. What about you? Is Cody coming?"

"No," Jim shook his head. "He called last week to beg off. He said the trip was too far for a long weekend. And in a way, he's right."

Sarah's heart hurt at the pain in his eyes. She wanted to put her arms around him and say she understood what it was like to miss the people you loved. But he was her investigator, and he was in love with Alexa. And emotional displays were always too risky, thanks to the eternal horror of Joey Menendez.

"So you and Alexa?"

"And you. If you'll come."

"No, I can't."

CHAPTER THIRTY-FIVE

Fourth Monday in December 2014, The Neptune, La Jolla

Jim entered The Neptune's overdone, sea-green palace on Prospect Street the following Monday at seven thirty. He verified George Dunn's reservation at eight by glancing over the shoulder of the attractive twenty-something blonde hostess in the figure-hugging black dress before taking up his lookout spot at the lavish gold bar accented with Poseidon's tridents.

He ordered a scotch and sipped slowly while he watched the white linen tables fill up with couples. It was unusual to see so many men in California out for an evening in sport coats. Maybe spending three hundred dollars for a meal didn't seem appropriate without one. Or maybe it was the proximity to Christmas that made them don more formal attire. The men were all accompanied by women with taut faces and large diamonds either in their ears or on their hands or both. They looked as if they all had extensive plastic surgery and never ate more than a lettuce leaf.

He grew tense as he waited. He'd checked a photographic data base, so he would recognize George Dunn, the forty-six-year old CEO of a successful biotech in San Diego, when he walked in with Elaina. Unfortunately, Mr. Dunn was very married and the father of three children; and Jim was worried about how to approach him, so he wouldn't think Jim was a process server sent by Mrs. Dunn.

Eight o'clock turned into eight fifteen, and then eight thirty. Jim tried to sip his drink slowly, so he wouldn't need to order another to have an excuse to remain at the bar.

He began to worry Mr. Dunn had decided to forgo his evening or had decided appearing in public with a call girl was too dangerous. He didn't want to feel anxious, but he did. He was counting on overcoming the loss of Jordan Stewart with evidence from Elaina Morales. She had to show up tonight. She just had to.

Finally, at nine, George Dunn entered, but with a tall blonde on his arm. Jim wondered if he'd decided to bring his wife, after all. Only one person could tell him what had become of Elaina. He hurried out to his car and was relieved when Maria Chavez answered on the first ring.

"Hallo?"

"It's Jim Mitchell. Your client just entered but with another woman. Elaina isn't here."

"Oh, I am so sorry, Mr. Jim. I forgot to call you back. I had to send Lucia for George. Elaina has gotten a bigger job."

"Bigger job?"

"Yes. Enrique Cervantes has hired her to cruise with him on his yacht for the rest of December and for January. He is a new client, and I am delighted to have him."

"The Enrique Cervantes who owns MexTel?"

"Yes. You know him?"

"Not personally. But I know his cell phone company."

"He is a billionaire. I'm hoping he likes Elaina. For her sake and mine."

"But I need to talk to her, Maria."

"I know. I am so sorry. I would do anything in the world for you. You know that. My offer is still open."

"No, Maria. No, thanks. Just tell me how to reach Elaina. She doesn't answer her phone when I call."

"I do not know why. I told her who you were, and that she should talk to you. That is all I can do."

"Are they already at sea?"

"No. They are flying to Cabo where Enrique keeps his yacht. They are spending Christmas and New Year's there, and then leaving on the cruise."

"Where are they staying?"

"The Esperanza. Why? Are you thinking of going? It's a fabulous resort, but very expensive."

"That doesn't matter. I *have* to speak to Elaina. It's a matter of life and death."

"Really?" Maria sounded skeptical. "Everyone says that, but—"

"But this time it is true. Elaina knows Alexa Reed didn't kill her husband."

"Ah—the beautiful little blonde woman. I have seen her picture in the papers. She does not look like a killer."

"Exactly. I need Elaina's help."

"So what will you do, Mr. Jim?"

"I will go to Cabo tomorrow night after court is over for the day. We have a three-day recess for Christmas."

"And do you want company? I would gladly give you the entire weekend with no charge. And who knows? Maybe you would forget the woman who does not see your heart in your eyes."

"Miss Chavez—"

"Maria, please. If I have to be in love with you, at least call me by my name."

"Maria, then. No. Thank you. I have to go alone."

"But I might be able to persuade Elaina to help you."

"If you can, please phone her. But I have to make this trip alone."

"Godspeed, then, Mr. Jim."

"Just Jim."

"I will say a rosary and light a candle for you, Mr. Jim."

* * *

He drove home cursing the bad luck that had put Enrique Cervantes in Elaina Morale's path. But just as he was turning into his drive, another thought struck him. He hurried into the house and dialed Alan Warrick's home number.

"How is the trial going?" Alan asked.

"Not well. We've lost our star witness. Maybe I should say, our only witness." Jim quickly summarized Preston Barton and his motion.

"Sounds like Coleman paid off Judge Tomlinson. Charlie knows collateral estoppel doesn't apply in this situation," Alan said.

"You are exactly right. It's entirely Coleman's doing. He called Sarah the night before and told her there'd be a 'surprise' the next day."

"Did those credit card records that I sent over help at all?"

"Yes, in a big way. But I've hit a wall in my investigation."

"How so?"

"The records helped me track down a call girl who was at Michael's the night he was killed. She may have seen the murder. The woman who runs the agency was going to set me up with an interview with her tonight. But she got a better offer from Enrique Cervantes–"

"Owner of MexTel and one of Coleman's prize clients." Alan finished for him. "I'm afraid Coleman has gotten the better of you on this one, too."

"But how did he know you'd given me Michael's records?"

"Coleman has moles in all parts of the firm. I wish that weren't true, but it is. I shouldn't have messengered them to you through regular firm channels. I'm sorry."

"Well, at least I know what I'm up against."

"What are you going to do?"

"Maria, the owner of the agency, says they don't actually depart from Cabo on the yacht until after the New Year. The court is dark on Wednesday, Thursday, and Friday for Christmas. I'm going to fly down tomorrow night and see if I can talk to her."

"Preston Barton has subpoenaed me as witness. I'm not looking forward to it. How's Alexa doing?"

"She's very tough. It's as if she's sitting in on someone else's trial. She makes notes all day, marking the issues she thinks will be important on appeal. Then she researches them all night. She's brilliant and methodical. All the years with Michael seem to have given her a super human detachment. I'd say she's coping. It's Sarah I'm worried about."

"Why?"

"She's drinking too much, refusing to eat, and she doesn't sleep. She's doing a great job in the courtroom, but she's deeply upset about something. And she's shut everyone out."

"Well, give Alexa my best. And I wish you success in finding that call girl. If there's anything else I can do, just let me know. And tell Sarah I said to take it easy. No one is going to blame her if the jury goes the wrong way."

* * *

Jim hung up and poured himself a scotch. He stood in front of Cody's pictures and studied his son's face. He wanted him back. He was sick of the divorce court shared-custody fiction that he had to espouse to keep his frail hold on the half-custody he was entitled to. In truth, he didn't want to share Cody with Josh or Gail or with his baby half-sister. Cody was his flesh and blood, and he wanted Cody all to himself. No more sharing. No more cancelled holidays. No more coming home to a cold, empty house at the end of the day. He wanted to help with homework and go to parent/teacher conferences and organize science projects. Jim drank a large swallow of scotch and said out loud, "I want my son back! Damn it, I want Cody back!"

And then he laughed at himself. Who was he to want his son back when he wouldn't even have been able to spend the holiday with him if he had come to San Diego for Christmas? *You're still obsessed with your work, he condemned himself. You still don't have a life of your own.* He thought of Maria and her offer and wondered if he should reconsider.

And then his phone rang.

"Jim, it's Sarah."

"You haven't been answering your phone. I've been trying to reach you all weekend."

"I turned it off. I've been trying to put a defense together."

"I just talked to Alan Warrick. He said to tell you no one is going to blame you if the jury goes the wrong way."

"I'll blame me." Her tone told him to leave that one alone. "Why were you talking to Alan?"

"The call girl didn't show tonight. I found out she's been hired to go on a cruise with Enrique Cervantes, who owns MexTel. I called Alan to confirm my hunch that MexTel is one of Coleman's pet clients."

"So Coleman has made her unavailable?" She sounded as exasperated as he felt.

"I'm going to fly to Cabo tomorrow night after court and try to talk to her. They don't start their cruise until after New Year's. Maria said they are at the Esperanza resort."

"That's fabulously expensive."

"Don't worry. I'm happy to dip into my old man's millions to cover it. If Coleman is buying this girl off, it's a good bet she hasn't got anything to say that the prosecutor wants the jury to hear. I'm going to come back with a defense, Sarah. I promise."

CHAPTER THIRTY-SIX

Christmas Day, 2013, Cabo San Lucas

On Christmas morning, Jim finished his breakfast on the terrace at the Esperanza around ten o'clock, and stared out at the resort's tranquil azure pools with the deeper blue of the Sea of Cortez just beyond. Maria had instructed him to wait for Elaina here. She could not give him an exact time when she would appear because she had to slip out after Enrique left for his golf game, and no one knew exactly when that would happen. But Jim didn't mind the wait. The serenity of the luxury resort was a stark contrast to the last two weeks he'd just spent in the gray, grimy halls of superior court.

He glanced at his watch. Ten thirty and no sign of Elaina. But Maria had promised him this meeting. His stomach tightened as he resolved to wait it out.

Suddenly Jim heard the sound of a woman's high heels clicking on tile. He looked up and saw Elaina Morales approaching. She was breathtaking in person. Five eight, masses of long dark curls, big soft brown eyes. In addition to a pair of sky-high heels, she was wearing a white bikini under a white robe that she hadn't bothered to tie. It was impossible for him not to react to her perfect caramel body in nearly full view.

He got up and went to meet her. "Jim Mitchell." He held out his hand.

"Elaina," she gave his fingertips a brief brush.

"Please sit down over here." He led her to the table where the remains of his breakfast had just been cleared away. "Do you want some coffee?"

"A margarita. Extra salt." She tossed her order at the waiter with the confidence of a beautiful woman whose every whim would be satisfied.

"More coffee for me," Jim told the departing waiter. He felt Elaina's eyes on him, and he shifted uncomfortably in his chair.

"What's wrong?" she asked playfully. "Don't you like being stared at?"

"Not especially."

"But you are a beautiful man as I am a beautiful woman. The world stares at beautiful people."

"At you, perhaps but–"

"No, at you as well. Why does that make you uncomfortable?"

"I don't know."

"Maria said you were a deep one. I was not going to meet with you, but she said I must."

Their drinks appeared, and Jim watched Elaina take a long sip of margarita. Her big brown eyes met his, mockingly. "What, you don't approve this early in the morning?"

"You don't need my approval."

"True, but I would like to have it. Maria said you were a beautiful man with kind eyes. And she said she had fallen in love with your eyes. And now I have, too. "

"So why are you drinking margaritas this early in the morning?"

"Because I have a long day ahead, pleasing a rich, whimsical man. I am good at my job, but it wears me down. And you, Mr. Jim? Are you good at your job, and does it wear you down?"

"Yes, to both."

"Maria said she offered to come here with you for free. This is a beautiful place, is it not? And Maria is very skilled at her job."

"I've no doubt. But I'm not looking for that."

"What are you looking for then?" She sipped her drink and batted her impossibly long eyelashes at him.

"I want to know what you heard and saw on the last night you were hired for a 'date' with Michael Reed. Did you see his murder?"

Elaina leaned back in her chair and stretched out her perfect legs, clearly putting them on display. "I cannot talk about that night."

"Of course you can. Alexa Reed didn't kill Michael, and you might be the only person in the world who can prove that."

"Maybe yes, maybe, no. But I cannot talk about what happened that night."

"But you were there. Of course you can tell me what you saw."

"I cannot." Her lovely face became very grave. She tossed back the last of her drink and signaled the hovering waiter for another.

"Didn't Maria tell you how important this information is?"

"Of course. She said you are trying to save the woman you love. She said you had a great love in your life. And she wished she had been that one. And now I wish it had been me. But, alas, no. You are embarrassed, but you should not be."

"Please, Elaina. Tell me what happened that night."

"I cannot."

"Why?"

"Michael's father has paid me fifty thousand dollars to remain silent. And he has arranged my cruise with Enrique for even more. I've dreamed of making this kind of money my whole life. I am not going to go back on my word. Even for you and your beautiful eyes."

"I can pay you more."

"No."

"I can. My father left me millions. I can top anything Coleman Reed offered. And you wouldn't have to go on any more 'dates' with Enrique."

Elaina reached for her second margarita as soon as it arrived. She took a long drink before she set the glass on the table and smiled at him. "No. Coleman Reed will have me killed if I take your offer. I support my mother and my orphaned nephews in Tijuana. What you are saying is too dangerous."

"Won't you even tell me off the record what happened?"

"I did what Maria asked. I met with you. And now I must go."

"Please."

357

"No."

"A life is at stake."

"My life is at stake. Goodbye, Mr. Jim."

CHAPTER THIRTY-SEVEN

First Monday in January 2014, San Diego County Courthouse

They swore the jury to try Alexa's case just after lunch on the first Monday in January. Jim didn't like the look of the jurors. Of the twelve, eight were white, middle-aged men who would readily identify with Ronald Brigman. The other four were female. Two were retired elementary school teachers, who might or might not sympathize with Alexa. One was a childless, African-American accountant in her mid-thirties, who frowned at everyone a great deal. The remaining juror was a small Asian woman in her late forties who helped run the family dry cleaning business. Listening to her responses during voir dire made Jim wonder how much English she actually understood. Sarah had tried to excuse her for cause and then had run out of peremptory challenges and now was stuck with her on the panel. Jim guessed she would be easily swayed by the authority of the middle-aged males.

The four alternate jurors were not much better. Three were middle-aged men, like the bulk of the jury, and one was a retired emergency room nurse. Maybe she, at least, had treated battered women in the ER, and therefore would have some feeling for what Alexa had been through. But none of them looked kindly at the three occupants of the defense table, and Jim knew they were in for a rocky ride.

As soon as the jurors were sworn and seated, the court turned the floor over to Preston Barton for his opening statement. For thirty minutes he recited the litany of evidence they had been struggling uphill against since their first day on the case, and then he went in for the kill.

"And so ladies and gentlemen, in summary, the evidence will show Alexa Reed is a liar who became a killer on the night of June 2, 2013. Driven by his wife's instability, Michael Reed filed for divorce to protect his young children, Meggie and Sam. Alexa responded by lying repeatedly to the family law judge, claiming her husband abused her. Even when one of the most highly esteemed psychologists in San Diego, Ronald Brigman, caught on to her game and told the family court Michael had never laid a hand on his wife, Alexa Reed kept scheming to get full custody of her children.

"She is one of the most highly trained lawyers in the country. She worked for a United States Supreme Court justice. Yet instead of doing an honest day's work like all of you, she turned her considerable legal talent to bilking Michael Reed out of child support to make sure she never had to work another day in her life.

"But Ronald Brigman caught on to her scheming and transferred custody of the children to Michael, ending her financial gravy train. And that is when Alexa Reed lost it, ladies and gentlemen. She lost it so badly that on the night of June 2, 2013, she drove to Ronald Brigman's with her Glock .9 and put five bullets into him and then drove to Michael Reed's and murdered the father of her children, knowing full well that those very young children were in the house and would be terrified when they heard the gunshots. The evidence will show that Alexa Reed is a scheming opportunist and a cold-blooded killer. In fact, she is such a cold-blooded killer, she stood over Michael Reed's dead body and called 911, disclaiming any knowledge of what she'd done. After you've heard the evidence, ladies and gentlemen, I believe you will easily reach verdicts of first degree murder for the tragic and senseless deaths of Michael Reed and Ronald Brigman at the hands of Alexa Reed."

Preston Barton threw the defense table an unmistakable smirk as he sat down. Jim was glad his remarks weren't on camera. Judge Tomlinson had refused television's request to tape the proceedings because, as Sarah argued, there was no way to guarantee Meggie and Sam wouldn't see some portion of them. But Jim knew the multiple reporters present had taken down every word, and the talking heads would be quoting all the lurid details on the five o'clock news.

Sarah, in her magnificent deep purple suit with the sunny starburst pin on her left shoulder radiating an optimism Jim knew none of them felt, stood up. "Your Honor, I am requesting a brief sidebar."

"Very well, Ms. Knight. Our jurors have been sitting for quite sometime. Why don't we give them a break?"

Jim watched the jurors give the defense table curious looks as they left the courtroom. They already think we've got something to hide, he thought; and his heart sank.

"All right, Ms. Knight. Now that the jurors are out of earshot, what do you want to talk about?

"I'm moving for a mistrial based upon prosecutorial misconduct." Sarah's voice was low and steady and emotionless.

Preston Barton jumped up from his seat at the prosecution's table. "Your Honor!"

Judge Tomlinson held up his hand. "Wait, wait, Mr. Barton. I haven't heard everything Ms. Knight has to say."

"I think it is very clear, Your Honor, that Mr. Barton did not confine his remarks to what he believes the evidence is going to show. He engaged in argument when he vouched for Ronald Brigman's expertise, accused my client of 'scheming,' and called her an 'opportunist.' There is no way the prejudice from this can be undone. My client cannot get a fair trial. I'm moving for a mistrial."

Judge Tomlinson had that look Jim had come to recognize when he was torn between knowing Sarah was right and what would happen if he ruled in her favor. He could almost picture Coleman Reed's hand in the judge's pocket.

"Your Honor!" Preston Barton was dancing up and down at his table, turning red.

"Mr. Barton, be quiet. I've just listened to you for a very long time. Ms. Knight has a point. You did cross the line on a number of occasions, but I'm not going to declare a mistrial. Instead, I'm going to reinstruct the jurors that arguments of counsel are not evidence. And then you can make your opening statement, Ms. Knight."

Jim saw Sarah swallow hard. "I'm reserving my opening, Your Honor, because you've ruled I can't have Dr. Stewart testify on Battered Women's Syndrome."

The judge's eyes held Sarah's for a long minute as if he were rethinking his ruling. But then he said, "Very well, Ms. Knight. Let's get the jurors back in here."

Sarah came back to the defense table and sat down. Alexa looked over at her and tried to smile, but Jim could tell the prosecutor's venom had deeply upset her.

"Ladies and gentleman, if you'll be seated quickly." Judge Tomlinson watched the jurors shuffle quickly back into their seats. "I'm going to remind you that the argument you just heard from Mr. Barton was only an argument. It was not evidence in this trial. The defense has a right to make an opening argument, but they have decided to reserve their statement for a later time. That means Mr. Barton is now going to call the state's first witness."

Preston Barton stood and announced, "The People call Officer Richard Nguyen."

Nguyen, a handsome, thirty-something Asian-American, was the officer who had responded to Alexa's 911 call. He was the one who had discovered Michael Reed in a pool of his own blood with Alexa's Glock . 9 beside him. Jim closed his eyes for a moment and wished he still believed in prayer because the trial had just begun and it felt as if they'd already lost.

* * *

First Tuesday in January 2014, San Diego County Courthouse

It all began again at eight thirty the next morning. Sarah, whom Jim had always seen in blacks and neutrals for the most part, was playing the color card for the jury. She was wearing an emerald green suit he had never seen before. Even with the scar shining against her thin face, she looked beautiful. And efficient and in charge. If he looked only at Sarah, he could almost convince himself they were winning.

Preston Barton recalled Officer Nguyen as a witness, and they labored through a morning of gruesome details about the position of Michael's body, the possible position of the shooter, and the trajectory of the bullets. It was dry stuff, and Jim watched the jury squirm with boredom. Some of them even smiled in the defense table's direction, giving Jim a sliver of hope that all might not be lost.

After lunch, the officer who found Ronald Brigman was called to testify. Officer Kyle Porter, who was tall and thin, with a full head of gray hair, came across like the gentle grandfather he probably was.

"Officer Porter, were you on duty on the morning of Monday, June 3 of last year?"

"I was."

"And were you working alone or with a partner?"

"I was alone in a black and white."

"And did you do a welfare check on Ronald Brigman at ten a.m. at 10924 Mountain View Drive in La Jolla?"

"Yes, I did. I received a call from dispatch telling me Dr. Brigman's ten o'clock appointment had shown up at his home office, and Dr. Brigman hadn't answered the door. The patient was concerned because Dr. Brigman always kept appointments. So I went to the location to see what was going on."

"And what did you find?"

"I found Dr. Brigman's patient in her car parked in the drive, waiting for me. After speaking briefly with her, I rang the bell and knocked on his front door but got no response."

"What did you do then?"

"I walked around to the back of his house where I found the screen door to the patio open. I stepped inside and saw Dr. Brigman, lying in a pool of blood. As I got closer, I could see multiple gunshot wounds, and I could tell he had been dead for some time."

"What did you do next?"

"I summoned backup and the coroner and the CSI team. Then I stayed with the body until Detective Rollins arrived to take charge of the investigation."

"How quickly did he arrive?"

"I'd say within fifteen minutes. He directed me to speak with Alice Snyder, the patient who'd had the appointment that morning; and then he told me to check the premises for surveillance cameras."

"And did you find any?"

"I did. Dr. Brigman had a camera focused on his front entryway."

"Were you familiar at that time with the defendant, Alexa Reed?"

"I knew she had called 911 on the previous night to report her ex-husband, Michael, been found dead at his house. I had not seen her at that point."

"Were you aware of the location of Michael Reed's residence?"

"Yes. He lived about a ten-minute drive from Dr. Brigman."

"Did you later become familiar with Mrs. Reed's appearance?"

"I did."

"And did you review the surveillance tape from Dr. Brigman's?"

"I did."

"And what did you observe on that tape?"

"At nine p.m. on the evening of June 2, Alexa Reed entered Ronald Brigman's front door."

"Was she alone?"

"Yes."

"Was she carrying anything?"

"A purse."

"Was the purse large enough to hold a handgun?"

"Yes."

"Did the surveillance tape show her exiting Dr. Brigman's house?"

"No, it did not."

"Thank you, Officer Porter. No further questions." Preston Barton smiled at the jury and sat down.

Sarah got up to cross-examine the officer, who continued to answer calmly in his soft, grandfatherly voice. He wasn't bothered by having to admit there was no surveillance camera on the back door, and he was not perturbed when Sarah forced him to agree Alexa could have left by the open back door long before the killer arrived.

But Preston Barton quickly won the point on his re-direct examination.

"Officer Porter, was the body of Ronald Brigman found closer to his front door or the open back door?

"The open back door."

"In your opinion, was the killer then more likely to have exited by the back door rather than the front?"

"Definitely by the back door."

"Thank you. No further questions, Your Honor."

Jim saw sixteen pairs of juror eyes focus on Alexa, sitting next to him in a white blouse and black suit. They didn't look sympathetic.

* * *

Second Wednesday in January 2014, San Diego County Courthouse

Next morning Detective Mack Rollins, a beefy man in his mid-forties, with large hands and rumpled clothes and equally rumpled salt and pepper hair, took the stand to establish Alexa Reed owned the gun found next to her ex-husband's body. Even though the detective's testimony was brief because he would be recalled later to go over all the details of his investigation into the two murders, Mack Rollins managed to convey by his tone and by his glances at Alexa his complete distaste for her. Sixteen pairs of juror eyes drank it all in, and Jim felt sick to his stomach.

After thirty minutes of Detective Rollins, Preston Barton called an expert on cell towers who spent the rest of Wednesday and all of Thursday boring the jury to tears as he traced the movement of Alexa's cell phone that night, emphasizing her proximity to Ronald Brigman and Michael Reed.

Jim watched Sarah focus on each witness, her face impassive, as she took careful notes. She cross-examined every one of them thoroughly and carefully, poking holes in their stories and conclusions where she could. But the jury continued to stare at the defense table and at Alexa, in particular, with stony eyes.

* * *

Second Friday in January 2014, San Diego County Courthouse

The interminable wrangling over the accuracy of tracking cell phones with cell towers continued for most of Friday. Finally, at two in the afternoon, Preston Barton called officer Brent McColly, a smug little man in a crisp San Diego Police Department uniform, who seemed only too happy to take the stand to testify against Alexa. He spent the rest of day doing everything in his power to make her sound as guilty as possible. He emphasized her admission that she was in the area of the murders close to the time they happened. Then, in an unexpectedly dramatic piece of showmanship, the prosecutor played the portion of Alexa's taped interview in which McColly had confronted her about the murder weapon. The jurors heard the officer say, "And can you explain, Mrs. Reed, why your Glock .9 was found next to your ex-husband's body?" Alexa's soft voice responded, "No. I hadn't seen my gun since mid-May when it was stolen." "And did you file a police report, Mrs. Reed?" "I did."

Preston Barton dramatically turned off the tape at this point and let silence fall over the courtroom before he asked, "And did you find a police report for the defendant's stolen gun?"

"No."

"So in your expert opinion, based on your eighteen years as an officer with SDPD, was a report made?"

"In my opinion it was not."

Sarah rose, majestic today in royal blue, "Objection!"

Judge Tomlinson barely glanced at her. "Overruled."

* * *

On the way home that night, Jim had been blunt with Alexa. "It didn't go well, today."

Out of the corner of his eye, he saw her mouth twitch. "We agreed not to post-mortem the testimony. It's hard enough to listen to it all day without having to drag myself through it again at night."

"But you can see how much we need the children to tell the jury Michael stole your gun."

"I'm not going to reopen that discussion. Meggie and Sam are not coming out here to testify."

"At this point, that's the only thing that could save your life."

"The answer is still no."

CHAPTER THIRTY-EIGHT

Second Monday in January 2014, San Diego County Courthouse

On Monday, Preston Barton called senior criminalist Cooper Kelly, his DNA expert, to testify that the DNA profiles on the murder weapon belonged to Michael and Alexa Reed. Jim watched the jury wilt under the hours-long onslaught of technical DNA information. By lunchtime, they were all squirming in their chairs like kids ready for recess.

Jim, Alexa, and Sarah adjourned to a corner of the courthouse coffee shop as far from prying eyes and ears as possible. Jim brought back three sandwiches although he knew only one would be eaten. Sarah was looking over a stack of paper Preston Barton had handed her as they were leaving the courtroom for lunch.

"Barton is boring the jury to death," Jim observed as he bit into the stale roast beef.

Alexa nodded as she unwrapped her sandwich, took a bite, and then put the whole thing down. "And when they're bored, they stare at me, and I wonder what they are thinking."

"Aren't you going to eat anything?" Jim asked Sarah.

She held up one hand as if to say 'wait,' without looking up from the report.

"In a minute."

"What's that?" Alexa asked.

"It's another report of the results of Cooper Kelly's DNA testing. I don't know why he had to give me another one. I've had this report for months—" Suddenly she was very pale.

"What's wrong?" Jim asked.

Her dark eyes met his. "They've gone back and done additional testing on the DNA swabs taken from the gun."

"And?" Jim prompted.

"And whereas the original report said the DNA on the gun was a mixture of Alexa and Michael Reed, now they are saying there is a third, unidentified profile that belongs to a woman."

Jim's heart began to race. "Do you realize what that means?"

But Sarah shook her head. "We can't talk about this right here, right now."

* * *

As soon as the court had come to order after lunch, Sarah stood up at the defense table. Jim noticed her hands were trembling as she gestured toward the DNA report. He hoped the jurors didn't notice.

"Your Honor, the defense has a matter to take up outside the presence of the jury."

Sixteen unhappy faces, who had just settled themselves for the rest of the afternoon, looked up at Judge Tomlinson, who frowned. "Can't this wait, Ms. Knight? We just seated everyone."

"No, Your Honor."

Jim watched the jurors file into the jury room, eyeing the defense table suspiciously. As the door closed on their unhappy faces, Judge Tomlinson turned back to Sarah.

"Ok, Ms. Knight. What is it?"

"Your Honor, I've received a new report from the prosecution that contains new information that could lead to my client's acquittal. I'm asking for a mistrial based upon late turnover of mandatory discovery and a violation of *Brady v. Maryland*, which requires the prosecutor to turn over anything that shows the defendant is innocent."

Judge Tomlinson frowned. "When did you receive this evidence?"

"Mr. Barton handed it to me as I was leaving the courtroom for lunch today."

"Your Honor!" The prosecutor was red-faced.

"What is the evidence, Ms. Knight?"

"This report says, for the first time, that the DNA evidence found on the murder weapon contained a third profile. Up until now, Mr. Kelly has insisted there were only two profiles found on the gun, Michael and Alexa Reed's."

Judge Tomlinson raised his eyebrows. "That does change things quite a bit. What is your explanation, Mr. Barton?"

"Mr. Kelly's supervisor was going over his work just before trial. He thought Mr. Kelly had overlooked another potential profile. He ordered some retesting. It's very weak, but the third profile is there."

"Male or female?"

"Female."

"Any leads on who it might be, Ms. Knight?"

"Not at this time."

"Then there's no one you can bring in and test to see if the third profile is a match?"

"Correct."

Jim's stomach tightened. He thought of Elaina Morales cruising with Enrique Cevantes.

"What about at the crime scenes? Does the profile show up anywhere else?" The judge looked at both attorneys.

"No," Preston Barton shook his head. "It's only this tiny bit of trace evidence on the gun."

"And Mrs. Reed's DNA was found at Ronald Brigman's?"

"Yes, Your Honor," Sarah answered. "But that doesn't prove she killed him. She was there often to drop off her children for therapy with Dr. Brigman."

"And the surveillance tape shows her entering Dr. Brigman's at nine that night," Preston Barton interjected.

"You have a DNA expert, Ms. Knight?"

"We do. Dr. Leo Spangler from UCSD."

Judge Tomlinson nodded. "He does good work. I'm not going to declare a mistrial yet. We are still going with the prosecution's witnesses. You've got time to get this to Dr. Spangler and get his thoughts on it. You should have time to prepare your approach to this new evidence. And I'll make Mr. Cooper subject to recall in case you want to put him on again later. I will also consider a jury instruction on late discovery when the time comes if you will draft one for me to review. Now let's get the jury back in here and get going with the afternoon's testimony."

* * *

"That DNA has to belong to Elaina," Jim insisted that night as he and Alexa ate in her little dining room. Sarah, as usual, had declined the dinner invitation. Jim hadn't changed out of his suit, but Alexa was wearing jeans and a long gray sweater.

Alexa studied him thoughtfully. "For a seasoned investigator, I think you're getting too excited about this and jumping to conclusions."

"No, it has to be Elaina. She was there that night. It's the only thing that makes sense."

"But she didn't kill Ronald Brigman," Alexa said.

The light went out of Jim's eyes. "We don't know that."

"Of course we do."

"Maybe she was sleeping with both of them. Tara was."

Alexa shook her head. "I wrote Justice Moreno's dissenting opinion in *Edwards v. Pennsylvania*. You know that case. The question was whether the DNA expert who did the actual testing has to take the stand."

"I know *Edwards*. But Cooper did the testing, and he's testifying."

"No, that's not why I brought it up. Justice Moreno was very concerned about the way everyone just assumes DNA is as unique as fingerprints. And it isn't. Many people have similar DNA. And in addition to that, DNA transfers easily. For all we know, that trace female profile could be a lab technician who forgot to put her gloves on."

Jim shook his head stubbornly. "I'm not buying that. It's got to be Elaina."

"You'd have to get her profile to find out. And she's on a yacht right now in the Pacific."

"There has to be a way. This is too important."

* * *

He left the cottage at eleven, drove home, took off his jacket, and poured his nightly scotch. Then he sat down on the sofa and dialed Maria Chavez.

"Mr. Jim! I am so glad to hear your voice!"

"Sorry, it's late, Maria."

"Never too late for you. Are you lonely? Do you want company?"

"No, that's not why I called."

She sighed deeply. "You are always too much business, Mr. Jim. Is this about the woman you love?"

"It's about the case I'm working on."

"So it is her. Okay. What can I do to help?"

"Is Elaina still on Enrique's yacht?"

"Yes. She does not come back for three more weeks. Do you need to see her?"

"I need a DNA sample."

"A DNA sample? Why?"

"Never mind why. It's life or death."

"Always life or death with you, Mr. Jim."

"Just Jim."

"No, I cannot. Not unless I sleep with you. And you always refuse."

Her return to the topic annoyed him slightly. "You and Elaina are friends, right?"

"We are close."

"Do you have anything that she has used? A toothbrush, a hairbrush, something?"

Maria thought for a minute. "Actually, she leaves a cosmetic bag here for times when she can't go home to get ready for a date."

"That's exactly what I need."

* * *

Jim sat back and savored his scotch. He was sure the third profile would turn out to be Elaina's. And maybe there was a link to Brigman, as well. Michael liked call girls. Maybe he'd turned Brigman on to them, too.

He began to feel as if they might have a shot at a not-guilty verdict. Originally he wanted to win Alexa's freedom for all the right, professional reasons. But now, if he was being scrupulously honest, he would admit Jordan had been correct. His personal feelings were involved.

Suddenly his cell rang.

"Jim, it's Sarah."

"Are you ok?"

"Someone tried to break in just now. Whoever it was came around the back and tried to get in through the French doors to the patio."

"Did he break the glass?"

"He tried, but couldn't. These are disguised security doors. I had them put in after the last break in."

"Have you called the police?"

"For all I know, it could be the police."

"I think you're going to have to make a report, though."

"Probably, but I'd like you here when I have to talk to them."

"Okay." He reached for his gun as he spoke. "I'll be right there."

* * *

Ten minutes later he knocked on Sarah's front door and called out, "It's me, Jim."

She opened it, white-faced and trembling. He hurried inside and held her close. She was even thinner than Alexa. He could feel her bones under the white cashmere sweater.

He released her and flipped off the hall light switch, taking his gun out of his holster as he moved silently toward her dark living room. Out of the corner of his eye, he saw her begin to follow him, but he held up a hand to warn her to stay put.

He crept across the floor, staying low because the curtains were open. As he drew closer to the door, the handle began to move. Then, as his eyes grew accustomed to the dark, he saw a figure in black on the patio. The face was covered by a ski mask.

The handle moved again, more urgently this time. Then gunfire burst through the door.

"Get down!" Jim yelled to Sarah as he hit the floor and rolled to the right, away from the path of the bullets.

The black-masked figure pushed the door open, but stopped at the threshold. Jim saw him turn toward Sarah, an easy target in the white sweater. She was crouching behind a chair, but her left shoulder was exposed.

As the gunman raised his gun to fire at her, Jim got off six rounds. He saw the man fall, then get up and run limping into the dark. Jim hurried out onto the patio, but there was nothing left but a trail of blood snaking toward the back gate.

He ran back inside to see Sarah was bleeding from her left shoulder, the red slowly seeping into the pristine cashmere and down her arm. He switched on a lamp to get a better look.

"I'm okay."

"No, you're not."

"Yes, I am. Get some scotch. Over there on the cupboard."

"What is this? The Wild West? I'm not giving you anything until the paramedics get here."

"No paramedics. I'm sick of hospitals."

"Be quiet."

"Call Tom, then, if I have to have a doctor. But I'm not going to the hospital. I'm not!"

Jim sighed. "Where's his number?"

* * *

By one-thirty, Tom Barrett had bandaged Sarah's shoulder which, luckily, had only been grazed by the bullet.

"You still need to go the hospital overnight for observation," Tom insisted as he put away his medical kit.

"No. I have to be in trial in the morning at eight-thirty." Sarah was lying on her bed, still in the sweater but with one sleeve cut away.

"You're in no shape for work." Tom laid a big gentle hand on the injured shoulder. He had a healer's touch, Jim thought. And he was a very decent guy. Sarah would be okay with him, but his heart turned over at the thought.

"Doesn't matter," Sarah mumbled. "I have to be there. I'm responsible for Alexa. She was dying, but I told her to come back for Meggie and Sam, and then she woke up. So I'm responsible for her, don't you see? I can't let her down. I've already let her down by telling her to come back."

Tom gave Jim a friendly smile. "I've given her a mild sedative. That's why she's rambling. She'll drop off shortly."

"Fine, good idea."

"I'd offer to stay with her, but I have surgery at eight in the morning."

"I'll look after her." Tom looked disappointed. He really cares about her, Jim thought and felt a twang of jealousy.

"Okay, then. But call me right away if anything changes. She could still go into shock."

"I'd like to get her out of here and take her to my place."

But Tom shook his head. "Better to let her stay still for now. I'll check with you tomorrow to see how she is. Call me if anything changes. Here's my number." He handed Jim his card.

Tom's steady brown eyes held Jim's. "You saved her life tonight."

"And you did, too."

"I was batting cleanup. You deserve the credit. Take care."

Tom patted Jim's back as if they were old friends and smiled as he turned to leave. Suddenly the night was still and quiet, and Jim was beyond exhaustion. Sarah had dropped off under the influence of the drugs. Jim looked around for a place to sleep but realized he was too exhausted to make it to the living room. He slipped off his coat and shoes, put his reloaded gun on the table by the bed, and lay down next to Sarah, wrapping his arm around her small, injured self. How did so much determination and courage live in one little human, he wondered as sleep mercifully overtook him.

CHAPTER THIRTY-NINE

Second Tuesday in January, 2014, La Jolla

But of course Sarah was in no shape for court the next morning. She opened her eyes when Jim's cell phone alarm went off at seven a.m. and then closed them again. Jim didn't feel much like getting up either, but he knew he had to make the court appearance for her.

He showered and shaved with a disposable razor he found in the bathroom, put on yesterday's rumpled suit, and was on time to pick up Alexa at eight. She looked especially beautiful in a light blue suit he had never seen before.

"Do you want me to ask for the continuance? You're not admitted to the bar in California," she said when Jim had filled her in on the wee hours of the morning.

He smiled. "You can't. You're the defendant, and you're represented by counsel. I'm admitted to the bar in New York and D.C. That will just have to do for today."

"Any idea who did it? It was Coleman, wasn't it?"

"No way to know. I managed to wound the guy, but he got away. I told you before, Sarah has a lot of enemies. Coleman, Tara, David Spineli. Take your pick."

"Who's David Spineli?"

"A particularly bad choice in a relationship she was involved in when she took your case. He made threats when she ended it."

"She never talks about herself. I didn't know she was seeing anyone."

"The neurosurgeon who stitched up her head when she crashed her car came over last night and did the honors on the shoulder. He's a nice guy, and he likes her."

"So maybe when it's over?" Alexa's eyes clouded the way they always did when the end of the trial came up. They had agreed to avoid that subject just as they had agreed not to talk over the witnesses' testimony at the end of the day.

"Maybe. Who knows?" Jim gave her a reassuring smile, and the sun seemed to come out in her eyes.

* * *

Judge Tomlinson continued the trial until the following Tuesday. Jim dropped Alexa at the cottage at eleven-thirty and then checked on Sarah, who was still sleeping soundly. He wished he could get her out of that bloody sweater, but taking it off would wake her, and he didn't want to do that.

Relieved that the nightmare of last night was over and that the world seemed to be coming back into focus, Jim called Maria, who agreed to bring the bag to the coffee house where they had first met. After Maria left, he telephoned Dr. Spangler and arranged to drop the bag by his office later that afternoon. And then he sat for a while, savoring his espresso and the freedom that a week's continuance gave him.

When Jim was new to the Bureau, he had quickly learned to follow his hunches. Now, as he inhaled the last drop of strong black coffee, he had the feeling he needed to drive by Ronald Brigman's.

He wound his way up Mt. Soledad and parked in front. The house was nondescript and ugly. *Like its owner*, he thought. No windows faced the street. It was a long, faceless rectangle of beige stucco punctuated by massive green double entrance doors, also without windows. The yard was brown and overgrown with weeds. Apparently the executor of Brigman's estate was doing little to maintain the value of the house. But even with a well-kept lawn, it had the air of a prison; and Jim shivered at the thought of Alexa being forced to drive Meggie and Sam here week after week for "therapy" designed to separate them forever.

He got out of his Range Rover, and walked across the stiff, dead grass and around the end of the garage to the back yard. As Alexa had said, this side of the house was all glass, with two massive sliding doors that opened onto a stone patio that ran all the way to the edge of the bluff. Jim stared down at the village of La Jolla, shrunken into miniature by the height of the mountain with the eternity of the Pacific shimmering beyond under the hard, crisp January sun.

He turned back to the house and walked up to the sliding doors. He wished one were open, but his hopes were disappointed. Suddenly a voice called out, "Hey, you there. What are you up to?"

He looked up to see one of the two next-door neighbors heading across the dead lawn toward him.

As she drew closer, he saw she was in her mid-forties, dressed in figure-hugging black and white workout wear, thin, and fit, with her long blonde hair slicked into a ponytail. A trophy wife at mid-life.

"I'm James Mitchell," he said as the woman planted herself on the stone patio in front of him. "I'm a private investigator."

"Oh, I thought you might be someone who wanted to buy the house. I was going to tell you it isn't for sale, yet. Too bad. You look like you'd make a very nice neighbor."

Jim looked at her left hand just to be sure the two caret diamond and the wedding band were actually there. "You are either Annalise Frederickson or Terri Morris."

"I'm Annalise. Terri lives over there." She pointed to the house on Jim's left.

"How do you know our names?"

"I work for the attorney who is defending Alexa Reed. The police interviewed you and Mrs. Morris a few days after the murder."

A knowing look came into Annalise's light hazel eyes. "I bet you've come for the surveillance tapes. My husband is a lawyer at King and White, and he said somebody would be coming to get them some day. Our cameras showed Dr. Brigman's back door."

Jim's heart leapt with relief and joy. "You mean you actually have surveillance tapes that cover Brigman's house as well as your own?"

"Oh, absolutely. And I have the ones from the Morris' camera, too, on the other side of Dr. Brigman's. Ted doesn't do criminal law, but he said someone would want them eventually. So he had them all duplicated and took charge of them. He actually has a copy at his office, but he won't mind if I give you the ones he kept here. He said to tell whoever came for them that the camera times on both our system and the Morris' system are accurate. And he said he would testify."

Jim handed her his business card. "We'll probably need him to authenticate the tapes. Would you give him my card?"

"Of course."

He hurried out to his Range Rover, got in, and yanked open his laptop. He didn't want to leave until he'd made sure the disks were operable. He waited impatiently while his computer whirred and spun to life. Then he inserted the first disk into the drive and held his breath until an image appeared on the screen. He clicked the play button and noted the time stamp, 6/2/2013, 21:30 hours. And, after a few seconds, he saw Alexa's thin figure leaving by Brigman's back door at nine-thirty just as she'd said. And a few seconds later, Brigman himself came out and stood gazing at the view for a few minutes before turning and going back into the house.

* * *

He was so excited he could barely breathe. He switched off his computer and drove straight to Sarah's. Her beige bungalow gleamed like a tranquil jewel under the benevolent midday sun. The little house set in the midst of its pristine green lawn, framed by the riot of feathery maiden hair ferns and ruby bougainvillea vines, gave no hint it had been the scene of blood and violence less than twenty-four hours earlier.

Laptop in hand, Jim knocked; but there was no answer. He took the key he'd grabbed on his way out that morning as a just-in-case measure and used it to open the heavy wooden front door. Inside, the house was cool and quiet.

"Sarah?" he called softly at first and then louder, several times, but no answer.

He made his way to her bedroom where he found her still sleeping, only she'd managed to wake long enough to shed her bloody clothes and put on black silk pajamas.

Her left cheek was hidden by the pillow, and Jim realized how breathtakingly beautiful she was without the scar on view. She'd been angry when he'd asked about it, but it looked like something plastic surgery could at least make less noticeable–if not erase. Why, he wondered for the millionth time, did she flaunt it?

She stirred and her long lashes fluttered, and then her lovely dark eyes opened and fixed on him.

He smiled. "How are you feeling?"

"Like a bus hit me."

"Shoulder hurt?"

"More than I want to admit."

"Tom left Vicodin, but you'll need some food to go with it. I'll go scramble some eggs. That is, if you have any." He was encouraged by her smile.

Fifteen minutes later, he was back with food and medication. He helped her arrange herself against the pillows and sat down on the side of the bed while she ate.

"I'm glad to see you're hungry."

"I've never been shot at before. I guess that's it. What happened in court this morning?"

"The judge has given us a week's continuance. Barton was his usual pompous self, but he offered no opposition. I'm sure he's worried about maintaining a conviction if he gets one because obviously your ability to provide effective assistance of counsel has been compromised twice."

Sarah sighed. "Well, that will be for the appellate geeks to argue years from now if we lose. For the moment, I have to get back downtown and keep trying to win this for her."

"Not until next Tuesday. And Judge Tomlinson seemed inclined to give you more days if you need them."

"But I don't want any more. None of us wants this to go on any longer. Except maybe Preston Barton. He loves talking to the reporters every afternoon at five."

"You haven't eaten all your eggs."

"I can't."

"Is the Vicodin making you sleepy?"

"Not yet."

"Then I've got something I want to show you." He smiled as he opened his laptop and pulled up the disk he'd just viewed.

He turned the computer around and set it on the bed beside Sarah.

She looked up at him. "What is it?"

"Surveillance footage of Brigman's back door at nine-thirty p.m. on June 2. Watch."

He studied her face as she stared at the computer, but her expression didn't change to happiness and relief the way he had thought it would.

She sighed and pushed the computer away when the segment ended.

"What's wrong? Aren't you glad to find this?"

"It helps, but not enough. It shows she left at nine-thirty, and Brigman was still alive. And according to the coroner he was alive for another hour and a half. But according to our client, she went back to his house at ten-thirty, which will allow Preston Barton to argue she had plenty of opportunity to kill him a half hour later."

"But there's more footage. I just haven't had a chance to look at all of it. She said she wasn't there for very long the second time, so it's likely we'll see her leaving again before he was killed at eleven."

Sarah's eyelids were drooped, and Jim realized the drug was taking hold.

* * *

Tired and discouraged, he folded up his laptop and left, being sure to lock the front door with his borrowed key. He stood on the stoop for a few moments in the softening early afternoon sun and smelled the brine in the onshore breeze that lightly whipped his cheeks. Overhead the seagulls rode the swift currents of air in wide arcs, crying their desolate refrain. *They make the loneliest sound in the world*, he thought; and he felt like the loneliest man in the world.

He got into his car and stared at Sarah's adorable stucco cottage with its terra cotta shutters and lush, bright landscaping and remembered the first night he'd seen her at the bar at Trend so beautiful and sleek and elegant. He wanted her to need him. He wanted her to stop shutting him out. He wanted her to tell him all her terrible secrets.

Suddenly his phone came to life in his pocket, and he remembered the other woman whose face was etched on his soul.

"Jim, it's Alexa. Could you come over to the cottage right now?"

* * *

He reached Crescent Court fifteen minutes later; and through the pines, Jim could see the sun still high above the blue Pacific, a ball of early winter fire on a January afternoon. As he got out of his Range Rover, he studied the little white house with its jaunty blue door and remembered Sarah's name for it, The Fairy Tale Cottage. He was tired and discouraged. His feelings for Sarah and Alexa were woven together in a tangle he couldn't sort out. He longed for some magic that would prove Alexa's innocence.

She met him at the front door, breathless with excitement. He had never seen her this way. Her eyes were shining with hope. She'd changed out of her suit from the court appearance that morning and was wearing jeans and a long white T-shirt. She was waving a business card in the air.

"Look, look, look what I found!"

Jim was still standing in the hall and had to close the front door himself. "What is it?"

"It's the business card the officer gave me the day I told him my gun had been stolen. He said he would write a report."

Jim's disappointment began to melt. "Let me see that." He looked down at a regulation San Diego Police Department business card for Officer Timothy Stratton. His badge number was in the corner.

"Where did you find it?"

"I have a file for miscellaneous papers related to the divorce. After you told me you were going over to Dr. Brigman's, I decided to go through it. Did you find anything over there by the way?"

"Yes. The neighbors' security cameras picked up Dr. Brigman's back door. Let me grab my laptop, and I'll show you the bit I've viewed so far. There's more that I haven't had a chance to look at."

He fetched his computer from the Range Rover and settled next to her on the sofa to show her the first disk. She was so close he could feel her holding her breath. Her light blue eyes seemed to darken as she studied the images on the screen. When the segment ended, he paused the disk; and she looked up at him and smiled.

"Wow. Just wow. It shows you everything happened just the way I said. Is the time stamp accurate?"

"It is."

"Has Sarah seen this?"

He sighed. "She's not feeling well this afternoon."

"In other words, she said it wouldn't help."

"Not exactly. She just pointed out that you were back again at ten-thirty."

"So maybe one of those disks is going to show that, too."

"That's what I'm hoping for. I was going to go over them this afternoon, but right now I think it's more important for me to find Officer Timothy Stratton. I'll be back for dinner."

"And shouldn't you take Sarah something?"

"I'll check in on her later."

* * *

Jim hurried home and changed into jeans and a t-shirt. He felt as if the suit he'd worn for the last two days had grown to his skin.

He had intended to start viewing the tapes, but luck and a data base he could access only because he was ex-FBI told him where Timothy Stratton lived. He didn't want to contact the police department for information because he was sure someone there would tip off Coleman Reed about his discovery. At four o'clock he braved the afternoon traffic on Interstate 8-East to find Officer Stratton's modest ranch house on a quiet street in La Mesa.

Mrs. Stratton, an attractive petite brunette in her early thirties, answered the door. "Oh, he's here. He just got home from his shift. And I just got home from school. I teach second grade. He's in the shower. Do you want to wait?"

Jim spent fifteen uncomfortable minutes on the living room sofa studying pictures of the Stratton wedding and the two Stratton babies, a boy and a girl, about two years apart, he guessed. He wanted to tell Tim Stratton to keep his priorities straight, so he would never be on the other end of a phone call saying his kids weren't coming to visit.

But Jim's musings were cut short by the officer's appearance. He was about five eight, but looked larger because his perfect six pack showed under his damp white t-shirt. He, too, was mid-thirties, very handsome, with striking brown eyes.

He walked over and shook Jim's hand. "Tim Stratton."

"James Mitchell, FBI, retired. Now private investigator for Sarah Knight—"

"Yeah, I know. The Alexa Reed case." Officer Stratton motioned for Jim to sit down as he turned his head toward the hallway and called out, "Caroline, could you come in here?"

"I'll be there in just a minute. I'm starting a video to keep the kids occupied," she called back.

Tim Stratton took a chair opposite Jim on the sofa and smiled, although he looked uneasy and uncomfortable. "Sorry, this is a big decision and we have to make it together."

"But I haven't told you why I'm here."

"Oh, I know. I wondered if Mrs. Reed kept the card I gave her that day."

"So did you write a report about her stolen gun?"

At that moment, Mrs. Stratton hurried in and took the chair next to her husband's.

"Sorry, but I know you don't want the children to interrupt us." She was still in her work clothes, a simple gray dress and red cardigan. Her cheeks were flushed.

"Did you write a report?" Jim repeated. "Preston Barton insists none was made."

Tim and his wife exchanged a long look. Then Caroline said, "Go ahead and tell him, honey."

"Even though it will cost me my job?"

"It's the right thing to do," she insisted. "What if I were in Alexa Reed's shoes? Shouldn't we try to save her life if we can? We've talked this through a lot, and we decided to tell the truth if anyone came asking."

Tim looked down at his big hands for a few minutes before he said to his wife, "You're right. That's what we decided. It's just hard to do, now that the time has come; but I just want to do the right thing and be remembered as an honest cop."

* * *

Second Tuesday in January 2014, Midnight

"Want me to stay?" Tom had been with her all evening. Sarah considered his offer. But she knew what she had to do that night even if she wished for an excuse to avoid it.

"Not tonight. I'm feeling sleepy."

"That's good, then. Lots of sleep is what you need." He gave her a goodnight kiss.

"Lock up."

"The second you leave."

"Call if you need me."

"In a heartbeat."

"Will call in the morning."

"Thanks."

And he was gone.

Her shoulder ached. She walked back through the house, leaving small lights on in the living room and the kitchen. If anyone was watching, she wanted him to think she was awake.

She settled herself in bed on her down pillows and opened the drawer in her night table. She took out a small jewelry box and lifted the lid carefully. She had prayed this time would never come. But Jim had the surveillance tapes, and that changed everything. She couldn't fail Alexa, no matter the personal cost. She took out the slip of paper in the box and dialed the number. A thick, male Hispanic accent answered.

"Juan? It's Sarah."

"I am not surprised. I've been expecting to hear from you."

"I'm going to need her."

"When?"

"On Thursday."

"Even if you expose the truth?"

"Especially if I expose the truth. No more lies, Juan. And much as I want to go on lying, I can't let Alexa Reed die."

"On Thursday, then."

CHAPTER FORTY

Third Tuesday in January 2014, San Diego County Courthouse

"The defense may call its first witness," Judge Tomlinson said to Sarah at nine o'clock the following Tuesday morning. Her shoulder was still stiff and sore. She had no idea who had tried to kill her. Since the gunman hadn't returned to finish her off, she suspected the attempt had been intimidation. Someone didn't want her to do her best job for her client. But nothing mattered now except saving Alexa's life. She knew she looked confident and poised in her black Marc Jacobs dress. The intricate faux emerald pin on her shoulder was there to rivet the jury's attention on her as she examined the defense's first witness.

"Thank you, Your Honor. The defense calls Officer Timothy Stratton."

Preston Barton leapt to his feet. "The People object."

Sarah had expected this reaction.

Unperturbed, Judge Tomlinson peered over his half-glasses at the portly prosecutor. "On what grounds?"

"Timothy Stratton was not on their witness list."

Sarah felt the jury's eyes on her as they waited for her response. "The defense only learned of Officer Stratton's existence last Tuesday. And we know Mr. Barton has known about Officer Stratton since the day the defendant was arrested because Mr. Barton tried to cover up evidence from Officer Stratton that will lead to Mrs. Reed's acquittal."

Judge Tomlinson looked grave. "Are you saying the prosecutor withheld *Brady* evidence?"

"I am, Your Honor."

Preston Barton was now red-faced and sputtering. "Your Honor, could we hold this hearing outside the presence of the jury?"

"I don't see why we should," the judge responded. "I haven't heard anything to suggest he shouldn't be able to testify. Let's not waste the jury's time. Go ahead, Ms. Knight."

Timothy Stratton, tall and handsome in his blue uniform, was sworn and took the stand. Sarah smiled at him, and asked, "Would you state your name and occupation for the record?"

"Timothy Owen Stratton. I'm an officer with the San Diego Police Department."

"And how long have you been an officer?"

"Ten years."

"Were you on duty on May 19, 2013?"

"I was."

"And did you answer a call for service at 719 Crescent Court in Pacific Beach at two p.m.?"

"I did."

"Is there anyone in the courtroom whom you recognize from that day?"

"Yes, the defendant, the woman in the light blue suit sitting over there."

"The record will show Officer Stratton has identified Mrs. Reed. You may continue," Judge Tomlinson intoned.

"What did Mrs. Reed tell you that afternoon?"

"Objection. Hearsay." Preston Barton was still bright red, Sarah noticed with satisfaction.

"Your Honor, Mrs. Reed has elected to testify. So Mr. Barton will have the opportunity for cross-examination." Sarah had tried to talk her out of it, but Jim had insisted she should. And she had listened to Jim, not Sarah.

"Very well. Continue."

"Why did Mrs. Reed call you to her residence on that Sunday afternoon?"

"She said she had a Glock .9 millimeter that she kept in the trunk of her car. She checked on the gun that afternoon, and it was missing."

"And did she have any idea how it came to be missing?"

"She guessed it had been stolen, but there was no sign of forced entry."

"Officer Stratton, are you experienced with car theft and break-ins?"

"I am. I've worked over a hundred cases."

"And in your experience, are there always signs of forced entry when a car has been broken into?"

"No."

"Now, Officer Stratton, did you prepare a police report based upon Mrs. Reed's information?"

"I did."

"When?"

"I wrote it that afternoon, and I filed it the next day in the department."

"So it was filed on May 20?"

"That is correct."

"And you are certain you filed that report?"

"Very certain."

Sarah noticed the jurors were hanging on Tim Stratton's every word and smiled inside. "So if Officer Brent McColly said he never found a report, would he be accurate?"

"No, he would not. He was aware Mrs. Reed had reported the gun stolen and that I had written and filed a report based upon her complaint."

"Officer Stratton, did there come a day when Officer McColly spoke to you about the report you had prepared?"

"Yes."

"And how did he contact you?"

"By telephone at my home. I was off-duty at the time."

"And was anyone else on the call?"

"Yes. Mr. Barton." Timothy Stratton looked over at the prosecutor, and all sixteen pairs of juror eyes followed his.

"Do you recall what day this happened?"

"June 3. It was the day Alexa Reed was arrested."

"Do you recall what Officer McColly told you?"

"Yes. He said Mrs. Reed had claimed she made a police report about her stolen gun, and I verified she had. Then Mr.

Barton asked me to destroy it and to lay low so the defense team wouldn't find me."

"Did he tell you why he wanted you to destroy the report and lay low?"

"Yes. Mr. Barton said it would be easier to convict Mrs. Reed of the murders if the report didn't exist."

"And what would happen if you didn't destroy the report?"

"I would lose my job."

"And are you afraid of losing your job for testifying here today?

"Objection. Relevance."

"Overruled. You may answer."

"Yes, I am."

"And did you do as you were asked and destroy the report?"

"I did at the office. But I kept a copy at home on my computer."

"And why did you keep a copy?"

"I knew destroying the report was wrong. I wanted to be an honest cop."

"And on the day you interviewed Mrs. Reed, did she tell you why she had the Glock .9?"

"Yes. She said she purchased the weapon and learned to use it because she was fearful for her safety and that of her children because of threats from Mr. Reed."

"Objection. Hearsay."

"I'll allow it. Continue, Ms. Knight."

"So she told you she had the gun because of threats from her ex-husband?"

"Correct."

"Did she say whether the gun was properly licensed, and if she'd taken firearms training?"

"Yes. It was licensed, and she had completed a course in firearms use and safety."

"Thank you, Officer Stratton."

With an inward sigh of relief, Sarah gathered her notes from the podium and resumed her seat at counsel table.

Judge Tomlinson looked over at Preston Barton. "Any questions for the officer, Mr. Barton?"

"Yes, Your Honor. A few."

Sarah watched Preston's stout little figure position itself behind the podium so the jurors could get a good view of his face.

"Officer Stratton, you testified you examined the trunk of Mrs. Reed's car and there were no signs it had been broken into?"

"That is correct."

"So other than Mrs. Reed's word that the gun had been stolen, did you find any additional evidence to back up her story?"

"No."

"Now you said I asked you to destroy this report?"

"Correct."

"And you said the reason given was it would be easier to prosecute her without it?'

"Correct."

"Are you an attorney, Officer Stratton?"

"No."

"So you aren't in a position to judge an attorney's tactical decisions, are you?"

"I am not."

"So if I had a tactical reason to want the report destroyed because it was based upon the unreliable statement of Alexa Reed, whom Dr. Ronald Brigman through psychological testing had found to be a liar, you would not be in a position to judge my reasons for the request, would you?"

Sarah leapt to her feet. "Objection, Your Honor."

"Counsel, approach the bench," Judge Tomlinson intoned. "Let me hear from you first, Ms. Knight."

Being careful to keep her voice low, so the jurors would not hear, Sarah said, "Dr. Brigman could not determine the truth of my client's statements through psychological testing."

"We've been through this," Preston Barton huffed. "Dr. Brigman's finding that she is a liar is conclusive."

"And that's legal error. This case is going to be reversed on appeal."

"Wishful thinking," Preston Barton shot back.

"That's enough," Judge Tomlinson said. "Rephrase your question, Mr. Barton, leaving Dr. Brigman out of it."

Sarah smiled inside, happy with her victory.

Preston Barton went back to the podium. "So, Officer Stratton, you would not be in a position to judge my legal reasons for directing you to destroy the report?"

"No, other than I was taught in the Academy not to destroy evidence."

"But did the Academy mention worthless and false evidence?"

"The Academy did not divide evidence up that way. Evidence is evidence."

"But you have, have you not, been instructed by my office and by your superiors in the department to destroy evidence that is old or stale or worthless from time to time in other cases?"

"That is correct."

"The Department has storage limitations, does it not, Officer?"

"Yes."

"So we can't keep everything, can we?"

"No."

"Thank you, Officer Stratton. No further questions."

"Do you have any re-direct, Ms. Knight?" Judge Tomlinson smiled politely.

"I do."

Sarah resumed her place at the podium and looked directly into Tim Stratton's earnest eyes. "Officer, when you interviewed Mrs. Reed that day, did you have any reason to believe she was not telling the truth about her gun being stolen?"

"No, not all. She was very open and direct. And she seemed upset that it had gone missing."

"And when you were asked to destroy your report, was it because it was old and valueless?"

"No."

"In fact, weren't you told, it had great value as evidence, and that is why the district attorney's office wanted it destroyed?

"Correct."

"And were you concerned about your professional reputation if you complied with the request to destroy it?"

"Very."

"And so that is why you kept the copy at home?"

"Correct."

Sarah looked up at Judge Tomlinson and said, "That's all I have."

"Thank you, Officer Stratton. You may be excused."

"Your Honor, wait! I have one more question." Preston Barton huffed to his feet, afraid he'd lose the opportunity.

"Very well, Mr. Barton. Sorry, Officer Stratton. If you would remain a little longer."

"Officer, did you ask Mrs. Reed who had a key to the trunk besides herself?"

"Yes. She said she had the only key."

"And you didn't take any steps to corroborate her story that the gun had been stolen, did you?"

"No. I wrote down what she told me, and I filed the report."

"Thank you, Officer Stratton. No more questions."

Anger welled in the pit of Sarah's stomach, but she tried not to show it as she looked over at the juror's faces. From their expressions, Preston had won that round. They didn't believe Alexa's gun had been stolen.

"Ms. Knight, you may call your next witness."

"The defense calls James Mitchell."

Sarah watched Jim approach the stand and be sworn by the clerk. He was so handsome in his dark power suit and red tie. The tailoring fit him perfectly and accented his broad, muscular shoulders. Unbidden, Sarah's memories of being in his strong safe arms broke through her professional concentration, and her heart began to beat hard and fast.

I can't feel this, she reminded herself. *He belongs to Alexa.*

Jim sat down on the witness chair and adjusted the microphone with an expert touch. The Bureau had trained him to testify, Sarah remembered. His gentle eyes focused on hers, encouraging her to begin.

"Would you state your name for the record?"

"James Chapman Mitchell."

"And how are you employed, Mr. Mitchell?"

"I'm self-employed as a private investigator."

"And what is your relationship to this case?"

"I was hired to be the defense investigator in August of last year."

"And what is your training and experience to do investigations, Mr. Mitchell?"

"I was a Special Agent for the Federal Bureau of Investigation for more than twenty years."

"And do you have a law degree in addition to your experience with the Bureau?"

"I do. I graduated from Georgetown."

"Now, Mr. Mitchell, turning to your investigative work in this case, did I ask you to review financial records of Ronald Brigman that I obtained by subpoena?"

"Yes."

"And do you have experience reviewing financial records?"

"I do. I worked over a hundred cases in the Bureau dealing with money laundering and organized crime."

"Will you describe the records I asked you to review?"

"Dr. Brigman had four bank accounts at Wells Fargo Bank, a personal checking account, a savings account, a business checking account, and a business savings account."

"And did you find any financial data relevant to the facts of this case when you reviewed Dr. Brigman's financial information?"

"Yes."

"Will you explain those for the jury?"

"I found a payment to Dr. Brigman each month from Michael Reed of four thousand dollars. It was transferred on the first of each month to Dr. Brigman's personal checking account."

"And how did you determine the payment came from Michael Reed?"

"Mrs. Reed provided the number of the account her ex-husband used to pay child support, and it matched the account he used to pay Dr. Brigman each month."

"Did you happen to notice when the payments to Dr. Brigman began?"

"Yes, in January of 2009."

"And did I ask you to obtain certified court records of the date Michael Reed filed for divorce from his wife?"

"You did."

"I'd like this marked as Defense Exhibit B. It's a date-stamped copy of Michael Reed's petition for divorce."

"And what is the date on this document, Mr. Mitchell?"

"January 15, 2009."

"And did I also ask you to obtain a certified copy of the minute order appointing Ronald Brigman as the child custody evaluator in the Reed divorce?"

"Yes."

"This will be Defense Exhibit C, Your Honor."

"What is the date that Dr. Brigman was appointed?"

"March 3, 2009."

Sarah saw the discrepancy register with some of the jurors, but she continued to nail down the point for all of them. "So the records show Michael Reed was paying Dr. Brigman four thousand a month from the time he filed for divorce in January and before Dr. Brigman became a part of the family law case in March?"

"That is correct."

"Did you reach a conclusion about the nature of this four thousand a month payment?"

"Objection!" Preston Barton was quivering with rage.

"Your Honor, Mr. Mitchell has established his reputation as an expert in investigating financial crimes."

"Very well. Overruled."

"I concluded that Michael Reed wanted to control the custody of his children by bribing Ronald Brigman, and he made that arrangement with him before he took action to divorce his wife."

"Now, Mr. Mitchell, I have one final area to cover with you. Did you become aware of surveillance cameras that covered the back of Dr. Brigman's house?"

"Yes, one of his neighbors provided me with footage from his cameras on the night of June 2, 2013."

"Thank you, Mr. Mitchell. No further questions."

Preston Barton leapt to the podium as Sarah sat down, but he managed to get a grip on his emotions. He began in a cool, confident professional tone. "So tell me, Mr. Mitchell, did you review all of the family court file?"

"Yes, I did."

"And did you read all of Dr. Brigman's psychological evaluations of Michael and Alexa and their children?"

"I did."

"And did you read Dr. Brigman's finding that the defendant had deliberately harmed the children's relationship with their father?"

"I read that. It didn't ring true to me."

"Your Honor, I ask that the portion of Mr. Mitchell's answer after 'I read that' be stricken as not responsive."

"It will be stricken. Just answer the question asked, Mr. Mitchell."

"And did you find a minute order that showed Dr. Brigman was appointed to do psychotherapy with the children?"

"Yes."

"And who paid for that therapy?"

"Michael Reed."

"And that would have been expensive therapy, would it not?"

"I am not versed in the costs of psychotherapy in San Diego, and that theory does not explain the payments in January before the divorce began."

"But what if Michael Reed was concerned about his relationship with his children and took them to Dr Brigman for an expert opinion in January 2009 leading him to decide to file for divorce to save his relationship with them?"

"Objection." Sarah stood up quickly. "These facts are not in evidence. Mr. Barton is asking the witness to speculate."

"That's true," Judge Tomlinson nodded. "Objection sustained."

"No further questions."

And to Sarah' great relief, the judge said to Jim, "You may step down."

"Ms. Knight, it's nearly four o'clock. Do you have another witness for today?"

"Yes, Your Honor. Ted Frederickson. He won't take long. I'll easily finish by four thirty."

"Very well. You may call your next witness."

Ted Frederickson presented well, Sarah thought as she watched the clerk swear in the tall, lanky, good-looking man in the obviously expensive Big Firm navy power suit and tasteful maroon tie.

"Good afternoon, Mr. Frederickson, please state your name and occupation for the record."

"Theodore Christian Frederickson. I am a partner with the firm of King and White."

"And do you practice criminal law, Mr. Frederickson?"

"No. I specialize in corporate buyouts and mergers."

"And did you have a connection to Dr. Ronald Brigman?"

"Yes. He was my next door neighbor for fifteen years."

"Did there come a time when my investigator, James Mitchell contacted you?"

"Yes. He spoke with my wife first, and then with me."

"And why did Mr. Mitchell contact you?"

"I have a surveillance system that covers the front and back of my house. And the camera in my back yard also picks up Dr. Brigman's back door."

"Can you describe the back door of Dr. Brigman's residence?"

"He had the same setup all of us on that side of the street have. Oversized sliding glass doors open onto a patio that gives us the best view from the edge of Mt. Soledad of the village of La Jolla and the Pacific Ocean."

"And I take it that is a pretty spectacular view?"

"Yes."

"And do you know if Dr. Brigman was in the habit of leaving his back doors open?"

"Yes. All of us along that side of the street liked to enjoy the view at night."

"Now, when Mr. Mitchell contacted you, was he seeking something in particular?"

"Yes. He had learned from my wife that I had saved the surveillance tape that showed the back door of Dr. Brigman's house on the night he was killed."

Sarah held up a CD. "I'd like this marked as Defense Exhibit D. It is a copy of the surveillance tape that Mr. Frederickson provided."

"No objection," Preston Barton mumbled.

"And have you viewed this surveillance footage, Mr. Frederickson?"

"I have."

"And does it accurately depict the area in question?"

"Yes."

"And is the time stamp on the footage accurate?"

"It is."

"No further questions."

"Mr. Barton?"

"Just briefly, Your Honor"

Sarah watched the prosecutor heft himself out of his chair and up to the podium.

"Mr. Frederickson, why did you provide this material to the defense and not to the police?"

"Because the police never asked for it. They took statements from my wife and me, and we told them about the tape, but they never came back for it."

"Why did you save it then?"

"I knew it was important evidence."

"Now you said that you have seen this footage?"

"Yes."

"And do you recognize anyone on it?"

"When I first viewed it, the only person I recognized was Ronald Brigman. But after I saw Mrs. Reed's picture in the paper, I realized she is there as well."

"Thank you, Mr. Frederickson. No further questions."

Judge Tomlinson looked up at the clock and smiled at the defense table. "And you were as good as your word, Ms. Knight. It is exactly four twenty-five. We will resume in the morning at eight-thirty."

CHAPTER FORTY-ONE

Next day, Wednesday, January 2014, San Diego County Courthouse

Sarah took several deep breaths as she stood at the podium next morning, ready to question Alexa, who had just been sworn as a witness. She looked quietly professional in her light gray suit and white blouse, and her face was open and gentle, without a hint of deception in those wide blue eyes, as she waited to begin telling her story.

Please let me do a good job, Sarah told the Universe as she felt Jim's eyes fixed intently on both of them and on the jurors, who were sizing up Alexa, some curiously, some with open hostility in their faces.

"Would you state your name for the record?"

"Alexa Harrison Reed."

Sarah took Alexa through the background they needed to establish her education, her work at the Supreme Court, her two children, and Michael's decision to initiate divorce proceedings.

The jurors' eyes stayed fixed on Alexa's face, and Sarah felt as if things were going their way for the moment.

"Now, Mrs. Reed, were there difficulties in your marriage to Michael Reed?"

"Yes."

"Could you describe them for the jury?"

"Michael had multiple affairs throughout our marriage."

"And was that the only difficulty?"

"No, Michael became increasingly violent with me."

Tears welled up in Alexa's eyes, and Sarah felt her stomach tighten. A little emotion might be good, but too much would look like a play for sympathy.

"Bailiff, would you put a box of tissues within Mrs. Reed's reach?" Judge Tomlinson observed mildly.

Preston Barton leapt to his feet. "The People request a sidebar."

Sarah sighed inwardly as she approached the bench. She already knew what the prosecutor was going to say.

"Your Honor, this evidence has been excluded because Dr. Brigman found it didn't happen."

"And the defense has brought forward evidence that Dr. Brigman was being paid by Michael Reed for opinions in his favor," Sarah countered. "The jurors are the ones who have to determine if Alexa Reed is telling the truth. The court of appeal is going to bounce this case back to you in a heartbeat if any more evidence is excluded in the name of Ronald Brigman's findings." Sarah took a deep breath when she finished. But she could see the shadow of Coleman Reed's phone calls hanging over Judge Tomlinson.

"I've made my ruling, Ms. Knight. If the court of appeal sends this case back, so be it. Dr. Brigman's finding that Michael Reed was not violent toward his wife is conclusive for this proceeding. Ask another question. It can be a leading question if necessary."

The jurors' eyes were fixed on her as she returned to the podium, and they did not look favorable.

"Mrs. Reed, would it be fair to say that because you asked your husband to cease his infidelities, he filed for divorce?"

"Yes."

"And did that lead to the loss of a significant portion of your time with your children?"

"Yes. In mid-May, Dr. Brigman gave ninety percent custody of the children to Michael beginning in September when they went back to school."

"And how old were they in May?"

"Meggie was five and Sam was four."

"And had you always been their primary caregiver?"

"Yes."

"And did Michael have time to care for the children?"

"No, he worked very long hours at Warrick, Thompson. During our marriage, the children and I rarely saw him."

"And did Michael Reed sometimes tell you he was working late in order to go on dates with other women?"

"Objection!" Preston Barton intoned, "Irrelevant!"

"I'll allow it," Judge Tomlinson said. "Please answer the question?"

"Yes, he often said he was out with a client when, in fact, he was seeing another woman."

"So your husband was often untruthful with you?"

"Objection," Preston Barton roared.

"On what grounds?"

"Relevance."

"I'll allow it. Continue, Ms. Knight."

Sarah breathed a sigh of relief and headed into deep waters with her next question. "Now, Mrs. Reed, I'd like to turn to June 2, of last year. Do you recall where your children were that day?"

"For the day, they were with me. But Michael came and got them at five p.m."

"And was this part of the new custody order Dr. Brigman had put in place?"

"Yes."

"And was that change difficult for you and for them?"

"Very."

"So what took place after Michael picked up Meggie and Sam?"

"I–I spent some time being emotional because I missed them."

"By 'emotional' do you mean crying?"

Alexa's eyes filled up again, and she nodded yes.

"I'm afraid you'll have to speak your answers, Mrs. Reed," Judge Tomlinson said gravely. "The court reporter can't take down head nods."

"Of course. I'm sorry. Yes, I spent some time crying because I missed my children."

"And then did something unusual happen?"

"Yes. About eight-thirty my phone rang, and it was Ronald Brigman. He said I had to be at his house that night by nine if I ever wanted to see my children again."

"What did you do?"

"I didn't want to go because I was afraid he was going to take away the time I had left with them. And I was terrified of going alone because anything that happened would be his word against mine."

"What did you do?"

"I called my attorney, Bob Metcalf; but he didn't answer. Finally I decided I would just have to do what Dr. Brigman asked because I didn't want to lose all contact with my children."

"What happened after you arrived at Dr. Brigman's?"

"He told me Michael had been paying him four thousand a month to get full custody of the children. He said he hadn't been able to give them to Michael as soon as he filed for divorce because they were so little, and they were primarily bonded to me. But Dr. Brigman said he'd been trying to change their attachment through his therapy sessions with them. He had been trying to get them to prefer Michael."

"And did that seem to be working?"

"No. Dr. Brigman's sessions with the children caused them a lot of stress and anxiety."

"What else did Ronald Brigman tell you that night?"

"He said Michael had stopped paying him; and since his therapy sessions to turn the children against me weren't working, he said I could have Meggie and Sam for two thousand a month. He called it 'the single mother discount.'"

"Objection, hearsay," Preston Barton intoned.

"Dr. Brigman's statements are declarations against interest," Sarah said. "He admitted to committing extortion."

"Objection overruled. You may continue."

"What did you say to Dr. Brigman's offer?"

"I was terrified. I didn't know whether to believe him or not. I still thought he was trying to manipulate me into doing something wrong or illegal to take away the rest of my time with Meggie and Sam."

"What did you do next?"

"I told Dr. Brigman I didn't have that kind of money, and I left. I was too upset to go home, so I drove around for a while. I needed to think. I tried to call Bob Metcalf again, but there was no answer."

"And what time did you leave Ronald Brigman's?"

"Around nine-thirty."

"Your Honor, I would like to play that portion of Defense Exhibit D that shows Mrs. Reed leaving Dr. Brigman's at nine-thirty."

"Certainly, Ms. Knight. If the bailiff could dim the lights so that the jury can get a better view on the overhead screen."

Sarah handed a laser pointer to the bailiff to give to Alexa. She glanced over at the jury and saw all eyes fixed on the tape as it played. Sarah hit the pause button when Alexa's figure appeared.

"Now, Mrs. Reed, are you in that frame of the surveillance tape?"

"Yes."

"Using the laser pointer, will you outline your image for the jury."

"Here." Sarah watched as Alexa traced her small form on the tape.

"And what are you doing at this point?"

"I'm leaving Dr. Brigman's by the back door."

"And could you point to the date and time stamp at the bottom of the tape and read it to us."

"June 2, 2013, 21:30 p.m."

"What is 21:30p.m.?"

"Nine-thirty."

"Thank you, Mrs. Reed." Sarah pushed the play button again and within a few frames a tall male figure appeared in profile. The man walked to the edge of the patio and gazed out over the mountain at the valley below.

"Do you recognize that person?" Sarah asked Alexa.

"Yes. It's Ronald Brigman."

"And what is the time showing at the bottom of that frame?"

"21:45 p.m., which is nine forty-five p.m."

"So Dr. Brigman was very much alive when you left at nine-thirty?"

"Yes, he was."

"Thank you, Your Honor. That is all of the surveillance tape that I am going to play."

The bailiff turned the lights back on, and everyone blinked at the bright light.

"Now, Mrs. Reed, you said that you left and drove around for a while?"

"Yes."

"What happened after that?"

"I decided to take a chance that Dr. Brigman was making a legitimate offer. I thought Alan Warrick would give me my job back if I told him why I needed two thousand a month to keep my children. I drove back to Dr. Brigman's to tell him I was going to accept his offer."

"What time did you arrive?"

"It must have been ten-thirty."

"And did you go to Dr. Brigman's front door?"

"No. He wasn't expecting me, and I was afraid he wouldn't answer. I felt I had to accept his offer that night, or he would take Meggie and Sam away for good. I guessed the back door was still open, and I went around that way."

"And did you enter Dr. Brigman's house through the back door?"

"Just barely. I stepped inside and called his name several times, but he didn't seem to be home."

"About what time was this?"

"Still around ten-thirty. It all happened very quickly."

"What did you do next?"

"I left and drove around again, planning to go back to see if he'd returned, so I could accept his offer. I was beginning to panic a little because I was so sure he would take Meggie and Sam if I didn't say yes that night."

"What happened next?"

"Around 11:15 Meggie called. She was crying because she and Sam were scared. Their father had gotten into an argument with a woman, and they were hiding in a closet and wanted me to come and get them."

"What did you do?"

"I drove to Michael's. The front door was standing wide open. I went into the front hall and found him lying in a pool of blood with a gun beside him."

"Did you recognize it as yours?"

"No. I didn't know it was mine until the police told me next day."

"What did you do next?"

"I called 911 and got Meggie and Sam into the car and took them home."

"Did you think you would be a suspect in this case?"

"No."

"And did you, in fact, kill Michael Reed and Ronald Brigman?"

"No."

"No further questions, Your Honor."

Sarah glanced over at the jurors as she sat down, and Preston Barton replaced her at the podium. Their faces were blank. She couldn't tell what they were thinking.

Preston Barton looked at Alexa Reed and began his cross-examination. "Mrs. Reed, did I hear you say you graduated first in your class from Georgetown?"

"That is correct."

"And you also said you were a clerk at the United States Supreme Court for Justice Paula Moreno?"

"Yes, I was."

"So Mrs. Reed, your educational achievements demonstrate you are in the top one percent of attorneys in this country, are you not?"

"I don't know how to answer that question."

"Well, let me put it this way: you know more than the average lawyer about the law."

"Again, I don't know how to answer that question."

"Now, Mrs. Reed, you assisted your attorney, Ms. Knight, in preparing your defense in this case, did you not?"

Sarah stood up quickly. "Objection, Your Honor. The question calls for information covered by the attorney client privilege and by attorney work product."

Judge Tomlinson frowned. "I'm going to allow it. He hasn't asked for any specifics, and a defendant has a right to assist his attorney in preparing his defense. He's just asked for generic information. Your client may answer the question."

"Yes, I did."

"So you were aware of all the witness statements and materials the prosecution turned over in discovery?"

Sarah shot up again. "Same objection, Your Honor."

Judge Tomlinson's frown deepened. "I agree with you this time. Sustained."

Sarah watched the prosecutor regroup. "Now, Mrs. Reed, you were in attendance at the preliminary hearing in this case, were you not?"

"Yes, I was."

"And you heard all the evidence presented against you there?"

"I did."

"And you've been in attendance every day in this trial, have you not?"

"Yes."

"And so you've heard all the witnesses' testimony?"

"I have."

"And that has given you the opportunity to fabricate this story about Dr. Brigman and bribes, hasn't it?"

"Objection!" Sarah roared to her feet. "The question assumes facts not in evidence and uses Mrs. Reed's Sixth Amendment right to jury trial and to confrontation against her."

"Overruled. You may continue."

Sarah felt the pit of her stomach tightening as Preston Barton moved in for the kill. She could see at least half the jury eyeing the prosecutor with approval.

"I haven't fabricated any stories," Alexa said, meeting Barton's eyes levelly.

Good, Sarah thought. She's standing up to him.

"Are you saying you've never fabricated any stories, Mrs. Reed?"

"Yes." Alexa's eyes never waived.

"But what about claiming your husband beat you? Didn't you tell Dr. Brigman that?"

Sarah was on her feet. "Objection!"

"Overruled. Mr. Barton is allowed to impeach the witness."

"Dr. Brigman refused to believe me when I told him about Michael's attacks."

"And could that have been because you are a liar, Mrs. Reed?"

"I am not."

"Are you sure?"

"I am sure."

The prosecutor shuffled through some papers on the podium and pulled out one of them. "Your Honor, I have here a report that Dr. Brigman prepared in the child custody proceedings dated April 2009. I'd liked this marked as the next People's Exhibit in order."

As he spoke, Preston Barton handed a copy to Sarah.

"Now, Mrs. Reed, you were aware that Dr. Brigman prepared a report for the family law court in April 2009, after he was appointed in February of that year?"

"Yes."

"And Dr. Brigman interviewed you in the course of preparing this report, did he not?"

"Yes."

"And did you tell him about an incident in December 2008, that occurred after you and Michael attended the Warrick, Thompson Christmas party?"

"Yes."

"And did you tell Dr. Brigman that your husband beat you that night and broke your arm?"

Sarah felt her stomach tighten.

"Yes."

"And did you tell Dr. Brigman that Michael then drove you to the emergency room?"

"Yes."

"And did you subsequently consent to Dr. Brigman's viewing your medical treatment records from the hospital that night?"

"Yes."

"And what did those records show you told the treating physician?"

"I told him I slipped and fell after we got home."

"So you didn't tell the ER doctor the same thing you told Dr. Brigman?"

Sarah saw Alexa's confidence snuffed out like a candle hit by a wind gust.

"No, I didn't."

"So you have fabricated stories, have you not, Mrs. Reed?

Alex bit her lip before replying, "That night at the hospital I did."

"No further questions, Your Honor."

Sarah felt Jim coiled like a spring beside her. She had time to scribble "Don't react" on her legal pad before Judge Tomlinson said, "Any redirect, Ms. Knight?"

"Yes, Your Honor."

Sarah gripped the podium to steady her shaking hands. Sixteen pairs of hostile juror eyes were fixed on her and Alexa.

"Now, Mrs. Reed, can you explain for the jury why you didn't tell the emergency room doctor that your husband had broken your arm that evening?"

Alexa's eyes said Sarah had just thrown her the lifeline she needed.

"Yes. On the way to the hospital, Michael said that if I told the truth—"

The prosecutor was on his pudgy little feet quickly. "Objection. Hearsay."

"It's not offered for the truth, Your Honor. It's offered to show Mrs. Reed's state of mind that night."

"I'm afraid it is hearsay. Sustained. Next question."

Sarah fought down the rising tide of panic in her gut and tried to keep her face impassive in front of the jurors.

"No further questions at this time."

"You may step down, Mrs. Reed."

Sarah was glad to see Alexa carried her head high as she crossed the courtroom and sat down. She saw Jim squeeze Alexa's hand sympathetically under the table.

"It's four-thirty," Judge Tomlinson observed. "We'll begin again in the morning at the usual time."

CHAPTER FORTY-TWO

That Wednesday night, January 2014, Alexa's Cottage, Pacific Beach

Jim studied Alexa's tired face in the dim light of her living room at eight-thirty that evening. He was sitting next to her on the sofa while a cheese pizza quietly congealed in its box on the coffee table. The three of them had met to talk over the situation, but the defense position was so dire, none of them had had the heart to start the discussion. Sarah had gone into the kitchen to finalize the arrangements with Dr. Spangler for tomorrow. He was the only defense witness left.

Alexa, who rarely consumed more than one glass of wine, was deeply into her third. In her jeans and t-shirt, she didn't look old enough to drink. Jim listened to Sarah's voice rise and fall in the other room as she talked to Dr. Spangler.

"You need to eat more if you are going to drink that much wine," Jim cautioned.

"Not hungry."

"You are sounding like Sarah."

Alexa's tired, tormented eyes fixed on his. "I shouldn't have testified. Sarah warned me. I just thought I could make the jurors understand what it was like that night."

"Don't give up yet."

Sarah appeared from the kitchen, putting her cell phone into her purse as she pulled out her keys.

"Aren't you going to stay long enough to eat?" Alexa asked.

"No, I've got too much to do before tomorrow."

Jim stood up. "I'll walk you out."

They stepped into the chilly night air, and Jim noticed Sarah pull her coat tighter around her.

"Cold?"

"Cold, tired, you name it."

"You should eat."

"Later."

"Don't work all night."

"I might have to. I need to be ready to question Dr. Spangler. He's my last chance to create reasonable doubt in the juror's minds that Alexa murdered them."

"Can you say anything to help Alexa stop blaming herself for today?"

"No. It's almost always a bad idea for a defendant to take the stand, and it is a disaster when a defendant has lied on the record. I told Alexa all that when you pressured her to testify, and she went ahead anyway."

She opened the driver's door and started to get in, but Jim put out his hand.

"Wait!"

She looked up at him in the thin, cold moonlight, her face dark and unreadable, and asked, "What is it?"

"I'm to blame for what happened today. You're right. I talked her into it."

"Mea culpa is quite noble, but blame isn't going to improve our situation with the jury. We're losing big time. You know that."

"I do." He stood in the drive under the sliver of moon until her tail lights vanished.

* * *

"Will you stay?" Alexa asked as soon as he came back inside. Jim's heart turned over because she'd been crying.

He sat down next to her on the sofa and put his arms around her and pulled her head onto his shoulder. He inhaled her light violet smell and stroked her soft cheek. I'm going too far, he told himself; but there's no one else to comfort her.

As he held her, wondering if he should give in and stay, he remembered the long nights in the hospital, listening to the steady rhythm of the ventilator as he willed her to live. A verdict of guilty would lead to the penalty phase of the trial where the jury would have to decide between life in prison or death. *There wasn't much difference between them*, Jim thought, as he realized Alexa's breathing had become more regular, and she had dropped off.

It was the wine. She'd drunk too much for a tiny body. But who could blame her after today? He carried her into her bedroom, pulled back the covers, and tucked her in. He was tempted to throw himself down beside her, but he couldn't go to court in the morning unshaven and in his jeans.

He wrapped up the unattractive cold pizza, put it in the fridge, and drained the wine bottle before tossing it into the recycle bin. He turned out all the lights except the small lamp in the living room in case she woke in the night, and went out, using her spare key to lock up. He paused on the porch to scan the drive for anything suspicious but saw nothing other than the night lit by the thin slice of silver moon. He made sure the door was locked one last time and then hurried to his Range Rover and headed home.

His answering machine's normally steady red eye was blinking in his dark kitchen when he came in from the garage. He punched the play button without turning on a light, and heard Cody's soft voice explain to him why he wasn't coming for the week of winter break, scheduled for February 1. He didn't want to leave his baby sister. He didn't want to leave his school friends. He didn't want to leave his mother and Josh. He signed off with "Sorry, Dad. I love you," splitting Jim's heart straight down the middle.

Jim was angry now. He was angry at the Universe that had separated him from his son. He was angry at the trial court for pandering to Preston Barton with the shadow of Coleman Reed looming over their heads. He was angry with himself for persuading Alexa to testify. And he was angry with Sarah for more reasons than he could count.

He changed into pajamas and a white t-shirt and poured himself a stiff scotch. He downed the drink in a hurry, hoping it would bring sleep. And mercifully it did.

* * *

But as he knew only too well, scotch-induced sleep never lasts. By midnight, he was wide awake. He lay in bed for a while, willing himself back into the oblivion of sleep. But too many images whirled through his head, like a torrent of leaves caught in an autumn downdraft. Alexa, on the witness stand in her gentle gray suit today. Alexa looking like a teenager in her jeans tonight, gulping wine to ease the pain of her searing defeat. Sarah, cool and elegant, in deep red, projecting confidence at the podium as she took Alexa through her story. Sarah standing by her car tonight, fierce but tired, desirable and distant as always. Above all, he was haunted by Cody's soft voice on the answering machine telling him there'd be no father-son winter visit.

The last blow was too much. Jim knew he wasn't going back to sleep. He poured another drink, hoping it would at least dull the ache in his heart, and turned on the lights in his living room. He sat down at his desk in the corner, booted up his laptop, and began to re-examine the Frederickson and Morrison surveillance footage. And what he saw made his blood run cold. He forgot everything else as he played and replayed the tapes and wondered what he should do.

* * *

Sarah's phone rang at midnight.

"Hello."

"It's Juan. I'm calling to let you know she has crossed the border."

"Thank you."

"She has her instructions. You are sure you want to go through with this?"

"I have no choice."

"There is always a place here for you in Mexico City. You don't have to stay in the United States and spend the rest of your life in jail."

"Thank you, Juan. When Alexa is safe, I'll decide what to do."

"You aren't to blame, Sarah."

"I know. But I can't change the way it looks."

CHAPTER FORTY-THREE

Then suddenly someone was pounding frantically on his front door. Instinctively he reached for his gun and went cautiously into the hall. As he was about to look through the peephole, he heard the pop, pop, pop of gunfire. A woman screamed, and a bullet flew past him. Then another and another.

The woman screamed again, but this time he could understand her. "It's Elaina!"

Jim ripped open the door and pulled her inside, firing all the while into the darkness, hoping to hit whoever was out there.

"Get down!" he yelled, and she threw herself onto the floor.

More bullets sped past him, as he emptied his clip wildly into the night without any idea where the shooter actually was. He was quickly out of ammunition, so he slammed the door and threw his body over Elaina's. He held his breath, hoping it was over.

They lay together in a terrified heap in the front hall, waiting for the next salvo to begin. But it didn't. Gradually, Jim felt the terror gripping him begin to ebb, and he became aware of Elaina's exquisite curves beneath him.

He eased himself off of her, and whispered in her ear. "Stay still. I'm going to look outside and see if I see anything."

He crawled back to the door, but instead of the peephole, he managed to peer between the blinds covering the narrow windows on either side. His heart sped up at the sight of a black Mercedes parked behind a white car in his drive.

"There's a black car and a white car out here. Which is yours?" he whispered to Elaina.

"White. A rental. Maria left it for me to pick up when I crossed the border tonight."

"There's a black Mercedes behind it."

"That's the car that followed me from San Ysidro. I thought I had lost it, but it appeared out of nowhere and opened fire. Is it still there?"

"Yes. No, wait. It's backing up. But stay down until I'm sure it's gone."

Another five minutes passed before Jim allowed her to stand up.

"Come this way."

He led her down the hall toward the living room, and she took a seat on the couch. Jim turned down the lights just in case the shooter was still around and poured each of them a scotch.

"Here."

She looked up at him with her beautiful almond-shaped eyes and said, "Thanks."

But as she downed the first gulp, Jim realized the left sleeve of her denim jacket was covered in blood.

"Wait! You've been hit."

Elaina looked down curiously. "I don't feel anything."

"It's probably not bad. Let's get your coat off."

He eased her jacket off and rolled up the equally bloody sleeve of her white silk blouse, wondering if he needed to call Tom Barrett; and, if he did, would Tom be with Sarah.

But it was only a scratch. "Thank God, it's nothing much," he told her. Come into the bathroom and I'll clean it up."

He led her into the guest bathroom off his second bedroom, and washed and cleaned her arm. He bandaged it with soft gauze and smiled. "Feel better?"

"Yes, much. But I need to get out of these clothes. I have new ones in the car."

"It's not safe to go out there tonight. I'll lend you some of mine."

She came back into the living room a few minutes later, her stunning body shrouded in his t-shirt and pajama pants.

She gave him the first smile she'd been able to manage. "Not exactly a fashion statement."

"You look lovely, anyway. I've topped off your drink. Do you want anything to eat?"

"No, thanks." She took the glass from him and curled herself onto the sofa, one leg tucked under her. Her color had come back, and she was heart-stoppingly beautiful once more. Jim tried not to feel what he was feeling.

"Let's start at the beginning," he said. "Who was shooting at you?"

"I am guessing men Coleman Reed hired. I lied to Enrique and said my mother in Tijuana was ill, so he would let me come home. I thought he believed me, but I must have been wrong."

"Why did you want to leave the yacht?"

"So I could come and testify."

"Why did you change your mind?"

"Does it matter?"

Jim took a long drink of scotch as he thought about her question. The lovely alcohol buzz was returning, and he felt sleepy once more. "No. Do you want to tell me what you saw that night?"

"Now is not the time to talk. Your eyes are almost closed. And I am tired. Tomorrow."

* * *

The call from Jim came at six a.m. Sarah had not slept at all, so she was awake and expecting it.

"Elaina Morales is here. She crossed the border last night. She is ready to testify."

Yes, yes. I know. I was the one who brought her here. But instead of the truth, she said, "Okay. I'll put her on before Dr. Spangler."

"I'll meet you at the courthouse with both Alexa and Elaina at the usual time."

"Of course."

Sarah looked around her little bungalow that morning as she left for the courthouse knowing she would probably never return. *I have to do this for Alexa*, she said to herself. *And for Jim, who loves her.* And the Universe replied, "*And you have to do it because it's your only chance of redemption.*"

CHAPTER FORTY-FOUR

Fourth Thursday in January 2014, San Diego County Courthouse

"Would you state your name for the record?"

"Elaina Sofia Diaz-Morales."

Elaina's beautiful dark eyes were fixed on Sarah, who stood at the podium in her most serious navy suit, her own face a study in concentration. Jim noticed the male jurors couldn't stop staring at Elaina's perfect figure in her simple black dress.

"And how are you employed?"

"I am an escort for Elite Call Girls."

"And how long have you worked for that service?"

"Seven years."

"And did you know Michael Reed?"

"Yes. He was a client."

"For how long?"

Elaina paused and turned her soft eyes toward the jury, thinking about her answer. "The first time I went on a date with Michael was 2007. So six years."

"And was he a frequent client during those six years?"

"Yes. More often after he filed for divorce."

"But he regularly went on dates with you while he was married to Alexa Reed?"

"Oh, yes. Michael was very open about being married."

"How was he open?"

"He talked about his marriage. He did not say kind things about his wife."

"What unkind things did he say?"

"Objection!" Preston Barton roared. He had looked as if he was going to have a heart attack the minute Elaina walked into the courtroom, and he still was red and sweating profusely.

"Your Honor, it is relevant to Michael Reed's state of mind."

"Overruled. You may answer."

"He often said his wife thought she was smarter than he was; but he said in reality she wasn't very smart because he could manipulate her through her children. He said he intended to destroy her by taking the children away."

"And did he talk about this often?"

"He tried to, but I usually turned the conversation in a different direction. I don't like to hear clients complain about their wives."

"Now were you with Michael Reed on the evening of June 2, 2013?"

"Yes. We had a date that night."

"And what time did that date begin?"

"I arrived at his house at eight p.m."

"And was anyone else there besides Michael?"

"His children. He had been boasting for sometime he would soon receive almost full custody of them. That night, they were with him."

"So how did you spend that evening with Michael Reed?"

"We put his children to bed between eight-thirty and nine. Then we ate dinner, drank some wine, and had sex."

"And then what happened?"

"Around ten o'clock someone began banging on the front door. Michael laughed because he thought it was his ex-wife, coming back to demand her children. And he said she had no right to have them that night, and he was going to call the police to arrest her."

"So did he call the police?"

"No. He put on his clothes and went to open the door. I checked on the children to make sure the banging hadn't awakened them."

"And were they awake?"

"No, they stirred a little. We had put them to bed in separate rooms, but now the little boy was sleeping on the floor on some blankets in his sister's room."

"What happened next?"

"I heard Michael raise his voice, and I walked into the front hall to warn him not to wake the children."

"And what did you see in the front hall?"

"I saw an older man arguing with Michael."

"Did you know the man's name?"

"Not until after he left. Michael told me then."

"And what was his name?"

"Ronald Brigman."

"Is this a photo of the man you saw in the hall that night?"

"Yes."

"Did you listen to the conversation between Dr. Brigman and Michael?"

"Yes. It became heated."

"Objection, hearsay!" Preston Barton roared again.

"That is her own observation, Your Honor."

"Agreed. Overruled. Continue."

"Why was the conversation heated?"

"Dr. Brigman told Michael he'd kept his part of the bargain and had given him almost full custody of the children. Now Michael had to pay up. He told Michael he was four months behind on his payments, and Dr. Brigman wanted his money by Monday afternoon."

"Objection!"

"The statements are declarations against interest, Your Honor."

"I'll allow it. Continue."

"What did Michael say?"

"He laughed and said he wasn't going to pay now that he had what he wanted."

"And then what happened?"

"Dr. Brigman said he'd give custody back to the children's mother. But Michael laughed again and reminded Dr. Brigman the reports he'd written had made her out to be so crazy and unstable no court would follow his recommendation if he said to give them back."

"And what did Dr. Brigman say?"

"He told Michael the court always followed his recommendation. He said there were ways he could rehabilitate Mrs. Reed, particularly because everything he had written about her was a lie that Michael had paid for."

"What happened next?"

"They shouted at each other, and then Dr. Brigman stormed off."

"What time was it?"

"I'm guessing about ten-thirty."

"What happened after Dr. Brigman left?"

"Michael was furious. I'd never seen him that angry before."

"What did he do?"

"He opened the hall closet and took out a gun. He started waving it around, and I was frightened."

"What did you do?"

"I tried to calm him down. I reminded him the children were in the house."

"Did it work?"

"He was a little less angry, but he still seemed very upset. He told me the gun belonged to his wife. He said he had a key to her car that she didn't know about, and he'd used it to take the gun out a few weeks earlier."

"What next?"

"I asked him why he wanted his wife's gun, and he began to laugh hysterically. He said he had been planning for sometime to kill Dr. Brigman using his wife's gun, so she'd be arrested for the murder. He said if he was lucky she'd get the death penalty. But either way, she'd never get out of prison; and she'd never see her children again. And he wouldn't have to pay Ronald Brigman another cent."

"What happened next?"

"He ran out, and I heard his car start. I was terrified. I don't like guns. I wanted to go home, but I didn't think I should leave the children alone in the house."

"So what did you do?"

"I put my clothes back on and packed up my things. I was going to leave the minute Michael got back."

"How long was he gone?"

"Not more than twenty minutes."

"What happened when he returned?"

"He came in holding the gun and bragging he'd killed Brigman, and everyone was going to think his wife did it. But then he realized he'd forgotten to leave the murder weapon with the body, so he said he'd have to go back and plant it."

Jim saw Elaina begin to shake. She looked over at him as if asking him to rescue her. At the podium, Sarah had become grim-faced.

"What happened next?"

"Michael had a horrible, wild look on his face. He said, 'I've got to take care of you, too. You know I killed him. But I can't shoot you because I'll wake up the children.' He put the gun down on the little table next to where we were standing in the hall, and he wrapped his hands around my throat."

"What did you do?"

"I screamed and lunged for the gun."

"And did you manage to get it?"

Elaina looked straight into Sarah's eyes. "Yes. I shot him as he was trying to strangle me."

"How many times did you fire?"

"I don't know. I was terrified, and I just kept shooting."

"And then?"

"I ran out and headed back to Tijuana where I live."

"So, Ms. Morales, did you kill Michael Reed on the night of June 2, 2013?"

"Yes, I did."

"And did Michael Reed confess to you that he killed Ronald Brigman between ten thirty-five and eleven-fifteen that night?"

"Yes, he did."

"No further questions, Your Honor." Sarah's eyes held Elaina's a minute longer before she sat down next to Alexa. Jim noticed her hands were shaking uncontrollably.

"Your witness, Mr. Barton."

He already looked defeated, Jim thought with satisfaction as the prosecutor shuffled to the podium.

"Ms. Morales, you testified you go on dates for Elite Call girls?"

"That is correct."

"And do those dates involve sex?"

"Sometimes." Elaina met Preston Barton's beady little eyes unflinchingly.

"Sometimes or all the time?"

"Only sometimes. There is a contract for every date. Some include sex, some do not."

"And what kinds of clients patronize Elite Call Girls?"

"Very wealthy clients."

"So what is the minimum charge for an evening with you, no sex?"

"Between five and seven thousand."

"And more with sex?"

"Correct."

"And have you ever been arrested for prostitution, Ms. Morales?"

"No."

"But your 'dates' for Elite Call Girls, are they not acts of prostitution?'

"Objection," Sarah said. "Calls for a legal conclusion."

"Sustained," Judge Tomlinson agreed. "You do not have to answer the question."

"No further questions," Preston Barton sat down, a defeated man; and Jim noticed the jury was looking at the defense table with new eyes.

"Any more witnesses, Ms. Knight?" Judge Tomlinson asked.

"No, Your Honor. The defense rests."

"Thank you, Ms. Morales. You may step down."

All eyes were on Elaina as she made her way out of the courtroom.

"We'll take a twenty minute recess," Judge Tomlinson said.

* * *

Sarah's heart was pounding. She got up and walked into the lobby to regain her composure. She wished her hands would stop shaking. She crossed the floor to stare at the passing traffic on Broadway, hoping that focusing on something else would clear her terror.

"Ms. Knight?" The dark, husky voice behind her was unmistakable. Elaina Morales stepped out of the shadows.

"Why did you wait for me?" Sarah's heart hammered harder. Her world was suddenly a vortex of terror, spinning faster and faster.

"Because I have a message for you."

"A message?"

"From my grandfather. He told me to say, 'Your secret is safe.'"

"I didn't expect that."

"I know. But he said you deserved it."

Then she turned and vanished into the lunchtime crowd swarming the sidewalk in front of the courthouse.

* * *

Jim was suddenly behind her. "The clerk has announced Judge Tomlinson is on his way back from chambers and is ready to reconvene."

Sarah struggled to regain her professional composure as she reentered the courtroom. But her terror only rose to a new level when she saw a group of dark-suited men occupying the first two rows of public seating.

Jim, walking beside her toward the defense table, leaned over and whispered in her ear, "FBI and U.S. Marshals."

Elaina had been wrong. Her secret wasn't safe. Sarah's mind whirled through the past which had caught up with her on this day, at this minute, with an innocent woman's life in her hands.

Judge Tomlinson entered and took the bench. He looked shaken to the core himself. Jim handed her a note scribbled on her legal pad, "Move for a dismissal."

She stared at him in disbelief. But he scribbled under the first note, "Just do it. Now."

On shaking legs, Sarah stood up at counsel table. "Your Honor, the defense moves for dismissal of all the charges based on Ms. Morales' testimony. The evidence is insufficient to submit the question of guilt to the jury. Alexa Reed did not murder Michael Reed or Ronald Brigman. We move for discharge of the jury and for an order exonerating Mrs. Reed and releasing her from custody."

Judge Tomlinson, looking old and weary, said, "Granted."

Alexa turned to her with tears of joy, just as the two rows of dark suits stood up as one man. Sarah could see their shoulder holsters under their coats and braced herself. But one group of them walked past the defense table and over to the prosecutor and took Preston Barton into custody. The rest approached the bench and handcuffed Judge Tomlinson.

Sarah watched the two being led out of the courtroom, still waiting for the other shoe to drop. Except it never did.

She turned to Alexa, but she was wrapped in Jim's arms and oblivious to everything else. Sarah quickly gathered her papers into her briefcase and hurried out the back way to avoid the chaos of the press in the hall. Her heart had split from top to bottom, but Alexa was free, and she and Jim could have a life together. And maybe now Sarah could start believing that Elaina had told the truth: her own terrible secret was yet safe.

CHAPTER FORTY-FIVE

Fourth Thursday Night, January 2014, Sarah's House, La Jolla

Her house was quiet and still at nine-thirty. She had begged off dinner with Tom.

She had called Juan to make sure Elaina had safely crossed back into Mexico. Now she sat on the couch in her living room with a celebratory bottle of zinfandel and contemplated the rest of her life. Had she earned her redemption today? Was her secret forever safe?

And then her phone rang. "Sarah, it's Jim. I have to talk to you."

"I'm too tired to come to Alexa's tonight." *And I don't want to see the two of you together,* she thought.

"I'm not at Alexa's. I'm parked in your driveway. I put Alexa on a plane to Dulles this afternoon. She's on her way to Meggie and Sam."

Sarah went to the front door and opened it, letting in the cool night air. She pulled her gray cashmere cardigan together over her yoga pants and silk camisole. Jim was wearing his jeans and hooded sweatshirt.

"Why are you here?"

"I have to explain some things."

"As in what happened in court today?"

"Yes. And I have a few questions for you."

Sarah's stomach tightened.

"Okay. Come in."

He followed her into the living room, and sat down on the couch.

"Glass of wine?"

"Not yet."

She picked up hers and refilled it from the bottle on the coffee table. "What have you come to say?" She sat down on the other end.

"That I'm not retired FBI. I was sent here from D.C. to work undercover on what we suspected were judges and others taking bribes and obstructing justice. We thought if it were going on, we'd certainly find evidence in the Alexa Reed case."

"So I didn't meet you by chance that night at Trend?"

"No. Although I had no idea how lovely you'd be."

Sarah felt her heart lurch and break one more time. "So you became my investigator to get close to Alexa's prosecution?"

"Yes. And I uncovered a lot more than I expected."

"Such as?"

"Today, in addition to the prosecutor and the judge in Alexa's criminal case, my colleagues arrested the judge in her family law case and Tara Jeffers. Tara, by the way, is facing attempted murder. She was the one who arranged for your car accident."

"Does Bob Metcalf know?"

"Yes, I called him myself."

"I felt a little sorry for Judge Tomlinson, though. He wasn't always in Coleman Reed's pocket."

"But he took Coleman's money in exchange for all those rulings in favor of the prosecution at trial, including keeping out Jordan's testimony. And he was on the take when he ordered the medications for Alexa that the jail psychiatrist then used to try to kill her."

"That explains why he was so upset when his ruling was abused and why he let her out on house arrest. Probably illegally, as he said," Sarah observed. "When he took that bribe, he didn't think they were going to try to kill her." *Why did Jim have to have the kindest face in the world*, she thought. "What about Timothy Stratton? Will he really lose his job?"

"Not now. But I'm going to see he's offered a better one with the Bureau. Tara and the prosecutor and the two judges are not all the arrests we made today. Tessa Spinelli was arrested for attempted murder. She sent the hit man to your house that night. She thought you were still sleeping with her husband. And Coleman Reed was arrested on charges of money laundering, obstruction of justice, and one count of attempted murder. His goons tried to kill Elaina when she crossed the border yesterday."

"So Alexa will be able to get her children back without Coleman being in the way?"

"Myrna will have them at the airport when she arrives."

Suddenly tears stung Sarah's eyes, and she knew her control was close to snapping. "Thanks for coming by and giving me the good news. But I'm really tired now, and I need to be alone."

"But I'm not finished," Jim looked very grave, and Sarah felt her hands begin to shake. "I need to ask you a few questions."

"Me?"

"Elaina lied on the stand today. The story she told me this morning was not the one she told in court."

"I have no idea what you are talking about."

"Yes, you do. I didn't show you all the surveillance tape from Ronald Brigman's neighbors. But I showed it to Elaina. She told me the truth. She lied to the jury to protect you. She didn't kill Michael Reed. You did. I had the other DNA profile on the gun tested. It didn't belong to Elaina. She never touched it."

"I don't know what to say."

"How about starting at the beginning with your real name, Beth Carter Rogers."

So her secret wasn't safe. Sarah studied the face of the man she loved with all her heart and considered the irony of confessing everything she had covered up for so long to him.

"How did you know that?"

"I'm an FBI agent, remember?"

She wondered when he was going to arrest her. Well, better in these last few minutes of freedom to tell it all. She was sitting on the other end of the sofa, facing him. She put her wine glass down and began to try to find the words.

"My story is a lot like Alexa's. I went to Yale, graduated high in my class, married a fellow classmate. My mother raised me alone in a suburb of Pittsburgh, and she died during my last year of law school. I thought I loved Bill Rogers; but in reality, I was desperately lonely.

"I wanted to stay on the East Coast, but Bill grew up in San Diego. He took a job at Brown, Thornton, and Gray, a mid-sized local firm here that long ago went under. I worked in their litigation section for a year, but when Matthew was born in 1995, I stayed home with him. Then, two years later, Ben was born."

Jim's steady eyes took in her story. "Where are they now?"

Tears stung Sarah's eyes, and she had to wait for a minute before she could answer. "They're dead."

"What happened?"

"Bill and Michael Reed have a lot in common."

"So he beat you?"

"And other things." Her fingers traced the scar on her cheek. "He did this on the day he had the divorce papers served. Then he convinced Ronald Brigman that I'd done it to myself to try to get full custody of the children. You've asked why I haven't had plastic surgery. Because it reminds me how foolish I was to believe that the truth would prevail or that God answers prayers."

"So Brigman was involved in your case?"

"He gave my babies to the man who murdered them." Sarah's eyes met his, daring him to dispute her story. "I don't know if he'd engineered his bribe scheme back then, but it was clear from the beginning he was in Bill's pocket."

"I gather he didn't try therapy on them the way he did with Alexa's children."

"No. He just declared me to be a 'crazy,' unfit mother even though I was their primary caregiver, had been a well-respected lawyer when I was in practice, and there were hospital records of Bill's attacks on me. Black eyes, two broken ribs, and a broken arm. And I didn't lie to the attending physician the way Alexa did. But Ronald Brigman ignored all that and took away my right ever to see Matthew and Ben again. Matthew was six and Ben was four."

"Near the ages of Alexa's children?"

"Yes." Sarah closed her eyes to hold back the tears. "I don't think I can tell this story. I never have. Putting it into words makes it real again. I can still see them leaving for the last time with their little suitcases. We were all crying. Ben had a bear that he loved the way Sam loved Mr. Wiggles. And Bill wouldn't let him take it with him. I kept it, but I was never able to look at it again." Sarah shook her head. "No, I can't tell this story. I never have because I can't."

Jim reached for her hands which were pressed together in her lap and squeezed them gently. "You can tell me. Go on. What year did you lose them?"

"2001. Bill immediately moved to Miami where he had gotten involved in real estate speculation. But it didn't matter where he took them, I was barred from contact."

"So you left San Diego and went to Craig, Lewis in New York?"

"I changed my name and took the New York bar. Hollis Craig gave me a job in white collar crime, and I made it my life."

"I know that Bill Rogers was killed in 2008, and his then wife and her lover were convicted of hiring a hit man."

"That's all true, except his wife didn't hire the hit man."

"You did?"

"Not exactly." Sarah looked away at the dark night filling the glass panes of the French doors. "Matthew and Ben were found beaten to death at their father's house in 2005. Bill managed to have his nanny convicted of double murder, but she didn't do it. He did."

"And how do you know?"

Sarah pulled her hands away from Jim's and was silent for a long time. Finally she said, "He told me. When he got drunk, Bill liked to call and boast about what he'd done to my children. He liked to tell me every detail of their last breaths. How they called out for me."

The tears that never came, overflowed, but when he reached out to comfort her, she shook her head.

When she could speak again, he asked quietly, "So you were responsible for killing Bill Rogers?"

"That depends on how you look at it. Bill was killed in 2008, six months after I won the acquittal for Joey Menendez. Joey was so grateful, he took it upon himself to order a hit on Bill. Juan Alberto Lopez, Elaina Morales' grandfather, was the hit man."

Sarah was glad to see Jim looked genuinely shocked for the first time. "Is that why she came back to testify?"

"Yes. I called Juan and told her we needed her. He made her come back. And this morning, just before you arrested everyone, she gave me a message from him: 'tell her her secret is safe.' Only it wasn't. How did you know about me?"

"You are on the surveillance camera going into Brigman's back door near eleven that night. I showed that tape to Elaina, and she told me what happened at Michael's afterward."

Sarah paused to sip her wine before she went on. "For years, I waited to confront Ronald Brigman about my boys' death. I don't know if I planned to kill him, but the firm in New York required its high profile criminal defense attorneys to have a legal weapon and to learn to shoot. I admit I had fantasies for years of watching Brigman die. Last January, I decided to come back and confront him. I'm not sure what I intended to do, but I opened the office here and bided my time.

"But Michael Reed learned my secret from someone in the Menendez family who had gone rogue. That same person turned him on to Elaina. Michael knew Juan killed Bill, and he knew Joey arranged it for me. As you figured out, Coleman was money laundering. Michael took that aspect of the family business over, and then opened his own branch in blackmail. He was demanding payments from me to keep quiet about the hit on Bill."

"Is that why you wouldn't work at Warrick, Thompson?"

Sarah nodded.

"So how did all this come together on the night of June 2?"

"It had been six months since I came back to confront Brigman. I decided to go up to his house that night. I took my gun. It was about eleven. As Alexa said, his back door was open. I went in and found him dead, and then I saw Michael Reed running out the front door. I was so angry that I'd been denied the right to confront Brigman alive that I pulled out my Glock and shot him twice in the head."

"And then I drove to Michael Reed's to confront him. I knew where he lived because I'd dropped the blackmail payments there."

"Were you going to kill him?"

"No. I even left my gun in the car. Maybe so I wouldn't be tempted. But as I came up the walk, I heard a woman screaming. The front door was open, and I went in. Michael had his hands around Elaina's throat. So I picked up the gun on the hall table and emptied it. Elaina ran out."

"Did you know she was Juan Lopez's granddaughter?"

"Not that night. But he called me later to say I'd saved her life. We were both hoping her identity wouldn't be revealed because Coleman would target her."

"What happened to your gun?"

"I drove to the ocean, and threw it away. I thought I had finally put the terrible past behind me. But then Alexa was arrested, and I wasn't sure what to do. If I came forward, I'd have to tell the truth about Joey's hit on Bill. And that would put my life in danger as well as Juan's because Joey would make sure neither of us survived to testify against him.

"All I could do was hope someone would find a way to get Alexa off without my secret being exposed. But then I was appointed on Alexa's case and that brought back all my own nightmares and left me this horrible dilemma. I knew that relying on Jordan wouldn't acquit Alexa, but it was all I had to work with until you found Elaina."

"Is that why you didn't want to talk to the Reed children? Because I'd find out about Elaina?"

"There were a couple of reasons I was afraid to interview them. First, as I said, I didn't know if they'd seen anything. And as you could tell, talking about it upset them. But I was also afraid that if they had seen anything, they'd have seen me shoot Michael and then my secret would have been out in the open."

"You must have been relieved when they didn't recognize you."

"On a purely human level, yes. But I had to save Alexa's life. I couldn't tell you about Elaina without giving my secret away, but I was glad when you found her on your own."

"But didn't you think she'd give you away?"

"Yes, but I knew I couldn't let Alexa get convicted. I was still hoping Jordan would win this by some miracle, but then we lost her; and Coleman bought Elaina off."

"So you were the one who got Elaina to testify?"

Sarah nodded. "After we lost Jordan, I had no choice. I had to save Alexa. I called Juan and told him we would both have to take the risk that Bill's murder would be revealed."

"And he was willing to do that?"

"Despite what you probably think, Juan is not a bad man. He saw what he did to Bill as justice for the deaths of Ben and Matthew. And, to be honest, so did I although, I didn't ask for Joey to use Juan to kill my ex-husband. But Alexa's being convicted would not have been justice. So Juan and I agreed about what we had to do."

"So Elaina risked her life to testify, and you thought she was going to tell the truth today in court?"

"Yes. I thought all those marshals and agents were there to arrest me for Michael's murder and for being an accomplice to Bill's. I assume that's why you're here now?"

Jim moved closer to her, and she smelled the wonderful, clean starch smell she loved. He smiled, his kind eyes melting her inside.

"No, that's not why I'm here. You killed Michael Reed in defense of Elaina, and you can't kill a dead man. Ronald Brigman was dead when you arrived. And you had nothing to do with Bill Rogers' death. That was all Joey Menendez's doing. And to be honest, it sounds as if Bill deserved Joey's brand of justice, as you said."

"Then why are you here?"

"To understand why you've kept me at a distance all these months."

Sarah held back tears with a super human effort. "I had to keep everyone out. I couldn't tell anyone this story."

"Well, now you've told me. And I have a proposition for you."

"Proposition?"

"I'm too far from Cody. This was meant to be a temporary job, and I'm going back to D.C."

Sarah smiled. "I know. To be with Alexa."

"No, not with Alexa. We're friends, and I care about her. I told you that. But she's grown wiser since she married Michael Reed. She knows she's in no place right now to start anything with anyone. She has to get her career going again and make a stable home for her children. I'm not interested in Alexa that way."

"I thought you were."

"I can see why, but no. Not Alexa. I've been in love with you, Sarah, since the night I saw you sitting at the bar at Trend. I knew that was going to make this job a lot harder, and it has. I'm not trying to tell you what to do with your career, but you know you don't belong in this town, unless you go to work for Alan. And he's offered you a partnership in the D.C. office. I want you to go back to D.C. With me."

He pulled her into his arms as he finished, and she put her head on his shoulder. She felt safe. And for the first time in more years than she could count, she was not alone.

TO THE READER

I hope that you enjoyed *Dark Moon* and will take time to let me know your thoughts about the story by leaving a review on Amazon.com. or Barnes and Noble.com or Goodreads.

I would also love to hear from you directly at dhawkins8350@gmail.com. You can connect with me on Facebook at https://www.facebook.com/deborah.hawkins.37 or on Twitter: @DeborahHawk3. And my my word press blog is found at https://dhawkinsdotnet.wordpress.com.

AWARD-WINNING FICTION BY DEBORAH HAWKINS

DANCE FOR A DEAD PRINCESS

ForeWord Reviews, Book of the Year, Finalist, 2013
Beverly Hills Book Award Finalist, 2014
Paris Book Festival, Honorable Mention

http://www.amazon.com/dp/B00C4HP9I0

RIDE YOUR HEART 'TIL IT BREAKS

**Beverly Hills Book Award, Women's Fiction, 2015
Paris Book Festival, Honorable Mention**

http://www.amazon.com/dp/B00RDJQB8Q

What readers are saying about novels by Deborah Hawkins:

"The work of an excellent and extremely talented storyteller and writer..." Top Shelf Books

"A very exciting page turner" Amazon Reviewer

"This tale of addictive love is a roller-coaster of emotion." Kirkus Reviews

"A simmering set of choices and consequences that will keep readers guessing until its satisfying conclusion." D. Donovan, Senior Book Reviewer, Midwest Book Review

DISCUSSION QUESTIONS

1. A dark moon describes the Moon during that time that it is invisible against the backdrop of the Sun in the sky. How is a dark moon a metaphor for crimes of domestic violence?

2. How does the metaphor of a dark moon explain the characters of Sarah Knight and Jim Mitchell?

3. Why is Alexa Reed unable to resist the attraction of Michael Reed? What pulls her deeper and deeper into the relationship? Why is she in denial about Michael Reed's dangerousness?

4. When does Alexa realize she is trapped with Michael? How does the legal system work against battered women to prevent them from leaving their batterers?

5. How does the family court system become an ingenious tool that Michael Reed uses to continue to abuse Alexa? How are Alexa's achievements used against her?

6. Domestic violence is the willful intimidation, physical assault, battery, sexual assault, and/or other abusive behavior as part of a systematic pattern of power and control perpetrated by one intimate partner against another. It includes physical violence, sexual violence, psychological violence, and emotional abuse. The frequency and severity of domestic violence can vary dramatically; however, the one constant component of domestic violence is one partner's consistent efforts to maintain power and control over the other. How does this definition apply to Alexa's relationship with Michael Reed? Name examples.

7. What function does Sarah's affair with David Spineli serve in her life?

8. Why is defending Alexa, Sarah's only chance of redemption? Is she redeemed at the end of the book? How?

9. Which characters are your favorites and why?

10. How do you think the court system should treat mothers who have been abused by the fathers of their children? What are some practical solutions that would empower these women over the men who have hurt and humiliated them?

11. Do you feel that people are less willing to believe Alexa when she says Michael has abused her because she is married to a wealthy husband? Would she be more likely to be believed if she were married to a poor man? Should being rich or poor be considered in determining the credibility of a woman who reports being battered?

12. Does the family law court give any consideration to Alexa's status as a full time mother when it makes its decisions about the custody of Meggie and Sam? Should the court consider which parent has been the primary caregiver of the children?

13. How does Coleman Reed stack the odds against Sarah? How does she stand up to him?

14. What is Sarah's most courageous moment? What is Jim Mitchell's?

15. What are the major themes of Dark Moon?

AUTHOR'S NOTE

Thank you for reading *Dark Moon*. I really hope that you enjoyed it so much that you'll decide to read more stories in the Warrick, Thompson files! I'm always at work on a new one. Sign up for my newsletter here to find out when the next book in the series will be available, deborahhawkinsfiction.com.

The idea for *Dark Moon* began to form in my author brain on a day when I asked myself a question. What would it be like, as an attorney, to represent a client who looked guilty in every way, but whom you knew for certain was innocent? What if you couldn't use the evidence of the client's innocence without ruining your own life? What would you do to save yourself and your client? And what if you had to chose which one to save? I hope you'll stop by Amazon.com and leave a review telling me what you think of Sarah's answers to these questions. And write to me at dhawkins8350@gmail.com. I love to hear from you.

A PREVIEW OF BOOK TWO

The hero of *Mirror, Mirror* is a very different kind of lawyer. Jeff Ryder's world consists of fast cars, beautiful women, big money, and making partner at Warrick, Thompson. But when Jeff is accused of violating the ethics rules and his fast track to partnership and riches evaporates, his only hope of restoring his fortune and his reputation is a lawsuit for former police officer and Navy SEAL, Chris Rafferty and his wife Beth. Jeff manages to toe the ethical lines until the night he sleeps with Beth and wakes up as a murder suspect, facing the death penalty. To read the whole story of Jeff's fall from grace, visit. https://www.amazon.com/dp/B0757GSP35

Or enjoy this preview.

PROLOGUE

Friday, May 20, 2016, 10349 New Salem Street, Mira Mesa, San Diego

Thunderous pounding on his front door. Jeff Ryder struggled out of sleep and picked up his cell phone. Six a.m. He had to be in court at 8:30 for a client who was accused of possession of methamphetamine for sale. His fee had been all of one hundred bucks, but it was all the two-bit dope dealer could afford; and Jeff needed the money. The days of pulling down $800 an hour as a Warrick, Thompson senior associate were over thanks to Professor Marian Pappas of the Southern Innocence Project at the California Western School of Law. She'd made his graduation from Berkeley in the top five percent of his class worthless. All those years of work obliterated by a bleeding-heart, liberal academic who didn't know a thing about being a prosecutor.

The pounding grew louder. He sighed. Some drunk couldn't find his way home.

It had happened before in this flea-bag apartment building in the low-rent district of Mira Mesa Boulevard.

Wearing only his boxers and his t-shirt, he headed through the tiny hall of his one-bedroom walkup toward the front door. It sounded as if the drunk were about to break it down. Jeff prepared to give the guy a piece of his mind as soon as he opened it.

But just as he reached for the door handle, the flimsy wooden door cracked and then fell onto the floor just as he stepped back to avoid being hit as it collapsed. Four policemen in uniform and one in plain clothes, all wearing body armor that said "POLICE" in large yellow letters, burst into Jeff's tiny, nearly empty livingroom, shoving their handguns in his face. His heart was in his mouth. He tried to find the words to tell him he was an attorney, and they were in the wrong place. But his lips wouldn't move.

"Police! Hands up!" one or all of them bellowed, and he obeyed, as he stared down the muzzles of those five guns.

"Jeffery Matthew Ryder," the one in plain clothes said, "I am Detective Charles Erwin, and I am arresting you for the murder of Professor Marian Pappas."

This had to be bad dream, Jeff thought. *I'll wake up any minute now.* "Murder?" his dry mouth finally allowed him to say. "But—"

"You have the right to remain silent," the detective began to recite as Jeff felt the cold steel handcuffs close around his wrists. "Anything you say can and will be used against you in a court of law. You have the right—"

"Damn it! I know my rights. I'm a lawyer! I didn't kill Marian Pappas or anyone else for that matter."

But the familiar litany continued. "You have the right to talk to a lawyer and to have him present with you while you are questioned. If you cannot afford a lawyer, one will be appointed to represent you before any questioning if you wish. You can decide at any time to exercise these rights and not answer any questions or make any statements."

"I didn't kill Marian Pappas," Jeff tried to speak more calmly this time, hoping they'd be willing to listen now that th Miranda formalities were out of the way. "She was alive the las time I saw her."

"Which was when?"

"Uh, a week ago." Jeff spoke with as much dignity as h could, standing before five armed officers while handcuffed ir his skivvies

"Right. When you went to her office and threatened he with a gun. And that was after last December when you wen to her office and threatened her because she testified against you in State Bar Court," Erwin sneered.

"I didn't kill her."

"Then why was your car at her house last night at 2 a.m. And why is the bullet the surgeon took out of her head in th ER going to match the ammunition in your gun?"

"I wasn't anywhere near her house last night. And neithe was my car or my gun. Blue Honda Civics are a dime a dozen.

"Maybe. But not the ones with this license plate numbe and this dent in the back quarter-panel." Detective Erwir pushed a photograph under his nose, and Jeff saw his car parker at a location he did not recognize.

He stared at it in disbelief. "That's my license plate, but didn't drive my car there. And I haven't the slighted idea wher that picture was taken."

"Of course you do. That's 1659 Tangier Drive. That' Marian Pappa's house."

"I've never been to her house. I don't even know wher Tangier Drive is."

"Well, your car does. As this picture proves. Come on guys, let's get this jerk downtown."

"No, wait!" Jeff stiffened as they tried to move him through the gaping hole where his front door had been.

"We can add resisting arrest to the charges," Detective Erwin said sarcastically.

But I have an alibi! Jeff had started to say. *I was with someone last night.* And then he realized that he had an alibi. But using it would destroy the woman he loved.

To read the rest of Jeff's story, vist
https://www.amazon.com/dp/B0757GSP35

Made in United States
North Haven, CT
26 September 2022

24595837R00286